ORUN AND AYE – HEAVEN AND EARTH

BOOK THREE

KEEPER OF THE SOULS

CAROLYN HOLLAND

ADDITIONAL TITLES BY CAROLYN HOLLAND

"Behind the Dark Veil"

"The Bliss of the Grave"

Published in the United States of America

Behind the Dark Veil LLC
Hillsborough, NJ 08844
USA

www.carolynhollandwrites.com

ISBN: 978-1-7324693-6-5 (paperback)
ISBN: 978-1-7324693-9-6 (ebook)

Library of Congress Cataloging-in-Publication Data is available upon request

Cover artwork and design by H. Dean Williams
Interior formatting by Damonza Studio

ACKNOWLEDGMENTS

I did not intend to write this book—at least not right now. I was two-thirds of the way through another novel when I came across an image on Facebook of the bullet-riddled, charred remains of a young Black woman who'd been taken by an angry white mob to the Folsom Bridge, about sixteen miles north of Valdosta, Georgia. She'd been bound by her feet, eviscerated, and hung from a tree with her head facing downward.

Try as I might, I could not erase the cruel image from my mind.

Research revealed her name was Mrs. Mary Turner, the eight-month pregnant wife of Hayes "Hazel" Turner, who'd been dragged from his home and lynched the previous day.

Her crime? It was the year 1918. Mrs. Turner forfeited her life after publicly speaking out against those who'd lynched her husband for a crime she knew he did not commit.

Soon thereafter, I was beset with those kinds of dreams that wake you up in the middle of the night and force you to reach for pen and paper. It was from those dreams—turned—nightmares, and that barbarous image, that *Keeper of the Souls* and its companion book, *Soul Contract*, were born. I pray my words bring Hayes "Hazel" Turner, his wife Mary, and their unborn baby heavenly peace.

This book is obsidian dark. There is no way I could have completed it without the protection of my heavenly family and the support and encouragement of Patrice McKinney and my Source of Knowledge Bookstore family. Thank you for giving my books a home and for providing a receptive fan base for those who wish to read them.

Patrice McKinney and Pame' Sawyer-Smith, I thank you from the bottom of my heart for being the best beta readers this writer could ask for! H. Dean Williams, the cover is fire! I don't have adequate words to thank you for sharing your time and your talent with me. Amit Dey, thank you for stepping in and doing what you do, expertly.

Thank you, Aliyah B. Reese, for providing me with the perfect title for this book. I may have changed your diapers, beloved niece, but you, my love, changed my life. Know that I shall always love you, no matter what comes.

Thank you to my bestie, Joan Morris-Belcher, for being you!

My beautiful editor, Tia Ross, the words "thank you" seem inadequate for all you've done, not only for me but for the culture of Black literature as a whole. Thank you for the Black Writers Collective and the Black Wordsmiths Network. I've made lifelong friends and have learned so much, all because of your genius! Thank you for your encouragement, your standard of excellence, and for riding with me on this crazy adventure called life. This is our third novel, Tia! I am truly grateful.

Brandy Patton, my eagle-eyed proofreader, thank you for agreeing to take on this project and for bringing your patience and your special skill-set to this novel. I am so thankful.

Kim C. Lee, author, web designer, and tech maverick extraordinaire, the website you designed for me suits me absolutely, positively, perfect. I'm so blessed that I met you.

Thank you to the members of the Black Writers Collective, my friends in the Novelist Spot, the Write Something Sundays and Wednesdays Tribes, and the readers whose support fuel Black literature. It's for you that I write.

The world of spirit is real. It is evidenced in every whispered warning that saves us from calamity and in every dream that gives us clarity. As always, I thank my Heavenly Family for allowing me to do this thing that I love so much!

Divine Creator, I give to you the highest praise.

Ayibobo!!!

CHAPTER ONE

A rural farm on Suqualena Road, Meridian

(Quitman County), Mississippi (August 2, 1964)

ELIZABETH ANNE FRANÇOIS fought her way out of a recurring nightmare, gasping like a woman held too long underwater. The remnants of the nightmare left her drenched in sweat, the bedcovers a damp, tangled mess around her limbs. This latest nightmare was far more vivid than all others that preceded it. It began with a hot, erotic coupling and ended with the hint of a horrific tragedy, leaving Elizabeth wet, wanting, and more frightened than she'd ever been.

Sometime during the night, her phantom lover lifted the hem of her nightgown and spread her wide, exposing her body for his taking. Her cheeks burned at the remembrance of his fierce possession.

The exotic taste of male essence that lingered on her tongue, and the soreness between her thighs, lent the lie to this being a dream. Elizabeth would much rather believe that a dark spirit cloaked in comely male flesh had slipped inside her bedroom during the night and rode her so hard she could barely remember her name, than admit the other alternative: that she may be going insane.

Is he still here? She wondered, hastening to cover herself lest the insatiable satyr play voyeur to her nudity.

It was always like this for Elizabeth once the demons of Morpheus took control of her thoughts—disconcerting, portentous, and unbelievably frightening.

"My name is Elizabeth Anne François," she mumbled through dry cracked lips to ensure she was no longer a prisoner of the all-too-real dream.

"I am the daughter of Calvin and Betty Johnson François. I am the granddaughter of Jethro and Tarry Carrole Johnson. I am the great-granddaughter of Morgan and Eunice Benoit Carrole. I am the great-great-granddaughter of Marcel and Anna Etienne Benoit. My great-great-great-grandmother, Shumaila bin Said el-Murgebi, was a Zanzibari princess who was tricked into slavery by her white lover and left to rot on Magnolia Hill Plantation, where she became known as Hannah. Mojuba, beloved ancestors whose shoulders I stand upon and by whom I am so blessed. Mojuba. Please tell me I am not insane."

With shaking hands, Elizabeth reached for the glass of water she always kept on her nightstand and drank deeply. She knew enough about the spirit world to know that dreams have meaning, especially recurring ones.

"What are you trying to tell me, beloved spirits?" she murmured.

When her question was met with silence, Elizabeth dragged her aching body out of bed to start her day.

◈

If someone was to ask Elizabeth Anne François to describe her life, she would tell them it was one long blues song, with notes that battered her spirit and left bruises on her soul. The kind of blues you feel when you try to eke out a decent living from a patch of land that keeps on giving you the middle finger. Land you can't bring yourself to leave because your no-count husband and three of your babies are buried in it.

No matter how hard the François family worked their small family farm, they could never make ends meet. It's like that when you are poor, and you live in a town no bigger than the produce section in a local supermarket. Add being Black to the equation, and you are down for the count before you get the chance to step inside the ring.

Just as soon as the François clan got a glimpse of the proverbial light at the end of the tunnel, something would always snuff it out. Today it was their ancient tractor. The damn thing sputtered and died mid-afternoon, with more than half the field left to plow. It was too late to call somebody out to look at it, so Elizabeth's brothers, Fruit and Junior, called it quits for the day. They reasoned the tractor will be just as broken come tomorrow, and so would they.

Fruit, Junior, and Jimmy Lee, one of the field hands who also filled in as Elizabeth's part-time lover, sat on the front porch sipping some of her potent homemade hooch over a game of cutthroat bid whist. Elizabeth was in the kitchen, elbow-deep in a sink full of fresh-picked greens, wondering where in the hell they were going to scrape up the money to get the damn tractor fixed. All the while, Brownie McGee was making love to the strings on his guitar, and Sonny Terry's harmonica was wailing on the floor model stereo in the living room.

But Terry and McGee ain't had nuthin' on Elizabeth, who was singing along with the scratchy record as if her life depended on it, whilst images of the man in her dreams continued to haunt her thoughts and stir up her nature. Elizabeth knew she would never meet a man like that in Meridian or anywhere else, for that matter. Maybe that was why she didn't sing nuthin' but the blues.

"If you ever change your mind about leaving, leaving me behind," she sang. "Oh, oh, oh, bring it to me. Bring your sweet lovin'. Bring it on home to me. Yeah. Yeah. Yeah."

Elizabeth put some down-home Mississippi stank on that song. Her voice could be heard soaring outside the walls of the kitchen to kiss the crops in the farthest corners of the field with tear-stained lips and failed intentions. Whenever Elizabeth sang the way she was singing now, gentle stalks of wheat leaned toward her rich, soulful voice and bowed their heads in sympathy. It was Elizabeth's way of acknowledging that all sweet lovin' ever got her was knocked up, fucked up, and heartbroken. Elizabeth knew all about the blues, alright. And just in case she'd forgotten, the fickle finger of fate was about to give her a sure 'nuf reminder.

Something foul was coming up the road, and it was stinking to high heaven.

Everyone in Meridian knew Elizabeth did spiritual work. She was born and raised in Mississippi by way of New Orleans, a legendary haven for Voodoo and hoodoo practitioners. By the time Elizabeth had her first menstrual, she was already formulating spirit-infused oils and potions and performing uncrossing rituals and the like. But hardly anyone knew anything about the soul snatching.

The first soul Elizabeth snatched belonged to that of her familiar, a midnight black cat with coal-black eyes and a shock of steel gray on its forehead in the shape of a star. She called the cat Àse. She was only seven years old when she put a load of buckshot into the body of a rabid bobcat that had Àse in the grip of its mighty jaws. She snatched the feline's soul and returned it to its dead body before the coldness of death set in, restoring its life. Other than a lost eye, Àse was no worse for wear.

Nearby farmers didn't know what to make of Elizabeth. Some referred to her as a mambo Voodoo priestess, a conjure woman, and even an Oogun Ika witch because of that eerie-looking one-eyed cat that always followed her around. Elizabeth was all of those things and so much more.

If someone suspected their significant other was cheating or thought somebody "put something on them," they sought Elizabeth out for help. She could work a root on somebody or lay down tricks that would have an unfortunate victim quacking like a duck, clucking like a chicken, or barking like a junkyard dog whenever they opened their mouth to speak.

Many whispered that she served the Loa with both hands, practicing both good and evil medicine. If your money was right, not only would Elizabeth have your enemy lying in a sickbed at sunset but, if she wanted to, she could have them dead by sunrise. Some even said she could raise a dead body and have it walking around like the zombies in a late-night horror movie.

Elizabeth also served as the local midwife, commonly known in the Deep South as a doula or baby catcher. Most of the babies in Quitman County, Clarke County, and thereabout received their first smack on the backside from Elizabeth. The nearest hospital, H. C. Watkins Memorial, was about thirty-eight miles away. It may as well have been 1,000 miles away since few of the Colored farmers had medical insurance or adequate funds with which to pay. Those who could pay were housed in the hospital basement or left to suffer in crowded hallways. Many preferred to bear their children at home.

Times were hard for everyone and especially for Colored folks. Farms across the state were failing, and the economy was in the toilet. One thing was for sure: Poverty never stopped Colored folks from makin' love. Hard times make for the sweetest lovemaking because lovin' is free. Folks in Meridian could not afford to feed nine or ten kids like they did back in the old days, yet seeds were catching every which way but loose. Abortion was legal in parts of Europe, but not in the United States. Word got around quickly when Elizabeth stopped catching babies to go into the more monetarily lucrative and spiritually bankrupt business of killing 'em.

For the right amount of coins, Elizabeth would steep one of her special herbal concoctions. A couple of cups of what Elizabeth liked to call her "baby killin' tea," mixed with pennyroyal, cotton root bark, devil's claw, and a few of Elizabeth's secret ingredients, would have you cramping in no time flat and miscarrying quicker than a swift kick in the belly. If the customer was too far along for the herbal abortifacient to work, Elizabeth would do it the old-fashioned way with some rubbing alcohol and a clothes hanger.

Before Elizabeth knew it, women were traveling from as far away as Louisiana and Texas to avail themselves of one or both of her special services. The money Elizabeth brought in from her root work and abortions kept the family afloat through many a lean time.

There is a price for walking the dark path, though. Most times, Elizabeth would dream about impending danger before it came knocking at her front door. For the past week, the spirits had been screaming out a warning to her. But she could neither see nor hear them. The anguished cries of all those unborn babies Elizabeth sent to heaven before their time drowned out their voices. That was why Elizabeth was unaware of the spiritual turmoil swirling around her like the worst kind of tidal wave—a turmoil that would leave her with blood on her hands no amount of soap could wash off.

CHAPTER TWO

ELIZABETH TRIED NOT to think about the money they would lose until they could get the tractor fixed, instead focusing her thoughts on Jimmy Lee. Jimmy Lee was a big, strapping, cornbread-fed, country boy ten years her junior with enough stamina to plow Elizabeth into next week if she had a mind to let him.

Jimmy Lee will help me forget my troubles, at least for a little while.

Elizabeth did not maintain any illusions about her personal appeal to the opposite sex. She was a fine-looking woman, and she knew it. Most men described her as a handsome gal with a healthy sexual appetite when, in fact, she was captivatingly beautiful. A foot of thick, bushy hair she couldn't keep straight, no matter how hard she pressed it framed her delicate heart-shaped face. Her rich, dark skin shone like polished ebony because of all the wholesome, natural foods she ate. Her eyes were as dark as onyx, with expressive, long lashes that curled at the tips. She was a beauty, alright. But it was her body that left men weak at the knees.

Elizabeth's body was a work of art. She was blessed with a busty, wide-hipped, hourglass figure that put one in the mind of Bessie Smith but with a waist so slender a man could wrap his hands around it. The only reason the men in and around Meridian called her handsome instead of beautiful was because she was dark-skinned. Dark-skinned girls were good enough to creep with, but not to court. That was fine with Elizabeth because creeping was all she had the patience for.

Not only was Elizabeth real easy on the eyes, but she kept a spotless house and liked to cook almost as much as she liked the feel of a good-looking, rugged man pressing down on her. Any man fortunate enough to slide inside Elizabeth François's warm, moist place would tell you she was more than comfortable in her skin. She was a Colored man's delight and a white man's wet dream.

Jimmy Lee didn't know it yet, but Elizabeth planned to give him everything she dreamed about giving to her mystery lover— or at least as much as she would give to any man. She planned to fuck him and send him on his merry way with a big old-fashioned Mississippi smile on his face. But first, she intended to fatten up the calf. Elizabeth knew one of the best ways to get a man to undo his belt buckle and share what the good lord gave him was through his belly.

She dipped the greens until the water turned brownish-green. Then she drained and refilled the sink and scrubbed those greens like she was washing clothes instead of cleaning collards.

Two fresh-baked apple pies were cooling on the kitchen table, and a savory combination of salt pork and beans was simmering on the stove along with the pork ribs cooking in the oven. The sugary sweet smell of apples, nutmeg, and cinnamon slow-jammed with the fragrant tobacco smoke coming from her brothers' hand-rolled cigarettes. The smoke wafting through the open kitchen window tickled Àse's nose as she sat on the sill dozing in the sun.

The record ended, temporarily plunging the house into a comfortable silence. Elizabeth found a sense of peace in the familiar sounds and smells of home. Suddenly, harsh words from the front porch disrupted the peaceful quiet.

"Naw, niggah, fuck dat shit! You reneged!" Elizabeth's brother,

Fruit, shouted, throwing the cards down on the porch like a bad sport. "You cut hearts three books back, and now you throwin' out an ace of hearts. You must think my ass is stupid, Jimmy Lee!"

Fruit's real name was Lawrence Alexander François, a big name for a man less than six feet in height. Their mother named him Fruit because he'd been such a pretty baby—as pretty as a girl. "He's as sweet as a fresh-picked piece of fruit," her mother would often remark. Back then, Fruit had the disposition to go along with all that sweetness. There was nothing sweet about Fruit now. Twenty-eight years of Mississippi livin' took care of that.

Elizabeth shook her head in dismay, not even bothering to listen to Jimmy Lee's response to Fruit's heated accusation. She had sense enough to know that it was just a matter of time before her other brother, Junior, jumped in, and the François boys double-teamed him.

Unlike Elizabeth, who inherited her father's rich brown complexion, Junior, whose given name was Johnny Heathcliff François, and Fruit were high yella with light brown eyes and curly hair, just like their mother. Both were favored over Elizabeth.

Fruit and Junior were as thick as thieves. There was no way Jimmy Lee could win an argument against them, especially when they had been drinking. Instead of telling Fruit he'd cut diamonds and not hearts earlier, Jimmy Lee grabbed his cap and hustled his thick, fine ass on down the road, taking the promise of his sweet kisses and Elizabeth's orgasms right along with him. Disappointed, Elizabeth watched his departure with a woeful expression.

"Shit! I guess I'm going to have to use five-finger Charlie on Palm Street to take the edge off," she mumbled under her breath.

Goddammit! She thought. *I hate sticking my finger inside myself. I swear, one of these days, Fruit's mouth is gonna write a check his yella ass can't cash. That boy always arguing about something and messin' shit up for everybody.*

Suddenly, the pie didn't smell so sweet, and the cooking didn't bring as much joy.

❧

Elizabeth was still at the sink, facing the kitchen window, when she sensed a presence behind her. She would know her son Calvin if she had to find him blindfolded in a field of a thousand kids. Calvin was the only something she'd done right in her life—that and killing his no-good, piece-of-shit daddy for beating her one time too many. She smiled before issuing an admonishment.

"Don't you let that screen door slam when you leave out of here, Calvin Lionel François!" she warned, without turning from her task.

Calvin, who had been trying to tiptoe past his mother, stopped dead in his tracks, wondering—and not for the first time—whether his mother was part bloodhound or had eyes in the back of her head.

Calvin responded with a respectful "Yes, ma'am." Then he filled two sixty-four-ounce mason jars with homemade hooch and headed for the kitchen door with the *Damballah Weddo Vévé* talisman his mama gave him at birth swinging from his neck.

Calvin had been in and out of the kitchen since his uncles came in from the field, replenishing everyone's drinks and fetching occasional snacks, a task he was thoroughly enjoying. Calvin swore the sun rose and set in his uncles' eyes. His uncles felt the same about him.

The homemade liquor was in a cast-iron container on the floor next to the icebox, right beside Old Lucy, one of three sawed-off shotguns Elizabeth kept in the house. Elizabeth named the other two shotguns Fred and Ethel, respectively. She named the razor-sharp serrated knife her brothers used to gut the pigs Ricky, after Ricky Ricardo on the *I Love Lucy* show.

Despite his mother's warning, the screen door slammed behind Calvin as loud as a shotgun blast.

Elizabeth shook her head and kept on cleaning the greens, mumbling under her breath, "Lord, I don't know what I'm gonna do with that chile."

⁂

Junior François, the younger of the François brothers at twenty-seven, was the first to notice the lone figure coming down the long dirt road leading up to the house. Junior set his drink down and pushed off the steps to stand. He swatted an annoying fly away from his face and raised his hand to shield his eyes from the glare of the orange and red setting sun.

That's when he realized the unexpected visitor was none other than Louise Sadie Krutchner, or Lou Sadie, as everyone in Clarke County called her—that is, when they weren't calling her a trouble-making, white trash whore.

The easy camaraderie the brothers enjoyed a few moments earlier vanished like a puff of smoke on a windy day, to be replaced by palpable tension. Junior stepped closer to the end of the porch with a frown on his face and a lit cigarette dangling from his lips.

"I'll be damned if that trifling gal ain't pregnant again," Junior said to Fruit with pinched lips. "Didn't Elizabeth scrape a baby out of her about four or five months ago?"

Fruit was quick to reply. "She sure did scrape a baby out that ho'. I ain't surprised she knocked up again. Everybody in Quitman County and thereabouts know she been fuckin' outta both pant legs since she was seven. All you got to do is rub the top of her head and her legs fly open," Fruit said with obvious disdain. "She bet not think I'm gone 'low her ass up in here," he added.

Junior, always the voice of reason, was quick to remind his older brother about their current financial predicament. They had a tractor that needed to be fixed and no money to fix it.

"Shit, Fruit, what the fuck you care? Long as she pay, she can get pregnant all she want. 'Cause with that broken tractor, we sure can use the extra money. I'm just saying."

Unfortunately, Fruit wasn't in a reasonable frame of mind. He rarely was where whites were concerned. He had inherited his mother's good looks and his father's volatile temper. Everyone referred to Fruit as the loose cannon in the François family, the hot-head. His next words confirmed it.

"Dat bitch got a lot of nerve showing her face down here!"

He skeeted a stream of spit through the gap in his pretty white front teeth while shoving a toothpick in his mouth as if he hadn't heard a word Junior said.

CHAPTER THREE

FRUIT FRANÇOIS WAS not one to forget a slight. He was still upset about an encounter he'd had with Lou Sadie several months ago after running into her at a local hole-in-the-wall in Lambert.

It angered him that Colored folk weren't allowed in any white establishments, yet whites felt comfortable invading the Colored joints and bringing their special brand of trouble right along with them. That was exactly what Lou Sadie had done.

Both she and Fruit were stinking drunk on the night in question and had exchanged words over something trivial. Lou Sadie spat in Fruit's face and called him a black nigger. Fruit blanked the fuck out.

Woman or not, it took Junior and three of Fruit's friends to keep him from putting his foot all the way up that peckerwood's ass. Seeing her standing at the bottom of the steps like she had every right to spit in a man's face and then walk in his house like nothing happened made Fruit a hundred kinds of mad all over again.

We might need the money, but I swear 'fore Gawd she ain't stepping one foot inside this house today, Fruit thought with determination. *The only way she is going to get past me will be over my dead body.* Fruit stood up, blocking her way.

"Elizabeth home?" Lou Sadie asked with that Mississippi twang, low-class whites were known for.

"Yup," Fruit replied, chewing on the toothpick stuck in the side of his mouth. He stared Lou Sadie down, daring her to make a move to get past him.

"Well, can I come in?" she asked, her patience growing thin.

"No, you can't come in," Fruit said unequivocally, mimicking her backwoods accent.

Fruit François was a proud man. Lou Sadie snatched a chunk of his dignity and all of his pride the night she spat in his face. Her mere presence made him feel slimy, as if she had spit on him all over again. It gave Fruit a great deal of pleasure to deny her access to his home and to his sister's special skills.

Junior recognized the storm clouds forming in his brother's eyes. He grabbed Fruit's arm in an attempt to calm him down, but it was too late. The liquor had taken over, and it was driving Fruit like an Indy 500 racecar with no brakes. Fruit François was on a roll. There was no stopping him now.

"You think I'm gon' 'low you to step foot in this here house after you disrespected me? You must think I'm a damn fool, Lou Sadie. This here," he said, pointing toward the front door, "is my house, and you ain't welcome in it.

"You need to take your nasty ass on out of here, Lou Sadie Krutchner. You need to do it right now 'cause you ain't going to get no help here! Bet you gon' think twice before you spit on some-body else and call them a niggah! Now git!" Fruit ordered with the authority of a Black man who was sick and tired of white people—this one in particular.

The tension between the adults mounted. It seemed everyone had forgotten all about Calvin, who took advantage of their inat-tention to drain what was left in Jimmy Lee's glass, as well as the contents of his uncles' glasses. Now that the glasses were empty, young Calvin's head was swiveling back and forth like the little white ball in a ping-pong tournament. All he needed was a bowl of his mama's homemade pork skins, and it would be just like going downtown to the picture show.

Elizabeth stepped out onto the porch, drying her hands on her apron, curious as to what all the commotion was about. She took in the situation in an instant. When Fruit was riled up like this, there was no talking to him. The liquor only added fuel to his anger. She knew to keep her mouth shut.

Lou Sadie narrowed her eyes at Elizabeth, waiting for her to override Fruit's order and grant her access to the house. When Elizabeth didn't open her mouth, throwing up her hand instead to make the sign to ward off the evil eye, Lou Sadie drilled her watery blue-eyed gaze on Fruit and then on Junior. She saved the last glare for young Calvin, scaring the living shit out of his little drunk ass.

Elizabeth expelled a breath she didn't realize she was holding when Lou Sadie turned without a word and made her way back down the road, leaving Elizabeth with a sick feeling in the pit of her stomach.

"I 'spect we ain't heard the last from that one." A worried frown accompanied Elizabeth's prediction.

Earlier that morning, before the sun stretched its arms to rise for the day, two demons named Agares and Margas observed a rabid dog rooting through one of the many trash heaps in the Epstein Barr Trailer Park, about five miles outside of Meridian. They were demonic henchmen serving Prince Hindrance, one of The Satan's five sons. The demon-flunkies were charged with the thankless task of securing a human vessel with a wide-enough chink of corruptibility in his or her soul to accommodate their master's evil spirit. Agares and Margas found exactly what their master was looking for in the form of a skinny blonde-haired human named Louise Sadie Krutchner.

The trailer park, a godforsaken place if ever there was one, served as an ideal location to rendezvous with their master as it was filled with poverty, disease, and despair. It sat squarely upon a barren patch of land where grass and trees were too afraid to grow. The demons watched and waited.

The mangy mutt's tail spun like a propeller when it finally came away with the reward of a malodorous baby's diaper, loaded with shit. The scurvy canine paid the demons no mind. It ripped the diaper open and was preparing to roll in the shit when a funnel of dark sulfurous smoke rose from a nearby patch of dry, dusty earth. Frightened, the animal bounded away with its pungent prize locked between its sharp teeth, its tail tucked between its legs.

Cloaked in the illusion of humanity and shrouded in a dense fog, the demon Hindrance chose that exact moment to coalesce. His subordinates, Agares and Margas, dropped to their knees before him to pay proper obeisance.

"Have you found me a vessel?" Hindrance asked in a voice which instilled a sense of abject fear in his lackeys.

"Yes, my lord," the demons replied in unison, their foreheads in the dust. "It is a female."

"Where is she?" he demanded, impatient to be on his way.

"She is in the next-to-last trailer." Margas pointed.

"Well, don't just stand there looking stupid. Take me to her immediately!" Hindrance commanded, already making his way down the row of dilapidated trailers, while his subordinates struggled to their feet.

A pack of wild coyotes chose that exact moment to howl at the moon. Their plaintive cries nearly drowned out the faint sound of country music coming from a trailer at the end of the trailer park. Other than the sound of the rabid dog, the coyotes, and the music, it was eerily quiet. The demons made sure that the occupants of all but one trailer were ensorcelled in a deathlike slumber before their master's arrival.

Agares and Margas, who were struggling to keep up, nearly barreled into Hindrance's back when he came to an abrupt halt outside of the trailer he sought. The faint sound of voices could be heard coming from inside the trailer. All three demons became invisible as they entered the trailer to hover in the dark shadows.

∾

"That's right, gal, suck it good!"

The order came from a wizened old man who smelled worse than the overflowing garbage cans stacked outside the trailer door.

"Lick my nuts," he ordered, pulling on the woman's greasy blonde hair, moving her mouth to the desired location.

"That's right, Sadie girl. Lick them balls clean as a whistle!" he chortled, holding her head between his widespread thighs. The woman's mouth was on his narrow pink cock, making wet slurping sounds while her head bobbed up and down between his hairy, boney thighs.

The old man squeezed his eyes shut, sucking in gulps of air. And then he froze, baring a mouth full of rotten black teeth that resembled pebbles, as his hot seed tunneled down her throat.

"Master, meet your new vessel Louise Sadie Krutchner and her father Neusome Krutchner," Margas said telepathically.

"Perfect," Hindrance said, wearing a wicked smile. "Absolutely fucking perfect!"

A veritable legion of demons had already set up shop within Lou Sadie's spirit and had, in fact, been directing her steps since the day she forced her way, red-faced, kicking, and squalling, from her mother's dead body. It was those same demons that guided her steps when she straddled the old man to gain her own satisfaction, despite his being her blood kin.

Hindrance's presence caused the demons inside of Lou Sadie to go into a frenzy. He stepped out of the shadows to give the demonic squatters the boot before he slipped inside Lou Sadie's frail human body like a hot knife in a soft stick of butter. Her flesh was a perfect fit.

Lou Sadie belonged to Hindrance now, mind, body, and soul. He intended to wear her flesh until the seams came loose and her soul split wide open—to ride that evil whore like a pony until her body gave out and her wicked heart exploded inside her chest. When she died—for surely she would, as do all of his vessels—he planned to be waiting for her arrival at the gates of hell so he could fuck with her some more.

His laughter rolled throughout the trailer park like thunder.

CHAPTER FOUR

AT A QUARTER past three in the morning, Lou Sadie, her paw, the Quitman County sheriff, and his deputy showed up at the François farm demanding to speak to Fruit. Junior had the foresight to grab his rifle as soon as he saw the lights from the caravan of vehicles coming up the drive.

No good ever comes from white folks showing up at your door in the early hours of the morning, especially if they are toting guns, he thought.

It was just after midnight when Byron De La Beckwith, a white segregationist and founding member of the infamous White Citizens' Council, shot Medgar Evers in the back, right in front of his home in Jackson. Then there was Reverend George Lee, who the crackers shot in the face as he drove home the day after Mother's Day, just because he was trying to register folks to vote. They gunned Lamar Smith down in front of the courthouse in broad daylight for doing the same thing as Reverend Lee. Junior knew not to trust any white man who showed up at his front door with a gun, no matter what time of the day or night. He was honor-bound to arm himself. He came out on the porch with his gun aimed directly at the sheriff, who was the first to get out of his car.

Madness came over the François family that morning—madness born of generations of stifled ambitions, thwarted dreams, and pent-up hatred that was bound to eventually come out. And young Calvin was right in the thick of things, witnessing it all. He blatantly disobeyed his mother's order to stay in the house and came out on the porch to join his Uncle Junior.

Fruit ran back inside the house to put on his boots and get the shotgun Elizabeth kept in the kitchen—the one she named "Old Lucy"—while Junior kept his rifle trained on the sheriff and his deputy, silently daring either of them to make a move. This show-down was a long time coming. The hatred the François brothers had for Sheriff Edgar DeLonge and his slimy deputy, Lester Stretch, was real.

❧

"Now you need to put that there rifle down, boy," DeLonge said, flabbergasted that a nigger had the nerve to train a gun on him.

Fruit stepped out on the porch to stand beside his brother, shot-gun in hand. "We don't need to do nothing but pay muthafuckin' taxes, be Black, and die," came Fruit's arrogant response. "We don't want no trouble, Sheriff. You and your deputy need to turn around and leave the way you come, and take that thang and her paw with you," he added, glancing toward the Krutchners.

"That's not going to happen, Fruit," DeLonge replied, spitting a mouthful of chewing tobacco near the toe of Fruit's boot. "I am here on official business. Put your firearms down now, and I might just forget you pulled a weapon on an officer of the law and let you live. If you don't, it's going to go hard on both of you," he warned.

Fruit chuckled. "Well, ain't that just some goddamn shit. This here muthafucka is running his mouth while me *and* my brother got rifles pointed at his ass. White people," he said, shaking his head in amazement.

Calvin stuck his head around the curtain of his mother and uncle's bodies to see the expression on the sheriff's face. He didn't like what he saw. The sheriff and his deputy were both known to have itchy trigger fingers.

Sheriff DeLonge reminded Calvin of an ugly, bald-headed Aunt Bea on *The Andy Griffith Show*. Deputy Stretch bore a striking resemblance to Barney Fife. The countrified version of the Keystone Cops shared a whispered exchange. Calvin hoped and prayed his uncles would give the sheriff and his Barney Fife lookalike deputy a good ole fashion, Mississippi, country boy ass-whipping and send them on their way. He was still too young to understand the inevitable consequences that would ensue from his uncles' foolhardy actions.

Calvin's attention was drawn away from the two mean-muggin' lawmen to focus on Lou Sadie's father, who began raising a ruckus. Elizabeth remained silent, letting her brothers do all the talking.

"Tell 'em what you told me!" ole man Krutchner shouted, smelling of musk, wet dog, and whiskey.

"I'm pregnant," Lou Sadie said with trembling lips, as if her protruding belly hadn't made her condition pretty damn obvious.

"Not that part, stupid! Tell 'em who done it!" her father barked.

Elizabeth held her breath, waiting for what she knew was coming next. And, of course, Lou Sadie didn't disappoint. The Krutchners were poor white trash. In Mississippi, it didn't matter if you were rich or poor. If you were white, you were right, even if you're as wrong as two left shoes put on backward. Elizabeth listened to Lou Sadie go into an act worthy of an Oscar nomination, as if she had written the nightmarish script herself. Àse, who had come out on the porch with the family, sensed Elizabeth's disquiet. The feline meowed at her feet.

"That's him!" Lou Sadie said, pointing the finger of certain death at Fruit François.

"That's him. Oh my God, that's him," Lou Sadie said dramatically, collapsing against her father for support. She sobbed uncontrollably.

"He raped me. And those two held me down while he did it!"

With those words, Lou Sadie Krutchner sealed not only Fruit François's fate but the fate of everyone in that house who had the misfortune to sport a set of testicles, fourteen-year-old Calvin included.

ʔ

Everything moved with lightning speed from that point on. One second, Elizabeth was standing on the porch in her nightclothes with a bed scarf covering a head full of sponge curlers, and the next she was screaming, "I swear before the Loa I will fucking kill you, you evil lying bitch!"

Somehow, Elizabeth propelled all one hundred eighty pounds of her full figure from the top of the porch all the way to the bottom without her feet touching a single step. She tackled those Krutchners like an NFL linebacker. All hell literally broke loose.

Dumb ass Barney Fife chose that moment to play Marshal Dillon. He went for his gun. Àse sprang off the porch to deliver a vicious swipe of her sharp claws across the deputy's face before disappearing somewhere under the bushes. Junior popped off a shot before Stretch could take aim, hitting him in his shooting hand. His gun flew in the air, landing several feet away, along with three of his fingers. The wounded deputy writhed on the ground, holding what was left of his hand, hollering his fool head off. That was when the sheriff finally snapped out of his what-the-shit-is-going-on stupor and decided his fat ass needed to take some action.

Niggers don't fight back in Quitman County, he thought angrily. *These high yella François boys and their goddamn sister are about to be some dead niggers!*

The sheriff took cover behind the squad car with his weapon drawn, callously leaving his wounded deputy to his own devices. There was no turning back now. Every member of the François family knew it. They were about to have a real live country-western shoot-out.

Lou Sadie, her father, and Elizabeth went down in a tangle of arms and legs to roll in the dirt at the bottom of the steps while the François brothers and the sheriff exchanged gunfire. Grunts of pain could be heard as Elizabeth's fist connected with the Krutchners again and again and again. If the circumstances had not been so dire, Calvin would have laughed at the comical scene.

Old Man Krutchner reminded Calvin of a cartoon character, lying flat on his back with stars floating around his head. It took one solid blow from Elizabeth's fist to shut him up. Lou Sadie wasn't faring much better than her father. Calvin's mama had a hand full of Lou Sadie's greasy blonde hair wrapped around her fist tight enough to pull that shit out by the roots. Elizabeth pounded Lou Sadie's head into the unforgiving ground. Neither of them seemed to care about Lou Sadie's enormous belly or what was in it.

⁓

It didn't take Lou Sadie long to come to her senses, and the demon inside of her to rear its ugly head.

Fruit François should have followed the sage counsel of his younger brother, the demon Hindrance thought, stroking the nipple on one of his vessel's swollen breasts. *He should have let my girl here go inside that piece-of-shit house he is so proud of, get that incestuous seed scraped out of her carcass, and called it a motherfuckin' day, but he didn't. And soon, very soon, it is going to be hangin' time!*

Oh, yeah!

⁓

Lou Sadie was fighting back tooth and nail, scratching and biting Elizabeth like a wild beast, all the while maintaining a wicked smile on her bloodied lips. Elizabeth was doing everything in her power to wipe that smile off Lou Sadie's face. Meanwhile, Fruit and Junior's bullets pinged against the side of the squad car like tin can target practice.

Junior provided cover for Fruit so that he could creep around the side of the car to get the drop on the sheriff. DeLonge spun around just in time to see Fruit behind him. The sheriff raised his gun to fire with a grim look of satisfaction. That look quickly turned to fear when all he got was a resounding "click" when he pulled the trigger. Fruit had been counting his rounds.

DeLonge is out of bullets. And now his fat ass is mine, Fruit thought, noting the bloody groove in the sheriff's forehead where one of his or Junior's bullets had winged him.

DeLonge was no match for Fruit, whose wiry muscled frame was made strong by years of backbreaking farm labor. It would not have mattered, however, if Fruit had been in a wheelchair and breathing through a respirator. His power came from an engine fueled by hatred.

The first blow was to DeLonge's midsection. Fruit felt like his fist was sinking into a stack of goose-feathered pillows. The sheriff doubled over in pain. Fruit followed up the gut punch with a right uppercut to his jaw. DeLonge's head snapped back like the lid on a treasure chest, giving up the gift of a bloody nose that leaked like a faucet. Calvin sprinted down the front porch steps and rounded the car to watch his Uncle Fruit in action.

The beating was thorough. *The sheriff's expertise is clearly of the hooded variety, where his victims are tied up and defenseless, and he is safe behind the anonymity of folks who look and think like him,* Calvin thought.

DeLonge was ill-equipped to stand and deliver when faced with a real man. Calvin stood there, taking it all in, as his uncles and his mama kicked some serious ass. He had never felt so proud. For the first time in his young life, he got to witness a situation where Colored folks prevailed. It was exhilarating.

CHAPTER FIVE

FRUIT'S PUNCHES TOOK on a life and rhythm all their own. The punches were cathartic, atoning for every time he had been forced to address the sheriff with a subservient "Yes sir" or "No sir" when he knew DeLonge was not good enough to scrape the mud off his boots.

Once Fruit got the sheriff down and cowering against the side of the squad car, he started kicking him. The kicks were for every time he had to grit his teeth and stand by quietly while DeLonge looked at his sister with lust in his rheumy blue eyes or made disrespectful comments about her.

Fruit kicked DeLonge in the side repeatedly, breaking several ribs. These kicks represented every time DeLonge sided with the white merchants downtown who willfully cheated the Colored farmers for the price of their crops. The successive boot stomps were for every time DeLonge made him feel less than a man, forcing him to choose life over his self-respect and dignity. Still not satisfied, Fruit picked up the sheriff's empty gun and pistol-whipped him with it.

"This is for you having the fucking nerve to bring that skank Lou Sadie Krutchner and her no-good paw on my property, and allow them to lie on me, my brother, and my nephew!" he said between each blow. Fruit's chest was heaving from exertion and his knuckles bloody when he finally stepped back to inspect his handiwork.

DeLonge was a god-awful mess. He was propped up against the squad car, sprawled on his ass in the dirt with his long legs spread wide looking like 'duh, what the fuck just happened here?' Calvin thought his Uncle Fruit was done after that, but he was wrong.

Fruit opened the car door and heaved DeLonge by the collar of his shirt. Cursing and grunting, he dragged DeLonge up against the footrest inside the open car door. Calvin couldn't believe his eyes when his Uncle Fruit repeatedly slammed the door on the sheriff's body like he wanted to break him in two.

Junior kept his gun trained on the entrance to the farm as his brother beat the sheriff's inert body with the car door and alternately kicked and punched him. Whatever they intended to do would have to be done right now. They didn't know if the sheriff had arranged for backup.

Old Man Krutchner was down for the count, but the battle between Elizabeth and Lou Sadie raged on. Despite the advantage of Elizabeth's size, the two of them were evenly matched now that the demon was orchestrating Lou Sadie's steps. Calvin ran to the porch to lean over the railing like an anxious spectator sitting ringside at a heavyweight boxing match. He shouted encouragement while his mama beat the shit out of Lou Sadie. Calvin's exhortations of excitement soon turned to shouts of despair when Lou Sadie tossed a handful of dirt in his mama's face, temporarily blinding her. The foul play maneuver tipped the odds in Lou Sadie's favor.

So intent was Junior's focus on the long drive leading up to the farm that he failed to notice the Barney Fife lookalike. The deputy retrieved his gun and, mangled hand and all, crawled to the squad car during the melee, leaving a trail of blood behind him. The sound of the wounded deputy cocking his weapon was as loud as cannon fire.

Calvin shouted out a warning. "Uncle Junior, he's got a gun!"

But the warning came too late. The Barney Fife lookalike held his left hand up with the mangled stump of his right wrist, took aim, and fired, temporarily distracting Elizabeth.

"Run! Get my son out of here! Save my baby!"

These were the last words Elizabeth could utter before Lou Sadie picked up a jagged rock and cracked her upside the head. Moments later, the deputy's second bullet slammed into her chest. Elizabeth dropped to her knees and toppled like a building hit with a wrecking ball.

The deputy tossed the smoking gun in the passenger seat of the squad car and sped down the long, dusty drive. It seemed like everything was moving in slow motion after that.

"MAAAAAMAAAAH!!!" Calvin screamed.

Without regard for his personal well-being, Calvin ran to his mother's side. With snot pouring from his nose, he screamed, "No, God! Don't be dead, mama. Please don't be dead!

He killed my mama!"

Calvin's gut-wrenching wail of agony echoed through the length and breadth of the farm to touch the sky. There is no way God and his angels did not hear him. Elizabeth's eyes were wide open, her pupils fixed and dilated. There was so much blood.

Fruit felt like some invisible force had doused him with a bucket of ice-cold water, immediately extinguishing the flames of his anger after his sister was shot. Hot tears ran down his face. He knew there was nothing they could do for Elizabeth. They had to save themselves. Fruit had to drag Calvin away from Elizabeth's body.

Lou Sadie chose that moment to jump on Junior's back like an attack monkey, trying to wrestle the rifle out of his hand. Junior knocked her out with one punch to the jaw. Calvin picked up his Uncle Fruit's discarded weapon and fired it at the speeding car. He was still firing the gun long after the squad car had disappeared from sight. Fruit had to pry the gun out of Calvin's shaking hands.

There was no time to figure out where Elizabeth kept the keys to the truck. Fruit took a moment to spit on DeLonge's prone figure, make the sign of the cross over his sister, and shoot down the road with young Calvin and Junior close on his heels. Lou Sadie came to just in time to witness their escape.

"You just as good as dead, Niggers! You just as good as dead!" she shouted at their retreating backs.

The sound of her wicked laughter followed them as they ran. Fruit wanted to go back and empty his rifle in her face, to silence her once and for all, but, unlike DeLonge and Stretch, he wasn't a natural-born killer.

The more pity, he didn't follow through.

❧

Courthouse Building, E. Church Street, Quitman, Mississippi

Mama always said one day Uncle Fruit's mouth was gonna write a check his yella ass couldn't cash. She didn't say nuthin' 'bout him getting us all killed though, Calvin thought with mounting fear.

A little less than three hours after they left the farm, the bandaged-up sheriff and his posse caught up to Fruit, Junior, and Calvin trying to make a run for it in Clarke County and hauled them back to the local jailhouse.

Calvin thought he was looking at a ghost when DeLonge limped up to his Uncle Fruit, all battered and bruised.

I should have known DeLonge was too damned mean to die.

Every Colored person in town knew to close their windows and draw their curtains when an all-white vigilante mob of about fifteen broke into the county jail on West Daniel Street with sledgehammers and crowbars, clamoring for blood. Still smarting from the ass-kickin' Fruit François gave him earlier, resulting in two broken ribs, and the bullet that grazed his skull, the sheriff didn't put up too much fuss when the mob dragged Fruit, Junior, and Calvin François out of their cells to mete out Mississippi's special brand of justice. In fact, he and his good buddy, Lester Stretch, who now looked like a one-eyed, one-handed pirate, were the ringleaders. The sheriff locked up the jailhouse and led the charge.

The scene unfolding in front of young Calvin's eyes was worse than the stories his mama used to tell him about how white people treated Colored people during slavery. His uncles were tied to lampposts in front of the courthouse when the real-life boogieman appeared as Sheriff DeLonge.

At first, Fruit was defiant. He knew he was going to die. So what did he have to lose? He said to himself, *Fuck it, I'm going out like a man.* Calvin let out a silent cheer when his uncle spat in the sheriff's face, just like Lou Sadie spat in his. His uncle's bravado didn't last long though. DeLonge was in his element. The only thing missing was his long white robe and hood.

Calvin knew the exact moment when his Uncle Fruit came to realize he wasn't dealing with humans—that he was dealing with a sociopathic, genetically flawed species unknown to man. No decent human could do what they did to Fruit and Junior François and still be able to sleep at night.

But who said they were decent? They are white devils, all of them, Calvin thought. *From now on, that is what I will call them.*

Calvin whimpered as his proud uncles stopped begging for mercy and started begging God to let them die. God must have been on vacation, or at the very least on lunch break because the members of the crazed mob beat them within an inch of their lives, only to revive them so that they could start all over again. Now all Fruit and Junior wanted was the blessed relief that comes with death, a bane it seemed God and the racist monsters were determined to deny them. The beating was vicious and, in the sick minds of the vigilantes, symbolic. They were feral beasts, like rabid animals getting off on the smell of fear, blood, and death.

They gouged out Fruit and Junior's eyes for looking at a white woman. They chopped off their hands for daring to touch a white woman. They castrated them and shoved their man parts down their throats so that they wouldn't be able to speak about being inside a white woman's body when they reached the Hereafter.

A member of the mob stood beside Calvin, forcing him to watch his uncles' mutilation. It was their intent that Calvin marinate in his fear so that he would serve up a piping hot pot of panic when it came his turn. It worked like a charm. Calvin was scared, alright. He was scared shitless.

One of the vigilantes snatched the *Damballah Weddo Vévé* talisman from around Calvin's neck and stomped it into the dust. Losing the charm was a physical kick in the gut. It was his last spiritual defense. The white devil kicked and punched Calvin every time he tried to close his eyes or look away from what was happening to his uncles, beating him so badly that his own mother wouldn't have recognized him.

They killed my mama, he lamented, reliving the sight and sound of the bullet slamming into Elizabeth's chest. *All this because of a white woman's lie,* he thought.

The irony of the situation was that, unlike other Colored men in the county who fantasized about being with a white woman, neither Fruit nor Junior had ever developed a fancy for white meat. His uncles always said, "The darker the berry, the sweeter the juice." They would never look at a white woman with desire, yet they would join the ranks of countless Colored men who died because of it. Calvin thanked God when his uncles finally stopped screaming and their heads slumped forward in eternal sleep.

Calvin's uncles were dead, but the white devils weren't done— not by a long shot.

Sheriff DeLonge put his dirty white pickup truck in reverse and backed that monster on wheels in front of the courthouse building. It had rained two days prior, and there was a thick layer of mud on the tires and the undercarriage. His appearance rendered Calvin numb with shock and fearful of what new evil the wicked sheriff would conjure up.

DeLonge was an enormous man. He heaved his bulk out of the truck, leaving the engine rumbling, and signaled one of his deputies to help him secure the dead bodies of Fruit and Junior François to the rear of the truck with sturdy chains. The entire process took less than ten minutes.

Fruit and Junior's bodies no longer belonged to them. They reminded Calvin of tin cans attached to the back of a newly married couple's car. Instead of the words "Just Married" written across the back windshield, Calvin imagined it would say, "Just Lynched," courtesy of the State of Mississippi, or something to that effect.

CHAPTER SIX

FLINCHING, THE SHERIFF hopped back inside his truck. He grunted as the truck dipped from his weight. He was clearly in a great deal of pain. Calvin was glad but didn't have time to gloat. The owner of the local tack and feed shop and the deputy dragged Calvin from the lamppost to cuff him inside a squad car. Calvin damned sure didn't go willingly. Unlike his uncles, he didn't put on a brave face. They had to drag him, kicking and screaming. His feet left runnels in the grass. His heart was pounding so rapidly, he thought he would have a heart attack. In fact, he prayed he would.

A heart attack will be more than welcome right about now, he prayed, not quite ready to give up on God.

❧

The white devils formed a caravan of sorts, with DeLonge's dirty white truck leading the fray. Hindrance ghosted into the back seat of DeLonge's vehicle and was immediately assailed with the pervasive stench that seeps from human pores when they are about to do evil. He leaned in closer to confirm his assessment and nearly came on himself from the subtle yet unmistakable perfume surrounding humans soon to be touched by the angel of death. DeLonge swatted his neck in annoyance, mistaking Hindrance's nearness with that of a pesky insect. The demon settled back in his seat for the ride, deriving an inordinate deal of pleasure, knowing the Caucasoid rat with no tail was not long for this world.

DeLonge glanced in his rearview mirror and nearly soiled his pants when he saw two bright orange eyes staring back at him. He turned to check the back seat and found nothing. Chiding himself for having an overactive imagination, he shook off the feeling that he was not alone and stuck his head out of the window.

"What in thunderation is the holdup? We ain't got all gol-dern day! Let's get this show on the road!" He shifted into gear and pulled off with a put-upon frown etched on his ugly face.

∿

DeLonge dragged Fruit and Junior's bodies through town, pausing once at a major intersection for all to see what happens to niggers who rape white women. Calvin gagged, sickened by the grisly trail of gore and chunks of flesh left in the wake of the white Chevy pickup truck.

Once DeLonge was certain the Colored folks cowering behind their closed curtains got the message loud and clear, he and the rest of his buddies exited town and headed for the highway. They eventually turned off at the exit for Shubata, a small town at the southern end of the county.

The sheriff turned on his right blinker, leading the cars behind him down a potholed dirt road. The dirt road wound past a cluster of abandoned cabins and eventually revealed a densely wooded area that widened to a fork in the road.

The caravan took another right at the fork, bringing into view the infamous Chickasawhay River and a rusty bridge. A crudely crafted sign depicting a skull and crossbones hung between the vertical rivets of the bridge for all to see. The sign read, "Danger, This Is You."

Hindrance knew they'd reached their destination.

&

Calvin's heart felt like it would explode when the caravan stopped at the banks of the Chickasawhay River and the rusty beams of the old Shubata Bridge came into view. Every Colored person in Mississippi knew about the infamous Shubata hanging bridge. Calvin fought not to be sick. At that moment, he wished he was as dead as his uncles were.

Two hulking, formidable men with cowboy hats and florid complexions detached what was left of Fruit and Junior François's bodies from the back of the truck. They dragged their grisly remains to the edge of the bridge like they were deer carcasses brought down during a hunt.

The word must have gotten out to the God-fearing town of Christians that there was going to be a lynching because now there were three times the number of spectators as there had been at the courthouse, including women and children. You would have thought they were preparing to watch fireworks instead of preparing to lynch two men whose souls had already left for points unknown. The mob lined the bridge.

Two giggling, tow-headed, children played a game of tag amongst the weeds and overgrown thickets while a man wearing butcher shop gloves and a pair of droopy jeans tied nooses around Fruit and Junior's necks and hoisted their limp bodies up from the steel girders to swing like bloody pendulums. Calvin could see the dead bodies of thousands swinging right alongside them.

Barring an act of divine intervention, I will join them soon.

One devil was taking Polaroid pictures as another good ole devil dog boy was blasting the local country and western station on his car radio and gulping from a bottle of corn liquor. Apparently, a lynching in Mississippi was even more festive than a Fourth of July celebration with fireworks and a roasted pig.

Calvin knew they were going to drag him out of the squad car and lynch him, the same way they had his uncles. He was going to die before he shaved or kissed his first girl, ending his life before he had a chance to live.

The mob finished stringing up Fruit and Junior. Still thirsty for blood, they turned their rapacious eyes on Calvin as he sat cowering in the back seat of the squad car. He listened to the anguished cries the blades of grass made as the angry white devils trampled upon them in their haste to steal his life.

Calvin's bowels opened like a trapdoor, soiling his bloody trousers with wet, muddy fear. The stink of shit and piss filled the inside of the squad car as mind-numbing terror threatened to choke Calvin to death. His sanity fled the scene as the distance between him and his tormentors closed, and the car door flew open.

One of them said, "It's your turn now, lil' nigra. We gon' do you worse than they did that Emmett Till."

They dragged him out of the squad car.

A red convertible carrying Lou Sadie Krutchner pulled up to the lonely dirt road in a cloud of dust, arriving just in time for Calvin's lynching. She jumped out of the car before it came to a full stop, sporting a black eye and a busted bottom lip, compliments of Elizabeth Anne François. Seeing her roughed up was minor consolation to Calvin considering what was about to happen. Despite her injuries, the she-devil was sporting a self-satisfied, shit-eating grin because, for the first time in her miserable life, she was getting what the whites construed as positive attention.

Lou Sadie adjusted her clothing and laughed at something the driver said. She had hitched a ride and gave up some booty in exchange for car fare.

Leering men cleared a path for her. Calvin watched her strut to the end of the bridge as if she was a queen and not the town harlot who was pregnant with her daddy's seed. And now, God help him, Lou Sadie *and* the demon inside of her would have a front-row seat for his execution.

Two devils dragged Calvin to the rusty beam, where his uncles were already swinging.

Lou Sadie watched the crowd pelt Calvin with vicious kicks and punches along the way. One of them hocked a nasty glob of spit in his face. The phlegm hung on his cheek like a shit stain on a nun's habit.

The kid looks like someone took a meat mallet to his face. The only thing missing for me to fully enjoy the show is a buttery bag of popcorn and an ice-cold Coke, she thought.

The Shubata Bridge was a truss bridge, a load-bearing structure composed of connected steel forming triangular units. The ropes were securely looped from the steel stringer attached to the bridge floor beam. Fruit and Junior's bodies dangled beneath, a few feet short of the muddy river.

Calvin was now in position on the bridge deck, so scared he could barely stand. A member of the mob sliced off one of Calvin's ears to take home as a trophy. Calvin's pain-filled screeches penetrated the tops of the trees and soared through the sky to bounce off the lowest level of The Heavens.

Awww sukey sukey now. It's hangin' time. Hindrance chortled with excitement, rubbing his leathery palms together in glee.

Someone tossed a length of hemp over the steel beam and looped the other end around Calvin's slender neck. A thick knot was looped in front to make the noose. The weight of the rope was a thousand-pound albatross around Calvin's neck. Lou Sadie moved closer. Neither she nor the demon wanted to miss a thing. They were one.

Calvin raised his eyes to a sea of evil-faced white people in search of one sympathetic face. There were none. All he wanted was his mama. Even though one eye was beaten shut and blood was streaming down his face, he zeroed in on his accuser, Lou Sadie Krutchner.

Calvin knew he wouldn't be getting any help from that quarter when the translucent image of a hideous demon with a black forked tongue departed the sheriff's truck to roll over Lou Sadie's body like a wave of smoke. He couldn't stop himself from begging, so desperately did he want to live.

"Please don't let them kill me. Please, Ms. Lou Sadie! I didn't do nuthin' wrong. I swear I didn't do nuthin' wrong!" he exhorted, with snot running from his nose and into his mouth.

"I don't want to die. I don't want to die. Please! I don't want to die!" The words spilled out of his mouth repeatedly, becoming a litany, to which a little white girl sitting upon her father's shoulders gaily clapped her hands.

The hate-charged atmosphere and Calvin's pleas for mercy fell upon deaf ears. Lou Sadie responded to his heartfelt plea by snatching a bottle of whiskey out of the sheriff's hands and bringing it to her lying lips, thrilled to have a ringside seat for Elizabeth's son's murder.

After that, all Calvin could do was scream. It seemed even that bane was denied him. Someone struck him with the butt of a hunting rifle to shut him up. Teeth flew out of his mouth. Now his busted lips were moving in what the demon inside Lou Sadie assumed was a prayer.

He can pray to He Whose Name I Cannot Utter, all he wants, Hindrance thought jovially. *All he will get is a 'return to sender' for his troubles because mercy and grace fled the scene a long time ago. The State of Mississippi and everyone in it belong to me!*

They strung the kid up. The demon felt Lou Sadie's panties get soaking wet. Four men stood in front of him. One of them, he knew not which, used his foot to push Calvin off the bridge. For a split second, Calvin was suspended mid-air, and then he plummeted toward the murky waters below, bouncing a few feet short of the surface.

Except for the sound of gagging and choking, it was eerily quiet on that bridge. The collective assemblage held their breath in anticipation of the death dance. They didn't have to wait long.

Calvin could not believe it was actually happening—that God was allowing these white devils to hang him after he'd prayed so hard, begging him not to. His mom always told him that the spirits and his ancestors would protect him. Maybe his protection left right along with his *Damballah Weddo Vévé*, or maybe they were on vacation or out to lunch with God. He wanted to curse God out, to call him a liar and a fraud, but he was way too busy dealing with the horrible burning in his chest, pumping his slender young legs and feet in search of ground to stand on and air to breathe.

His struggles caused the noose to tighten around his neck, further cutting off his air supply. His eyes bugged out of their sockets, and his throat and chest burned as if they were on fire. His tongue swelled to twice its size. One foot was bare. Loose, watery stool ran down his leg and dripped around his twitching ankles. The demon had to admit the kid was putting on a damn good show. He nearly came on himself watching Calvin dance on thin air.

All too soon, gravity won out. With his neck twisted at an odd angle, Calvin's body jerked a few times before it grew still, allowing death to take over. Now his body was swaying to the same discordant beat as his uncles.

Alas, the show is over. I will depart this place and leave the minor demons to scramble over the three new souls claimed this day. I have much bigger fish to fry, Hindrance thought. And with that, the demon departed Lou Sadie's body as quickly as he had entered it.

CHAPTER SEVEN

ELIZABETH ANNE FRANÇOIS'S enemies would soon learn that it would take more than a bullet and a rock upside the head to kill her. She had the favor of the spirits upon her, and it was not her time to go.

As fate would have it, after learning of Fruit, Junior, and Calvin's deaths, Jimmy Lee doubled back to the farm to find Elizabeth lying bloody and unconscious at the bottom of the front porch steps with that blasted one-eyed cat sitting on her chest. Deputy Lester Stretch's bullet struck Elizabeth in the upper chest area and exited through her back, thankfully sparing any vital organs. Àse watched Jimmy Lee lift her mistress's inert body and carry her inside the house, where he patched her up as best he could.

The sheriff should have finished Elizabeth off while he had the chance because an enormous ball of festering hatred filled the space where love for her brothers and her son once lived.

Elizabeth and Jimmy Lee waited until the wee hours of the morning, when the stench of betrayal had settled, to head out to Shubata. Together, they performed the solemn task of loading Fruit, Junior, and Calvin's bodies into the back of Elizabeth's pickup truck to take them back to the farm for burial. Through it all, Elizabeth didn't so much as flinch at the physical exertion nor did she shed a single tear.

Once the grim task was completed, Jimmy Lee did everything in his power short of dropping to his knees and begging Elizabeth to leave town with him. There was no safe place for Elizabeth in Mississippi, and he knew it.

Once the sheriff learns she is not dead, he will finish the job, just as sure as my name is Jimmy Lee Lawson.

"I love you, Elizabeth. Always have and always will," he said haltingly. "I ain't never been much for flowery words, but I always thought we'd be together. The time is now, Elizabeth. There is nothing left for you here. I'm leaving for Texas tomorrow. I want you to come with me. My uncle has a modest farm in Austin. We can stay with him until we get on our feet. We can have a good life together. Come with me, Elizabeth. Let me take care of you. Please."

Elizabeth was moved by the sincerity of Jimmy Lee's words, but she had different plans. She intended to leave town alright, just not with Jimmy Lee. He'd already gone out on a limb for her. She would not repay his kindness by getting him killed for associating with her. He was just shy of twenty years old, with his whole life ahead of him. He deserved better than that.

"Jimmy Lee, I swear before God, I will be grateful to you 'til the day I die," she said in a voice filled with emotion made gruff from unshed tears.

"Had it not been for your courageous act of sneaking through the woods and back to the farm to tend my wounds, I would be dead, and my son and brothers would have swung from that godforsaken bridge until the buzzards picked their bones clean. Thank you for helping me bury my family, baby," she said, gently stroking his cheek with a work-roughened hand.

Jimmy Lee lowered his head for the kiss she'd always denied him. The thought of their tongues dancing in that familiar way had always stoked a fire in his lower belly. It made Jimmy Lee hunger for the elusive, sensuous woman he'd never been able to tame, no matter how hard he tried. At the very last moment, Elizabeth turned away so that his kiss landed on her cheek instead of her lips.

Not once in all the years they'd known each other had she allowed him to kiss her. Tonight was no different. Both of them knew they would never see each other again, at least not in this life; yet, she stubbornly refused to give him the one thing he craved.

He pulled her closer to him, consigning her softness and lush curves to memory. They would have made love atop the freshly dug graves had Elizabeth not had the strength to pull away. She ran her thumb over his full bottom lip before she doused his hopes and dreams forever.

"I have a score to settle," Elizabeth said. "Maybe I will see you in the next life."

And with those final words, she turned to leave. She did not bother to look back.

The headlights on Sheriff Edgar DeLonge's dirty white Chevy pickup truck illuminated a fat, lazy possum crossing the road. He slowed down to allow the possum to pass. Overgrown vegetation encroached upon both sides of the dirt road leading up to the farmhouse he called home. He saw no reason to maintain it. Other than hosting an occasional Klan meeting, DeLonge rarely had any visitors.

The truck rumbled past a gnarly limbed, oak tree partially obscuring a sign that read "Old Hill-DeLonge Plantation, Old Hill-DeLonge Road, Meridian, Mississippi (circa 1723)." Not long thereafter, the farmhouse in which five generations of DeLonges had lived and died came into full view. The house sat smack-dab in the middle of nowhere, just south of Collinsville, ten minutes north of Meridian proper and about three and a half hours from New Orleans. There wasn't another soul for miles, which suited DeLonge just fine.

DeLonge pulled in front of the house and killed the engine. He sat behind the wheel, staring at nothingness, too sore and too tired to move. The adrenaline rush of the kill had subsided, allowing the aches and pains of a beaten middle-aged man to set in. Fruit François's beating and the events of the day were finally taking their toll.

DeLonge was a burly man, at least six-foot-four. In his younger days, his build had been as solid as the oak trees leading up to his house. A sedentary lifestyle, however, and too much drink and rich food conspired to pile fat over the muscles that made up his 325-pound frame. He heaved his body out of the truck, and made his way to the front door and into the house with carefully measured steps, wheezing like an asthmatic.

DeLonge entered his house to find the TV still on. He'd been eating a TV dinner while watching the evening news, and fuming over the current state of affairs in the country when Neusome Krutchner showed up on his doorstep the night before, demanding justice for his daughter.

Except for the mouse that was feasting upon the congealed remnants of the Swanson meatloaf dinner, everything, including the rancor DeLonge felt when the newscaster made reference to the signing of the civil rights act a month earlier, was as he'd left it.

DeLonge vowed then and there, that as the duly elected Sheriff of Lauderdale County, to make it his mission to ensure that the Colored residents of his district didn't get any dangerous ideas about equality. After barely listening to Krutchner's allegations, DeLonge pushed away from the snack tray and grabbed his gun.

Later that night, DeLonge, his deputy, and the Krutchners set out for the François farm, determined to make an example of the proud Colored farmers who resided there. DeLonge reasoned that if he brought down the proudest among them, the others would easily fall in line.

And now, Fruit, Junior, Calvin, and Elizabeth Francois were dead.

DeLonge and a few of his buddies stuck around after the lynching to have a go at Lou Sadie. He was determined to wash the whore's stink off his body. Once inside, he wasted no time shedding his clothing and heading for the bathroom to stand under a scalding hot shower.

DeLonge was in the habit of shitting, shaving, and showering with the bathroom door wide open. There was no need for modesty. He was a sixty-nine-year-old bachelor, residing all alone. He had no children, at least none that he knew of. Other than the few curious birds, squirrels, and night creatures that occasionally scurried by the open bathroom window, there was absolutely no one to observe his nudity. He didn't even have to lock his front door. He liked it like that.

DeLonge hummed a drunken tune as he scrubbed away at his flesh, getting "Zestfully clean." He was far more concerned with the possibility of catching something from Lou Sadie than he was about the role he played in the dastardly events of the day.

This would not be the first lynching he took part in, and, if he had his way, it damn sure would not be his last. DeLonge, like his father and grandfather, was a long-standing, card-holding member of the local White Knights of the Ku Klux Klan and a firm believer in their precepts.

DeLonge watched the news and he read the papers. The Coloreds were rioting and tearing stuff up all over the country. He was sickened by the Civil Rights Act signed into law. It was his job as sheriff to put the fear of God in the Coloreds in his county so they didn't get any bright ideas about doing the same shit in his jurisdiction.

I'll kill every single one of them before I allow that to happen.

His narrow slit for lips nearly disappeared altogether as his left temple throbbed from the bullet that nigger Junior François fired at him.

I'm lucky the bullet merely grazed and didn't kill me, he thought.

Unsightly purple bruises covered his face and body. It hurt like hell whenever he took a deep breath. He feared one or more of his ribs might be cracked from that door-slamming stunt Fruit François pulled.

Those François boys were light-skinned uppity niggers who needed to be taught a lesson, and by golly I'm glad I was the one to teach 'em. I wish I could bring their Black asses back to life so that I can kill 'em all over again.

DeLonge was as hirsute as a gorilla, with hair growing out of his nose and ears. Even his back and buttocks were covered in a dense coat of thick gray hair. Despite the surfeit of hair on his body, save for a solitary strand on his crown, and a Bozo the Clown cap of gray around his ridiculously oversized ears, he had very little hair on his head. DeLonge's dome was as bald as a cue ball.

The steamy hot shower water sluiced through the thick coils of hair covering nearly every inch of his body, turning the pale skin beneath the hair an unhealthy shade of pink. By the time DeLonge felt clean, the smell of Zest soap and steam filled the bathroom, coating every surface with liquid fog. He turned sideways, grunting as he squeezed his oversized body out of the outdated shower stall, glistening all over and dripping water onto the dirty tile floor. He made for an unattractive sight with his big bloated belly, flat hairy ass, and colt thin legs.

A white cotton towel, made dingy from too many uses and not enough washes, sat atop the closed toilet seat. He used it to dry his face and then his body, oblivious to the sour smell rising from the damp material. That was when he noticed the three words scrawled in the condensation on his bathroom mirror.

"It's payback time!"

He dropped the towel and went for his gun.

CHAPTER EIGHT

EDGAR DELONGE STRUGGLED into the soiled pants he'd worn earlier, mindless of the specks of blood and particles of brain matter embedded in the fabric. The task was made especially difficult since he had to keep his eyes peeled for imminent danger and hold on to his gun.

He searched the totally dark interior of the house one room at a time with eyes narrowed, and his pistol cocked and loaded. This was the only home he had ever known. DeLonge knew the interior like the back of his hand. He didn't need light.

Someone was in my house while I was showering. They may still be here.

DeLonge could feel the imprint of their presence in his space. If the burglar escaped, they could not have gotten far. Thinking he might need some backup, he picked up the phone in the kitchen to get one of his deputies out there.

The line was dead.

DeLonge was heading to his basement when a sound from outside gave him pause. Next came a loud whinny. He hurried to the stable where he kept his prized mare, Lullabelle. His grip tightened on the gun.

I will put a bullet between the eyes of anyone trying to steal my horse and ask questions later. I paid a lot of money for that horse, he silently declared.

For the past five years, DeLonge had been running his mare in the Kentucky Derby. She hadn't placed yet, but it was just a matter of time before his investment paid off. Woe unto anybody fool enough to mess with his Lullabelle. He cautiously opened the door to the stable.

⌘

Elizabeth was lying in wait behind the stable door tightly gripping the shovel DeLonge used to scoop horse manure. She chose that moment to strike.

She swung the shovel like she was Mickey Mantle, up to bat in the fourteenth inning of the World Series with bases loaded.

She swung with all her might, hitting DeLonge square in the center of his face, mindless of the pain from the bullet his deputy plugged in her a few hours earlier. The shovel made a loud clanging sound at the same time his gun went off and flew out of his hand.

The impact of the shovel flattened DeLonge's nose and fractured multiple bones in his face. He went down like a crippled kid in the ring with a heavyweight boxer. Elizabeth went to work as soon as he hit the ground.

In less than five minutes, she had DeLonge bound, gagged, and trussed tighter than a fat hog in a hog-tying contest. The finishing touch was the long length of rawhide she tethered from his prized mare's saddle to the rope wrapped around his shoulder. When she was done, she pulled up a wooden stool she spied near a bale of hay, sat down, and waited.

DeLonge came to a few minutes later smelling of fear, sweat, and Zest. Choking sounds issued throughout the stable. Elizabeth had shoved an old oil rag down his throat, making it impossible for him to beg for his miserable life.

DeLonge blinked through the pain to clear his vision and damn near shit on himself when he saw who was sitting on a wooden stool beside him with her chin in her hand. Elizabeth François resembled a medical student studying a particularly odious body for dissection. There was a miniature black cauldron on the floor next to her.

What in the blue-blazin' fuck! We left that Black bitch for dead, he thought, with his eyes bugging out of his head. *I saw Stretch cap her in the chest with my own eyes.*

Elizabeth looked down at the sheriff's fat belly and wrinkled neck dispassionately. She took her time to look at every inch of him, watching him shrivel before her eyes.

A smile crossed her pretty face when she saw the flesh wound on his temple from where a bullet had grazed him.

That is not the result of the recent shovel attack. That is a bullet wound from one of my brothers.

Elizabeth was first to break the silence.

"I come from a long line of Zanzibari witches. My maternal great-grandmother three times removed was Mehwish Shumaila bin Said el-Murgebi. She was a Zanzibari princess, tricked by her white lover, and enslaved on Magnolia Hill, one of the most infamous plantations in Louisiana. The whites stole everything from her, even her name. They named her Hannah," Elizabeth said, as if she was confiding a bit of information she found to be rather distasteful.

"No matter what the whites did to her, they could not break her. She survived years of enslavement by chipping away at the core of her masters' dark souls, one spell at a time. Her patience paid off. One day, she burned the plantation to the ground with everyone in it," Elizabeth confided with a smile. Hannah was eventually captured and executed, but not before her only daughter, Ann, escaped north and continued our bloodline.

What in the gawdallmighty hell is this crazy Black nigger bitch talking about? DeLonge wondered. *She can shove her jungle history lesson right up her fat ass*, he thought hatefully, forgetting all the times he had lusted after that same ass.

If she would just shut her pie hole for a minute, maybe I can convince her to change her course of action and get myself out of this predicament. Hell, everybody knows niggers are stupid. Promise them some money, and they will do just about anything.

"I guess you are wondering why I brought you here and why I am providing background information about my family," she said, as if she could read his mind. "I just want you to understand the kind of folks I come from and the significance of your actions, Sheriff DeLonge.

"You should have *asked* somebody before you fucked with me and my family. I work with multiple hands," she said proudly. "I guess somebody like you wouldn't know anything about Orisha, Palo, Hoodoo, Voodoo and such. I am what you white folks would call a witch or a sorceress," she said, pointing her finger at her chest.

"I took my brothers and my son down from that bridge and gave them a proper burial. I saw what you animals did to their bodies." She paused to control her rising temper.

"You had no right to touch my family! You will suffer the same fate as them. You see, I believe in an eye for an eye, literally."

"This here is Ricky." She brandished a wicked-looking hunting knife seconds before she dug the tip of the blade into DeLonge's left eye, scooping the blue orb right out of the socket. The resultant muffled scream was so blood-curdling it raised the hackles at the base of her skull. Other than a sense of annoyance, she felt nothing for DeLonge's suffering.

Gag and all, DeLonge howled like a wolf shouting at the moon. The sound was sweet music to Elizabeth's ears. She wanted to stand up and dance. Instead, she waited patiently for the agonizing sounds to subside and soft whimpers to take their place. DeLonge struggled against the ties that bound him as she continued with her personal monologue.

"We Françoises ain't never bothered nobody. We tended our land and minded our business. We never killed nobody who didn't deserve to die. Most folks have the good sense to leave us the fuck alone. That bitch Lou Sadie Krutchner lied on my brothers and my son. You knew it, and you still let those pale-skinned animals lynch them—probably even took part in it. That makes you a liar too. Well, guess what, motherfucker? You won't be lying no more!"

Elizabeth pulled the gag out of his mouth, and before he could catch a full breath or yell for help, she cut out his tongue and wiped the bloody blade on his fat, quivering belly.

"You should have left us the fuck alone, Sheriff. That was your first mistake. Your second one was not making sure that I was dead."

She scooped out the other eye just as nice as you please, leaving three bloody sockets in DeLonge's face, where his eyes and tongue had once been.

Elizabeth paced back and forth in front of DeLonge's body, brandishing the knife with a wicked smile on her face. Unable to see, Edgar DeLonge shifted his head back and forth as if he could sense, or maybe even smell, her intentions.

Humh, the bastard doesn't look so important now, Elizabeth thought, looking down at the mess she had made of the sheriff.

DeLonge had been running roughshod over the Colored folks in Quitman County for years. *That shit is gonna stop today.* Finally growing weary of the wicked game she was playing, Elizabeth decided it was time to finish him off.

"Sheriff DeLonge?" she asked to make sure he was still with her. After all, his ears were still intact.

"I am going to cut off that little Vienna sausage you got between your legs and shove it down your throat, just like you did to Fruit and Junior. I must admit though, my brothers had a lot more to work with." She reached inside his pants to grab his tiny manhood. "And after that, I am going to let your prize mare over there drag your body all over this farm until the skin peels off your body. And when you are good and dead," she whispered theatrically, "I will chop off your head and steal your soul so that you will never know a moment's peace."

The light of the moon caught the surface of the knife as Elizabeth brought it to DeLonge's crotch.

"This is for my son!" She sliced his manhood off, lobbing a mouthful of spit on him.

"If anybody deserves to die, it is you. Payback is a bitch, and revenge is a motherfucker!"

CHAPTER NINE

ELIZABETH SLIPPED INSIDE the Krutchner trailer with the stealth of a seasoned cat burglar. Once inside, the first thing she noticed was the smell. It was godawful.

Consistent with the rotten, filthy souls of its occupants, the interior of the trailer was as filthy as she expected it would be. There was trash, dirty clothes, and decayed food strewn about everywhere in the cramped living room area. A box with a half-eaten pizza sat on the coffee table next to several empty bottles of beer.

A forty-watt bulb lit the hallway outside the open bathroom door. Elizabeth frowned after peeking inside. A plumbing leak, raw sewage on the floor, and a full toilet contributed to the overall noisome smell.

There was a closed door next to the bathroom. Elizabeth assumed that was where Lou Sadie slept. She could hear the whirl of an oscillating fan on the other side of the door.

Neusome Krutchner lay snoring on a dingy gray couch with his hand inside the open zipper of his trousers. Elizabeth stood over him with Ethel, her sawed-off shotgun, waiting for him to sense her presence. It did not take long for the snoring to stop, his rheumy blue eyes to open, and his brain to register he was not alone.

"Who's there? Come into the light. I can't see you," he said.

A nasty gust of foul breath filled the confines of the filthy living space the minute Old Man Krutchner opened his mouth, assaulting Elizabeth's stomach more effectively than the smell in the filthy bathroom.

More than happy to oblige, Elizabeth stepped to the left so that the light from the moon could better shine on her through the dingy trailer window. She stooped and placed a small wrought iron pot at her feet.

I want him to know who is going to end his rotten life. And if his lying whore of a daughter is in the back room, as I suspect she is, I have a bullet with her name on it, too.

"What the fuck are you doing in my house, nigger!" Neusome sputtered while struggling to get up from the couch.

Without a word, Elizabeth cocked that rifle, shoved it in his mouth and pulled the trigger. There was a loud thud as brain tissue and crimson-coated sofa feathers flew like wounded butterflies. Before heading to the back bedroom, Elizabeth paused to whisper to what used to be Old Man Krutchner's face.

"You want to know what this nigger is doing in your nasty house? Killing you, that's what." She spat on him and hastened to the back room before Lou Sadie could arm herself.

Lou Sadie, the sheriff, and several others remained at the Shubata Bridge, passing around a bottle of corn liquor long after the spectators at the François lynching headed back to town. It was not too long before they were passing pregnant Lou Sadie between them, within a few feet of Calvin's sightless eyes. And now, her head was pounding like a herd of buffalo was running through it. She ached all over.

With Elizabeth François dead, Lou Sadie had no hope of getting a safe abortion in Meridian. She urged the men to use her hard, hoping they would fuck her daddy's bastard right out of her.

She lay sprawled atop dingy bed linen in the grips of the worst hangover of her life and far too drunk to remember which of the men brought her home. It didn't matter. She had been well-used by all of them and intended to sleep for the next two days, if not longer.

Her eyes flew open.

Was that a shot I just heard?

Before Lou Sadie could sufficiently rouse herself to investigate, Elizabeth François strode through the door on her long, sturdy, farmer's legs, dressed in unrelieved black with a camel-colored canvas sack on her shoulder and a sawed-off, double-barreled shotgun in her hand.

Lou Sadie's eyes darted around for a means of escape. She saw none. Her lips were trembling when she addressed the woman whose life she had ruined, based upon a filthy lie.

"You know they gonna hunt you down like a dog for this, Elizabeth. They gonna hang you right beside Fruit, Junior, and your boy," she warned.

Lou Sadie kept talking when her statement was met with silence. She needed to buy herself some time to figure out how to get out of this.

I am too young to die.

"If you leave right now, I promise I won't tell nobody ya come here. It'll be our little secret. Shit, my paw needed killin'. He been putting babies in me since I started bleeding. You did me a favor by killin' him."

Elizabeth appeared to contemplate Lou Sadie's words. "I might consider letting you live if you tell me where Lester Stretch lives."

Before long, Lou Sadie was singing like a jailhouse snitch. She sighed in relief when Elizabeth leaned the shotgun up against the wall and walked closer to the bed, placing a small black pot on the crate Lou Sadie used as a nightstand. Her relief was short-lived. Elizabeth reached inside the canvas sack to brandish a razor sharp, serrated knife.

"This here is a special knife," Elizabeth said, carefully running her gloved finger against the edge so as not to slice through the cloth. "It's a basic buck knife. Fruit and Junior used to use this knife to gut the pigs," she said in a matter-of-fact voice. "I named it Ricky."

"I 'spect you came by my house yesterday so that I could help you get rid of that baby growing inside your belly. And that's just what I intend to do," she said, adjusting the fingers of her gloves.

Lou Sadie's screams could be heard for at least twenty minutes before a deathlike silence embraced the trailer.

&

A stream of hot, pungent urine splashed against the side of Lester Stretch's utility shed. Stretch was in the doghouse again…literally. He came home after a couple of rounds with Lou Sadie to find all the lights out and his house locked down tighter than a jailhouse cell.

His wife, Susan, warned him what would happen if he came home soused again. Not only had Stretch come home drunk as a skunk, but he came home seriously wounded and smelling like that cheap whore, Lou Sadie, had smeared her nasty essence all over him.

Shit, I might be minus a few fingers and have a pirate patch on one eye, but there is nuthin' wrong with my dick, he thought with pride.

When Lester called his wife to inform her of his injuries, she let him know in no uncertain terms that she was sick and tired of his shenanigans and that he would have to find someplace else to sleep. Stretch zipped up his pants and prepared to bed down in the toolshed with Buster, the family dog.

Stretch staggered through the narrow flower-lined pavers leading to the shed, only to run smack-dab into Elizabeth François.

"What are you doing here? DeLonge said you were dead," Stretch said, his speech slurred from way too much alcohol.

"As you can see, Mr. Stretch, I am very much alive," Elizabeth replied. "Your bullet hit me here," she said, raising her hand to show the bandaged area where the bullet entered and exited her upper shoulder. In doing so, she had to undo the top buttons of her blouse, deliberately drawing attention to her soft ample breasts. Stretch licked his lips like a hungry man tempted by a bountiful feast.

"What do you want?" he asked, reluctantly tearing his eyes away from Elizabeth's feminine curves.

"I need your help, Mr. Stretch. My brothers did wrong, and they paid for their actions with their lives. I know the sheriff is still powerful mad, but my son Calvin is innocent of any wrongdoing. Do you think you can find it in your heart to talk to the sheriff and get him to release Calvin's body for a proper burial?" she asked. "It would mean the world to me," she added, stepping closer to run her hand along his chest.

Stretch's breath quickened. He was so intoxicated by the liquor and Elizabeth's closeness that he didn't have the presence of mind to question her motives. What he saw was a woman who would do just about *anything* for his help.

He glanced at the back of his house. Except for the back porch light, which cast a faint illumination on the yard, the house was totally dark. The inherent evil in Stretch rose to the surface like a pot left too long on the stove. The decision was made. Maimed hand and all, he planned to bend Elizabeth François over the workbench in his shed and have at her right under his wife's nose.

That ought to fix Susan for locking me out of my own house, he thought spitefully.

I plan to fuck Elizabeth François real good. And when I've had my fill, I'll turn her over to the sheriff. Shit, we might even have ourselves another hangin', he thought.

His lascivious gaze raked Elizabeth from head to toe. It wasn't until that moment when he noticed the canvas sack hanging from Elizabeth's good shoulder.

"What you got in that there bag, Elizabeth?" His man part took on a life of its own when Elizabeth's pink tongue came out to moisten her luscious lips.

"Well," she said, shyly. "I was kind of nervous, being that I was going to be asking for a favor and all. I didn't want to come empty-handed, so I brought some of my homemade hooch…you know, to relax me a bit."

Her words were uttered in a breathless Marilyn Monroe voice with a southern lilt that made the flesh at the apex of Stretch's bony thighs throb like a toothache. He wanted to throw Elizabeth down on the ground and ease that ache inside of her lush body.

If Elizabeth François needs some liquid courage to spread those pillow-soft thighs of hers, then so be it. She can drink all she wants for all I care.

Elizabeth reached inside the bag to pull out a bottle and two plastic cups.

"Hold on," he said, cradling his bandaged hand. "We can go in the shed. But first I need to chain the dog up so he doesn't wake up my wife."

CHAPTER TEN

ELIZABETH WAITED OUTSIDE the shed while Stretch slipped inside to secure the dog. Moments later, a dim light came on from within. Stretch poked his head out of the cracked door and motioned her inside.

As soon as Elizabeth shut the door behind her, a vicious beast of a dog vaunted himself at her with savage fury, straining against its chain with snapping jaws and wild rabid eyes that burned with malevolent intent. She flattened her back against the shed wall, as the dog barked and snarled, its teeth bared, desperate to tear into her.

"Shut up, you damned hound!" Stretch ordered.

The dog stopped barking at its master's command, but it kept its angry gaze locked and loaded on Elizabeth, its growl low and menacing.

"It's mighty hot in here," Elizabeth observed, undoing two more buttons at the top of her shirt to expose a generous amount of cleavage. "I'm going to pour myself a drink. You going to let me drink by myself, Mr. Stretch?"

Elizabeth was no stranger to the lustful ways of men, especially the white ones. She knew what Stretch wanted. The irony was not lost on Elizabeth that she still had to address him as "Mister," despite what they were about to do.

"Hell no," he responded, his eyes glowing with unbridled lust. "No way will I let a sexy gal like you drink alone," he declared.

"So, you will drink with me," she confirmed shyly.

"Don't mind if I do," Stretch said enthusiastically as Elizabeth offered him the first cup. Elizabeth poured a second cup for herself and raised it to Stretch in a toast.

"To us," she said with a smile.

&

Stretch noticed a change in Elizabeth's demeanor immediately after he took the first sip. There was a cunning look in her eyes he'd failed to notice before. His teeth, hands, and feet went numb before he could finish the drink. A debilitating weakness took control of his entire body. The cup fell from his fingers.

Elizabeth watched dispassionately as Stretch swayed on his feet and toppled like a house built of sand. He finally dropped to his knees before her. She could tell he was in distress by the erratic cadence of his breathing. She imagined each breath was a gift that could be snatched away at any moment. Elizabeth kicked him over, causing him to roll onto his side. The sweet tone of voice she'd used earlier was gone, replaced by something devoid of emotion or humanity.

"I guess you are wondering what is happening to you? I lined your cup with a poison extracted from a puffer fish, which causes immediate paralysis. I can do anything I want to you, and you won't be able to defend yourself or call for help. How does it feel to be helpless and at the mercy of someone who thinks you are less than worthless, Lester? She asked.

"Let me explain how this is going to go. You will be in a state of unresponsive wakefulness. I will break it down for your dumb, backwoods, racist ass if my words are too big for you to comprehend. What that means is that you are going to feel every single thing I am about to do to you; the pain, the fear, *everything*!"

The stupid dog chose that exact moment to start his infernal barking again.

"Wait a minute. I'll be right back," Elizabeth said politely.

She walked up to that dog like the badass farm girl she was and kicked him square in the head with her sturdy, serviceable saddle shoes. After she let him know who the boss was, the frightened hound curled up in a corner whimpering like a three-month-old puppy somebody stomped on. Elizabeth pulled out good old "Ricky" and slit the dog's throat so deep, she damn near decapitated him. She felt no remorse. Buster was the same bloodthirsty canine Stretch used to sic on innocent Colored children for walking past his house.

"Sorry 'bout that." She wiped the bloody blade across the front of Stretch's shirt. "I didn't want him to wake up your wife," she said. "Sure wouldn't want to have to kill her, too. Now where was I?"

In response, a growing pool of pungent pee appeared between Stretch's legs.

"That's right!" Elizabeth snapped her finger. "I was about to show you what happens to folks dumb enough to fuck with my family."

Elizabeth slipped outside the shed to retrieve the cloth-covered trap box, the set of metal tongs, and the duct tape she'd hidden behind a bush prior to Stretch's arrival. She hurriedly carried the items back to the shed. With tongs at the ready, she dragged the trap box beneath the naked bulb in the shed and slowly raised the lid.

Stretch's eyes were frozen with terror as Elizabeth used the tongs to slide the crumbled newspaper in the trap box aside. She took her time, prolonging the process and savoring his fear. A soft rattling sound played duet to Stretch's labored breathing.

With a sure hand made steady from years of practice, Elizabeth locked the head of a four-foot-long, stout-bodied copperhead between the lips of the metal tongs. The snake's flesh was bubblegum pink and accented with dark wide bands that resembled miniature hourglasses.

She grabbed ahold of the snake by the top of its head and the bottom of its jaw between her thumb and forefinger, effectively clamping its mouth shut and trapping its lethal poisonous tongue. The snake thrashed about and squirmed, attempting to wrap its body around her wrist. She didn't release the tongs until she was certain she had a firm grip. As long as Elizabeth had it by the head, she was in control.

Taking measured steps, she walked toward Stretch with a self-satisfied expression and dropped to her knees beside him. Without a word, she pried Stretch's mouth open and shoved the head of the venomous snake between his parted lips.

Seeking a dark, moist place, and lured by the sweet smell of alcohol, the snake did what came naturally. It tunneled down Stretch's throat until there was nothing visible but the slender tip of its colorful tail. Elizabeth slapped a piece of duct tape over Stretch's mouth, silently watching him choke to death.

She hurried to retrieve a miniature wrought iron pot from her bag to capture his soul before it could escape to points unknown. Her lips moved as she silently chanted the magic spell to separate Stretch's soul from his body as the light went out of his eyes. She shut the lid and sealed it tight.

The soul was now hers to command.

❧

Hindrance had a front-row seat inside Elizabeth François's lush body, literally moving in tandem with her as she picked off the ringleaders who murdered her family, one by one. He allowed her warm human blood to flow through and over him and the beat of her heart to slow down after her latest kill, hoping she had another victim in mind. And now he was in a full-blown frenzy.

In all the demon's millennia of existence, he had yet to see a human as exquisitely and decadently vengeful as Elizabeth Anne François; that she was a soul-snatcher made him desire her even more. Soul-snatchers were far and wide between. Humans with the unique talent to snatch souls are virtually nonexistent in The Hells.

Any demon would be proud to have one such as this human at his back, in his bed, and on her knees. The thought of riding the wild human to submission made his scaly demon dick as hard as the impenetrable gates of hell.

With a female like this by my side, I can rule all seven levels of The Hells, he thought. *With her ability to snatch souls, I can make the evil souls she captures a part of my army and be invincible.*

The demon laughed to himself. *I wonder how she will react when I disclose the role I played in her family's demise, for tell her I shall. I will wait until after I've fucked the life out of her to divulge that tidbit of information,* he thought, grabbing hold of his bloated crotch. *I shall make this human my dark queen,* he vowed.

Hindrance exited Elizabeth's body and was about to manifest in his true form to ravish her on the dirty shed floor when his father telepathically summoned him from The Hells. He hesitated but a moment, taking the time to observe the object of his desire gathering the materials she'd used to commit cold-blooded murder with practiced precision.

He wanted nothing more than to tarry but dared not. One doesn't keep The Satan waiting.

⁓ℱ⁓

Elizabeth made her escape from Meridian with eleven hundred miles before her and nothing to do but drive and think. She was headed east, with everything she owned in the back of her old beat-up truck—that is, everything but her heart. She left *that* back in Mississippi.

She had a long trek ahead of her and was figuratively holding her breath every mile of the way, fearful a pack of devils with pale faces and badges were nipping at her heels or setting up a trap ahead of her. Her rational mind told her all white folks weren't bad, but her life experiences dictated otherwise. She slid her hand beneath the driver's seat to touch the cold metal of her sawed-off shotgun and felt a modicum of relief.

Elizabeth could physically distance herself from Mississippi, but she could never distance herself from the memories.

CHAPTER ELEVEN

KILLING WASN'T NEW to Elizabeth. Like a dog that has been kicked one time too many, she learned to bite before the next kick came. She made her first kill when she was only sixteen, right after her forty-nine-year-old husband tried to beat Calvin right out of her belly. In hindsight, maybe it would have been better if he had.

She could vividly remember every detail of the day the darkness came out to play. Her husband subjected her to a brutal beating after catching her doing a little spirit work. He'd already warned her that he didn't want any of that mumbo jumbo hoodoo shit in his house. Elizabeth could no more stop talking to the spirits or performing ancient African rituals passed down by her mother and grandmother than she could muster up the courage to remind him he was living in *her* family home, not his.

Elizabeth patched up her wounds as best she could and, while her husband was still out working in the fields, she cleaned the house from top to bottom, scrubbing down every surface with Florida water and soap, singing "Àse, Àse, O," and praying as she worked. Elizabeth knew there was no problem that a prayer and a spell couldn't cure.

That evening, Elizabeth prepared her husband's favorite supper:

oxtails, fried cabbage, candied yams, and cold water cornbread. She placed a heaping plate of steaming hot food and an ice-cold bottle of beer in front of him along with all the necessary utensils, basically doing everything for him short of tucking the napkin in his collar, chopping up his meat, and spooning the food into his mouth.

Her husband was old-school. He was of the mindset that a woman's place was to serve. Elizabeth didn't mind. She'd been in the kitchen with her mama since she was a little girl. She liked to cook and clean. She just didn't like to cook and clean for *him*. Not only did her husband expect her to wait on him hand and foot, but he forbid her to make a plate for herself until he gave the say-so.

Elizabeth dutifully pulled up a chair to watch him eat. He pointedly ignored her while pretending to read the newspapers.

The asshole never did learn how to read.

That night, her husband thoroughly enjoyed what Elizabeth liked to refer to as the last supper, even demanding seconds. Elizabeth jumped up, happy to oblige.

The rat poison took effect halfway through the second helping, she recalled, laughing to herself.

Her husband knew she'd done something to the food the minute his belly started cramping. He lunged across the table with murder in his eyes, doing his best to get at her, knocking over his chair in the process and swiping everything on the table to the floor. Elizabeth calmly picked up a cast-iron skillet and brained him.

Later that night, she rolled his body in a sheet, hefted him inside a wheelbarrow, and dragged his ass to the patch of vacant land behind the cornfield. It was a fitting spot to plant him. Her husband always did enjoy a good buttery ear of corn.

"From the earth we came, and to the earth we shall return," were the last words she whispered over her husband's grave before she spit on it. The act of spitting on that grave expressed her loathing and contempt far better than words ever could.

By the time the authorities came to investigate several weeks later, Elizabeth's husband was feeding the boll weevils and the worms, and Elizabeth had a brand new baby boy to love. She named him Calvin after her late father, who, unlike her husband, knew how to treat the females in his family.

Her brothers Fruit and Junior came back from 'Nam to find themselves minus a brother-in-law and overjoyed that they had gained a brand new nephew. Neither of them asked any questions about Elizabeth's absentee husband, and Elizabeth volunteered no answers.

Somebody should have told that sonofabitch who the fuck he was dealing with, she thought, reminiscing about the look on his dead face when she tossed the first shovel of dirt on him.

Everybody around town knew not to mess with the François family. They never started trouble, but they would damn sure finish it. Elizabeth's husband was the first somebody to fertilize the cornfield, but not the last. Back then, nobody gave a damn when somebody Colored turned up missing.

Elizabeth was proof positive that the first kill is the hardest, and the rest come easy. She didn't want to kill, but she would do it again if she had to.

⚘

Elizabeth drove in a trance-like state, her mind a jumble of discordant thoughts and memories—some good, but mostly bad. Her life flashed before her eyes as the wheels on the old truck ate up the miles on I-59 North, and from there I-75 and I-81. Her only company was Àse, who she kept in a carrier in the passenger seat.

She'd been driving on pure adrenaline for eight hours, on the verge of falling asleep with her eyes wide open and perilously close to slamming into the divider. A sudden jerk of her hand on the steering wheel and the blare of a nearby motorist's horn snapped

Elizabeth out of her trance, saving her from being yet another victim of the dreaded white line fever. She looked at the gas gauge.

I'm getting low on gas, and I'm dog-tired. A perilous combination, she thought. *We need to stop somewhere.*

The million-dollar question was where? She may have escaped a lynch mob in Mississippi, but she was still in the Deep South where Colored motorists were known to disappear and never be heard of again.

Although the Civil Rights Act was passed last month, a lot of whites either couldn't read or didn't give a damn. Colored travelers still had to be careful where they stopped to get gas and food. Some rest stop proprietors refused to serve Colored people, and if they did serve them, thanks to that sonofabitch Thomas Dartmouth "Daddy" Rice, after whom the phrase "Jim Crow" was coined, the accommodations were separate and always inferior.

Rice became rich performing a minstrel routine based upon a fictional Black slave named Jim Crow. His act portrayed a demeaning and extremely insulting caricature of a clumsy, dim-witted, Colored buffoon, which was apparently how white folks felt comfortable in viewing Colored people.

Elizabeth would do just about anything to snuff out the light behind Rice's eyes while he was in his blackface get-up. But he was already dead and buried in an unmarked grave somewhere in New York.

I'll have to find his grave so that I can take a piss on it, she thought uncharitably.

Elizabeth kept one eye on the road while she referred to the dog-eared copy of the *Negro Motorist Green Book*, an annual guidebook for Colored travelers that Jimmy Lee had given her years ago. There was a Colored-friendly rest area in Greeneville, Tennessee, between the end of I-81 to the south and the Virginia state line to the north.

It was about thirty miles outside of Johnson City, which was the halfway mark between Mississippi and her final destination.

Elizabeth glanced at the cooler on the passenger-side floor, where she'd placed DeLonge's severed head, and felt a fleeting sense of satisfaction. She had no way of knowing she'd be driving into the eye of the storm when she followed the sign for exit 41.

❧

CHAPTER TWELVE

610 Lee Place, Plainfield, NJ 07063

OVER ELEVEN HUNDRED miles from Mississippi, and metaphorically worlds apart, young Daniel Calhoun's day was beginning like any other. He opened his eyes just in time to see a dark shadow dart from the foot of his bed to the other side of his bedroom. Daniel couldn't tell if it was a spirit or the remnants of a dream reluctant to let go. He blinked, and the image disappeared behind the partially open door of his closet. Daniel wasn't frightened. Before she passed, his granny told him he was born with a veil, so he was used to seeing stuff like that. The sound of a closing door and someone walking down the hallway sliced through the post-dream fog, rendering Daniel fully alert. The desperate need to relieve himself forced Daniel to sit up in bed. Before he could make it to the bathroom, he heard the shower come on and his dad singing a gospel song off-key. There was only one bathroom in their tidy two-bedroom house. Daniel waited it out until his belly was about to burst rather than share space with his father. Every Sunday morning, his dad would get up early to read his bible. Right after, he would shit, shower, and shave to prepare for the 11:00 A.M. church service, where he would sit in the section reserved for the deacons and deaconesses, all sanctified and shit.

But Daniel knew there wasn't a thing sanctified about his father. He couldn't stand his father's self-righteous, fake Christian ways. Daniel remained seated on the side of his bed with his eyes closed and his stomach tightening into knots, pretending he didn't have to pee so badly his teeth hurt. He was determined to hold his water until his father was out of the bathroom, but his bladder had other plans. Grumbling to himself, he thought: *When you gotta go, you gotta go.* Resigned that he would have no choice but to engage with his father or piss on himself, he stood up and headed for the bathroom.

Fifteen minutes into his father's ablutions, Daniel stumbled into the bathroom, scratching his belly and rubbing sleep crust from his eyes. He wrinkled his nose when the pervasive stink of Magic Shave and Ivory soap pinched the inside of his nostrils. Heedless of his father's presence, he headed straight for the toilet and whipped out his little wooden soldier to relieve himself.

"Aaah," he said, groaning in relief as a long stream of first-morning urine splashed against the inside of the commode. His ass cheeks vibrated as a wet bullet of flatulence evacuated his belly, adding to the overall stink. He flushed the toilet and dragged his bare feet to the twin vanity.

Father and son stood side by side, brushing their teeth—one in a pair of dingy boxers and the other with a damp towel wrapped around his hips. It was Sunday morning, and the Calhoun men had officially started their day.

"Mawnin', Dad," Daniel mumbled with a froth of Colgate foam spilling out of the sides of his mouth.

Franklin Calhoun paused to ruffle his son's messy afro. Daniel stiffened at his father's touch. Franklin couldn't remember the last time his son suffered his touch without flinching or had looked him in the eye while talking to him. Today was no different.

"Mawnin', son. You sure you don't want to come to church with your old man this mawnin'?" Franklin teased. "There is going to be a guest speaker from Philly," he added as enticement.

"Naw, Dad," Daniel replied, looking everywhere but at his father. "I have a test tomorrow. I'd better stay home and study." Daniel reached for the bottle of Listerine to gargle, making a point not to touch his father while doing so.

Hard as he tried, Franklin could not figure out how his son, an otherwise straight "A" student and presiding track star, had failed gym.

How in the hell do you fail gym? He asked himself.

Not only did Daniel accomplish the impossible but to avoid being left back and as a caveat for reinstatement on the track team, his son had to attend summer school.

Franklin's droopy eyes inspected his son. Daniel was rail thin like his late wife's side of the family, with long skinny arms, a puny chest, and nutmeg-colored skin.

That boy could eat me out of house and home and not gain a pound, he thought.

Daniel usually hid his long-lashed, expressive, brown, eyes behind a bookish pair of thick, black, David Ruffin-style, glasses that constantly slipped down the bridge of his narrow nose. The only thing Daniel inherited from his father were his pearly whites and his lousy eyesight. Everything else came from his mother. Franklin's wife, Merle, took her last breath at the same time Daniel took his first one.

The Lord giveth, and the Lord taketh away, Franklin thought sadly, peering at his reflection in the mirror.

Daniel thanked God every day that he didn't look like his father.

He probably wouldn't look half bad if he didn't have more craters on his face than the surface of the moon and a nose that looked like he'd caught the wrong end of a pair of brass knuckles, he thought obdurately.

Franklin was not a good-looking man by any stretch of the

imagination. He bore an uncanny resemblance to the cartoon character Touché Turtle, with prominent, heavy-lidded sleepy eyes and an oddly shaped oblong head.

What Franklin lacked in looks, he more than adequately compensated for in other ways. He was a college-educated man with a weakness for wide-hipped women, Lincoln Continentals, and fine threads. Quite a few members of Bethel Baptist Church were more than willing to overlook Franklin's ugly face because of his professional credentials and the prodigious package he was holding.

Franklin took it upon himself to service as many church matrons as were willing. He considered it his duty as an upstanding Christian to help those sisters in need, focusing his attention on married women to avoid any unnecessary entanglements. He was a confirmed bachelor, and he intended to stay that way.

Yeah, I might be ugly, he thought, examining his image in the mirror with a smirk on his face when he caught his son looking at him, *but I bet I get way more trim than that Casanova cat on his best day.*

Franklin's mind drifted to the night before when he had Deaconess Lottie Poole pinned up against the counter in the church kitchen with her cotton drawers around her ankles and her skirt around her waist. Franklin immediately got hard. He thought the act of fornicating in a house of worship constituted a negligible sin that could easily be remedied by placing more dollars in the collection plate or praying a few minutes longer. Little did he know that there was not a collection plate that was big enough, nor enough money in the world, to close the festering fissure bubbling inside his godforsaken, rotten soul.

I am the chairman of the Deacon Board, he thought proudly. *It would be unseemly of me to show up at church with a boner.*

Franklin forced his thoughts out of the gutter and hurried from the bathroom to get dressed, but not before his son was utterly disgusted by the sizable tent his prodigious member made in the front of his towel. Less than twenty minutes later, Franklin was dressed and ready to go.

Franklin believed clothes made the man and not the other way around. "I cut a fine-looking figure in this here lightweight seersucker suit, off-white shirt, and powder blue tie," he declared, preening in front of his bedroom mirror. He wore a jaunty off-white straw hat tipped back on his head and a pair of off-white Stacy Adams he picked up on Branford Place in Newark to complete his outfit.

✍

It promised to be a scorcher out. Franklin draped the jacket over his arm in deference to the heat. He would put it on just before he made his grand entrance into the church. He paused at the door to give his son some last-minute instructions.

"Daniel," he said in his best Sunday morning, Martin Luther King Jr., voice. "Run to the corner store and pick me up a bag of charcoal briquettes. I might want to throw something on the grill when I get back. It's too hot to turn on the oven. Make sure you take out the garbage and pull the cans to the curb before you leave out of here. The garbage man is coming tomorrow morning."

It was a good thing Franklin didn't see Daniel roll his eyes at him behind his back. There would have been hell to pay.

"I want that nasty bedroom of yours tidied up by the time I come back from church. And I don't want no kids rippin' and runnin' in my house, you hear? That includes your cousin Muscles. That boy is keeping bad company. I don't trust him and don't want him in this house while I'm not here."

"Yes, Dad," Daniel said dutifully.

Sometimes Daniel felt like the male version of Cinderella. Daniel loved his cousin Muscles. Sometimes Muscles would come by the house, and they would get high together. Muscles didn't seem to care that Daniel wasn't into the same stuff as his other friends.

I wish my dad would shut the fuck up and just leave. I can't wait until I turn eighteen to get my own place, Daniel thought.

"Alright," Franklin said, pausing to preen in front of the decorative living room mirror one last time. "I've got a Deacon Board meeting right after church, so I'll be late. See you this evening."

"Okay, Dad, bye."

"I thought I told that boy to drag those trash cans to the curb," Franklin mumbled, slowing down in front of his driveway. Anger-propelled steam was burning a scorching trail up his neck. It didn't take much to set Franklin off. Church let out early. He was hot. He was hungry. *And* he was in a foul mood.

He barely missed hitting a towering, dark-skinned man who was blocking his driveway. He leaned on the horn, letting the stranger know his displeasure. The man took his time getting out of the way. Franklin wanted to roll down the window and jump bad with the dude, but something told him to let him be.

Despite the insufferable heat, the man was wearing a pair of black leather gloves, a crazy-looking full-length red velvet cape thingamajig with a red, black and green knit apple cap, and red patent-leather platform shoes. Franklin couldn't see the man's eyes because he was wearing a pair of Ray Charles sunglasses. The crazy get-up looked more like a Halloween costume than something a grown man would wear out in the street.

He must be crazy, he thought. *Best to let sleeping dogs lie.*

CHAPTER THIRTEEN

FRANKLIN MANEUVERED HIS Lincoln into the narrow driveway, where both metal trash cans were still sitting outside the garage, seemingly mocking his authority. His anger meter crept up yet another notch.

He sat in the car, reluctant to turn off the ignition and the air-conditioning that went along with it.

It's hot enough to fry a slab of Taylor ham on the sidewalk. And wouldn't you know it? On the hottest day of the year, the blasted church air-conditioning gave up the ghost.

Black folks generate heat on a cold day. The mercury was kissing one hundred degrees inside that church, and the church had the nerve to be packed. Without the benefit of air-conditioning, it was nigh on unbearable.

They suffered through regular church service, but Pastor Nelson canceled the Deacon Board meeting scheduled to take place right after. He told everyone to go home and try to stay cool. Franklin intended to do just that.

If my old arthritic left knee is any indication, there is going to be a downpour of epic proportions. The sky is getting darker by the minute.

I won't be doing any barbecuing outside today. I sure hope the rain will cool things off a bit.

A bucket of crispy fried chicken with all the fixings and a homemade glazed pound cake rode shotgun in the passenger seat, right alongside Franklin's trusty *King James Bible*. He purchased the chicken, biscuits, and mashed potatoes from Kentucky Fried in North Plainfield. The cake, however, was compliments of Deaconess Lottie Poole, a silver-haired fox with a pretty set of big brown legs that Franklin crawled between whenever her husband, a traveling salesman, went out of town.

Just because I'm a Christian doesn't mean I'm dead. I'm a man, and a man has needs, he thought, to justify his breaking God's commandment not to covet thy neighbor's wife. *Shit, the Pooles live on the other side of town.*

Lottie told Franklin her husband would be out of town again next weekend.

I have to stop by Lottie's house and properly thank her for this here pound cake, Franklin thought, laughing to himself as he dug the house keys out of his pocket and got out of the car.

Franklin dragged the trashcans to the curb and returned to the car to get the food. An oily sheen of sweat was taking up residence on his skin by the time he walked the short distance from the car to the door. He pushed his hat back to wipe the sweat off his brow with his forearm.

His dark eyes narrowed at the familiar smell of weed that greeted him at the front door. Stevie Wonder's "I Was Made To Love Her" was playing loud enough to disturb the next-door neighbors.

Daniel knows I don't allow no finger-poppin' devil music in this house, he thought angrily. *This here is a Christian household. He's supposed to be studying.* Franklin was a firm believer in the "spare the rod and spoil the child" rule. Daniel could attest to that.

It's been a long time since I've seen fit to whup Daniel's ass, he reasoned with an itching hand. *I plan to beat Daniel's ass all the way into next week for disrespecting my house.*

By the time I get finished with his narrow ass, I bet he won't be smoking no more weed or playing sacrilegious music in my house or any-where else, Franklin thought, placing the food on the kitchen table.

His lips were a straight line of Southern Baptist Christian indignation as he walked down the hallway looking like a death row executioner. Each footfall was a determined step of self-pro-claimed righteousness.

❧

Franklin's feet carried him down the carpeted hallway, past the custom-framed pictures of the white Virgin Mary and the white Jesus. With every step he took, the smell of musky man and weed grew more pronounced. He followed the smell to his son's bed-room door and tried the knob. The door was locked. By this time, Franklin's anger meter was creeping dangerously close to the point of no return.

Hell no! Ain't no locked doors allowed in my house 'less I'm the one locking 'em. I pay the cost to be the goddamn boss!

He raised his hand to knock. *Maybe Daniel is burning incense that smells like weed. Maybe I've got it all wrong. The boy could be in the room jerking off or something. That would explain the locked bedroom door.*

Hell, I have lost count of the times I beat the Bishop, he thought, joking to himself.

Then Franklin heard a deep guttural moan, followed by a voice that bore an uncanny resemblance to that of his son, exhorting, "Yes! Right there. Eeew shit, *pah-leeeeze* don't stop! Stir that gravy up nice and slow!"

Acting on sheer instinct, Franklin sprang into action. He took a step back and raised his Stacy Adams–clad foot to kick that door in like he was Plainfield Vice. The door crashed into a poster of the Supremes hanging on the wall behind it, leaving a noticeable dent in the image of Diana Ross's feet.

The sordid tableau playing out in front of Franklin hit him so hard he had to grab hold of the door frame to keep from falling. Franklin didn't know at what point he had started crying, but he was crying like a frightened three-year-old left out in the woods late at night.

His son. His namesake. His fucking *seed* was lying face down on the bed with his ass elevated while a heavyset teen plowed about nine inches of thick, glistening cock up his ass. The kid's dick was buried so far up Daniel's ass, Franklin was surprised it didn't pop out of Daniel's mouth.

Franklin stood rooted in that doorway, temporarily immobilized. Both youths turned in his direction at the same time, like they were actors in one of those old-fashioned silent movies. Franklin moved his head from left to right in denial of what was right in front of him. He knew he was probably grasping at straws, but he thought, maybe, just maybe, this kid had forced himself on Daniel. That was something he could handle.

Then he noted the tube of anal lube conspicuously sitting on Daniel's nightstand. That put the lie to any assumption he may have harbored that his son was an unwilling participant in an act he considered the most reprehensible, abhorrent sin before God and man. In Franklin's mind, the tube of lube was an irrefutable indictment.

Franklin knew his son had some sugar in his tank, but never in a million years did he think it had gone this far. Then he remembered the times he had turned a blind eye when he caught Daniel jumping rope with the neighborhood girls, or when Daniel would cry when he wouldn't allow him to play jacks or other games traditionally played by little girls. He thought Daniel was just going through a phase.

I should have known better.

❧

"This is the devil's work," Franklin said, raising his eyes to whatever demon was controlling his son 'cause it sure as hell wasn't the lord.

"I should have nipped this shit in the bud a long time ago," he said, removing his leather belt from around his waist.

"By the time I am done with you, boy, you will either be straight or dead. I will not knowingly suffer a sodomite under my roof. Hallelujah!" he proclaimed, raising a fist in the air as if almighty God was cosigning his every word.

Then, to Daniel's chagrin, his deranged father started stomping around the bedroom, doing the Holy Ghost dance and speaking in tongues. Ernie Wilson, Daniel's lover, stared at Franklin, stunned by the outlandish display.

Daniel felt sick to his stomach. He scrambled to the head of the bed and, with shaking hands, snatched the bedsheet to cover his nakedness. His action left his lover ass out and totally exposed to Franklin's baleful glare. This was Daniel's worst nightmare come true.

Ernie's erect phallus was dangling between his thick thighs like a pendulum. Franklin watched the offending appendage shrink before his eyes. The sight of it caused Franklin to lose his fragile hold on sanity. It was like someone stuck a stick of dynamite in his mouth and lit the fuse.

Franklin lost it.

"You muthafuckin' faggots!" he bellowed at the top of his lungs. Daniel flinched as the vile epithet shot out of his father's mouth. Everything in that bible Franklin left in the front seat of his car flew out the window, right along with his façade of Christian righteousness.

CHAPTER FOURTEEN

SENSING THINGS WERE about to get ugly and afraid to make any fast moves, Ernie cautiously slid out of the bed and reached for his pants.

Daniel's dad has a crazy look in his eyes. I need to get the fuck out of here before he snaps, Ernie thought.

He didn't make it. Daniel's father was on him before he set one foot on the floor.

"Dad! No!" Daniel shouted, as if words alone could prevent what was coming.

Franklin rolled up his sleeves and charged Ernie like a bull with a red cloth waved in front of him. As soon as he got ahold of Ernie, he put him in a chokehold and literally dragged him to the floor. Ernie didn't go down willingly. He was five-foot-seven and easily a buck-ninety-five. He fought all the way, kicking and punching. Despite all of his efforts, Ernie was no match for Franklin's homophobic-fueled rage. Franklin manhandled the brawny youth as if he weighed next to nothing.

"You fuckin' cocksucker!" Franklin spat. Franklin's eyes filled with hatred when Ernie bit down on his arm until his teeth met in the middle. Franklin uttered a vicious curse and released the chokehold. A chunk of flesh from Franklin's forearm flapped away from the bone like a cheap toupee. Enraged, Franklin hauled back with his mighty fist and punched Ernie in the face hard enough to loosen his two front teeth.

Ernie's arms pinwheeled as he crashed into the stereo against the wall behind him. The needle jerked across the record, making a loud scratching sound. The record skipped, causing Stevie Wonder to sing the phrase, "You know my papa disapproved it. My mama boohooed it. Yeah. Yeah. Yeah," over and over again.

Franklin sounded like a fire-and-brimstone preacher as he quoted bible verses between brutal punches. His clothes clung to his body, delineating every muscle in his powerful arms as he battered Ernie.

"Thou shalt not lie with mankind as with womankind," he quoted, spit flying out of his mouth.

PUNCH!

"It is an abomination!"

PUNCH!

"Leviticus 18:22!"

PUNCH!

Daniel scrambled to his knees on the bed, gasping in horror as his father pummeled Ernie with his angry, balled-up fists. Every horrible *thump* of fist meeting flesh felt like a fist to Daniel's belly. Daniel wanted nothing more than to grab his clothes and get the hell out of there and leave Ernie to fend for himself, but fear had him rooted to the spot.

Daniel literally shoved his fist in his mouth to keep from crying out when Franklin straddled Ernie, pressing his full weight down on Ernie's chest. Franklin's lips formed an ugly sneer as he repeatedly banged Ernie's head, leaving a bloody dint each time Ernie's skull connected with the unforgiving wall. Ernie's eyes rolled to the back of his head. All Daniel could see were the whites. Franklin continued to beat Ernie long after his body went limp.

"'If a man also lie with mankind, as he lieth with a woman, both of them have committed an abomination: they shall surely be put to death; their blood shall be upon them.' Leviticus 20:13!!!" Franklin snarled, making the words of the bible profane, while Daniel ad-libbed his own private chorus, screaming, "Dad, stop. Please. You are going to kill him!" For all the good it did him.

Daniel's words were as ineffectual as a fly standing up to a fire-breathing dragon. If anything, Daniel needed to worry about his own ass because he knew his father was coming for him next.

Blood was everywhere. It sprayed out of Ernie's nose and mouth like an uncapped geyser, splashing against the walls and sinking into the thick fiber of the bluish-gray carpet. Ernie lay sprawled on the floor with his back against the wall beneath a black light poster depicting the peace symbol, his arms spread as if he was offering up his life. His body involuntarily jerked from the impact of each punch, as Franklin's fist continued to pound away at him.

Franklin beat that kid like he was a grown-ass man who owed him a whole lot of money. He beat him like he was fighting for a heavyweight championship worth millions. He beat him like he caught him pissing on his wife's grave. And then he beat him some goddamn more.

Daniel couldn't take it anymore. He leaped off the bed to stay his father's arm, only to receive a vicious backhand to the face for his efforts. The blow sent him flying across the room like a car with no brakes. Daniel's body slammed into his dresser bureau like a villain in an old-time western. He slid to the floor, with stars bursting behind his eyelids and a loud ringing in his ears, unable to move.

Franklin turned away from Ernie, but not before hacking up a thick glob of phlegm and spitting in his face. At that point, Daniel knew without a doubt his father was crazy.

With a heaving chest and murder in his eyes, Franklin turned his bloodshot, red eyes in Daniel's direction.

"You want to be a woman? You want a fucking dick up your Black ass?" Franklin shouted, cracking his bloody knuckles. Spit flew out of his mouth.

"Negroes are fighting in the street right now," Franklin said, "getting shot at, having dogs sicced on them, dying even, just for the right to be treated like men. And you," he paused and spat, "you let another man take you like a woman!"

Franklin concluded his diatribe. "I brought you into this world, lil' muthafuckah, and I will take you out." His voice was a deadly calm that struck more fear in Daniel than his previous ranting and raving. Daniel knew he meant it.

Franklin jerked the extension cord attached to the stereo from the wall. The stereo came crashing down like London Bridge, silencing Stevie Wonder's voice forever. Franklin took his time, never once taking his eyes off Daniel, as he wrapped a length of cord around his busted bloody fist and moved to the corner of the room where Daniel lay shivering with a cum-stained sheet wrapped around his body, too frightened to move.

"Please don't hurt me, Daddy!" Daniel begged, curling up in a protective ball to brace himself for the blows he knew were coming. By now, Daniel's body was slick with sweat generated from fear. He covered his head and face with his arms. This wouldn't be the first beating his father gave him, but somehow he knew it would be the worst.

Franklin dragged Daniel out of the corner, then began whipping Daniel's ass with that extension cord like a Negro caught spying at a Klan rally. Soon, a tapestry of bloody stripes covered Daniel's naked flesh from his calves to the back of his neck. There was not a place on Daniel's body that didn't know the fiery kiss of the extension cord's merciless forked tongue. Each blow burned like fire. Daniel's flaccid penis and balls danced along with his feet as he vainly attempted to escape the vicious stings raining down on him like the vengeance of

God. His screams rose to the attic and fell to the basement, bouncing back and forth against the walls like a rubber ball.

Daniel raised his arms to ward off the attack, only for his father to bring the cord across his forearms and hand, slicing the flesh open. Desperate to stop the beating, Daniel somehow grabbed hold of one end of the extension cord.

"Let the cord go," Franklin demanded, between clenched teeth. Franklin looked like an escapee from an insane asylum, his face slick with sweat and his chest heaving.

"Dad… please," Snot ran from Daniel's nose, his face awash with tears. "Please! I'm not gonna do it no more, Daddy. I promise. I'm not gonna do it no more!"

"You damn right, you ain't gonna do it no more. I'm gonna see to that. I'm not going to tell you again, boy," Franklin warned. "Let go of the cord." There was not a shred of sympathy on Franklin's face. He was as implacable as a mountain.

Even though his hand was slick with blood and sweat, Daniel was determined to hold on to the end of that cord for all he was worth. He would hold on to that cord 'til the cows come home, 'til kingdom come, 'til hell froze over if he had to. Daniel's steadfast refusal to let go of the instrument of torture only whetted Franklin's anger.

Franklin drew his leg back and kicked Daniel in the nuts with his pointy-toed Stacy Adams. Daniel screamed like a woman giving birth. He clutched his injured testicles, leaving his face and upper body vulnerable to his father's vicious attack.

"You are not my son! You should be dead, not your mother!" he shouted, with tears streaming down his face. "I'm 'bout to rectify God's oversight right now!"

The extension cord came alive in Franklin's hand, coiling itself around the nerve endings on Daniel's young skin with every crack, leaving the gift of a stinging bloody welt in its wake. Daniel was on the floor against the side of the bed in the fetal position, his arms crossed in front of his face, while Franklin repeatedly swung that extension cord, delivering liquid fire with each swing.

Swish. Swish. Swish.

The extension cord sliced through the air to bloody Daniel's flesh. A beat-down with an extension cord hurts like hell under the best of circumstances, but it is fire-coated agony when you are butt-naked and covered in sweat. Daniel knew, as sure as day turns into night, his father was going to kill him. As if Franklin could read his son's mind, he bent to wrap the cord around Daniel's neck and pulled the ends together.

Daniel's gaze remained fixed on his bedroom window while the curtain of consciousness behind his eyes closed. His life's light grew dim. It was midday, yet it was pitch dark out. A streak of lightning rent the sky. A loud clap of thunder laughed in Daniel's face as his father choked the life out of him. And then, as if the angels were weeping right along with Daniel, the sky broke open, and it began to pour.

CHAPTER FIFTEEN

ERNIE RELUCTANTLY DRIFTED out of the darkness and into consciousness. At first, he thought he was dead. Then an avalanche of pain, the likes of which he had never known, came tumbling down on him, causing his whole body to tremble. The pain let him know he was very much alive. Unbidden, his mind played back the recent events.

Daniel's father caught Daniel and me together. He went buck-wild on me, he thought, becoming more fearful by the moment.

The sound of gagging and choking forced him to open first one and then the other eye. He couldn't believe what he was seeing. Mr. Calhoun was actually strangling the life out of Daniel.

I have to do something, he thought in desperation.

Ernie staggered to his knees. His eyes scanned the destroyed bedroom, frantically searching for something, anything he could use to stop that sick motherfucker from committing murder.

His gaze landed on a set of dumbbells stacked in the opposite corner of the room. He grabbed a ten-pound dumbbell and swung it into the back of Franklin Calhoun's head with all his might. Ernie was stunned when nothing happened. He thought he would have to strike him again. Finally, after what seemed an inordinately long time, Franklin's knees buckled, and he folded like a deck of cards.

Ernie dropped the dumbbell and limped over to where Daniel lay gasping on the floor. It took a while but, with Ernie's help, Daniel could finally stand on wobbly feet. The room was spinning around Daniel like he was on a roller coaster, and the inside of his throat felt like it had been painted with battery acid. But he was alive, and that's all that mattered.

"Is he dead?" Daniel croaked after a body-jolting fit of coughing.

Like a skittish animal who'd been kicked one time too many, Ernie stepped into his trousers, his eyes locked on Franklin's prone figure. Afraid his tormentor would spring to life and resume his attack, Ernie slipped his sneakers on and pulled his tee shirt over his head, prepared to run if need be. He stood a distance from Franklin, afraid to touch him.

"He's alive, alright," Ernie replied, watching his attacker's back rise and fall. Anxious to depart, Ernie tossed Daniel his shirt and trousers, assisting him in pulling the shirt over his lacerated flesh when he moved too slowly.

"If we don't get out of here, he's going to finish what he started. Please hurry, man," he said, begging as Daniel cautiously slipped into his pants, keeping his eyes on his father the entire time.

"What are we going to do? Where are we going to go?" Daniel cried, wiping the blood from his face with a portion of the sheet. "He will find us!"

"I don't know," Ernie replied, following Daniel's lead. "We can figure out what we are going to do after we get out of here. Hurry!"

Ernie expelled an audible sigh of relief when Daniel was finally dressed and ready to go. They limped out of the house into the pouring rain like two wounded warriors. Neither of them noticed the odd-looking, dark-skinned man standing in the rain, wearing a long purple-and-red cape and a red, black and green apple cap.

Apple cap transmitted a telepathic message to his master's henchman to apprehend the human youths.

❧

Daniel and Ernie ran out the back door of Daniel's father's house as if the KKK and a pack of police dogs were after them. They ran as if hellhounds with dynamite strapped on their backs were nipping at their heels and the entire block was about to blow. The boys were desperate to put as much space between themselves and that monster named "Franklin Calhoun" as possible. They ran for their lives.

Heedless of the pain scoring every muscle in his body, Daniel's long, lean legs cleared his father's backyard fence like he was competing in the Penn Relays. The much larger, and significantly less agile, Ernie huffed and puffed behind him, valiantly struggling to keep up.

Old Lady Cabbell, who lived on the opposite end of Lee Place, caught a flash of the boys through her kitchen window. She came rushing out of her house with a pair of ratty bedroom slippers on, allowing the screen door to slam behind her.

She would later tell the police that they shot past her like streaks of lightning, trampling the begonias and laying waste to the Lincoln rose bush in her backyard. She shouted at them to stop, but they didn't bother to look back.

Daniel and Ernie cut through yard after yard, trampling flowers, knocking over decorative planters, and decimating shrubbery. They eventually exited through the alleyway between the Foster's and the Evelyn's houses on the corner of South Second and Lee Place. And now their sneaker-clad feet were pounding on the rain-soaked sidewalk, due east, toward Grant Avenue.

It was hot—the kind of heat that makes your clothes stick to your body and sweat pop out thick and oily on the surface of your skin. The heat made it difficult to run. Daniel was a track star, but Ernie was not. The fact that Ernie was about twenty-five pounds overweight and asthmatic didn't help. Ernie's chest was burning, and his feet felt like they were weighed down with bricks, yet he continued to do his best to keep up.

They ran, and they didn't stop running until Ernie stumbled and nearly fell over an uneven pavement at the corner of South Second Street and Grant Avenue. The lumbering youth caught himself in time to break his fall. But now Ernie was bent over, sucking wind, and desperate to catch his breath. Daniel, who was nearly a block ahead, jogged back to his side, exhorting him to keep on running, while constantly looking over his shoulder for his father.

Ernie hissed when the simple act of straightening up to stand woke a tsunami of pain throughout his body. A look of incredulity covered his face.

"Are you fucking kidding me?" he asked between bouts of sputtering and nearly throwing up. "Did you crack your skull and lose your mind?" There would be no more fence hurdle jumping for Ernie. He was done. And as soon as he caught his breath, he made it a point to tell Daniel.

"Your crazy father is just going to have to kill my fucking Black ass," Ernie declared. He narrowed his eyes and jerked out of reach when Daniel tried to grab hold of his arm and urge him to continue running.

"I swear before God, Danny, I can't take another step," he said, wiping the sweat from his eyes.

Daniel opened his mouth, fully prepared to convince Ernie to keep running. He was determined to carry his lover on his back if he had to.

All Ernie wanted to do was go home and act like today had never happened, and he hastened to tell Daniel that as well.

"Look, man," Ernie said, with a serious look on his face. "I think we should cut our losses and go back home. You can always go to your Aunt Selma's house if you are scared to go back home.

Whatever punishment we have coming has got to be better than being stuck out here in the rain."

"I can't go back home, Ernie," Daniel responded. "And I can't go to my Aunt Selma's house. When my father comes to, he is going to break his neck to tell my Aunt Selma what he caught us doing, and he'll probably do it in graphic detail."

Ernie was quick to remind Daniel of an earlier conversation. "I thought you said your father and your aunt weren't on speaking terms?"

"They aren't," Daniel replied, grim-faced. "But you best believe they will call a truce for this. And when they do, my aunt will tell your parents as quickly as her little fat fingers can dial their phone number. Once the word on us is out, I doubt anyone will even bother to help us."

"And just in case you forgot, Ernie," he added flippantly. "We weren't caught sneaking one of the neighborhood girls in the house for a make-out session. We got caught fucking each other!" he shouted, totally losing his cool.

That admission hurt Daniel to the core. He loved his aunt more than anything. But she was a bible-toting, bible-quoting woman of the church. Daniel didn't know if she would continue to love him once she found out he was what the bible called a sodomite. Something inside Daniel made him twist the metaphorical knife in Ernie's belly even deeper.

"Shit," he said, with his lips twisted in a bitter grimace. "They may even change the locks on us and forget we were ever born. The way I see it, we are on our own," he said solemnly, as a sizable drop of rain plopped on his cheek.

"Well, what do you suggest we do?" Ernie said in resignation.

"Let's stick with the plan and go to the park," Daniel responded.

"Green Brook Park?" Ernie asked hopefully, since the park was less than a block away.

"No. Let's go to Cedar Brook Park. I want to get as far away from my house as possible. We can stay there overnight and decide what our next move is in the morning."

Ernie had a better idea. "You got any money?" he asked.

"No, I didn't think to snatch my wallet while we were running for our lives," Daniel retorted.

"Well, then, we will just have to hitch a ride, that's all," Ernie said, deliberately ignoring Daniel's sarcasm. "My cousin goes to Livingston College. We can hole up in his dorm room until the heat dies down or until we can figure out what we are going to do. It beats sleeping in the park," he concluded.

No sooner did the words slip out of Ernie's mouth when a white dude in a fancy car pulled up beside them.

"You guys need a ride?" he asked.

Something about the guy just didn't sit right with Daniel, and he told Ernie so.

"Listen, man. Maybe we should wait for somebody else. I'm not feeling this dude."

"Man, you must be crazy. I don't know about you, but I'm getting in that car. You coming?"

They got in the car. There was an unsavory-looking character sitting in the back seat wearing a funky brown suit and a greasy fedora. Daniel knew they'd made a mistake.

CHAPTER SIXTEEN

1294 Arlington Avenue, Plainfield, New Jersey 07060

LORETTA BURKETT LAY on her side with her eyes closed, feigning sleep while listening to the rain pounding against her bedroom window. She quickly opened her eyes when she saw the world and every shameful thing she'd done in it through the curtain of her lowered lids.

The bedroom door opened in increments.

She braced herself, waiting for her husband's side of the bed to dip and accommodate the burden of his weight.

Please, God, don't let him reach for me, she prayed.

Albert grunted, positioning himself beside her, smelling of peanut butter, pound cake, and lunch meat. In less than five minutes he was fast asleep, leaving Loretta to envy his ability to escape his troubles in slumber while she could not, and thanking God that this time her prayer was answered.

Albert has his secrets and God knows I have mine, she conceded, while her husband snored loud enough to bring the house down.

❧

What seemed like an eternity later, her eyes heavy-laden with fatigue, Loretta finally drifted to sleep, only to have the shrill ring of the phone slice through her guilty slumber to mock her.

What time is it? She wondered, battling nearsightedness to decipher the blurry green numbers on the alarm clock.

It's only 3:35 A.M. Bad news always arrives on the wings of late-night phone calls, she thought, preparing herself for the worst.

Biting her bottom lip, she debated whether she should reach over the ponderous mountain of her husband's belly to silence the incessant ringing or hope the late-night caller gets the message and hangs up.

She'd been receiving hang-up calls of late and was fearful that a past indiscretion, or her most recent one, had come back to haunt her. The second and third rings demanded a response.

God sure don't like ugly, she thought as an invisible hand gripped her belly with fear.

Loretta held her breath as the phone lit up like the top of a police squad car, its shrill ring resounding like a siren.

⚬

Albert sputtered awake to reach for the fancy new electric push-button system Bell Telephone, with touch-tone dialing. The phone was the only concession to modernity, besides Albert's extensive wardrobe, that he allowed in their house. Albert didn't like change.

"Hello," he croaked, struggling to sit up in bed, as an invisible hand reached inside Loretta's belly, gripping her bowels with fear.

"No, it's no trouble at all," he lied in response to whatever news the late-night caller relayed. Loretta strained her ears, desperate to hear what was being said.

"Thank you for letting me know. I'll make the hotline call." He placed the handset in its cradle with a somber expression.

"What's wrong?" Loretta asked, her voice tentative and fearful as she sat up in bed.

"That was Deacon Albright," he replied, running a baseball mitt-sized hand down the surface of his round face. "Daniel Calhoun and

Ernie Wilson have been missing since last Sunday. They were last seen getting into a car with a strange white man and are presumed the victims of foul play."

"I have to make my hotline call to the Fullers," he mumbled. He dialed a number they both knew by heart.

He made the call, and within moments promptly fell back to sleep, leaving Loretta back where she'd started, disconsolate and drowning in guilt.

There'd been a rash of missing children in Essex, Passaic, and Union counties, all of them Colored. To date, not a single one of them has been found alive. Loretta didn't know any of the previous victims. Their innocent faces represented dashed dreams, lost hope, and fear. But this was different. She knew both boys.

Daniel was Deacon Calhoun's only son, and Ernie cut their grass in the summer and shoveled their steps and walkway in the winter. *This is personal*, she thought, already thinking of Daniel and Ernie in the past tense. Ten minutes later, Loretta drifted into a troubled sleep.

Sooner than they would have wanted, the Burkett's front door was squealing like something out of a Bela Lugosi movie, and Albert was pulling it closed behind him. He stood on the porch with a jangle of keys in his fat pudgy hand and a dog-eared bible tucked beneath his left arm, dressed and ready for church. It was an unseasonably hot Sunday morning, with the dog days of August proclaiming owner-ship of the day. Albert paused to take in his surroundings and adjust to the unexpected roar of heat.

Sometime during the early hours of the morning, a torrent of heavy rain ripped through the city, bringing with it a ferocious storm and raging flash floods. The brook that gave Cedar Brook Park its name rose to overflow, leaving in its wake a hot pocket of humidity and standing pools of water across the street from the Burkett's house.

It won't be long before the standing water joins forces with the insufferable heat and attracts hordes of blood-sucking mosquitoes, Albert thought, adjusting his sunglasses to better see his wife through the condensation on the lenses.

Loretta hasn't said ten words to me all morning. She turned away when I tried to kiss her, and she has yet to look me in the eye. Albert's belly tightened with fear. He sensed something was wrong.

Does she know the predicament I've gotten us into?

From the foot of the steps, Loretta could see the worry lines marring Albert's brow. *How can I tell Albert that I am grappling with the kind of guilt that will contaminate him if I admit to it? That I ran into an old lover and, within five minutes, was in the back seat of the car Albert purchased, spread wide for the taking? The telling will be so much worse if it comes from someone else. The last thing I want to do is hurt my husband.*

Not only had Loretta cheated on him the day before, but a sworn enemy bore witness to the deception. She tensed as Albert grabbed hold of the front porch rail, fearful that it would no longer support the five-hundred-some-odd pounds that taxed his beautiful heart or that she might break it with the truth.

He knows something is wrong.

She watched Albert position himself sideways to carefully descend the steps in his two-toned Brogue Oxford lace-ups, noting, and not for the first time, how small Albert's feet were compared to his overall girth. Feet like that were far too small to bear the weight of his insecurities. She knew her husband well enough to know that he tried to hide behind well-tailored clothing and the lenses of his dark sunglasses to shield himself from pain.

Loretta listened to Albert's labored breathing as he slowly made his way down the front steps. She let out a breath she hadn't realized she was holding when he finally reached the last step, a light sheen of sweat on his smooth, round face. Ever the gentleman, Albert hurried ahead to open the passenger-side door of their new Cadillac for her.

Look at us, she thought, watching Albert lumber to the driver's side, huffing and puffing like an overheated coal furnace. *The town whore and a compulsive eater preparing to sit in church all gussied up with bibles in hand and our dark, nasty secrets neatly tucked away. And poor sweet Daniel and Ernie will still be just as dead,* she worried, trying on the ugly reality for size.

The car dipped like a listing ship as Albert stuffed himself behind the wheel and struggled to close the door behind him.

The short ride to the church was fraught with an uncomfortable silence. Both were holding on to secrets they were too ashamed to disclose to the universe or each other.

Bethel Baptist Church, Plainfield, New Jersey

The devil sure is busy, Loretta thought as Albert maneuvered their car into the church parking lot. They'd arrived earlier than usual, only to find reserved signs blocking off ten spaces in the nearly full lot.

"I wonder what that's all about," Albert said, his meticulously groomed thin mustache joining his lips in a frown.

No sooner had the question passed his lips before a car bearing vanity plates for New Jersey Governor Thomas Wallace pulled into the lot, trailed by his ever-present media detail.

"He's probably up to no good," Loretta replied with pinched lips painted a vibrant red.

"Sweetheart, you and I both know the only time a white

politician steps foot inside a Colored church is when they are lagging in the polls and ready to tell more lies to get the Colored vote," Albert replied.

Loretta watched the governor and his retinue pull into the reserved spaces. "Well, the presidential election is coming up on November third. It looks like that demon is looking to sway the Colored vote so that Barry Goldwater creature can capitalize on our grief, and get himself a free photo op in the process."

CHAPTER SEVENTEEN

D UE IN LARGE part to Deacon Franklin Calhoun's well-orchestrated call to Pastor Stuart E. Nelson and the church's efficient hotline, the members of Bethel Baptist Church were the first to receive the disturbing news about Daniel and Ernie—but not the only ones.

Pastor Nelson called the associate pastors, who called the members of the trustee board. The trustees called the deacons and deaconesses. Each member called their assigned numbers, and so on and so forth until every member of the 3,000-plus Bethel Baptist Church family was alerted to the sad news. No one thought to question why it had taken Franklin Calhoun an entire week to alert the authorities that his only son was missing.

By sunrise, word of the missing teens would spread throughout the state and all the way to the governor's mansion like a field of parched kindling kissed by a lit match. The white political engine wouldn't think of missing an opportunity to capitalize at Colored folks' expense, nor would they think about doing anything about it.

"Lawd, have mercy. Satan done brought two of his demons with him," Loretta exclaimed when she caught sight of the pockmarked face of Plainfield's Police Chief, Scott McCullough. Among the unwelcome visitors making up the caravan was Wayman Hetfield, the slimy racist newspaper reporter for the *Courier News*. Everyone in the Colored community knew Hetfield was on the governor's payroll to whitewash their shady back-room dealings in the media. Wallace, Hetfield, and Chief McCullough were as thick as thieves.

McCullough's sins were too many to count. Loretta was a ten-year-old runaway when the chief found her wandering the streets of Plainfield, frightened and hungry. Instead of protecting and serving, the chief molested her, and callously returned her to her aunt's house, for further abuse.

❦

Albert and Loretta remained in the car with a feeling of impending doom churning inside their gut. They solemnly watched the white men make their way to the front entrance of the church, laughing and joking amongst themselves like they didn't have a care in the world.

"There's a spot over there, Albert," Loretta said, turning away from the chief's ugly visage and the dark memories that accompanied it. "You think you can maneuver into it?" She pointed to the only space available on the far side of the lot against the fence.

"It'll be tight, but I think I can negotiate it," Albert replied, allowing a hint of his British West Indian accent to peep through. "Why don't you get out and leave the parking to an expert?" Albert suggested, in a failed attempt to interject levity where there was no space for it.

Loretta turned to her husband, her expression softening.

"Sounds like a plan, Sweetheart."

Loretta surprised Albert with an unexpected kiss on the cheek, grabbed her choir robe from the back seat, and headed to the back entrance of the church. The feel of Loretta's sweet lips lingered on his cheek long after she got out of the car.

"Everything is going to be alright," Albert vowed, as he hastened to claim the parking space.

❦

An angry sun scorched the weathered bricks of Bethel Baptist Church as one car after another paused out front to discharge elderly worshippers. Others circled the block in frustration, searching for parking spaces close to the church they would not find.

The church was packed to the rafters, with a throng of worshippers bottle-necked at the entrance. It seemed everyone in the City of Plainfield and the surrounding towns wanted to hear what the outspoken pastor of Bethel Baptist had to say about the two missing boys, members and nonmembers alike.

With her choir robe and purse in one hand and her bible clutched in the other, Loretta struggled through the crush of people obstructing the stairway to the lower level of the church, where the members of the choir would meet.

She smiled her thanks when Renee Fuller, a member of the Junior Usher Board and the only child of her friends, Leila and Leroy Fuller, held the door open for her and offered to carry her choir robe.

"Thank you, sweetie. It's a zoo out there!"

"It sure is. I haven't seen this many folks in church since The Clark Sisters concert last year," Renee replied, then added, "I love to hear you sing."

"Thank you, Renee. That's so nice of you to say. As a matter of fact, I have been asked to sing today," she replied, eliciting a teenaged squeal.

"Well, I'd better get back upstairs," Renee replied, leaving Loretta to savor her sweet smile.

❦

It was because of the unusual congestion, and the news team taking photos of Governor Thomas Wallace and the police chief, that not much attention was paid to the slovenly white man dressed in a stained brown suit made shiny from excessive wear.

Holding his signature dirty brown fedora in hand, Frankie Palermo slipped inside the vestibule along with the governor and his cronies with his head down and his mean-spirited, mud-brown eyes zeroed in on two well-dressed, middle-aged Colored men grinning, shaking hands, and patting the backs of Wallace and the chief like they were part of the second coming. Frankie thought it odd that Colored people would welcome someone such as him and the sleazy white politicians in their midst, when they would sooner slit their Black throats than look at them.

"So, Governor Wallace, what brings you to Bethel Baptist on this fine Sunday?" Hetfield asked, as if he didn't already know. He held the mic up to the governor's face, waiting for his response.

"I've come to convince the members of Bethel Baptist Church to vote for Barry Goldwater, the Republican candidate for President of the United States and the best man for the job."

Determined to shake things up, Frankie locked eyes with Wayman Hetfield, who hurriedly whispered something in the chief's ear while staying just out of range of the flashing cameras. Satisfied when their plastic smiles disappeared and the color leaked from their faces, Frankie offered a brief mocking nod and turned away.

He shouldered his way through the throng to accept a church program from a pleasant, gray-haired Colored woman standing sentinel outside the interior church doors. She opened the ornate wooden doors leading to the sanctuary, where a much younger woman offered to usher him to his seat.

Vile thoughts unsuitable for church or anywhere else flooded the cesspool that was Frankie's mind as his rapacious eyes followed the sway of the pretty Colored usher's round hips into the belly of the church. He was a stone-cold killer eager to draw blood. The unwitting usher paused halfway down the aisle and, with a welcoming smile, extended a white-gloved hand to indicate where he should sit.

Frankie squeezed past seven or eight worshippers, leaving an unpleasant smell of salami and musk in his wake. He took a seat dead center between an elderly woman wearing a wide-brimmed peach hat, and a little boy who looked to be nine or ten years of age, who sought to engage him in a staring contest.

Keep it up, little nigger, and I'll make sure you earn a spot right next to your friends Danny and Ernie, Frankie silently vowed. His lips curled in a wicked yellow-toothed smile so frightening, the child scooted away from him and his sour smell.

Frankie settled in to watch as the people of God silently streamed in, not one smile among them.

I guess they're wondering what happened to those two Colored kids, he thought with a wolfish grin. "But I'm not telling them," he whispered in a sing-song voice so low only the frightened child could hear. Satisfied that he'd made his point, he turned his attention elsewhere.

An avid reader, Frankie found the concept of enslavement and human bondage fascinating and, time permitting, sought to learn as much on the subjects as possible. He'd read an article in *National Geographic* or *Time Magazine*—he could not recall which—that during slavery times, you could easily determine if a nigger was free or in bondage by the quality of the clothing they wore.

Either by diabolical design, or an ingenious means to perpetuate the overall sense of separation and self-loathing necessary to keep the slaves in line, the daily uniform of those held in bondage comprised rough-hewn flax or flesh-irritating hemp.

The more compliant slaves were rewarded once or twice a year with a superior quality of cloth to make a second set of clothing. The latter set of clothing would be worn on Sundays, when all and sundry were given leave to attend their enslaver's sanctioned church service, where the God-given sanctity of their enslavement would be reinforced.

Based upon what Frankie saw at Bethel Baptist Church, dressing in their Sunday best, or Sunday-go-to-meeting wear, remained a long-standing tradition, making for an enslavement far more insidious than the whips and chains of old, for this was an enslavement of the mind.

Frankie snapped out of his reverie as the service was about to begin.

A stalwart, good-looking, Colored man, identified on the church program as Deacon Nelson, made his way to the front of the church to lead the responsive scripture reading, which was printed on the back of the church program. Following everyone's lead, Frankie stood to his feet.

All but Frankie, who chose to visually scour the crowded sanctuary in search of his mark, repeated each line on the printed program in unison.

And then he spotted him.

Bingo!

The man he intended to kill stood less than ten rows away in the first pew in the center section of the church, repeating the words to the responsive reading with a fervor that would suggest he'd been given a free pass to heaven.

Frankie zeroed in on the thick rolls of fat holding court on the back of his meaty neck, taking particular note of the cut and custom fit of his navy-blue sports jacket and white linen trousers.

Frankie's narrow, dark-eyed gaze remained locked on his mark long after the responsive scripture reading was concluded, and the congregation was instructed to sit.

Everybody wants to go to heaven, but nobody wants to die, he thought. *You, my fat friend, will pay every penny that you owe me, and then you shall die very hard.*

CHAPTER EIGHTEEN

THE FIRST STRAIN of the organ swelled throughout the sanctuary, interrupting Frankie's murderous thoughts and temporarily soothing the savage beast that was his constant companion. Frankie's attention was drawn to the front of the church where a slender, middle-aged Colored man, dressed in unrelieved black, sat comfortably on the bench, swaying as his magical fingers danced across the surface of the keys to make the organ sing.

Frankie swiveled his neck to the back of the church, where over seventy-five members of the Bethel Baptist Church gospel choir streamed in from the vestibule to fan down both sides of the center pew. Frankie listened as the clear alto voice of the most beautiful Colored woman he'd ever seen soared throughout the church.

Loretta belted out Mahalia Jackson's "Trouble of the World" in down-home southern revival style as the Bethel Baptist choir members made their way toward the choir stand, humming and swaying to the rhythm of the strong gospel beat.

She led the choir to the front of the church with her head held high, aching inside, as she proclaimed, "Sooner I'll be done with the troubles of the world." By the time she got to the chorus where she sang, "I'm going home to live with God," half the church had forgotten Loretta's checkered past to stand on their feet.

Loretta sang like she was singing to almighty God and not to a church filled with heartbroken members, most of whom had gossiped about her behind her back.

She sang for Daniel and Ernie, for lost innocence, and for the childhood she never had.

She poured her pain on the church floor for all to see, hoping and praying her sins would be forgiven, but fearful they would not.

∾

The spirit reached out and touched everyone within hearing of Loretta's sweet voice—everyone but Frankie Palermo, who was enraptured by the beauty of the music and the woman singing, but unmoved by the faith-filled sentiment of her song. Through it all, Frankie remained focused on the sick things he would do to her if only he could get her alone.

Frankie didn't believe any of it. Never had and never would. He didn't believe there was a God. And since he didn't believe there was a God, he certainly didn't believe the God he *didn't believe in* had a son named Jesus who was crucified and rose from the dead.

The name Jesus was as common back then as the name Smith is today, he thought, looking at the graphic depiction of Christ on the cross which took up much of the wall behind the pulpit.

Rise from the dead? Ludicrous! Once you are dead, you're dead. Case closed. I should know, having put my fair share of dead bodies in the ground. Not a one of them has come back to take me into account.

I believe in me. Everything that I have, everything that I am, and everything that I ever hope to become, are from my efforts and my efforts alone, not some mythical all-seeing being in a fanciful realm from which no one has returned to verify its existence.

Frankie found it difficult to hide his disdain as worshippers waived their hands in the air, thanking the lord for everything from waking them up that morning to healing the corns on their shuffling ashy feet.

They are weak, he thought, *all of them—weak little black slugs looking for a savior to make their miserable, pathetic lives better instead of doing something about it themselves.*

If I can't see it, touch it, fuck it, or kill it, goddammit, it doesn't exist.

❧

The atmosphere within the church was charged with Holy Ghost energy. Frankie settled in for the show. He knew he wouldn't be disappointed when the heartbeat of Bethel Baptist, their beloved pastor, Stuart Nelson, entered the sanctuary flanked by his oldest son, Assistant Pastor Nathaniel Nelson, and his second in command, Associate Pastor Thomas Cathcart.

The sheep literally went wild when their shepherd and associate pastor took their seats in the pulpit, and Assistant Pastor Nathaniel Nelson took to the podium with his rock star good looks to render a rousing opening prayer. At the conclusion of the prayer, the woman sitting next to Frankie shouted, "Hallelujah. Praise the Lawd!"

In a strong southern Baptist stentorian voice, the assistant pastor declared, "The next voice you will hear shall be that of our esteemed pastor, Reverend Dr. Stuart Nelson!"

❧

The choir members were now in the choir stand, having sung their hearts out. Still on a spiritual high from the rousing gospel music, people fanned themselves with paper fans donated by Brown's and Judkin's Funeral Homes, both of which Frankie knew well, having kept both establishments busy with a steady stream of dead bodies since his arrival in town.

Loretta stood in the choir stand, watching how her dearest friend

Althea Collin's eyes automatically lit up at the sight of Nathaniel Nelson, who'd asked her to marry him eight months ago. Loretta was genuinely fond of the handsome assistant pastor and thrilled to learn that her closest friend would become a part of Bethel's first family. And yet, she couldn't help but feel a sharp pang of envy at Althea's good fortune compared to her own.

The parallels were marked. Pastor Stuart and first lady Ida Mae adored their future daughter-in-law, while Loretta's late in-laws had despised her 'til the day they died.

Althea and Nathaniel's wedding would be featured in *Jet Magazine* while Loretta and Albert got married at city hall in secret. Their witnesses were Albert's high school guidance counselor and a stranger they pulled off the street for twenty-five dollars.

Loretta initially had mixed feelings when Althea asked her to serve as her matron of honor and assist in planning the wedding of the century her parents wanted for her. Althea was the kindest person she'd ever met. She deserved every good thing.

Loretta battled those unworthy thoughts now as she had then. *Get thee behind me, Satan*, she silently commanded, recognizing the author of her thoughts was nothing but the devil and realizing that it didn't make a damn bit of sense for her to harbor negative thoughts toward her best friend.

Althea has her cross to bear, and I have mine. Please, dear God, let her know the joy she brings.

All conversation ceased, and the congregation collectively held their breaths as, with a grave expression, Pastor Nelson took to the lectern.

❧

"Good morning, church!" Pastor Stuart Nelson said in a voice that reverberated throughout the sanctuary without the need of a microphone.

The response to his greeting was an immediate and resounding, "Good morning, Pastor!"

Pastor Nelson waited patiently as two senior ushers opened the doors of the church while the others hastily placed folding chairs at the end of each aisle to accommodate the late arrivers. Soon there was a field of colorful birds from the balcony to the main floor fanning themselves. Frankie jerked to attention at the pastor's next statement.

"Before I start today's sermon, I want to thank Sister Loretta Burkett, our Gospel Cavalier Choir, and our renowned choir director, Eldridge Hargrove, for sharing their gifts with us this morning. You truly made a joyful noise unto our lord and savior and blessed this church. Amen?" He peered over his reading glasses as if he was asking a question to which he already knew the answer.

"Amen," came the collective response of the children of God. But none of them said amen louder than Frankie.

Well, well, well, I don't know how that lovely songbird is related to fat boy Burkett, but I certainly intend to find out, he speculated before returning his attention to the pulpit.

"I didn't come here this morning to name-drop," Pastor Nelson said, eliciting a dutiful chuckle from the congregation. Pastor Nelson was a storyteller extraordinaire. Everyone was eager to see where his opening remarks were going, Governor Wallace, Chief McCullough, and Wayman Hetfield included. Wallace whispered an off-color comment to the chief, generating an inappropriate guffaw from Hetfield and a frown from a woman sitting nearby.

"However," the pastor continued, "I would be remiss if I did not let you know that my sons and I were amongst a select group of clergymen invited to attend a civil rights conference which took place at the Ebenezer Baptist Church in Atlanta, Georgia." He made it a point to drag out the words "the Ebenezer" and "Georgia" in dramatic fashion.

Uninterested in hearing about the pastor's recent sojourn in what the chief disparagingly referred to as Coon Town, Georgia, the white trio engaged in a personal conversation that had absolutely nothing to do with Sunday worship or the missing boys.

✑

"As many of you know," Pastor Nelson continued, "our first lady was born and raised in Valdosta, so we made a brief detour to spend time with the family.

The conference was a grand affair. Malcolm, who'd just returned from a pilgrimage to Mecca on May 21st, was gracious enough to attend, along with Reverend Ralph Abernathy and a host of preachers and Jewish leaders from across these United States, all of whom have taken up the Black man's struggle, with a fervent desire to do Gawd's will.

I had the privilege and honor to have a lengthy conversation with my good friend Martin, who hosted the event."

The pastor appeared to grow in stature after speaking the name of the well-known civil rights activist. "Martin and I are Morehouse men and Alpha Phi Alpha brothers," he added proudly.

"As I said earlier," he said with a self-deprecating laugh, "I didn't come here to name-drop. However, it was with a great deal of joy that I was able to bring my two sons, Nathaniel and Deacon, to this historical event and introduce them to men on the battlefront for freedom and justice. The main topic on the agenda was the Civil Rights Act, which President Lyndon Baines Johnson signed into law on July 2nd.

Since the signing, a white off-duty police officer shot and killed a Negro teenager in Harlem, and still has his job. A young Negro woman was beaten and wrongfully detained by the police in the

Lafayette Gardens Public Housing Complex in Jersey City, and when a gentleman intervened on her behalf, he too was manhandled and arrested. Unlike the Negro victims, the officers involved are still gainfully employed."

"It's a shame before God how they treat us!" someone shouted from the packed balcony, buoying the pastor on.

"While we were in Georgia, we learned of the lynching of two men and a fourteen-year-old child from what is commonly known in Mississippi as the hanging bridge. I doubt those murderers will be brought to justice either. The president may have signed that act, but without enforcement, it amounts to little more than elegantly written words put to expensive parchment paper.

From that day forward, I couldn't look at a tree in Georgia without wondering how many Negroes were lynched from it, and I still had to rely on the *Negro Motorist Green Book* to get my family home safe! Is this what civil rights looks like to you, church?"

The pastor removed his glasses and picked up a white handkerchief to wipe the sweat from his face.

"Take your time, pastor!" shouted a gray-haired old man sitting at the front of the church.

"I know Rome was not built in a day, but how long before they do right by us, church? How long!"

Frankie knew the pastor was about to dive into shark-infested waters when a member of the church missionary group ascended the pulpit to theatrically present him with a fresh handkerchief and a cool glass of water. Pastor Nelson's next words would prove him right.

"The evil institution of racism is not just a southern problem. It is a morally bankrupt, spiritual one! I say woe be unto those who refuse to do right by us!" he said, getting the congregation stirred up.

CHAPTER NINETEEN

"**O**VER THE PAST two months, I couldn't turn on the television without a spokesperson from the Westfield, Short Hills, or Chatham Police Departments alerting the public to a rash of missing children between the ages of twelve and eighteen," Pastor Nelson said.

"Since the beginning of May, thirty-nine known teens have been reported missing. A task force comprising all three police departments has exhausted all resources to locate the missing children, nineteen of whom were found dead. Until recently, the victims were all white.

"Last month, the bodies of nine Negro children residing in Plainfield, Newark, and Irvington, respectively, were found drained of blood. Not only did our babies receive no media attention, but the elected officials whose salaries we pay with our tax dollars have made no attempts to locate our children. Instead, they have the unmitigated gall to come into the house of the lord to get Barry Goldwater, a known enemy of our people, elected to the highest office of the land.

Is it me, church, or is something wrong with this picture?" he asked, looking directly at the white interlopers. Not one of them was man enough to make eye contact with the pastor.

"Last night, I received a call from our own Deacon Franklin Calhoun, informing me that his son, young Daniel, whom I've known since the day he was born, and Ernie Wilson, a fine young member of this church family, have gone missing and are presumed victims of foul play."

The pastor's pronouncement was met with a theatrical gasp, as if he'd delivered some shocking news they didn't already know.

"I recall looking at the clock on my nightstand before answering the phone. It was 3:00 A.M., a period of time frequently referred to by those in the occult world as the witching hour. Make no mistake about it. Such a thing as the witching hour is as real as the evil deeds that occur during it."

He leaned forward conversationally. "God helps those who help themselves. If we want to find out who is responsible for these heinous, reprehensible, patently evil deeds, we obviously cannot rely upon law enforcement. We will have to solve these crimes on our own." He looked directly at Governor Wallace and Chief McCullough. "After all, prayer without work is what, church?"

The walls of the church rocked with a unanimous response: "Death!"

✦

"Each of you should give what you have decided in your heart to give, not reluctantly or under compulsion, for God loves a cheerful giver, and God can bless you abundantly, so that in all things at all times, having all that you need, you will abound in every good work," the pastor said, as the organist played softly in the background.

Frankie admired how the pastor moved on to the collection phase of the service, quoting the second book of Corinthians 9:7, as if he hadn't issued a fuck you and kiss my Black ass to three of the most powerful white men in the state.

Frankie murmured, "You are one smooth operator, alright,"

exhibiting an unaccustomed show of respect. "I'll be sure to come back for your funeral because you just signed your death warrant," he added under his breath as the male ushers fanned through the church with brass offering plates to take the collection.

&

The tone of the sermon took a dangerous turn, reminding Frankie of an attack dog he once owned that would let a thief in but tear them to shreds when they tried to leave. The governor, police chief, and Hetfield may have been welcomed into the church with what appeared to be open arms, but Frankie sensed they would leave with their egos bloodied and flayed. Now, Wallace, McCullough and Hetfield sat stone-faced, silently taking in the pastor's words and the worshippers' reactions to them. All three stubbornly refused to put so much as a dime in the collection plate.

Frankie could taste Wayman Hetfield's anger in the back of his throat. It was palpable, reaching out to touch every member in the congregation like a virulent infection.

I suspect Wallace, McCullough and Hetfield have heard enough.

Frankie's suspicions proved correct when all three of them abruptly rose to leave. Wallace led the pack, shooting down the church aisle toward the exit like an angry Brahma bull with a stick up his ass as Pastor Nelson recited Matthew 6:24-26 in a booming voice of condemnation.

"No man can serve two masters, for either he will hate one and love the other; or else he will hold to one and despise the other. Ye cannot serve Gawd and mammon!"

Wallace's body jerked like a demon doused with holy water with each of the pastor's condemning words.

Frankie Palermo, whose eyes missed nothing, saw Hetfield's back stiffen and his hand freeze on the door. Frankie knew without a doubt that the pastor's words had struck home, and that whatever he said next would hammer the nails in his coffin.

"Yeah, though we walk through the valley of the shadow of death, we need fear no man or his wicked purpose. You see, the Gawd we serve shall always create an inhospitable environment for darkness wherever and whenever it rears its ugly head."

Pastor Nelson concluded his biblical beat-down. "My Gawd is a champion. He maketh so the bearers of darkness shall always flee in his mighty wake. Get thee gone, unclean spirits!"

All eyes, including those of Albert Burkett, were riveted on the rear of the church where Wallace's pale veiny palm pulsed like a moldy stain against the sacred wooden door. Their departure was met with a thunderous applause when the demons in sheep's clothing pushed through the church doors to make their ignoble retreat.

◈

Albert Burkett stood out like an over-fed prince amongst farm hands in a navy-blue sports coat, crème-colored shirt and trousers, and a navy, silver, and crème striped silk tie that looked more expensive than Frankie's entire wardrobe.

Frankie had to give it to him: For a fat guy, Albert looked casket clean.

Albert murmured a brief prayer of thanks that the governor and his cohorts were no longer present to befoul the house of the lord and was prepared to express his sentiments to Leroy Fuller, who was sitting to his right, when every drop of blood drained from his face.

Sitting not ten rows behind Albert, wearing the same wolfish grin he wore on the day he threatened to gut him and burn his house down with him in it, was Frankie Palermo. And Palermo wasn't alone.

Albert swayed on his feet when he saw the familiar hateful glare of his late father, Albert J. Burkett, II, sitting right next to Palermo.

This can't be real, Albert thought, blinking to clear his vision. He was suddenly beset with a crippling mixture of fear and guilt when the image remained.

My father told me exactly what he would do to me if I messed up. He swore he would come back from the grave and beat my fat ass. Albert's fear escalated to full-scaled terror at the realization that he'd messed up... badly.

Please, dear God, don't let this be real, he prayed, shaking all over and desperate to escape. Albert wobbled on his feet, generating a look of concern from Deacon Leroy Fuller.

"Pardon my candor, Brother Burkett, but you don't look well," Leroy said, taking in his overall pallor and the damp sheen of sweat covering Albert's plump round face.

Unable to move or speak, Albert issued a loud wet belch from the depths of his gut, coating his throat with an acidic mixture of everything he'd consumed in the past twenty-four hours. Moments later, the bones in his lower back joined forces with his sour stomach to beat a persistent throb, and a stream of hot urine ran down his leg.

"You disgust me," the image of his father said. "I warned you what would happen if you fucked my shit up, now didn't I, Albert?"

I must be losing my mind, Albert thought as a sharp, crushing pain pounded inside his chest, drawing tears.

"Does it hurt?" his father whispered from some place inside Albert's subconscious.

"Did you feel that, Albert? All I did was pinch your aorta like so."

Albert gasped as he was sent into a spiraling vortex of pain. This time, Albert knew he was not imagining things—the voice was real. He placed his hand on his chest to shield his heart from further attack.

"That's what it feels like when fat clogs the arteries in your heart, causing the muscle to die," Albert Sr. added conversationally. "You are having what is commonly known as an acute myocardial infarction. Simply put, you, worthless tub of lard, are having a good old-fashioned heart attack."

The statement was punctuated by a sharp, crushing pain that radiated from the tips of Albert's fingers to his neck, finally setting up residence in the center of his chest where it refused to let go. Albert was in too much pain to respond.

The last thing Albert recalled before he toppled to the church floor was the sound of splintering wood, Loretta's anguished cry, and Leroy Fuller shouting, "Someone dial 911!"

CHAPTER TWENTY

Greeneville, Tennessee Rest Area —

Interstate 81, Greeneville, Tennessee

ELIZABETH WAS DOG-TIRED and barely able to keep her eyes open when she got off the interstate at Exit 81 in Greeneville, Tennessee.

She followed a long, winding stretch of road she hoped would lead her to the Colored-friendly rest station mentioned in the *Negro Motorist Green Book.*

After what seemed an interminably long drive past grazing cows and a corn silo, a bright blue sign with white lettering advertising water, restrooms, and vending machines for road-weary travelers assured her she was headed in the right direction.

The battered truck limped into the sparsely crowded parking lot, moaning, groaning, and clanking like an orchestra of pots, pans, and tin cans. The pickup truck was twenty-plus years old and not built for long highway hauls. But then again, neither was Elizabeth. She parked the truck, killed the engine, and slumped down in the driver's seat, where she promptly fell asleep.

❦

Elizabeth woke several hours later to find the sun had slipped behind the moon to give way to darkness and two eighteen-wheeler semi-trucks sandwiching her in.

"It smells like cat pee and poop in here," she said to her feline companion, wrinkling her nose. "How 'bout I take care of that nasty old litter box and get you some fresh water while you stretch your little furry legs." She smirked at her failed attempt at normalcy.

Àse meowed in agreement.

Elizabeth emptied the litter box and sat on a nearby park bench staring at the stars, while Àse did her business and darted into the nearby wooded area. She had no concerns about whether Àse would return. The feline possessed a wild nature similar to hers. The two were tethered in spirit. They were one. Elizabeth returned to the truck and placed Àse in the front passenger seat to act as a guard.

"I'm going to throw some water on my face and make myself presentable. If anybody tries to get in this truck, I want you to scratch both their eyes out and rip open their throats, you hear?" Elizabeth stroked Àse's tail with affection. The bloodthirsty, one-eyed cat acknowledged the assignment with a rounded back and loud hiss.

Satisfied Àse's needs were met, Elizabeth reached in the back seat for the bag with her toiletries and exited the truck. The little nappy hairs at the nape of her neck stood on end as she headed with determined steps toward the rest area entrance, sensing she was being watched.

❦

The interior of the rest stop was little more than a two-thousand-square-foot cavern with institutional steel gray walls, a newsstand, and a bank of vending machines. Across from the vending machines were two doors painted a darker shade of gray in contrast to the walls—one with an image of a stick figure in a wheelchair and a white image of a woman, and the other with the likeness of a male.

A map showing every rest area in the State of Tennessee, bearing the notation "you are here" in bold red letters, was placed in a prominent position on the wall above a rack of local brochures. Elizabeth walked toward the massive wall map.

She'd been on the road nearly six hours. After calculating the distance from where she was and her ultimate destination, Elizabeth purchased a newspaper and a bag of pork rinds from the newsstand, filled a canister with water from the fountain, and headed to the restroom, silently praying the truck would start up when she was ready to leave. She no longer felt safe.

The light inside the restroom was unnaturally bright. Elizabeth checked each stall to ensure they were empty before spreading her belongings on the counter. She splashed her face with water, gargled, and grabbed a paper towel to dry her face. Avoiding her image in the mirror, she unfolded the newspaper.

The headline read "Massacre in Mississippi" with graphic photographs of the mutilated bodies of her two brothers and her son swinging from the Shubata Bridge for all the world to see. The newspaper fell from fingers suddenly gone nerveless to flutter to the dingy restroom floor. Elizabeth had to grab hold of the cold porcelain sink to keep from passing out. Even that boon was denied her at the sound of two or more people approaching the bathroom door.

Taking a deep breath, she quickly pulled herself together and bent to gather the scattered pages from the floor, finding refuge behind the locked door of the handicapped stall seconds before a laughing group of women entered the restroom. Elizabeth lifted her skirt and lowered her panties to sit on the toilet, settling in to read.

A local photographer, who conveniently asked to remain anonymous, had taken pictures of the lynching while it was happening and leaked them to the press. Photos of her family were all over the national news, sparking outrage in some, apathy in others, and an indescribable sense of sorrow in Elizabeth. And now the media, the FBI, the NAACP, and the Congress of Racial Equality had descended upon Quitman and Clarke Counties like biblical locusts to make sense of the irreconcilable act of barbarism.

Reference was made to the brutal execution-style killings of Sheriff DeLonge, Lester Stretch, and the Krutchners. The article made no mention of DeLonge's missing head or of an escaped Negro murderess. In fact, based upon what Elizabeth read, it appeared the authorities assumed she'd met a fate similar to that of her family, ending with her body being tossed in the river.

While the nation was focusing on the lynchings, the residents of Mississippi were focused on who killed their local heroes, DeLonge and Stretch. Even the Krutchners made the *good white folks* list.

One thing about white folks, they know how to band together when it becomes necessary to bring down somebody Colored, Elizabeth thought.

She heard the stalls opening and closing and the women's subsequent departure. What she didn't hear was the flow of running water or the pull of paper towels.

"Nasty-ass bitches," she mumbled before returning to the article with her nose turned up at the odor they left behind.

The residents of Meridian and thereabout suspected it was an outside Black vigilante group that orchestrated the murders in retaliation for the lynching. There was a hue and cry for the killers to be caught and brought to justice immediately but no such outrage for her family. Elizabeth suspected they were eager to have another lynching. If she were to fall into the hands of the authorities, the next one would be hers.

Elizabeth waited until the foot traffic died down outside the restroom before she hastily shoved the newspaper inside her sizable canvas bag. With a sense of reverence, she retrieved the knife she'd used to kill Lou Sadie. Twenty minutes later, she exited that bathroom with her long, thick hair shorn within an inch of her skull. She put on a scarf, purchased a cheap pair of reading glasses, and headed for the door.

Elizabeth could name each of her ancestors, dating back to the first slave brought to Louisiana from Zanzibar. She thought it best to adopt her mother's maiden name. That way, she could not possibly get tripped up if questioned about her newly adopted identity. From that moment forth, Elizabeth Anne François was dead, and Betty Johnson was born.

CHAPTER TWENTY-ONE

New Jersey Turnpike

ELIZABETH RUMMAGED THROUGH her purse to find the folded piece of paper she'd stuck in the side of her wallet almost four years ago. The number belonged to her cousin, Anahita Benoit.

My family in Jersey is all that I have now.

Armed with a steely resolve and a stack of coins, she stopped at the next gas station with a pay phone to place the call, and almost went crazy when she learned the number was no longer in service. She opened the phone book and let her fingers do the walking.

"Hello?" Elizabeth's cousin asked after the phone rang only two times.

It was late. Elizabeth felt guilty about disturbing her at this time of night, but this was an emergency.

"May I speak to Anahita, please?" she asked in a soft voice with a heavy southern accent.

"This is she? Who is this?"

Elizabeth recognized her cousin's voice immediately. She was so glad and hastened to tell her so.

"Oh. Thank the gods it's you, Anahita! I thought I would never find you! This is your cousin Elizabeth from Mississippi." She added the last by way of reminder, even though she knew it wasn't necessary. Both Anahita and her twin sister Anita knew her well. Over the years, both had frequented the farm in Mississippi to avail themselves of Elizabeth's special baby killing services.

"Anahita, I need your help."

"How did you get this number?" Anahita hissed.

"I called your old number only to find it was out of service. I went through the Yellow Pages and called every Benoit listed, hoping to find you."

"What do you want?" Anahita asked, her tone cold.

"I need somewhere to stay, just for a little while until I can get on my feet. I…"

Anahita cut Elizabeth off before she could utter another word.

"You listen to me, you little nappy-headed, backwoods, country bumpkin!" Anahita spat. "I don't give a flying fuck what you need. You can sleep in an alley or on top of a city steam grate for all I care. But you had better not *ever* call this number again, and I fuckin' mean it!"

And with that, Anahita hung up the phone, temporarily leaving Elizabeth dumbfounded. Elizabeth's hands were shaking when she placed the receiver in the jack and stepped out of the phone booth.

What in the world am I going to do now, she lamented, as she made her way back to the truck, weary in mind, body, and spirit.

I have to find a job, she thought, diving back into survival mode. She had hoped her cousin would be in a position to help her with that, or at least put her up for the night. *After that bitch went all Three Faces of Eve on me, I know not to look for any help from that direction. I am on my own.*

It took all but ten seconds for the rage to set in.

There was no time for her to act on her anger, but one day, she fully intended to pay Anahita back in spades.

❧

I-287E, Exit 10, Metuchen/Perth Amboy, New Jersey

Elizabeth exhausted a significant amount of the money she found in Edgar DeLonge's house for gas, and was now down to a measly $147.33. Angered and more than a little hurt by her cousin's unexpected rebuff, she had no choice but to use some of her meager funds on somewhere to stay for the night.

A little past midnight, Elizabeth turned into the potholed parking lot of the Rainbow Motel in Green Brook, New Jersey, killed the engine, and sat outside the main office, staring at the Vacancies sign prominently displayed in the window.

It costs sixteen dollars a night to crash in this sleazy motel, money I can ill-afford to spend.

But she couldn't drive another mile, even if her life depended on it. Like it or not, this was where Elizabeth would lay her head, at least for the night. She dragged herself out of the truck to get a room. Ten minutes later, she was locking the door behind her and kicking off her shoes.

Tomorrow I will drive to the nearest town to find some work. It's warm out. I'll sleep in the truck if I have to. The spirits took care of us from Mississippi to Jersey. I will trust them to take care of us tomorrow, she thought, stroking her cat's velvet fur. She laid her weary body down to rest.

❧

No sooner did Elizabeth allow her eyes to drift closed when the rhythmic sound of a passion-propelled headboard banging against paper-thin walls startled her awake.

The occupants in the room next to hers were engaged in the kind of lovin' that will sweat out your press-n-curl and give you a sore throat the next morning from sucking air and hollering your fool head off. Elizabeth lay atop the dingy hotel sheets, listening to the staccato beat of the headboard, the soprano screams of surrender, and the bass moans and groans of possession.

She covered her head with the flat, funky motel pillow to drown out the sounds, to no avail. One minute the woman was cursing up a blue streak, and the next she was screaming like her lover was killing her.

Elizabeth was all for somebody getting their itch scratched, but she'd been on the road for nearly sixteen hours straight and desperately needed some sleep.

She wanted to bang on the wall with one of her clunky shoes and scream at them to keep it down, but something in her spirit told her not to. The last thing she wanted was to draw any undue attention.

God forbid if someone calls the cops, she worried.

In hindsight, it may be best that I stay awake. Sleep means dreams, and dreams will force me to relive the darkest hours of my life.

The spirits tend to slip between the pages of Elizabeth's dreams to direct the narrative. Most nights she welcomed them, but not tonight. She feared what they would say if given the chance to speak their minds. There would be no sleep for her on this night.

Elizabeth stepped out of the motel room and into the midmorning sunlight with eyes burning from lack of sleep. The motel appeared even tawdrier under the microscope of the unforgiving light of day.

It was 11:00 A.M., and the couple responsible for disturbing her sleep were leaving their room at the same time as Elizabeth. She had already painted a mental picture of them as she lay awake listening to them pleasure each other. They looked nothing like she imagined.

The young woman looked to be no more than seventeen or eighteen, if that. She wore her thick, straight hair pulled back in a neat ponytail, with random wisps of curls framing her brownish-yellow oval-shaped face like a lovely portrait. Elizabeth noticed a light dusting of freckles across the bridge of her nose. She was beautiful and innocent looking. Elizabeth knew better.

The man she was with was considerably older and equally attractive. He had golden brown skin, light-brown eyes, a mustache, and close-cut curly hair with reddish blond highlights, giving him a Puerto Rican or Brazilian look. The way he was putting it down the night before, Elizabeth could have sworn he was Colored. They were a striking couple.

Elizabeth wondered if the girl's parents knew she'd spent the night with her legs gapped open in a nasty motel with a man who looked far too old for her. She wagered they did not.

✺

"Excuse me, please. Excuse me!" Elizabeth shouted, running to catch up with the couple in her serviceable clodhopper shoes. From the look on their faces, she could tell they were relieved to see it was a stranger hailing them and not someone they knew.

"Good morning," Elizabeth said, slightly winded. "Sorry to bother you good folks, but I'm from out of town, and I was wonderin' if you know where I can find work around here?" she asked politely.

The young girl was quick to respond. "You probably want to go to Plainfield if you are looking for work. There are a lot of Black people from down south living in Plainfield," she stated, picking up on Elizabeth's prominent accent. "In fact, I hear they are hiring at Muhlenberg Hospital.

We are originally from Newark, but I hear tell people can get jobs at Chelsca Fan Corp., Mack Truck, National Starch, and Chemical Corp. You might also want to try the 7-Up bottling plant or Plainfield Iron and Metal. They have a scrapyard on the west end of town. Yup, Plainfield is your best bet."

Up close, the girl looked even younger than Elizabeth initially thought and far too juvenile to be spending the night in a rundown motel. Elizabeth found it difficult to believe the lustful noises of the previous night came from those innocent lips.

"Thank you," Elizabeth said with an appreciative smile.

Elizabeth stopped the couple again when they turned to go.

"One more thing. Do you happen to know where I might rent a room by the week?"

This time the man spoke up. "I'm also from Newark, so I can't help you with that. You know anybody, Renee?"

"I'm sorry. I can't help with that," she stated apologetically. "I attend church in Plainfield, but I live in Newark. I recommend you see what's in the classified section of the *Courier News* or the *Star Ledger*." She reached inside her purse for a pen to write down the names of the local newspapers. Her boyfriend, whom she called Billy, eventually found a wrinkled napkin bearing the motel logo to write on.

Well, ain't that just nuthin', Elizabeth thought. *Church folks sinnin' on Saturday night and praying on Sunday morning. Some things never change.*

Elizabeth could read people. She didn't need to pull out her Tarot cards or a crystal ball to know that the couple standing before her was destined for a sad end. There was an aura of foreboding surrounding both of them, which told Elizabeth they were racing toward heartache.

She thanked the couple and let them be about their business, watching them with a look of sorrow. Elizabeth wondered why the spirits would reveal dark clouds swirling around two virtual strangers, but not the storm clouds that swept her family away.

CHAPTER TWENTY-TWO

NEARLY A WEEK had elapsed since Albert's shameful collapse in church, and yet the words of the young emergency room physician remained etched in Loretta's memory.

The little shit marched into Albert's hospital room on the day he was admitted with his officious chart in hand. Without so much as a greeting or any form of eye contact at all, he summarily announced, "Mr. Burkett, sir. You lucked up this time. What you experienced was a stress-related panic attack. However, if you don't lose a substantial amount of weight, and do it quickly, you are going to die."

After delivering those ominous words, the cold-hearted bastard left the room, leaving both of them wracked with worry—Loretta from guilt, and Albert from something he was not yet ready to reveal.

Albert is my anchor, my friend, my everything. When he passed out in church, I feared that I'd lost him.

Loretta never learned how to care for herself. There'd always been a man around for that. She didn't know what she would do without Albert.

While Loretta despaired over Albert's health, all he could think about was the threat that Frankie Palermo presented and the mounting medical bills.

❧

After a heated exchange between Albert and the discharge attendant, with Albert declaring he could walk just fine, Albert grudgingly sat in the wheelchair. There was an uncomfortable silence between Albert and Loretta as the hospital discharge attendant pushed Albert's wheelchair onto the service elevator and pressed the button for the main lobby.

When the hospital social worker recommended they look into the Duke Weight Loss Center in Durham, North Carolina, Loretta knew they had to act immediately. She called the following morning to arrange for Albert's admission. All she needed was the insurance information to get him admitted.

Loretta sensed Albert didn't want to go, but she was determined to fight for his life even if he wasn't. Loretta was first to alight when the elevator doors opened.

"I'll pull the car up," she said, leaving Albert and the attendant inside the hospital double doors to enjoy the frigid air-conditioning for a moment longer. It was blazing hot out, and Loretta sought to spare her husband as much discomfort as possible. When Loretta returned with the car, Albert was quick to take charge.

"I'll drive." He extended a fat baseball mitt-sized hand for the keys.

Exhausted, Loretta acquiesced. Afraid to stay in the house alone, she'd been traveling back and forth between the hospital and her friend Althea's home in Newark. She welcomed her husband taking the wheel, if only for the short drive home.

Her eyes fluttered shut as soon as Albert got her settled in the passenger seat and closed the door behind her. She was already drifting off by the time Albert exited the hospital parking lot. Within minutes, the sound of soft snoring could be heard throughout the car. For the briefest of moments, Albert didn't have a care in the world. He was going home.

It wasn't until Albert made the right turn from Randolph Road onto Park Avenue that he noticed the familiar scarred, brown, Pontiac following close on their heels and who sat behind the wheel.

Suddenly, Albert felt sick all over again. He glanced at his wife, who let out another soft snore. More petrified for Loretta than himself, he picked up speed with his heart lodged so deep in his throat he thought he'd choke on it. Albert knew better than most what Palermo was capable of.

I can't allow that monster near my wife, he thought, clenching the steering wheel for all he was worth as a nauseating pain ripped through his chest.

Desperate to shake Palermo, Albert made a quick left at the light seconds before it turned red. He issued an anguished moan when his nemesis ran the light to stay hot on his tail. More frightened than ever, Albert floored the gas, passing his street to take the winding route through the park on two wheels. There was a baseball game in session. The stands were full.

Surely, he won't try anything with so many witnesses? Albert prayed, as he picked up speed, violently jerking Loretta awake. Alarmed by the break-neck rate of speed, Loretta held on to the dashboard to prevent tumbling out of the passenger seat.

Moments later, Albert careened into their driveway on a sharp turn, striking the decorative curbside mailbox. Loretta held her breath as he applied the brakes just short of crashing into the garage door. Temporarily unable to speak, she sat with her palm pressed to her chest to slow down her racing heart.

"What the heck has gotten into you, Albert? You scared the living daylights out of me!"

She was far too upset to notice how shaken her husband was or the white man behind the wheel of the nondescript, brown, Pontiac that sped past their residence. Her eyes were fixed on her husband's lap.

"Albert, did you pee on yourself?"

❧

1290 Arlington Avenue, Plainfield, New Jersey.

"Lord have mercy, it's hot out here," Selma Calhoun-Barksdale said, stating the obvious.

Selma sat on her front porch in a faded sundress with her knees spread wide and a pair of dingy pink bunny rabbit bedroom slippers on her feet.

The seventy-plus senior was fanning herself with the *Home and Garden* section of the local newspaper hard enough to make the bangs on her steel gray wig flutter against her forehead.

"Sure is," her neighbor Trudy Scott replied. "Just stuff me inside the icebox and close the damn door behind me."

The loose flesh on Trudy's upper arm flapped like bat wings when she raised her forearm to swipe her sweaty brow.

Selma didn't know what the current temperature was, but at noon it was hovering near the one-hundred-degree mark and rising. It was now 6:00 P.M., and the humidity was so thick and the air so heavy she could barely breathe. It was hot, alright. Blazing hot.

The two friends started their visit in Selma's living room but came out on the porch hoping to catch some kind of breeze. Their complaints about the heat did nothing to deter them from imbibing their third glass each of Selma's potent rum-laced lemonade.

Trudy, who was recently widowed, owned a bi-level on the opposite end of the street. Since her husband passed, she'd taken to spending quite a bit of time at Selma's house, primarily because she'd treated her late husband badly and was afraid to be alone at night. It was also because Selma always poured her alcohol with a heavy hand. Trudy rarely left until the bottle containing whatever they were drinking was empty, and she was drunk enough to sleep without the fear her husband would pay her a visit in retribution for past mistreatment.

Selma didn't mind. With her nephew, Daniel, missing and her grandson, Muscles, locked in his bedroom twenty-four seven mourning him, she welcomed the company.

"You know it don't make a damn bit of sense to be this hot out," Selma said for lack of anything constructive to say.

"Uh-huh," Trudy replied, only half-listening to Selma ramble on about the weather. She was far more interested in what was going on at the house two doors down.

With her right eye nearly closed shut from a recent stroke and the right side of her mouth lifted in a misshapen sneer, Trudy watched through her Coke-bottle spectacle lenses as Albert Burkett careened into their driveway like an escapee from Rahway State Prison with the cops blazing hot on his tail. She frowned when she saw his pretty, young wife in the passenger seat. Trudy sat poised like a snake, waiting for her unsuspecting neighbors to leave the protection of their car.

"What makes no sense is for somebody to let themselves get that damn big," Trudy declared as a beat-up brown Pontiac sped down the street, leaking oil. She now had Selma's attention.

"Who you telling, Trudy? If you ask me, he's gotten even bigger than he was before. Who the hell gains weight eating nasty hospital food?" Selma wondered aloud, lighting a Camel cigarette and letting the smoke tunnel through both nostrils like a locomotive.

"Shit, I bet that young wife of his has been sneaking food to him in the hospital so she can kill his fat ass off and collect the money from The Melting Pot." Trudy grinned.

Selma playfully rapped Trudy on the leg with her makeshift fan. "Girl, hush your mouth." She snickered. Selma was nosy, but not unkind. Trudy was mean-spirited by nature and brought out the worst in others.

Mean or not, Trudy wasn't the only one who questioned Loretta's motives in marrying Albert Burkett. Plainfield was a little big town with more than its share of wagging tongues. The combination of a beautiful woman with a shady past and a rich, socially inept, morbidly obese man makes fertile fodder for gossip. Wrapped up in the moment, Selma let slip something she'd been holding on to for years.

"His mother told me she caught Loretta in bed with their youngest son, Andrew. His parents like tah had a fit when Loretta and Albert eloped."

Selma regretted the hateful words the moment they passed her lips. Despite her disclosure, she was genuinely fond of the young couple and, unlike Trudy, had no desire to hurt them.

"I knew it!" Trudy said, latching on to the information like a detective on a career make-or-break case. "I always wondered why Andrew left town and never came back. The only thing Albert has going for him is the family business. Why else would someone like Loretta want to be with him?" she asked, referring to Albert being the heir apparent to Burkett's Melting Pot, the oldest and most profitable Black-owned business in the state.

"This is how I see it," Trudy said. "Loretta couldn't snag the good-looking son, so she sunk her claws into fat Albert. I don't trust that gal as far as I can throw her, and you know I got a bad back. Give me one of those Camels." Trudy extended her hand.

Trudy ran the tip of the match against the coarse surface of the matchbox, threatening the sweetness of Selma's potted lilies with the unpleasant smell of sulfur. Selma was afraid Trudy would repeat her slip to someone else.

Despite her recent stroke, Trudy filled her lungs with the smoke from the unfiltered cigarette and reached for the potent rum and lemonade cocktail to wash the smoke down. The nasty, wet rumble of Trudy's cough was evidence that her lungs were as diseased as her spirit.

The two-faced busy-bodies sat in temporary silence, watching

Albert and Loretta Burkett close the car door behind them and slowly walk toward their front door.

§

"Good evening, Deacon Burkett. How you doin', Sister Burkett? Glad to see ya'll back home again," said two-faced Selma.

"Missed you at choir practice this evening, Sister Burkett," Trudy said, lying through her teeth. She hated Loretta and her lovely singing voice.

Selma discarded the newspaper to vigorously fan herself with a fan bearing the Brown's Funeral Home logo. "I declare, you sure gave us a scare, Deacon Burkett."

Albert cringed at Selma's mention of the frighteningly embarrassing incident which occurred during last Sunday's church service. It began with him passing out at the sight of Tony Palermo and the hallucination of his dead father, and culminated with him being taken to the emergency ward. Then, as he'd done now, he soiled his pants.

He later learned that the front doors of the church had to be removed, and several of his fellow deacons drafted, to assist the EMTs in getting him out of the church and into the ambulance.

His round face burned beet-red with shame.

"For a minute there, I thought we'd lost you." Selma piped in with all the sensitivity of a sociopathic serial killer.

Albert ignored the comment. Loretta threw up her hand in greeting and kept it moving.

"Lord have mercy," Trudy whispered under her breath as Albert struggled to make it up the steps, huffing and puffing like an out-of-commission freight train. Loretta followed close on his heels to shield him from embarrassment, lest the neighbors see his soiled trousers and run with the information.

"If you need some help negotiating them there steps, I can send my grandson, Muscles, over." Selma offered the help loud enough for residents in the next town to hear.

"That won't be necessary, Mrs. Barksdale, but thank you," Loretta replied in that soft, polite tone that never failed to work Trudy's nerves.

"Hmph, that heffa ain't foolin' nobody, talking all prim and proper. I got her number," Trudy said. Loretta Burkett had done nothing to earn Trudy's scorn other than be young and pretty.

"Let's see what we can find out," Trudy said with the devil in her good eye.

Trudy limped down the steps and onto the sidewalk in a pair of her late husband's bedroom slippers and a floral scarf partially covering a head full of sponge rollers. She turned to Selma once she reached the sidewalk.

"You coming?"

❧

"Let me do that for you," Loretta insisted with an outstretched hand after Albert's second attempt to open the door failed. A colony of wasps flew around the porch light, adding to her anxiety as Selma and Trudy drew closer.

Moments later, the loud click of the lock disengaging proved the third try was the charm. The door to 1294 Arlington Avenue yawned open like a foul-mouthed belch, albeit too late to avoid an encounter with Selma Barksdale and Trudy Scott, who were standing at the foot of their steps.

With a sigh of resignation, Loretta handed Albert her purse. "You go inside and clean yourself up," she said as Selma and Trudy converged on her. "I will get rid of them."

CHAPTER TWENTY-THREE

"LORD, JESUS, I thought they'd never leave," Loretta mumbled under her breath after successfully fending off Selma and Trudy's intrusive questions. The front door squealed in agreement as she locked it behind her. She kicked off her sandals to find the interior of the house hotter than a blazing funeral pyre.

"Godda…" She caught herself just shy of using the lord's name in vain.

I swear, the least Albert could have done is turn on the air before he went upstairs.

Sucking her teeth, she hurriedly turned on the air-conditioning unit in the living room window and plopped down on the plastic-covered sofa in front of it.

"Lord knows, I hate this house!" she groused.

Mentally and physically drained, Loretta closed her eyes and promptly drifted off.

It might have been minutes or just a few seconds before a strange sound penetrated her subconscious, nudging her awake. Trapped within the walls of that murky place between sleep and wakefulness where dreams blend with reality, Loretta reluctantly opened her eyes.

For a split second, she could have sworn she saw her deceased mother-in-law leading Albert by the hand to the door. The dream seemed all the more real at the sound of the squeaking front door opening and closing behind them.

She blinked twice to dispel the unpleasant image, which vanished just as quickly as it appeared, leaving her more than a little shaken. Loretta said a silent prayer and dismissed what she'd seen for what it was—the remnants of a disturbing dream.

Now fully awake, Loretta canted her head sideways to better discern a strange sound coming from the kitchen. The yellowing plastic that covered every piece of furniture in the living room crackled in rebuke as she got up from the sofa to investigate.

Moments later, Loretta was standing in the entryway to the kitchen, staring at Albert, who was sitting at the kitchen table as close as his enormous belly would allow. His keys sat on the counter next to her purse. All was dark save for the light from of the open refrigerator door.

Oblivious to Loretta's presence, Albert sat hunched over a platter of leftover baked ham. His fat fingers, mouth, and chin glistened with pork grease as he shoveled pieces of the salty pork in his mouth so fast Loretta feared he might choke. The disgusting image of Albert eating like a pig at a trough, with his legs splayed open and a drying piss stain at the apex of his crotch, would abide with Loretta for the rest of her life.

Loretta saw red.

She marched into the kitchen, her lips a straight line of resolve, lifted the heavy glass serving platter from the table and slammed it to the floor. Shattered glass and pork grease littered the old-fashioned black-and-white tile flooring, as the partially ravaged eight-pound glazed ham rolled to the opposite side of the kitchen floor like a severed head.

Determined to feed the ravenous beast of his addiction, Albert rose from the table like a colossal behemoth and, like a man possessed, lumbered toward the open refrigerator to retrieve a roasted chicken.

This time he was ready for Loretta. Cradling the chicken to his breast like a football, he spun around and, with an expression Loretta had never seen before, raised his fist as if he intended to knock Loretta's lights out if she even thought about coming between him and that chicken.

Loretta instinctively threw her hands up to protect her face, an action that snapped Albert out of his craziness more effectively than a bucket of ice water in his face.

"What, Albert?" Loretta said, staring up at him with defiance. "You fittin' to beat my ass so you can eat that chicken?" she taunted now that the imminent danger of the blow had passed. "Well, don't let me stop you. Go ahead. Eat it! And while you are at it, you can eat this too."

Loretta ran over to where the greasy ham rested and tossed it at Albert, striking him in the chest. The ham fell to the floor, leaving a sizable grease stain on the shirt she'd ironed for him that morning.

"Here! Eat these, Albert. Wouldn't want you to miss out on your protein."

She reached inside the refrigerator for a carton of eggs. One by one, she pelted Albert with the contents of the carton. Loretta reached inside the fridge for the gravy boat. She scooped the congealed gelatinous mess with her bare hands and slapped Albert in the face with it. A bag of flour and powdered sugar came next.

"I bet you are mighty thirsty, aren't you, Albert." She tossed a full pitcher of ice-cold Kool-Aid in his face.

It wasn't until Loretta saw Albert swaying on his feet, covered with food, that the white-hot power of her blinding rage was finally appeased. She slumped against the counter like a party balloon someone had let the air out of.

"I thought I could trust you, that I would be safe with you, but I was wrong," she stated, delivering a one-two punch to Albert's heart.

I'm no fool. I know Loretta will never love me passionately. What woman in their right mind could? I mean, look at me. I'm a mess, he thought, disheartened.

Theirs was not a fiery, passionate love, but it was a good love, built on acceptance and trust. Loretta had given him something far richer than passion. She'd entrusted him with her heart and her secrets. Albert knew better than most how difficult it had been for Loretta to let down her guard, to let him in. He'd never raised a hand against anyone. To finally do so against the woman he treasured more than his next breath was unthinkable.

Prior to this blow-up, Albert's relationship with his wife had been a deep abiding friendship forged in the knowledge that no matter what their life accomplishments, they would never measure up to the expectations of the people who raised them.

They were two misfits, equally yoked in their emotional trauma. And now, because of him, that trust was shattered. He feared his actions would cause irreparable damage to their marriage.

I abused her trust, he thought in despair. *I have to make this right.*

"Please forgive me. I swear I didn't mean it, Loretta. I worship the ground you walk on." Albert extended a hand, his eyes begging her to take it.

"I love you."

"You don't love me, Albert," she said. "Shit, you don't even know how to love yourself," she added, throwing her religion out of the window. "Why else would you head straight for the refrigerator as soon as you walked through the front door, huh?"

Her question was met with silence. "Right! Just like I thought."

"Please." Albert tried to stop the rollercoaster of words he knew would destroy whatever respect Loretta had left for him. Loretta could not be stopped. She'd been silent too long. She was determined to have her say.

"I'm no fool, Albert. I can feel in my gut that there is something more going on that you aren't telling me." Her words caused the color to drain from Albert's face.

"So don't you dare give me that I love you garbage because if you really loved me, you would do everything in your power to stay alive! How many times have I asked you for the health insurance information, Albert?"

She was sick of his stalling tactics. When that question was also met with silence, Loretta picked up a box of garbage bags and prepared to clean up the mess in the kitchen.

Dejected, Albert struggled upstairs to clean up.

Albert was showered and closeted in his office by the time Loretta set the kitchen to rights. The mere thought of Albert made Loretta's head pound like a base drum.

She was rummaging through her purse in search of her migraine medicine when she came across a piece of folded white paper tucked amongst the greenbacks in her wallet. She would later swear that the devil himself had placed it there to ensure she would see it when she was at her lowest. Her hands shook uncontrollably as she unfolded the paper bearing a phone number written in a bold hand. No name was needed. Loretta knew who the number belonged to.

Moments later, she was back in the kitchen, standing before the yellow phone mounted on the wall. Strangely enough, she had no recollection of how she had gotten there and would later characterize her next action as an out-of-body experience.

The dial tone seemed inordinately loud when she lifted the receiver from the jack. She placed her hand over the earpiece to muffle the sound, all the while keeping her ears peeled and her eyes locked on her husband's closed office door.

Holding her breath, she inserted her middle finger into the circular hole corresponding with the first number. Each number she dialed on the rotary represented a bullet she was locking and loading in the chamber of the gun she would use to kill her marriage.

The phone rang once and then twice. She was relieved the universe had saved her from herself when the phone rang for the third time. She was ready to hang up, but the devil wasn't ready to let her off the hook. Someone picked up on the other end.

"Hello?" Her voice trembled with uncertainty.

"Hey, baby. I was wondering when you would call," came the deep masculine reply.

Loretta took exception that he said "when" and not "if." She hated that he still found her so predictable, but not enough to change the disastrous course she was set on.

"Let me take you out to dinner," he said.

"I can't get away."

"Then why the fuck you call me?"

"I just wanted to talk."

"Liar," he replied in that deep sensual tone that always turned her inside out and made her want to touch herself. "We both know what you want, now don't we?" He was referring to what happened between them a week earlier while Loretta and Althea were in Newark selecting floral arrangements for Althea's upcoming wedding.

They'd been in the florist shop for a little over an hour when Loretta, fearful of getting a ticket, hurried outside to feed the parking meter. She dropped two quarters in the meter and was about to rejoin Althea when a burst of deep masculine laughter overshadowed all sound, rendering her deaf and dumb to her surroundings.

I'd know that sound anywhere, she'd thought. Against her will, Loretta's eyes sought the source and froze.

Sitting on a bench near the colossal bronze Wars of America monument between the busy intersection of Broad and East Park Place was the man who'd ruthlessly taken advantage of Loretta when she was far too young and damaged to defend herself—a man who had a tether on her spirit only permanent distance could break.

Like a feral animal sensing nearby prey, Chester "Chet" Palmer stopped mid-sentence in an animated conversation with two other men to turn in Loretta's direction. A slow predatory smile lit his wicked lying lips when his eyes unerringly landed on her.

Had Loretta's feet not been metaphorically locked in two-ton blocks of cement by the memory of his touch, she would have beat feet to the safety of the florist shop and left through the back door. Instead, she stood like a frightened child, awaiting her fate.

As if by majick, Chet was standing before her, sucking the oxygen out of her space and exerting his considerable will on her.

Then, as he'd done now, he said, "Hey, Baby."

Something inside of Loretta shriveled and died when Althea came out to see what was keeping Loretta to find her and Chet in the back seat of her car. Althea was not alone. Hester Kay, who had every reason to hate her, stood gloating right next to Althea. What bothered Loretta more than getting caught in an illicit act by her dearest friend and her worst enemy was that, given the chance, she would do it again.

Chet Palmer and Loretta Lawson Burkett had history, and none of it was good.

"Meet me in the industrial park off Frelinghuysen," Chet commanded, redirecting her train of thought. "I'll be there at eleven."

"I have to go!" Loretta said, nearly jumping out of her skin as the door to Albert's office sprang open, and he walked out with a questioning look.

"Who was that?" he asked, afraid he'd given up the right to ask her anything.

"It was Althea. I was talking to Althea," she stuttered, surprised at how easily the lie rolled off her tongue. "A few days ago, she asked me if I could tag along for an appointment with a wedding vendor. I was just confirming I would be there. The appointment is tomorrow at 8:00 A.M. I thought I would spend the night."

Loretta relayed the information like a rehearsed speech, far too guilty to look into Albert's pleading eyes. The die was cast. She would do what she always did when faced with a life crisis. She would spread her thighs to dull her pain.

Realizing she was still upset with him, Albert returned to his office and closed the door behind him.

CHAPTER TWENTY-FOUR

L ESS THAN AN hour after Albert questioned Loretta about the phone call, he heard the staccato beat of her high heels descending the stairs. He held his breath, hoping, no praying, she would crack his office door open to bid him goodnight.

Initially, Albert thought nothing of Loretta's plan to spend the night at Althea's house, even though it was more a statement than a request. But when the screaming door opened and closed behind her, without a goodbye, he wasn't so sure.

He shook off his insecurity and pounded away at the keys on his calculator. His swollen kielbasa-shaped fingers flew across the keyboard as he tallied his monthly expenses again and again. No matter how many times he added them up, he still came up $3,200.79 short.

A waterfall of sweat ran down Albert's face. What didn't get caught within the folds of flesh on his triple chin pooled at the base of his neck and saturated the collar of his crisp white dress shirt. He was a man thrown overboard without a life jacket, drowning in a sea of debt.

Albert reached for a cotton handkerchief with the initials AJB, III monogrammed in fancy script. He mopped the sweat from his face and neck and, with a pained expression, paused to look at the collage of photos on the dark paneled wall facing him. His father, Albert J. Burkett, II, died over a year ago, and yet he could still feel the ache of judgment boring into his spirit.

Hanging in a prominent place amongst the photographic memories was an old black-and-white photo of his dad and his grandfather, Albert J. Burkett, I. Their eyes followed Albert in condemnation, lest he forget any of his shortcomings. The photo was taken at the ribbon-cutting ceremony for Burkett's Melting Pot, the oldest and most successful Black-owned family business in the State of New Jersey—that is, until Albert took over.

When Alfred's younger brother, Andrew, informed their father that he had no desire to take over the family business, instead choosing a career in the military, their father grudgingly passed the reigns of the business to Albert. If Albert lived to be one hundred, he would never forget the last conversation he had with his father.

"I paid off the mortgage on this house years ago. We own it all, the house, the Burkett Melting Pot building, and the business personalty, free and clear. Not many Colored folks can claim that kind of accomplishment," he'd boasted. "Both canceled mortgages are in the safe in my office, along with the banking and title information, so don't do anything stupid like letting white folks talk you into borrowing money from them. Once you go down that rabbit hole, there is no coming back.

And trust me, they will try. The business is in a prime location. They've been trying to get their thieving hands on the land and the building for years. You'll find the life insurance policies and burial instructions there too."

Albert began to cry at the mention of his death.

"Pay attention, Boy!" his father demanded in a voice that was surprisingly strong for someone who was about to kick the bucket.

"I regret making you my namesake because you're weak. But with Andrew gone, you are the only one left." He fanned his rotten death breath in Albert's face and cut him to the core with his mean-spirited words.

"And don't you dare waste my hard-earned money on that whorish gal you married either. I mean it, Albert. If you do, I swear I'll come back from the grave and beat your fat ass until you are just as dead as I will be," he said with a vitriol usually reserved for a hated enemy.

"You had better not fuck this up," his father added, drilling him with a milky-eyed stare. Before Albert could reply, Albert Burkett, II released one last breath and died.

Albert counted to one hundred before alerting the private duty nurse. He needed to make sure the bastard was dead. To this day, Albert regretted not summoning the courage to stand up to the old man and defend his wife's character.

Of course, I did exactly what you thought I would do, he said, locking eyes with the image of his father in the photo.

I fucked everything up. Don't I always?

❧

An invisible hand clutched Albert's heart, filling him with dread. *Loretta asked me for the insurance information so that she could complete the Duke Weight Loss Center admission application.*

How can I tell her I allowed the health insurance policies to lapse long ago? He anguished, suddenly sick to his stomach. *To make matters worse, I cashed in our life insurance policies. If I drop dead tomorrow, Loretta will be hard-pressed to scrape up the money to bury me.*

"Father God, I don't know what to do." He wailed as tears and snot burned his tongue.

Albert struggled to press his fat fingers into his side pants pocket to retrieve a clean handkerchief. Finally giving up, he used the sleeve of his crisp white shirt to wipe his nose.

"I am going to lose the business that has been in my family for three generations. I am going to lose our home. I am going to lose my wife. And if I don't come up with the money I owe Palermo, I'm subject to lose my life."

The jarring ring of the phone sliced through the silence, disrupting his distressed thoughts. Albert nearly jumped out of his skin. He cleared his throat before answering.

"Hello?" He hoped to hear Loretta's sweet voice.

"Hey, Albert." It was Althea. "May I speak with Loretta?"

Albert's belly churned with fear. "She's not with you?"

"Why, no. Should she be?" Althea asked, becoming an unwitting party to her best friend's deceit and Albert's fear. "What's going on, Albert?" She grew more anxious by the minute.

But Albert didn't hear the sudden barrage of questions Althea was lobbing at him. He'd already hung up.

Loretta lied to me. If she's not with Althea, then where is she? And more importantly, who is she with?

Albert realized it was selfish of him, but the thought of another man giving her what he could not was driving him crazy.

Grunting, he used the desk as an anchor and heaved his corpulent body from his chair, desperate to do what his brain had programmed him to do whenever he faced a stressful situation.

I need something to eat.

The floorboards of the old house moaned in protest with every uneven step as Albert lumbered toward the kitchen as fast as the edema in his swollen feet would allow. Save for a pitcher of water, the refrigerator was as empty as it had been on the Sears and Roebuck showroom floor. Alfred slammed the refrigerator door shut.

Loretta had done a thorough sweep of the house, the garage, the basement, and the backyard shed. She'd even emptied the garbage before leaving for only God knows where.

Albert grabbed his car keys off the occasional table in the foyer and headed to The Melting Pot, his home away from home.

❧

The Melting Pot, 1201 South Avenue, Plainfield, New Jersey

Albert entered the restaurant through the service entrance in the back. Without the hustle and bustle of the cooks and wait staff, the space seemed sterile and as eerily quiet as a morgue. All that was missing were the drawers to accommodate the dead bodies.

Tomorrow, he thought, gently placing his keys on the counter, *the restaurant will come to life. Its dining hall will be filled with hungry patrons, cooks, wait staff, and other workers eager to please, all soon to be unemployed. But tonight, the restaurant and all that is in it belongs to me. It is my sanctuary and my place of quiet peace.*

Once he entered the pristine commercial kitchen, Albert zeroed in on the Master-Bilt walk-in combo cooler/freezer as if he were a guided missile and the fridge a homing device.

The door to the refrigerator made a sucking vacuum sound when he disengaged the closure latch. A burst of cool air dried some of the sweat on his face. The interior bulbs immediately came on, revealing the refrigerator contents in a burst of bright light.

Albert didn't care that much of the food he was eyeing had been catered for a party on the morrow. He was like a dope fiend faced with his drug of choice. Nothing and no one mattered except that he feed that hungry monkey hanging on his back.

On a shelf on the left side of the walk-in fridge was a rectangular metal pan containing a twenty-two-pound turkey that had been marinating in The Melting Pot signature sauce for two days, deep-fried, with the meat pulled from the bone. He quickly placed the heavy pan on one of the stainless-steel working stations behind him.

I will just eat a little, he promised himself.

Next, his eyes fell upon an elaborately decorated sheet cake with the words "Happy Sixtieth Anniversary, Mom and Dad" etched on the top in decorative floral script. The sheet cake was a modified torte, comprising eight extremely thin layers of rich lemon cake slathered in homemade butter crème icing and pineapple and coconut compote. He placed the cake next to the pan of fried turkey.

I shall eat about an inch from one end of the cake, even it out and apply fresh icing, he reasoned. *No one will know.*

And then he sat down to eat, wheezing as he squeezed his enormous body into one of the kitchen chairs. The circumference of his waist and belly were so rotund, he was hard-pressed to pull himself close enough to the work counter to eat comfortably.

All was quiet except for the soft hum of the commercial grade appliances and Albert's snorts and grunts as he packed as much food into his gaping maw as possible, dropping food and dripping grease on his white cotton shirt in his haste.

Albert ate like a man possessed. He ate like he was afraid someone would snatch the food from his grasp and prevent him from ever eating again. His eyes darted furtively around the chrome and stainless steel industrial kitchen as he shamelessly routed through the massive amount of food like a starving animal.

Albert couldn't stop himself. He ate and continued to eat like a man hypnotized. When he came to his senses, he'd nearly eaten all the sheet cake and had placed a significant dent in the pan of greasy fried turkey, yet still the void in his spirit was not filled.

Blinded by the potent pain of inadequacy, Albert stood, causing the stool to topple to the floor with a thunderous crash. He was drunk on gluttony, staggering and lurching to the open refrigerator with grease and cake-covered fingers to find something—anything he could shove into his mouth.

His next target was a metal mixing bowl containing the leftover homemade buttercream icing used for the sheet cake. He scooped up a can of Hershey's chocolate syrup in one hand and the bowl of icing in the other, and swiftly placed both items on one of the stainless-steel working stations behind him.

Not even bothering with a spoon, Albert dipped his bare hands into the bowl of icing and filled his mouth with its sickening sweetness. Before swallowing, he used his icing-befouled hands to squeeze the ice-cold Hershey syrup into his open mouth.

At last, he'd found nirvana.

He moaned in satisfaction as an explosion went off in his head. His heart sputtered and seized like a car running out of gas. His last thought was of his beloved Loretta as he crashed to the restaurant floor.

CHAPTER TWENTY-FIVE

The No Name Bar, 24 Wright Street, Newark, New Jersey

CHET INSISTED LORETTA leave her car in an industrial park off Frelinghuysen Avenue, citing a scarcity of parking spaces where they would dine. She thought his request was odd but complied, hastily removing her wedding rings and placing them in the glove compartment immediately upon his arrival. Moments later, she was sliding across the smooth black leather seats in Chet's Lincoln Continental and into the familiar, yet questionable security of his waiting arms.

The interior of the car smelled like a combination of vanilla and the spicy pheromone that covered the surface of Chet's rich dark skin like the sweetest cologne. If food was her husband's addiction, Chester Allan Palmer, a/k/a "Chet," was Loretta's anesthetic for the pain that plagued her and her deadly drug of choice.

Chet drove the short distance to the restaurant one-handed, with his body in a serious gangsta' lean. He strummed Loretta's sensibilities, languidly massaging the center of her palm with the middle digit of his free hand, mindfucking her as he drove like the consummate sybarite he'd always been.

Loretta realized her mistake in accepting Chet's invitation the moment they arrived at the intended location. Lincolns, Caddies, El Dorados, and several Mercedes lined both sides of the busy street, some double-parked, with the windows rolled down and a babel of radios blasting popular tunes. Even the loudest car radio couldn't drown out the music thumping from inside the rundown commercial building that sat in the middle of the block like a skid mark in a drunk's dirty drawers.

Loretta took in the aged pylon sign on the building's roof. The letters of the No Name Bar were lit up like Times Square on New Year's Eve. The second 'N' rested on a loose shingle, like a tear that refused to let go. A group of well-dressed, unsavory-looking characters stood to the left of the flashing neon sign advertising beer and package goods, reminding Loretta of a past best left behind.

I no longer frequent places like this, she thought, wondering what the heck she'd gotten herself into.

My husband and I are active members of our church. Albert is a deacon, and I teach Sunday school and sing in the gospel choir—facts she should have considered before she picked up the phone to dial Chet's number.

"Chet, is this where we are having dinner?" she asked in disbelief.

Chet shifted into park in the middle of the busy street, and turned to her with a level glare.

"What? This place ain't upscale enough for you? It's not up to fat boy's standards?" His words caused her to flinch. "Don't forget where the fuck you came from, Rette," he added in an ominous tone, making her feel like a nasty wad of gum on the bottom of his tan suede Ballys.

Chet knows about the gutter I crawled out of when I married Albert. It is incredibly cruel of him to remind me of it. But then again, Chet has always been cruel. So, then, why am I here? Loretta asked herself, then immediately answered her own question.

I'm here because I'm a slut, just like my mother, and this is the treatment I deserve.

Old habits die hard.

"It's just that I don't feel comfortable being in a crowded bar where I can easily run into someone I know," she said, trying to backpedal. This was only partially true because Albert would never have brought her to a place like this.

Acting as if the issue was settled, Chet rolled down his window to motion over one of the unsavory guys standing in front of the bar.

"My man," Chet said with a toothsome smile as he got out of the car.

"What can I do you for, brutha?" the dude replied, flashing a gold rim on his left front tooth.

"Can you see my girl inside while I park my ride?"

"No doubt, brutha."

He bent to peer inside the car and locked his predatory gaze on Loretta, making her feel like she needed to take a bath in a tub filled with bleach. Chet instructed Loretta to go with the shady-looking character without bothering to open the car door for her.

Had Loretta remained in Chet's car but a few minutes more, or even turned around to address him, she would have seen fourteen-year-old Renee Fuller strutting down the street on her way to the bar. But Loretta didn't turn around. She'd been too hurt to do so, and too afraid to chastise Chet for bringing her to the No Name Bar. There was nothing she could do to avert what would happen later.

⚘

Renee Fuller's breath hitched in excitement at the sight of a group of brothers dressed in tailor-made silk trousers with slick-looking button-down shirts and stingy-brimmed hats, each one finer than the next. Some were leaning against cars that looked like they'd just come off the showroom floor. Renee dug in her pocket for a stick of Juicy Fruit gum, popped the gum in her mouth, and tossed the wrapper on the sidewalk.

"Aaaw shit now! They playing my song!" she yelled, snapping her fingers to the beat of the music and belting out the chorus. "You beat me to the punch," she sang as she did the signature Jersey strut across the street on a set of the prettiest bow legs in Newark.

The music pulsed through her body, calling to her and igniting something deeply primal within her spirit. She'd chosen the perfect night to sneak out of the house. Her only disappointment was that her partner-in-crime and best friend Rayna wasn't able to enjoy the night with her.

Rayna's grandmother paid them an unexpected visit from the Bronx and ended up staying the night. Rayna was forced to give her grandmother her bedroom while she shared a room with her bed-wetting, nosy-ass little sister.

The little bitch can't get up to go to the bathroom, but she could damn sure wake up to clock Rayna's actions. Rayna couldn't sneak out as planned.

Renee hadn't invited her other close friend, Joanne, because her mouth ran like water and she'd already used her as an alibi last weekend. Her parents thought she was attending a sleepover at Joanne's house. She spent one night at Joanne's house and the rest of the weekend in the Rainbow Motel screwing the shit out of her man, Guillermo "Billy" Torres, the finest Puerto Rican in Newark.

Tonight, Renee would have to get in trouble all by herself.

I'm going to have a stinkin' good time, she thought. *And I can't wait to tell Rayna all about it.*

Renee knew all eyes were on her, and she reveled in the attention. She walked the ghetto gauntlet of cat-calls and whistles, wearing the form-fitting blue dress she took from her much smaller mother's closet and the matching blue suede shoes she'd stolen from Bamberger's like she owned the world and everything in it.

"Hey, Little Mama! You want some of this?" a player named Darryl called out from inside his Caddy with a fat joint in his hand.

Renee was tempted but politely declined. *Once I hook up with Billy, I can have all the smoke, coke, and drinks I want.* Not only was Billy super-fine, but he was also one of the biggest drug dealers in the state.

There was an overall atmosphere of revelry with everyone talking loud, laughing, and flirting while Martha Reeves and the Vandellas lookalikes danced the jerk in the middle of the street in thigh-high boots and indecently short skirts.

Renee saw Ralph, the neighborhood number runner, slip into the alley between Rick's Barbershop and Murphy's Meat Market with Pam and Rosa Russell. The twins, although not much older than Renee, had been in and out of foster homes most of their lives. Renee assumed Ralph and the twins weren't in the alley to straight or box their numbers of choice. Her assumption proved correct when Rosa pushed Ralph against the wall and dropped to her knees before him, while Pam stood watch in the mouth of the alley.

Ralph saw Renee watching them, her gaze lingering a bit too long. An unspoken understanding passed between them at that moment. Though he was married with nine kids, Renee knew he would keep her secret if she kept his.

I can't point the finger at nobody. After all, I'm a sinner too.

Renee spotted her boyfriend Billy's black-on-black Deuce, shining like new money in front of the bar. She picked up her pace, striding across the uneven pavement like a paid professional in her stolen high heels. Smiling to herself, she knocked on the blacked-out driver's side window, prepared to greet the man she had risked everything for with a sexy, "Hey, Baby," as the window descended.

But it wasn't Billy. Tony Columbus, the crooked mayor of

Newark's ne'er-do-well son, rolled down the blacked-out window, releasing a billow of pungent smoke. Bright blue eyes rimmed red from excessive alcohol and drugs took in her stylish attire.

"Where's Billy?" Renee asked, not bothering to hide her disappointment.

She scanned the vicinity, searching for the man she had lied to her parents about repeatedly, all to spend time with him. The steady rhythm of her gum popping matched the music playing everywhere around them.

"Well, hello back at you, young stuff," Tony replied affably. "Does your bible-toting pappy know you're out this late at night?"

I got your pappy, motherfucker, she thought, glaring at him.

Renee didn't like white people, especially those who try to act like they're Colored. And she hated it even more that Tony referred to her father as somebody's "pappy," like he was a slave or something.

Daddy always said, 'Give white folks an inch, and they'll take a mile,' she thought with a bitter taste in her mouth.

"If anybody should keep their ass in the house, it's you," Renee replied, rolling her eyes. "Didn't you just do a bid in Annandale for possession?" She looked at him like he was a hot turd stinking up her man's car. "And here you are smoking weed and hanging out where you have no business, and you still on probation."

"Hold up, baby girl. No need to get salty." Tony hunched his shoulders and raised his hands in defense of his statement. "It ain't safe for a pretty little church girl like you to be out with us sinners." Tony ignored Renee's reaction to his earlier comment. "I'm just saying there are a lot of bad people who might want to eat a sweet young thing like you up."

I wish one of them would try. I belong to Guillermo "Billy" Torres. Only a fool would try to touch me, she thought with pride.

"Do you know where Billy is or not?" Renee was determined to get a straight answer out of Tony.

"Maybe." Tony smirked with his noncommittal reply.

I didn't climb out of my goddamn bedroom window, nearly breaking my neck, to do a fucking back-and-forth routine with White Boy Tony, she thought, still thinking about her recent rendezvous at the Rainbow Motel with Billy. Then, unlike now, she'd been able to lay up with her man all night.

"I don't have time to play with you, Tony. You know my time is limited! Either you know where Billy is, or you don't."

"Feisty little one, aren't we? Tell you what," Tony said, raising a joint to his lips to take a deep, leisurely drag. "Why don't you hop in the ride? Let me get your head straight, and then I'll tell you where Brother Bill is."

"Well, alright now," Renee said, promptly changing her tune. That was all the incentive she needed to get her little fresh ass in the car.

Tony leaned in to give Renee a shotgun as soon as she closed the passenger-side door behind her. She inhaled deeply, experiencing euphoria the second she exhaled the acrid smoke.

This is some good shit, she thought, closing her eyes to savor the mellow feeling.

When she opened her eyes again, Tony was close enough for Renee to see the pores on his pale cheeks. She could smell the combination of weed and peppermint on his breath and the subtle citrus fragrance of his cologne. He was close enough to kiss her. Instead of reclaiming her personal space, Renee held her breath, curious to see what his next move would be.

CHAPTER TWENTY-SIX

"YOU ARE SO damn pretty," Tony whispered in a husky voice. He ran his finger along the side of Renee's cheek. "Your skin is so soft, so smooth, like velvet." His voice trailed off.

Renee knew Tony dug her. *And why not? I'm fine as fuck*, she thought. It was evident he wanted her by the way he looked at her when he thought no one was watching—the way he was looking at her right now. She also knew he wanted to kiss her.

My question is: Does he want me bad enough to jeopardize his relationship with Billy? She knew Billy and Tony were more than partners-in-crime, and that they had been best friends since grade school.

Tony must have remembered where he was and whose chick he was pushing up on because he immediately backed off, leaving Renee heady with the knowledge that she could bring Tony to his knees if she wanted to.

"Brother Bill is inside handling some business." He nodded toward the bar.

Renee got out of the car with a self-satisfied smile on her lips and the feeling of Tony's eyes burning through her clothes. She couldn't help but mess with his head one last time. Walking backward toward the bar, she blew him a kiss. It was okay to play with Tony. He was a nice guy and kind of cute for a white boy, but he wasn't Billy.

❧

Loretta watched Chet make his way through the crowded bar, stopping along the way to exchange greetings, shake a hand, or pat someone on the back, like he was campaigning for city council. At a whopping six-foot six, he stood head and shoulders above most of the men in the bar.

I should have asked him to order me a double. No, make that a triple glass of whiskey instead of that tired sloe gin fizz I requested. I'm going to have to get drunk to deal with this shit, she thought, grim-faced.

Chet had the temerity to accuse her of acting bourgeois when she insisted they sit in a dark corner in the farthest reaches of the crowded bar. Loretta may have acted the fool when he reminded her where she'd come from, but on that point, she remained adamant. She wanted to be as far away from everyone as possible, hoping— no, praying she didn't bring any roaches home with her and that no one she knew saw her enter the bar with somebody else's husband.

That's right, dammit, she thought, rolling her eyes toward a woman who'd given Chet an over-ebullient greeting when they first arrived, even inquiring about his wife and kids after pointedly ignoring her.

Not only is Chet married, but his crazy-ass wife will beat the brakes off my ass if she catches me with her man again.

She nervously massaged the two-inch keloid scar marring her otherwise perfect complexion, recalling how she'd come by it. If Loretta lived to be one hundred, she would never forget that day.

Chet's wife, Toni, came home from work early to find her seven-month-old baby in his crib crying and Loretta, their fourteen-year-old babysitter, in their marital bed riding the shit out of her husband.

Toni dragged Loretta outside butt-naked. She beat the living shit out of her in front of the neighbors and would have killed her had Albert's younger brother, Andrew not been riding down the street on his five-speed bike and pulled Toni off her. Andrew removed his jacket to cover her shame. She would eventually thank Andrew in the only way she knew how—with her body—and fall in love with him, for all the good it would do her. Andrew left Plainfield and Loretta behind on his graduation day and never looked back.

During and after the beating, Chet didn't lift so much as a finger to help her, instead throwing her to the wolves. *And yet, I still melt at the mere sight of him.*

He obviously has no respect for me. She rooted inside her purse for her cigarette case and her signature tube of fire engine red lipstick. *Why else would he bring me to a place like this?* She applied a fresh coat of lip color to her full lips. *But then again, no respectable married Christian woman would be so brazen as to allow herself to be paraded around in public with a married man.*

She returned the tube to her purse and retrieved a Benson & Hedges Menthol 100 from the gold-trimmed mother-of-pearl cigarette case Albert gave her last year for her birthday. She always chain-smoked when she was nervous.

Everything circles right back to Albert, doesn't it? She thought with a rueful, self-deprecating smile.

No sooner did Loretta have the cigarette in her hand before a tall, lanky dude wearing a stingy-brimmed straw hat sprang out of the woodwork to light it. His hopeful, wide-mouthed grin revealed two gold caps on his front teeth.

Men had always been the bane of Loretta's existence. She was a naturally pretty woman with an earthy, yet sophisticated aura about her. Members of the opposite sex flocked to her like butter-flies to nectar.

Serves my hot ass good and right! Loretta thought, dismissing the pimp-looking dude with a curt "thank you" before giving him her back. *It ain't nothing but the devil and sinful lust that motivated me to see Chet again.*

Why am I like this? She asked herself, as if she could forget her aunt's constant reminder that her mother had been a whore and so was she, one of many cruel claims Loretta was ill-equipped to refute.

The last memory Loretta had of her parents was of her father shooting her mother and the man she would later learn was her mother's lover before turning his gun on himself when she was just five years old.

❧

Loretta agreed to go out with Chet, knowing full well that a meal and a few drinks were merely a prelude to what she really wanted.

Perhaps my mother was a whore. It makes no difference, since I am who I am. I crave the feel of a man's hardness pounding inside me. But I'll be goddamned if I agreed to this. She tapped her high-heel-clad foot under the table.

Loretta thought Chet was going to take her somewhere nice and dressed accordingly. She looked and felt as out of place as a princess in a pigsty, garbed in a white linen dress and a strand of pearls. Her thick, reddish, sun-bleached, blonde hair was pulled back in a sleek classic chignon. She'd even worn the expensive perfume Albert purchased for her last Christmas in anticipation of a memorable evening.

A group of women at a nearby table were looking at her sideways and making nasty comments like they wanted to start something. The last thing Loretta needed was for word to get back to members of her church that she'd been seen in a bar, rolling around on the floor like she didn't have a bit of sense, or that she was in jail for sticking her foot all the way up somebody's ass. She had worked too hard to clean up her act and had too much to lose to allow those low-class slags to drag her in the mud with them.

The No Name Bar. Hmph, places like this don't deserve a name, she thought spitefully, taking in the topless go-go dancer and the throng of horny men shoving greenbacks inside of her minuscule G-string with their tongues hanging out of their mouths.

Chet promised Loretta dinner, drinks, and that he was going to "bust her back out." His words, not hers.

I guess dinner will comprise a choice between fried whiting or chicken wings on Wonder Bread with a side of coleslaw or greasy fries. She glanced over at the long line of people waiting to pick up orders from the two short, fat, elderly ladies manning the kitchen. Loretta was nobody's snob. She'd had her fair share of dive bars and grease-laden soul food.

It's just that I had hoped things would be different this time. Disappointment washed over her. *I should have known better.*

Some things never change, she thought, as her stomach growled in protest.

This isn't the first time I let Chet sweet-talk his way inside my panties, but I swear before Almighty God that it will be the last, she vowed with a pinched expression.

So he'd better do me good enough to last a lifetime.

The object of her fizzling affection laughed loudly while conversing with a group of guys at the bar. *I wish Chet would hurry back.* She brooded. *Maybe we can cop a couple of fish sandwiches and a bottle and conclude this at a hotel. Better yet, maybe I should get out of here while I'm ahead.*

Granted, I am not physically attracted to Albert, but that man would give me the world if he could. He's a good man, and he loves me despite my past. I am married to an imperfect but kind, loving, godly man who pulls out chairs, opens doors for me, and treats me like a queen instead of using me up and tossing me away like every other man in my life. Albert honored me by giving me his last name.

She suddenly had an epiphany.

Here I am, a twenty-nine-year-old woman with the unenviable distinction of having the worst reputation in town being given an opportunity at respectability. And what do I do with it? I choose to lay up with someone who will bruise my insides and walk away leaving me a sullied, filthy mess. There is something wrong with this picture.

So what if Albert doesn't make me weak at the knees when he walks into a room. I'm nobody's prize, and God knows that I've had enough sex to last me a lifetime. I will not allow that self-destructive streak in me to mess things up!

That being said, she thought, *I sure would like to feel Chet's sweet meat stretching my insides one more time before I settle into a marriage in name only.*

⁓

"Wait one damn minute!"

Loretta did a double-take. *Is that who the hell I think it is?*

She sat forward in her chair to get a better look as Leila and Leroy Fuller's daughter, Renee, switched her little narrow ass through the bar on the arm of a grown man like she was twenty-one, and old enough to vote. Loretta's dark eyes followed the couple as they went into one of the back rooms and closed the door behind them.

Well, I'll be double damned! That little heifer can't be more than fourteen or fifteen if she's a damned day old.

That Renee was around the same age Loretta had been when Chet took advantage of her was a bucket of ice-cold water in the face of her desire, effectively dousing the flames of lust.

Loretta knew Renee's parents very well. They all attended Bethel Baptist Church in Plainfield. Renee's mother was best friends with the pastor's wife, and her father, Leroy, sits on the Deacon Board.

Her hands were itching to snatch Renee by the ear and drag her out of the bar, but she couldn't confront Renee without compromising her own reputation.

What a goddamn mess this is, she thought, her lips a straight line of indignation. *It just goes to show that what you do in the dark always comes out in the light. I'm getting the hell out of here just as soon as Chet returns with our drinks.*

CHAPTER TWENTY-SEVEN

THE DEMON KNOWN throughout The Hells as Tyranny floated like a storm cloud above the weathered marquee of the No Name Bar, cloaked in a majikal blanket of impenetrable invisibility. His broad, scaly chest swelled with vainglorious pride as he looked down upon the two-legged cockroaches reveling below.

My father, the ruler of all seven levels of The Hells, did not choose my brothers Hindrance, Salacious, Travail, or even his favorite son, Incarnadine, for this routine reconnaissance mission. He chose me, he thought.

I've been charged with the task to find a human witch named Sharon Samuels, and I shall not fail him!

Tyranny was honored to be part of his father's plans to destroy The Heavens and the Earth and take his rightful seat on the throne of He Whose Name He Dared Not Utter. The cruel despot saw this mission as an opportunity not only to test his mettle in the human realm but to prove his worth to his sire. But first, he and his team planned to have a little fun.

The tyrannous prince handpicked Andros, Drusiel, and Claniel to accompany him on this important mission, primarily because they were members of the powerful Dominion order of fallen angels and secondly, because they are mercenary killers who'd yet to wet their horns in human blood. Most importantly, each of the chosen demons knew how to follow orders. He turned his yellow reptilian eyes on the trusted cadre of demons under his command.

"As this is your first time walking among mortals, it is imperative you follow my lead. We must disguise our natural appearance so that we may move freely and undetected. Toward that end, our first order of business is to snatch some bodies," he said, capturing their undivided attention.

Tyranny spoke with authority as he, like his father, had walked the width and breadth of the earth many times and knew his way around.

It was a well-known fact among the residents of The Hells that a human must have a chink in their soul for a demon to claim his or her body as its vessel.

Tyranny was sure they would find an abundance of suitable vessels in or around the No Name Bar. Godlessness and corruptibility hung in the air like a homemade stink bomb.

The demons scanned the crowd below in search of easy prey. It wasn't long before all but Tyranny sensed humans vibrating at a satisfactory degree of corruptibility to house their demonic natures in the form of several young drug dealers peddling their products in front of the bar. One by one, Andros, Drusiel, and Claniel did a dive bomb act through the skulls of their unsuspecting vessels, leaving Tyranny alone on the roof.

Less than ten minutes later, a man exited the driver's side of a black-on-black Deuce and a Quarter illegally parked in front of the building. The human closed the door behind him and approached the bar entrance with his head bowed.

Tyranny snapped to attention when the human shared a greeting with a bearded, shirtless, human wearing a straw hat and a bright red suit who'd just exited. A thick cloud of despair surrounded him, drawing Tyranny in like the hypnotic wail of a practiced flute to a cobra.

"Hey, Tony," the red-suited human said. "What it be, baby?!"

The human named Tony appeared to shake off what was previously plaguing him as if it never existed. "It gon' be what it be, baby."

And then the two humans shook hands.

Ah, one white human in a sea of darkness, Tyranny thought. "Alas, I have found my vessel."

He closed his eyes and floated to the sidewalk below. The human jerked like a car with a stalled engine when Tyranny sat behind the wheel of his body, prepared to drive. Tyranny eased into the seat of his soul, immediately liking the fit and feel of Tony Columbus's body. Despite excessive use of drugs and alcohol, the human was still a relatively healthy specimen.

I'll be able to get plenty of traction out of this one, Tyranny crowed.

Not only did Tyranny have possession of the good-looking human's flesh, but he also owned his thoughts, feelings, and every single one of his memories. Right about now, the white human named Tony was terrified. He'd broken the drug dealer's cardinal rule to not become addicted to the product he peddles. Not only was he hopelessly addicted but he owed his partner a boatload of money and had no means to recoup the loss. His mind was running like an engine nearing empty as he tried to think of someone he could pin the monetary loss on. Tyranny liked the way Tony Columbus Jr. thought. Deciding to take the body for a test ride, he entered the hot, crowded bar.

Tyranny could tell Tony was well-liked by the enthusiastic greetings he received upon entering. The demon thought it ironic that the darker-hued humans would suffer whites in their midst, even though the favor is seldom reciprocated.

Well, I'll just have to see what I can do to bring them to their senses, the demon thought with a sinister chuckle.

❧

The lighting inside the bar was dim, the music was loud, and the patrons were guzzling down liquid forgetfulness faster than the three washed-out barmaids could raise their hands to pour it.

After pointedly ignoring several greetings directed to the human whose flesh he'd appropriated, Tyranny pushed ahead of several patrons to order a drink from the bar.

The barmaid placed Tony's usual drink in front of him with a worshipping smile.

"What the fuck is this shit, you ugly, gap-toothed bitch?"

The demon carefully watched the barmaid make his replacement drink through Tony's bright blue eyes to make sure she didn't spit in it.

Guess she won't be speaking to Tony anymore, he thought, so happy he could sing at the discord he'd sown.

"Next time, wait until I tell you what the fuck I want, you stupid cunt!" he snapped before swaggering off without paying her.

With his drink in hand, Tyranny moved toward a corner, where he took a minute to laugh at the barmaid's hurt expression and survey his surroundings.

The smell of chicken and fish frying in century-old grease competed with the pungent odor of hemp, human body odor, and cheap drugstore perfume. Drug transactions were taking place in bathrooms that hadn't seen a mop or any kind of soap and water since the No Name Bar opened back in '54.

This was the perfect environment for demons to ferment evil, and Tyranny and his motley band of aerial demons were smack-dab in the thick of things.

Tyranny locked eyes with a stripper resembling the whore of

Babylon. She returned his stare unflinchingly, while grinding on a slick pole anchored in the center of a raised dais in the middle of the bar. Glassy-eyed humans stuffed wrinkled paper money inside her sweaty G-string.

Tyranny whispered, "I see you, witch," in a voice only she could hear. Her soulless black eyes narrowed in recognition.

It was hot as seven Hells inside the bar, the kind of heat generated by too many human bodies in a confined space. And yet Tyranny felt right at home wearing the purloined flesh of his human vessel like a cheap suit from Sears and Roebuck against the rough, scaly surface of his skin.

He turned away from the Oogun Ika witch to focus on Claniel, who was shamelessly grinding on a woman in the middle of the dance floor who appeared to be so drunk she could barely stand.

She probably doesn't know where she is, what she is doing, or who the hell she is doing it with, Tyranny thought, giving a brief nod in Claniel's direction, indicating he'd chosen well.

Several women in the bar were shaking their heads in disgust as the demon took outrageous liberties with the incoherent woman for all to see.

Maybe Claniel will invite the bitch to his apartment so that he can show her his etchings and we can all have a crack at her, Tyranny thought, grinning with Tony's handsome pink lips.

Wondering what devilment Andros and Drusiel were up to, Tyranny trained his demon eyes near the area right off the bar where food was being sold and used his preternatural abilities to search through the walls.

Two human whores were in a back room, selling lap dances and anything else the horny little humans had the money to buy. Drusiel and Andros were back there with them. Andros sat in a wooden-backed chair, a woman wearing a snug purple dress and black fishnet stockings knelt before him. Tyranny couldn't see her face. But he couldn't help but notice the matted nape of her dusty wig and the big hole in the calf of one of her stockings. Andros had an unbreakable grip on the back of her head. The demon wore a twisted leer as he shoved his human cock down her throat. Tyranny laughed to himself when he realized the human was choking and on the verge of passing out.

By golly, my boys are having a funky good time. Oh yeah!

Drusiel had his hand over the mouth of the other working girl to muffle her screams while plowing his human cock in and out of her fat ass so hard it came out covered in shit and blood.

Cool. Cool. Cool. Now that's what's up! Tyranny thought, effortlessly picking up the human lingo stored in Tony's head.

⦦

Tyranny's eyes scanned the crowd in search of one face alone: Renee's. His host's body was still thrumming in excitement from that innocent kiss she'd blown in his direction.

The hell with Billy and the money I owe him, he thought, bolstered by the surfeit of alcohol and coke floating through Tony's bloodstream.

Tony wanted Billy's money, reputation, and his young girl/woman. In fact, Tyranny knew Tony was heartily sick and tired of being Billy's trusty sidekick, the Tonto to his motherfucking Lone Ranger, the Step-n-Fetch-It Robin, while Billy played the star role of Batman.

That shit is gonna stop tonight.

A high stakes card game was going on in yet another back room, and some guys were playing pool. Claniel had already been back there. In less than ten minutes, he had wagered and lost the profits from the drug sales his human host made that day—profits that rightfully belonged to the drug dealer named Billy. And now he was on the dance floor, jerking his human body to the beat of the music like he was having a seizure.

Billy Torres and some of his crew were in the back room discussing how the flunky had shorted him. The demon closed his eyes to savor the scent.

Yes. Sweet Renee is back there with him.

"Uh-oh," Tyranny sang to no one in particular. "Looks like somebody's in trouble." At the same time, the Marvelettes belted out "Don't Mess With Bill, no, no, no, no" on the jukebox.

Tyranny suspected it was a popular tune because the humans were packing the dance floor like a herd of cattle at round-up time. The next thing he knew, Billy and four other cats wearing angry expressions were parting the crowded dance floor like Moses parted the Red Sea. Tyranny was impressed that not one human on the dance floor missed a beat.

It suddenly occurred to Tyranny that Billy's ire could very well be directed at him. *After all, my boy Tony has stolen over fifty G's in product and half that much in cash from him*, he speculated.

His human heart went into overdrive when he realized that Billy and his crew were making their way toward Claniel and not him.

And boy, do they look mad!

Claniel pushed his drunken dance partner at Billy. She stumbled and hit the floor. Billy stepped over her like she was trash as Claniel pulled out a shiny knife.

It was on.

Tyranny loved nothing better than a good old-fashioned human fight, but he had more important things to do. He quietly made his way through the crowd to the back room.

CHAPTER TWENTY-EIGHT

TYRANNY MET UP with Drusiel, Claniel, and Andros on Frelinghuysen Avenue, a few blocks away from the No Name Bar. He stripped off his shirt and used it as a towel to wipe the blood off his face and hands, then he tossed the offensive garment on the ground in a nearby alley. Without being told, Drusiel took the shirt off his back and gave it to Tyranny. The night was warm. His undershirt would suffice.

Now that they were all cleaned up, the four of them looked as normal as any other group of good-looking young men in search of a good time.

Claniel was bouncing back and forth on the balls of his feet like a heavyweight champ warming up for a bout in the ring. "Did we or did we not wreak some havoc in that damn bar tonight?"

"That we did, Claniel," Drusiel replied, while counting the thick wad of cash he'd just taken out of his pocket. "That we did. In fact, I believe we put that little hole-in-the-wall on the map. I wager the No Name Bar won't be nameless when they write about what happened tonight in the human newspapers."

Drusiel cleaned out both registers behind the bar while the free-for-all was raging. And now he had a pocket full of money and a desire to get more.

Claniel was still too excited to stay still. His chest swelled with pride. Drusiel may have robbed the place, but he'd been the first to draw blood. As far as Claniel was concerned, bloodletting trumped a run-of-the-mill robbery any day of the week. He'd cut Billy Torres pretty badly. It had been a gut hit.

He could still feel the sensation of his knife sinking into the human's flesh and the look of absolute astonishment on Torres's face when he did it. Once he'd gotten the knife in real good, he'd twisted it to do maximum internal damage, and it felt just fucking wunnerful. What made it even better was that everybody in the bar will think one of Billy's own men had done it.

Fucking priceless!

"Not bad for our first night out, huh?" he crowed. "Tyranny, did you see me shank that Torres dude? Huh? Did you see it?" Claniel was acting like a human child seeking the approval of a respected elder. "I would have slit his throat had police sirens not diverted me from my purpose."

Tyranny just looked at him without bothering to respond.

"Humans have a hard time recovering from gut wounds," Claniel said without pausing. "If he lives, that Puerto Rican can tell everyone he knows he was literally saved by the motherfucking bell!" Spit flew out of his mouth as he started laughing at his own joke.

Well, all four demons thought that was just plain hilarious. In fact, they were bent over laughing with tears streaming out of their eyes.

They'd only just begun. The night was still young, and there was a lot more shit to get into. By the time the authorities came looking for them, they will have abandoned their current bodies and be in possession of new ones, leaving the dumbfounded humans, who will have no memory of how their flesh was used, to pay the price for the crimes they committed.

Tyranny couldn't help but laugh as Claniel relayed the story. He laughed even harder when he thought about the little present that was waiting for whomever was first to enter the back room.

He shouted to the skies, *"Walking around in human skin is fucking groooooovy, man!"*

They were still laughing and trying to decide what additional turmoil they could stir up before they had to complete their assignment and report back to The Hells when they saw a human female approach from across the street.

Somehow, Loretta and Chet got separated during the melee. Raw, unadulterated fear doused the heat of Loretta's desire like a bucket of ice-cold water on a campfire. Gone were all thoughts about Chet, the motel they planned to lay up in, and all those nasty little things he promised he would do to her while whispering in her ear back at the bar.

Chet needs to take his Black ass home to his goddamn wife!

As far as Loretta was concerned it was done, over, *finito* the minute the fight broke out, and the man she'd seen Renee with got stabbed.

No romance tonight, buddy.

She hoped and prayed Renee made it through the crazy barroom brawl because she didn't have the guts to go looking for her. All Loretta wanted to do was make it to her car, put the key in the ignition, and fly west down Route 22 as if the City of Newark was going down like Atlantis.

Dear Lord, I am not a bad person. I swear upon your almighty name that if you let me get out of here before anyone sees me, I will never, ever, as long as I am Black and have a hole in my stupid ass, even think about cheating on Albert again.

All this was said as Loretta did a combination run/walk in her haste to place as much distance between herself and the No Name Bar as possible.

❧

Tyranny couldn't believe their luck. They were heading across the street toward the woman when a brand spanking new 1964 black Ford van with shiny hubcaps cruised past them. The van slowed down at the next corner and stopped. The music coming from the van shook the sidewalks upon which they stood, even though it was a half block away.

And then the driver put all 55,000 pounds of that highly polished black steel on wheels in reverse and backed her up to stop right in front of where the demons were standing.

Uh-oh, Tyranny thought. *We were looking for trouble, and it looks like it has found us. How convenient.*

The passenger door slid open as the van idled in the middle of the street with the music blasting. Andros sensed that whatever opened that door wasn't human. He was proven correct when out stepped a six-and-a-half-foot demon from a class and order he didn't recognize. Jimi Hendrix's "Are You Experienced?" was playing on the radio loud enough to rattle his human vessel's teeth.

Other than his penchant for loud rock music, he was perfect in every way, and looked almost human in a pair of jeans, construction boots, and a lightweight black hooded sweatshirt. The lower portion of his face was covered with a black mask. His body and overall stance oozed aggression.

It was not unusual for one class of demon to attack another without provocation. After all, they were demons. It was their nature to stir up trouble wherever they could find it. Tyranny smacked his lips and rubbed his hands together in anticipation of a good fight.

If ya can't get along, get it on!

Tyranny's team was evidently of the same accord. The adrenaline in the human bodies Tyranny and his team inhabited was flowing like river rapids. Claniel was still doing the rope-a-dope, mimicking the actions of the human named Muhammad Ali. Drusiel was swaying back and forth, shaking his hands out and cracking his knuckles. And Andros took a second to stretch the kinks out of his neck before he drew the pistol he'd taken from Billy Torres. All Tyranny could say was, "Let's get ready to rumble!"

He took a quick look inside the open door of the van. Unless someone was lying in wait on the floor or hiding in the trunk, it appeared there was only one other demon in the van. He was sitting behind the wheel, busy thrumming his fingers on the steering wheel and bopping his head to the squeal of Hendrix's crazy guitar as if he didn't have a care in the world.

With the driver being the only occupant left in the van, which made it two against four. It sounded like perfect odds to Tyranny, who was breathing heavy with excitement.

The lone demon stood outside the van in a wide-legged stance, glaring at Tyranny and his team like he could take them all down with one hand tied behind his back.

I'd like to see you try, Tyranny thought, then said, without taking his eyes off the demon, "I don't know about you guys, but I, for one, am raring for a good fight. What say you?"

Claniel snorted. "You ain't said nothin' but a word, Thunderbird."

Tyranny rolled his eyes. Clearly, Claniel has been watching way too much human TV.

Andros was the next to respond. "I say we kick that arrogant motherfucker's ass, snatch the other fucker out of the driver's seat, and take that nice shiny black vehicle of his."

"Sounds like a capital idea to me, boys." Claniel turned to Drusiel for his vote.

Wary of this being that stood before them with a challenge in his eyes and no fear, Drusiel said cautiously, "I'm in," even though his instincts told him he should run in the opposite direction and not look back.

CHAPTER TWENTY-NINE

TYRANNY REALIZED THE fight might not be as easily won as he'd previously thought. The demon moved like a strike of lightning. One minute he was standing in front of the van, and the next he was literally flying to deliver a vicious kick to the side of Tyranny's head.

The blow was brutal, causing blood to flow out of his human vessel's nose to bloody his crisp white shirt. Tyranny hit the sidewalk hard. He had barely crawled to one knee before his attacker grabbed him by the collar like he was little more than a scruffy mutt.

He dragged Tyranny down the sidewalk, peeling the flesh off one side of Tony Columbus's face. It burned like hellfire. Try as he might, Tyranny couldn't shake him loose. Finally, the demon swung Tyranny into his team members like he was a shot put, knocking Claniel and Drusiel down like bowling pins in a *Three Stooges* episode.

What form of demon is this?

Claniel and Drusiel made a quick recovery. They were excited about the encounter before, but now they were enraged. Both pulled out knives. Andros cocked his gun and fired it directly between the demon's eyes.

But then the strangest thing happened. The demon vanished,

only to reappear behind them and deliver yet another damaging blow—this time to Andros, who dropped like a bag of rocks. His weapon clattered to the sidewalk, out of reach.

The demon delivered a vicious kick to Drusiel's groin, shooting pain all over his body. Before Drusiel could recover, a follow-up knee to his jaw sent his head snapping backward, causing him to bite his tongue in half. He howled in pain, spraying a nasty mixture of red and oily black demon blood.

⁕

The preternatural being behind the wheel of the van was oblivious to the fighting going on around him. There was no doubt in his mind that his partner could handle the demons. He was preoccupied with the human female standing beside a midsized white car directly across the street from the van.

His dark eyes were locked on the human female. Clearly in shock, she stared right back at him, unable to turn away, reminding him of a deer caught in the scope of a hunter's rifle.

For some inexplicable reason, the woman's fear called out to him like a dark night creature to its mate, punching through his chest to chip away at the brick wall around his heart. It screamed at him louder than the strings on Hendrix's guitar.

She is lovely.

The bloodlust from the violence taking place on one side of the street and the enticing bouquet of the human's blood stroked his predatory instincts, causing his fangs to punch through his gums. Wanting her to see how she affected him, he pulled down his mask.

The woman gasped, snapping out of her state of shock. With hands that shook uncontrollably, she frantically tried to unlock her car door, only to cry out in frustration when she dropped the keys and had to root around for them on the dark street.

He shook his head like a shaggy dog to clear his thoughts. She reminded him of someone he knew a long time ago, when he could still feel. There was no room in his mind to care about what happens to anyone—especially not a human.

Hell, I don't much care about what happens to me, he thought, finding it difficult to reconcile his current feelings.

Whether he cared what happened to the frightened woman or not, there was one thing that he knew for damn sure. *If one of those motherfuckers whose asses my partner is kicking all over the sidewalk even thinks about going near her, I am going to rip them apart with my bare hands.*

No sooner did the thought cross his mind when one of those motherfuckers slipped right past his partner. He was headed toward the woman who was frantically trying to unlock the door to her car to make her escape. Out of habit, he adjusted his mask and consigned the human's license plate to memory, FLY-69X, before springing into action.

⧉

Claniel remembered the tasty morsel across the street. He had every intention of using her as a human shield to escape a battle they were clearly losing. Claniel looked at the van to find it still in the middle of the street with the engine running, and the driver nowhere in sight.

Suddenly, the demon who'd been sitting behind the wheel materialized in front of him. Before Claniel could refocus enough to wage an offense, the demon had pummeled him to the ground.

And now there were two of them fighting side by side—one dark and one light. Both possessed the ability to implement sorcery that Tyranny and his ilk could not counter while in the bodies of their human vessels. And with each of them severely wounded, they could not revert to their natural, much stronger demonic bodies.

Tyranny and his demonic motley crew never knew what hit them.

They were no match for the two mysterious beings who moved quicker than a thought and had the power of 10,000 men. No match at all.

Demons fight dirty, but these beings took dirty to a new low. The dark demon became two then four exact replicas of himself. It was like walking inside a human carnival house of mirrors and seeing images of yourself everywhere you turn. Tyranny and his team could not determine which image to attack until it was too late.

The other demon was a fire-breathing beast. Each time Tyranny or a member of his team raised a hand to strike, the demon caused a burst of fire to heat their weapon. They had to either drop the weapon or risk incinerating the hand holding it.

⁊

Loretta took in the unbelievable scene from across the street. "Surely, I didn't just see the fang-toothed dude who was sitting in the car disappear right in front of my eyes! No, I didn't. No, I didn't. No, I didn't, Lord." She whimpered the phrase in a sing-song voice as tears streamed down her face and her body shook uncontrollably.

Not only had the driver pulled an *I Dream of Jeannie* move, but now he was across the street with the other brawny masked guy putting a serious can of whup-ass on all four of the men. That was all Loretta had to see. She broke three fingernails getting the key in the car door.

When Loretta finally slid behind the wheel, she shouted, "Thank you, sweet Jesus!" and peeled down the street, not bothering to look left or right.

Anything that gets in my way is going to get ran the fuck over.

⁊

A little more than a half hour after her ordeal, Loretta pulled into her driveway, still shaken. Two cops approached her before she could get out of the car.

"Are you Mrs. Loretta Burkett?" one asked, to which she replied in a shaking voice that she was.

The other officer said, "We are sorry to inform you that your husband has died." The rest of the officers' words came to Loretta through a wind tunnel as she fainted.

CHAPTER THIRTY

TYRANNY THOUGHT HE and his team were as good as dead. But instead of outright killing them, their attackers beat the living shit out of them and tossed them in the back of the black van. The next thing Tyranny knew, he and his entire squad were locked in individual cells in a makeshift jail in the basement of a house somewhere in west bum fuck Newark. Shit didn't look good at the moment.

First, they hauled Drusiel from his cell. Next, they came for Andros. An hour later, Claniel was dragged out of his cell kicking and screaming as someone played the eerie, hauntingly beautiful strains of Beethoven's "Moonlight Sonata" loud enough to shatter glass. This was a far cry from the Hendrix piece that had been playing in the van.

Apparently, our captors have an eclectic taste in music, Tyranny thought nervously.

The music was deafening, but not quite loud enough to drown out Claniel's agonizing screams for mercy. Neither Drusiel nor Andros were brought back to their cells. Tyranny doubted Claniel would return either.

And now Tyranny was the only one left. His imagination was conjuring up one nightmarish image after another when suddenly everything went totally silent. Tyranny grew as still as a statue, straining to hear what was going on down the hall. He heard a single set of footsteps approaching. A chill ran down his spine.

Satan help me, one of them is coming for me! Maybe I can bargain with them. Maybe I can convince them to see reason. Everyone has a price.

And if I can't, then what?

Tyranny struggled against the chains that bound him, desperate to get loose. But it was useless. Each link was forged in the shape of a heptagram, turning them into demon-binding chains that drained what little power he had left, rendering him virtually helpless.

Depictions of the deadly seven-pointed star were chiseled into the cement floor and each wall of his cell. He looked up to see a grand heptagram on the ceiling. He never stopped to question how a fellow demon could circumvent the powerful wards.

Far too soon, a being that was built like a human linebacker stood before him in a long plastic slicker. Tyranny sniffed the surrounding air.

It doesn't smell like a demon, but it damn sure isn't human, he thought, taking in every detail of his captor beneath lowered eyes.

It had plastic booties on its feet, a cap covering its hair, and the same half mask that was covering its nose and mouth when Tyranny was captured. Its raiment was covered from head to toe in black demon blood.

With the cunning and guile inherent in all things demonic, Tyranny feigned unconsciousness, allowing his body to go slack while the immortal being dragged him by the collar of his shirt down the dark hallway, and into what appeared to be a miniature operating room. He hoisted him onto a gurney. Tyranny was immediately assailed by the familiar metallic stench of demon blood and excrement. It clogged the air, nearly choking him.

I'm not dead yet. And if I play my cards right, I might just be able to get out of here alive.

Hoping against hope that the unidentified demon would fall for his ruse and release him from his chains, Tyranny formulated a plan. *I will pretend to be unconscious and turn on my attackers when the opportunity arises.* Tyranny held his breath and waited.

The air-conditioning was set at sub-zero temperature. His teeth chattered from the bone-chilling cold. Demons don't like the cold. Tyranny fought to keep his eyes closed, but he couldn't stop the human body he had invaded from shaking from the cold. Chill bumps covered the surface of Tyranny's flesh.

His eyes flew open as sharp talons ripped across his chest, stripping him of what remained of his shirt and ripping the mortal flesh to shreds. The furrows in his chest burned like acid.

So much for trying to play possum. The gig was up. *When I get out of this, I will eat their fucking hearts for breakfast,* he vowed, as his eyes sprang open.

Tyranny thought he was back in one of The Hells. There was blood everywhere. The floor was slick with it and strewn with gore, viscera, and body parts, which presumably had once belonged to the members of his team. Even the ceiling served as an abstract canvas painted in demon blood.

There were two of them. One of his captors strapped his head to the cold metal table, limiting his mobility. Tyranny couldn't control his hiss of pain. A blinding operating room light glared down from the ceiling directly into his eyes, while the other, who was similarly dressed, stood waiting on the sidelines, admiring their handy work.

Tyranny's captors were masters at the art of torture. They remained silent, giving the demon a moment to take in his surroundings. They watched him with studied intent as he squirmed upon seeing the body parts they'd deliberately left out. This was a form of psychological torture which had proven to be extremely effective for them in the past.

The dark-skinned one knew the exact moment when the demon's eyes landed on the assortment of power tools on a table against the wall. The demon struggled against the chains like a trapped animal, desperate to escape.

Tyranny's struggles amused the dark demon. *We have yet to touch him,* he thought, closing his eyes to allow the music to wash over him.

Not only had the demon's level of anxiety reached a crescendo without their laying a hand on him, but his fear rose in concert with the discordant notes of *Fortuna,* taking his heartbeat along for the deadly ride.

Ah, the beauty of it all. Music is a wonderful accompaniment to the suffering of one's enemies, the mysterious dark-skinned being thought.

He was particularly fond of this piece. It made him feel like he was invincible, like he could single-handedly slice away at an entire army of demons and fell them one by one with his bare hands.

"Enough with the mind games, brother," his golden-skinned companion said. "It's time to play hardball."

Tyranny ceased to struggle, too shocked to move. *These were no ordinary demons.* That fact was born out when the one who dragged him into this death trap touched the heptagram without ill effect.

What the fuck are they? And then it hit him.

"Nephilim!"

Tyranny decried as the one who had dragged him down the hall finally pulled his face mask down, displaying a preternatural handsome face with a soul patch and mustache. The only thing more dangerous to a demon than a Nephilim is a warrior angel. Tyranny knew right then and there his ass was double-fucked.

"I see you know what I am, demon. Do you know who I am?"

the half-breed angel asked in a voice reminiscent of Clint Eastwood in *Hang 'Em High*, but raspier.

Tyranny knew who he was, all right, as did every demon on the seven levels of The Hells and beyond. He was Simeon of the House of Ramuel, firstborn of Chief Watcher Angel Ramuel and namesake of that same angel who abandoned The Heavens to stick his angelic dick inside a worthless mortal woman.

He was also the same Nephilim who had escaped imprisonment in the lowest level of The Hells, and a member of the corps that had been dogging Tyranny's steps ever since. All demons feared him, including Tyranny.

This is not going to end well.

"I asked you a question. Do you know who I am?" Simeon repeated.

"Y-y-yes," Tyranny said. "Yes. I know who you are. You are Simeon, a member of the Brothers of the Dark Veil, the group of half-breed angels that escaped Tartarus after two centuries in captivity."

The Nephilim cracked something closely resembling a smile, apparently satisfied with the demon's answer. Something inherently self-destructive in Tyranny wouldn't allow him to stop there.

"You cannot speak above a whisper because The Satan sliced your throat deep enough to take your head off your shoulders."

That wiped the smile off the princely looking half-breed's face.

Simeon backhanded him, caving in the back of his human skull as it slammed into the cold, hard surface of the metal table. Tyranny immediately regretted his moment of bravado.

The force of the blow opened his left cheek to the bone. Teeth broke away from the gums, threatening to choke him as they shot down his throat. Tyranny's lacerated tongue shot out to lick away the blood on the side of his mouth. His mind swirled with unanswered questions while he spat out pieces of Tony Columbus's pretty white teeth.

I know there are Gibborim in town. Those pesky sons of bitch are everywhere. But I had no idea the Brothers of the Dark Veil were in Newark as well, Tyranny thought, mentally tracking the history.

North America used to be Ajuma Akibeel's district. But their king did a little shuffling back in the 1700s, and now the continent of North America was under the jurisdiction of Nicodemus Urakabarameel. Tyranny knew for a fact that Urakabarameel was off the grid, having done a disappearing act about forty years ago. Rumor had it he was somewhere in the south.

Well, if Simeon of the House of Ramuel is here and Urakabarameel is incommunicado, who in The Hells is the other Nephilim?

As if his thoughts had been uttered aloud, the other Nephilim pulled down his mask and Tyranny actually shit on himself. The smell of his acrid fear polluted the air.

Ajuma Akibeel! By all that is unholy, tell me I am not looking into the wicked green eyes of Watcher Angel Akibeel's spawn, the blood clot issue of the angel who taught the forbidden art of astrology to the humans. Say it isn't so!

Tyranny was in the clutches of a renowned Nephilim monster, a half-breed abomination who acted more demon than angel—a merciless sadist more evil than The Satan and his four brothers combined.

Ajuma Akibeel, former commander of an army of 365,000 bloodthirsty Gibborim, stood before him, growling under his breath with an ink black full beard and death in his eyes. The shocking contrast of the black beard with the Nephilim's fair skin made his piercing green eyes impossibly bright. He looked like a rabid dog poised to attack.

"Now that we have introduced ourselves, would you like to tell us who you are?" Simeon asked in a deceptively polite voice.

"I am Tyranny, son of The Satan."

The half-breeds' sensual lips turned up in slow, wicked smiles, sending a chill down Tyranny's spine.

"Well," Ajuma said, stroking his silky beard, "Tyranny, son of Satan, there is someone we'd like you to meet."

CHAPTER THIRTY-ONE

TYRANNY CAME TO, stripped bare, his body slick with sweat, and the inside of his mouth pulsing like a nasty tooth-ache. He tensed when the door to his prison cell swung open, allowing the thing that had been torturing him for the past two nights to pick up where he'd left off.

Tyranny identified himself as the son of Satan, and was immediately returned to his cell. He thought, surely they were arranging to ransom him. He could not have been further from the truth. They'd returned him to his cell so that they could leave him to the none-too-tender mercy of a third Nephilim whose treatment of Tyranny made his team members' death seem merciful. He surveyed his surroundings.

There were no windows in the cell to determine the time of day or night. The only way Tyranny could discern that it was nightfall was because "it" was back from the dark cave he presumed it had crawled into to sleep during the day. Nephilim are vampires and cannot tolerate the sun.

His hands were suspended by demon-binding chains forged in the shape of a heptagram and bolted into the cell wall approximately two feet above his head. Depictions of the deadly seven-pointed star were chiseled into the cement floor and on all the walls.

Tyranny squeezed his eyes shut to keep the hot, salty beads of fear-laced sweat from rolling down his face to blind him, and surreptitiously raised his eyes toward the ceiling. The grand heptagram on the ceiling mocked him, leaving no doubt that the sole purpose of this place was to detain and destroy those of his kind. Tyranny knew his chances of escape were slim, but not impossible.

It was impossible for him to kick out, as his feet were secured by the ankles, and bolted into the cement floor. He was trussed by the wrists, causing his arms to tingle from the neck to his pits like they were being pulled from the socket. Tyranny was a prisoner of the human body he'd usurped, and virtually helpless.

He'd been given neither food nor drink, something he could do without, but not the vessel housing him.

Surely, that is a bad sign. One doesn't bother to feed what it plans to kill. Tony Columbus is dying. If I don't figure out a means of escape, I could very well be trapped inside Columbus's corpse with no means to exit, he despaired. Even more troubling was the fact that during the entire time he'd been held captive, not one demand had been made for a ransom.

I refuse to accept that my existence will end in a dingy basement in the human realm, he vowed. Tyranny waited, poised for what would come next.

The Nephilim was dressed in a thobe similar to the garments worn by Bedouins of ancient time. Except for the area surrounding his eyes, every inch of his powerfully built body was covered in unrelieved black. Tyranny could see that its hands and the skin around the eye area were as dark as those of an Andalusian Moor.

Seeing no benefit to continue feigning unconsciousness, Tyranny raised his head to sniff the surrounding air, locking eyes with the Nephilim. From the smell of him, he appeared to be a member of the first or lowest of the nine angelic choirs—that of a mere angel and, therefore, the least perfect. Tyranny, although fallen, was a member of the angelic order of Thrones and, as such, was exponentially more powerful than his captor. He spat on the cell floor, allowing a low growl of warning to roll off his tongue at the sheer indignity of the situation.

Unimpressed by the demon's display of disdain, the Nephilim boldly maintained eye contact with Tyranny, forcing him to be the first to look away.

I am Tyranny, the third son of the ruler of all seven levels of The Hells!

He found it incomprehensible that he was tethered to a wall by his wrists and ankles like a fuckin' Mississippi slave by a lowlife Nephilim mongrel angel.

There was a time during the good old days when demons roamed the earth freely and the chosen knew their place. Apparently, this Negro didn't get the damn memo. He growled again, his eyes narrowed to swollen slits.

Everyone has a price. I have but to ferret out what the half-breed wants, and then be prepared to negotiate. But first, I must establish a rapport. Deciding to try one last time to reason with him, Tyranny dove in head first, breaking the silence.

"What do you want from me, Nephilim? Name it, and it is yours. I am worth far more to you alive than dead—trillions, in fact!" he boasted in the same beguiling voice the serpent used to tempt Eve.

"Spare me, and my father will reward you handsomely. He will make you rich beyond your wildest dreams."

Without a word of acknowledgment, the one who held the privileged son of The Satan captive walked right past him and silently busied himself setting up a Super 8 camera, lighting a match to Tyranny's volatile temper. Rage bubbled to the surface of Tyranny's throat, threatening to spill out of his mouth.

How dare that black mutt ignore me! When I get out of here, I swear before all that is unholy that I will slice off the top of his head and brain fuck this arrogant Black bastard into the gutters of the lowest level of The Hells! The camera was up and running. Its glare so harsh, Tyranny was forced to shut his eyes and turn his face away.

May hap I will be ransomed after all, he thought. *Could it be he is filming me because he intends to ransom me? Maybe he intends to offer the video to my father as proof of life,* Tyranny thought, unable to contain his excitement.

The Nephilim removed his *aba,* the sleeveless coat he wore over his thobe, to don a hooded plastic slicker, effectively dashing the demon's hope like breakers crashing against the ocean floor.

His action left no doubt that things were about to get messy.

⁓

Jihad of the House of Akibeel knew what the fallen angel-turned demon was thinking. *He's thinking he will be ransomed, can bribe his way out of this, or somehow free himself and kill me.*

Little does he know, there is not enough money in the universe that can buy him his freedom by ransom or by bribery. And as to him freeing himself, he can squash those thoughts immediately. I've been waiting a long time for an opportunity to watch this piece of garbage squirm. I shall not allow him to escape.

If Jihad could torture and kill Tyranny a million times for holding him captive in The Hells, robbing him of his memories, and making him into the mindless animal he had become, he would do so gladly.

Jihad picked up the same pair of pliers he'd used to pull out what was left of the demon's teeth the night before, closely observing Tyranny's struggle to hide his fear, but his eyes gave him away.

I can smell your fear, even taste it on my tongue, Tyranny. I'll be damned if this doesn't feel as good as, or better than, some hot, sloppy, wet sex, he thought, cupping himself.

He'd deliberately placed the bloody pliers and a host of other tools and instruments in plain view for Tyranny to mull over as he contemplated his fate. Thanks to Tyranny and his siblings, Jihad knew from firsthand experience that fear of what is coming oftentimes is far more torturous than the pain itself. He returned the pliers to their place on the table and slipped on a set of brass knuckles with wicked-sharp metal spikes.

Jihad took steady, measured steps toward Tyranny. Each step magnified the level of menace surrounding him. Tyranny struggled against the demon-binding chains, shredding the flesh around his wrists and ankles in a futile attempt to escape what he knew was coming.

The empty expression in Jihad's deep-brown eyes didn't change. Seconds later, his mallet-sized fist barreled toward Tyranny's face, landing dead center. The vicious blow caught Tyranny on the bridge of his nose, slamming his head into the concrete wall behind him with a sickening thud, smashing his fractured nose to smithereens. Tyranny squealed like a stuck pig, writhing against the damp prison wall in agony, like someone shoved a shiv in his face.

No sooner did Tyranny recover from the shock of the first blow before another came behind it. A brutal succession of blows followed, breaking the flesh and spraying blood like a fountain, until Tyranny lost count of the hammering fists slamming into the once handsome face of the human he'd taken possession of.

Motivated by a fiery, all-encompassing hatred that would not burn out until Tyranny was dead, and maybe not even then, Jihad paused to admire his handiwork. Satisfied with the severity of the beating, he reached for a nearby towel to clean his hands of the demon's blood, and turned his attention back to the camera.

Determined to keep the unconscious demon hovering on an exquisite razor's edge between anguish and death, Jihad tossed an ice-cold bucket of water in his face, forcing him back to consciousness.

The demon sputtered and choked. Tyranny would soon discover the beating had only been a warm-up.

Jihad walked over to the table where his instruments were laid out, thinking, *It is time to make Tyranny sing.*

Tyranny could not see beneath the cloth concealing his face, but for the first time in two decades, Jihad of the House of Akibeel was wearing a smile.

❧

"It looks like you are having difficulty breathing," Jihad stated. "How about you let me help you with that, huh? Give me a minute and I will open an airway for you." He chose a pencil from the table.

Fisting Tyranny's long blond hair in his hand, he pulled his head back to expose his vulnerable human neck, and jammed the lead pencil into the front of his throat, performing an excruciatingly painful makeshift tracheotomy.

"Whew Hoooo!" He chortled, at the wheezing, bubbling sound that emanated around the lead pencil. To intensify the demon's discomfort, Jihad moved the pencil back and forth in Tyranny's throat, watching with great satisfaction as the vessel gave up the ghost.

Jihad didn't bother to hide the hitch of excitement that raced through his body when Tony Columbus Jr. expired. He always felt like fucking when he got his hands wet. Truth be told, nowadays, that was about the only time he felt like fucking.

As a reward for his efforts, Tyranny let out an extended mournful moan upon realizing he was trapped inside a dead human body, with no means of escape. The moan grew into a screech that echoed off the ceiling and all four walls.

Oh, yeah, Jihad thought. *This is the best foreplay in the world.*

A loud, wet rumble erupted from the pit of Tyranny's belly that echoed throughout the cell. Seconds later, his bowels evacuated, coating every gasp of air he sucked in with deadly demon stink.

Tyranny is afraid, Jihad thought in amazement. *I have scared the living shit out of one of the most infamous fallen angels in existence. Ah, it doesn't get much better than this.*

CHAPTER THIRTY-TWO

ONE MINUTE THE psychotic Nephilim was shoving a pencil in Tyranny's throat, and now he was standing before him with some kind of razor in his hand. Tyranny flinched at the sight of it. He didn't know how much more of this he could take. With the vessel dead, there was no one to share the pain.

The Nephilim ran the razor-sharp edge of the coring knife from the surface of Tyranny's upper thigh to his knee. The flesh peeled away like the skin on an apple. With just one stroke, the Nephilim had sliced through the epidermis and the dermis to expose the glistening connective tissue below. There was a split-second delay before white-hot pain shot to the back of Tyranny's eyeballs.

Jihad responded with a long "Yesssssss" as the demon mewled like a stomped kitten. "Aaaaaah sing for me, Tyranny. Sing for me, baby," he whispered in a dark seductive voice before he began to dance.

Tyranny watched in misery as the mad half-breed spun around in wild abandon with the sharp, bloody instrument in his hand, his movements like a wild Indian hyped-up on peyote. The hem of his desert garb flowed with his body as he danced to a tune no one could hear but him. Unable to take anymore, Tyranny closed his eyes and turned his head, not wanting to see what would come next.

Jihad suddenly stopped dancing. He needed to see the fear in Tyranny's eyes as he tortured him.

"Open your eyes," he ordered, a command which Tyranny stubbornly refused to obey.

Jihad captured Tyranny's bloody ruined face in one of his rough callused hands and sliced off the demon's eyelids, harrumphing at his cruel handiwork. Pain surged through Tyranny's body like an electric current in water.

"I have information!" Tyranny wheezed through ragged bloody gums.

Jihad looked at the mess he'd made of the human vessel, thinking, *I have broken the mighty Tyranny. And all it took was a few human household items: a pair of pliers, a fruit corer, and a goddamn number two lead pencil.*

Tyranny took a deep breath and opened his mouth to speak again. This time he would make it count. "I have information… about the Nephilim traitor. I can tell you about Moultrie!"

Now *that* got Jihad's attention.

❦

Jihad's movements were as graceful as a world-class surgeon as he returned his bloody instrument to the nearby table as if it were no more than a fork he'd been using to eat a gourmet meal.

"Speak," he said in a voice that reminded Tyranny of the mysteries of the grave, as his dark, soulless eyes bored unflinchingly into Tony Columbus's mangled face.

Tyranny knew from the look in those eyes that the pitiless Nephilim who refused to show his face was not only going to kill him, but that he would enjoy doing it. He hoped to provide information that would change his mind.

"I have knowledge of the one you seek. I will give it to you gladly if you will give me your word of honor that you will spare my life. Please," he panted, hoping there was some good in him—that he would be foolish enough to offer some compassion.

Jihad paused but briefly before responding, "You have my word on it. Now tell me what you know."

That was good enough for Tyranny.

Tyranny's words spilled out of the vessel's decaying mouth in a rush as he told the Nephilim almost everything he knew about the one known as Moultrie The Wizard. He disclosed information that would earn him a death sentence in The Hells if The Satan learned it originated from him. At this point in the game, he had nothing to lose.

"Moultrie of the House of Armers is in New Jersey as we speak," he said. "I have seen him with my own eyes. He is in possession of the Sigil of Solomon and has promised to locate certain items that have been hidden in the human realm. In exchange, he's asked that an army of demons be placed at his disposal. Moultrie has already used the sigil to open gateways all over the world for the aerial demons to come through. That is how I came to be here."

Jihad listened with keen interest. The story of King Solomon was taught to Nephilim young while on their mothers' knees. The one known throughout history as King Solomon was, in fact, Amenhotep III, Pharaoh of the Eighteenth Dynasty of Egypt who, like himself, wore black skin. Amenhotep had used the infamous seal to command demons and to speak with animals. It appeared Moultrie intended to do the same, but for different reasons.

Moultrie has been on the Nephilim Most Wanted List since the 1700s, with a fifty-million-dollar bounty on his head. The Brothers of the Dark Veil have been trying to capture the traitorous but extremely illusive Nephilim for centuries, without success.

Any source of information as to Moultrie's present whereabouts, even if from a lying, conniving, deceitful fallen angel-turned demon, would be thoroughly investigated. Jihad's full attention was on Tyranny's every word.

"Moultrie has opened a gateway for the aerial demons right here in Newark."

"Why here?" the Nephilim asked, with a furrow in his brow. He casually lit a cigarette.

Tyranny took a deep, painful breath of the smoke swirling around the cell, glad the Nephilim was finally listening to him.

Maybe I will get out of this alive after all.

"The ancient books point to the North American East Coast. Whatever my father is looking for is in one of these human cities and is of such importance that he is willing to join forces with a hated Nephilim in order to find it. No one but Moultrie and my father know exactly what it is they seek, or why." He offered up the partial truth easily.

"There are three human thwarts, one of whom is a powerful witch sent by He Whose Name I Dare Not Speak, who are preventing Moultrie from finding what he seeks."

Something inherently evil in Tyranny kept him from telling Jihad the true purpose of his visit on earth. His orders were to search out the witch and ascertain the location of a book of majick his father wanted, and thereby elevate his status throughout The Hells. His enemy must never know about *that.*

"Moultrie has enlisted the services of a rival coven of *Oogun Ika* witches to uncover the witch's secrets and to destroy not only her, but her entire bloodline. Once she is killed, the other thwarts will be easy to find and kill. The threat to my father dies along with them."

"Who is this witch The Satan wishes to destroy?" Jihad asked, warming to Tyranny's revelations.

"I do not know her name. All I know is that she must die before the next full moon, or the window of opportunity within which The Wizard can locate whatever he is looking for will close for the next quarter century."

Jihad knew about heavenly thwarts. The Emerald Tablet

authored by the ancient Egyptian sage, Hermes Trismegistus, states, "As above, so below. As within, so without," meaning: What the lesser of us do in the physical world will reflect itself in the spiritual realm, and vice versa.

The Ancient of Days will suffer no man to endure evil without its anecdote, correlating directly with the requirement that there be balance in all things. For every demon, there is an adverse angelic being, and no darkness without the promise of light.

Human thwarts are born into the world to protect mankind from the evil that dogs their every step. The thwarts Tyranny spoke of must be protected at all costs.

"You said there were three thwarts," Jihad said. "Who are the others, and where can I find them?"

"One is a preacher, and the other is a simple man of faith. Both are unaware of the role they play in balancing the universe. The witch is their protector. Their identity and location will not be revealed until she dies."

Jihad took a moment to marinate on the information. It made perfectly good sense. The Satan needed someone who could walk the earth to do his bidding. According to the Book of Revelation 20:7-10, The Satan shall remain imprisoned in The Hells for a period of 1,000 years after the commencement of the son of God's millennial reign.

When that time is up, The Satan shall be loosed from his prison, where he will be free to deceive nations in all four corners of the globe. He will gather those who worship him together and spark the flame for the Gog and Magog War against Israel. The resulting deaths shall be more numerous than the grains of sand on every shore.

Who better to do The Satan's dirty work than a quasi-immortal Nephilim who can walk on earth and throughout The Hells in his own flesh? Jihad knew what he had to do.

I need to relay this information to my king. It is imperative we find out what The Satan is searching for and take possession of it before he can get his hands on it. And the three thwarts must be found and protected at all costs.

"Do you know anything else?" Jihad asked politely. He intuitively knew there was much that Tyranny was not telling him.

Tyranny shook his head that he did not, hoping that what he had already divulged would be enough to save him from any further torture and possibly secure his freedom.

I just want the pain to end. If I get out of this alive, I will have to immediately go into hiding. The little I told the Nephilim is a betrayal to my kind. I dare not allow my father or my brothers to get their hands on me.

The Nephilim casually picked up the dreaded coring knife. Tyranny's belly dropped in fear.

"Have mercy… please. I don't want to die," the once powerful demon said in a weak whisper.

Choked-up with emotion, he barked out a painful cough that sounded like a sputtering engine.

Jihad could tell by the demon's agonized expression that the cough had cost him dearly.

"Ouch, I bet that hurt."

Tyranny's lidless eyes were bright with fever and pain. "You said you would spare my life if I told you what I know!" His voice exuded disbelief.

I am the son of The Satan. It is not supposed to end like this! He declared.

Jihad observed the edges on the coring knife to ensure it didn't need sharpening before responding with two simple words. "I lied."

Tyranny lived another four agonizing hours while the Nephilim methodically skinned him alive. Jihad finally grew bored and beheaded him.

CHAPTER THIRTY-THREE

O N THE OTHER side of town in a seedy hotel off the Broadway Strip, General Ajuma Akibeel was preparing to deliver a Super 8-millimeter tape to Nicodemus Urakabarameel when the words "Late Breaking News" flashed across the television screen. The image of the star in the one-man play scripted, directed, and shot by Jihad of the House of Akibeel was front and center.

Camera flashes were going off like the red carpet at the Academy Awards with overzealous reporters snapping pictures of Mayor Anthony Columbus and his tearful wife making a poignant appeal for mercy after the recent abduction of their twenty-six-year-old son, Anthony Columbus Jr.

The cameraman panned in to get a close-up of the woman's tear-stained face as she made an impassioned plea to her son's abductor. "Please just let my son go. I don't know what he's done wrong that you had to take him away from his father and me, but I am begging you to please let him go. I know he is not perfect. He's had scrapes with the law, but he's my only son."

At this point, her voice broke. The mayor wrapped his arms around her and turned to the cameras. "His family needs him. I need him," he chimed in.

The camera panned back to the reporter. "The distraught mother just referred to her son's arrest record. According to a New Jersey Department of Public Safety source, Anthony Columbus Jr. served a five-year prison sentence after pleading guilty to felony drug possession—this on the heels of an investigation into allegations of conspiracy and extortion against Columbus Sr. The Columbus family is offering a monetary reward for anyone with information as to Anthony Columbus Jr.'s whereabouts.

"Anthony Columbus Jr. was last seen three days ago at the No Name Bar at 24 Wright Street in Newark, the scene of a horrific attack on a female minor," the reporter said, seemingly as an afterthought.

"Anyone having information relating to the person or persons responsible for the disappearance of Anthony Columbus Jr. should call 1-800-Cop-Tips; that's 1-800-267-8477."

It wasn't lost on Ajuma that the human law enforcement agents were focused on finding Columbus and not on apprehending the individual who assaulted the melanated child. The slight served to make Ajuma hate Caucasoid humans all the more.

When the camera panned on Mrs. Columbus, she expressed her fear that whoever took her son may well come for her. "I am so scared," she said in a shaking voice. "Thank God they didn't come here looking for Anthony while I was alone. I simply don't know why this is happening." She shuddered.

Ajuma stood before the television, his lip curled in derision, at the wrinkle-faced, thin-lipped white woman's last statement.

No self-respecting Nephilim would fuck you if he hadn't been with a woman in a thousand years.

Ajuma used his mind to turn the TV off and departed.

❧

837 Ramapo Way, Westfield, Union County, New Jersey

General Nicodemus Urakabarameel's bedroom looked like a scene from a Roman orgy. Discarded champagne bottles, cigarette and cigar butts, and the smell coming from an ornate vintage glass hookah, half filled with hashish, mingled with the sweet smell of female essence and musky male. Eclipsing every other smell was the pervasive metallic scent of blood. The combined effluvium created a heavy pall of stink that only an open window and a liberal dose of Lysol spray could dispel.

The lovely wife of a Rephaim councilman and two other females whose names he didn't know had been waiting for him when he got back from Oklahoma during the wee hours of the morning. The Nephilim general, known as Nico, was back, and they were so damned glad that he was.

Three females were sprawled on Nico's stadium-sized bed in an elegantly decorated bedroom with ceiling-to-floor windows. Each window was hidden beneath custom blinds that were set on a timer to close at dawn and open at sunset. To ensure no natural sunlight filtered in, the blinds were covered by thick brocade drapery.

All three females were utterly and thoroughly spent, with blissful smiles of satisfaction on their sleeping faces. It seemed even in exhausted sleep they didn't want to let Nico go. They held on to him like clinging vines, their beautiful bodies vulnerable and shamelessly exposed atop 1800-thread-count Egyptian sheets made sticky from sweat and their combined bodily fluids, rendering it nearly impossible to determine where one ended and the other began.

The hand of one of Nico's lovers rested on his taut belly, a burnished blonde's head was on his broad chest, and the last female, a dark bushy-haired beauty, was using one of Nico's thick muscular thighs as a pillow. She had passed out with her lips around the tip of his manhood.

Each of the women bore deep puncture wounds in their necks, upon the tops of their breasts, and on the insides of their thighs. The mighty Nephilim general had fed well.

Nico lay in the center of the bed like a well-fed cheetah, having been fucking like a satyr all day, drinking like a sailor all night, and sucking on the hookah pipe like a male whore working hard for his money a few short hours ago. The thick column of pleasure-giving flesh between his muscle-bound thighs, temporarily sated.

A soft snore slipped between his sensuous lips as his massive, muscular body relaxed in slumber. Nico was out cold, making good on a promise to get some sorely needed sleep, when he heard shattering glass and an auto alarm going off outside his home. Thinking he was under attack, he sprang out of bed with his male meat swinging. He pulled on the pants he'd discarded on the floor the night before and ghosted outside to investigate.

Nico stood beside one of his favorite cars with a scowl on his handsome face and lips tightened in anger. The words "Dirty Black Whoring Bastard" had been keyed into the driver's side door of his custom Corvette, and the passenger-side window had been shattered. A construction site brick sat on the tan leather bucket seat amid a prism of shimmering glass, mocking him.

His dark, penetrating eyes scanned the vicinity for a trace of the vandal. But whoever did it was long gone, leaving nothing behind but the humid night air to caress his shirtless body and the trill of a northern mockingbird singing to its mate.

Nephilim of the Rephaim upper class, to which Nico belonged, are extremely acquisitive. They like expensive planes, sleek boats, and fast cars. Even though he had more money than God, and could easily replace the vehicle, this was an affront on every level imaginable.

The act positively reeked of a female scorned. Nico didn't have a clue which one of the many females he was dealing with might be responsible. And since he drew the line at putting his size sixteen-foot up a female's ass unless she was a demon, the only thing left for him to do was to chalk the situation up to the unfortunate price of being a player and see if his mechanic could repair the damage.

"I will have to remember to lock my vehicles in the garage behind the house from here on out," he muttered, crestfallen.

He went back inside to tell the sleeping females the party was over. It was time for them to take their sexy asses' home.

Less than a block away, Rena of the House of Artael sat slumped behind the wheel of a navy-blue sedan. A baseball cap concealed her thick head of auburn curls as she cried her eyes out.

Rena couldn't remember a time in her life when she hadn't been madly and hopelessly in love with Nicodemus Urakabarameel. She also couldn't remember a time in her life when she'd been so angry. It was a mixture of anger and unrequited love that made her vandalize Nico's beautiful custom-built car.

Just this rising, she'd overheard her parents discussing Nico's imminent return to the East Coast. Rena knew she absolutely had to see him—to let him know how deep her feelings for him were. She decided right then and there to go to his house. It was a bold move, but one she was determined to make.

That was why it hurt so badly when she arrived at Nico's house to find him ushering in not one but three females, all of whom were probably in his bed right now—a bed that she yearned to share with him more than anything.

Rena was beautiful, and she knew it. She was also willful, selfish, and accustomed to getting her way. Her parents spoiled her, giving her any and everything she wanted. Rena wanted Nicodemus Urakabarameel, and she was determined to get him, even if she had to play dirty to do it. A cold, calculating look took over as she angrily swiped away the tears with the heel of her hand.

I bet Councilman Armers will be interested to know how his beloved wife Delia spends her time while he is out of town, she thought spitefully. Rena waited for Nico to go back inside before she started the car and drove away.

CHAPTER THIRTY-FOUR

Wiggins Auto Body, 413 West 2ⁿᵈ Street, Plainfield, NJ

THE HUM OF a powerful engine heralded Nico's arrival as he pulled the defamed bronze Corvette L88 into a space under the Wiggins' Auto Body sign advertising "We Work While Others Sleep."

In the right corner of the sign was a middle-aged Black man standing next to a horse and buggy, wearing a leather apron, and holding a horse shoeing tool. The image on the business sign bore a startling likeness to the current owner, who was at that moment rushing toward Nico with a wide grin. The males clasped hands.

Wiggins' Auto Body is as popular among humans as it is among Nephilim because they are open when the other shops are closed and do exceptionally good work for reasonable prices.

Few humans realize that the sign is actually the original one the Wiggins family put up when they first went into business shoeing horses and fixing buggies and carriages back in the 1800s. Nor did humans have any way of knowing that the man depicted on the sign was, in fact, Abe, the current owner.

A large community of Nephilim reside among humans in

Plainfield, mostly of the Anakin or Gibborim lower class, blending in seamlessly with the human population.

Nephilim of the Rephaim, or upper class, who live among humans generally do so not by choice but as a punishment, although there are some kinky Rephaim who are not averse to slumming on occasion.

Nephilim are everywhere, always have been and always will be. It was the Brothers of the Dark Veil's job to keep the humans ignorant of their presence and to protect members of the Nephilim Nation from demons at night and from humans during the daylight hours when they are most vulnerable.

Even though the weakest Nephilim is exponentially stronger than their human counterparts, they are cursed with xeroderma pigmentosum, a skin condition that makes it impossible for them to tolerate the rays of the sun. The Brothers of the Dark Veil are the only Nephilim able to tolerate sunlight, and that only sparingly. All others burn to a crisp upon impact.

Yet another vulnerability of the Nephilim Nation is their insatiable need for blood. They consume food just like humans. But blood to the Nephilim is as vital as water is to mankind. They weaken and die without it.

Working class Nephilim, known as Anakin, who are not fortunate enough to secure positions in a Rephaim household behind the Dark Veil, hide their identity and derive a livelihood by working the unpopular graveyard shifts eschewed by most humans. They leave town just before the fact that they don't age at the rate of humans becomes apparent, only to return later as the child or grandchild of themselves.

Other than the Nephilim king, Nico was the most powerful Nephilim in North America with forty percent Seraphim blood, forty-five percent Cherubim blood, and only fifteen percent human blood flowing through his veins.

His father took his mother to the very brink of death, nearly draining all of her human blood and replacing it with his superior angelic blood, before impregnating her. With all that pure angelic blood running through his veins, Nico still didn't hesitate to pull the Anakin mechanic whose work clothes were covered in dirt and oil toward him in a warm embrace.

Abe's eyes were sparkling with genuine affection. Nico was one of his favorites among the king's seven Brothers of the Dark Veil. He'd been in the southern part of the country for the past forty-three years protecting the Nephilim in the greater Oklahoma City area, and he'd been missed.

Abe's daughter Anya and his son-in-law Ismael reside in an encampment behind the Dark Veil in Boley, Oklahoma, not far from the Greenwood District of Tulsa, where a thriving community of melanated humans were massacred some forty-some odd years ago. Abe kept tabs on the general's exploits through regular phone calls from his daughter. Nicodemus was a fearless warrior.

"You have been sorely missed, General. How are things?" he asked.

"It is good to see you as well, old friend. Other than my new auto situation," he said, turning toward his car, "I am well."

∽

Abe immediately saw the reason for Nico's visit. "Pardon my asking, but do you have female problems, General?" It was obvious even to Abe that only a female would take out her frustration on a male's favorite car.

"It seems that way, doesn't it?" Nico replied affably.

Nico was a legendary womanizer. He couldn't seem to keep that legendary dick of his inside his pants. The Nephilim he cuckolded tended to overlook that shortcoming, since he was such a nice guy and far too powerful to be messed with.

But from the looks of Nico's car, Abe guessed Nico had been messing around with someone who wasn't too keen on sharing. Unable to take it out on him, they took it out on one of his beautiful cars.

Abe shook his head in disgust. "Who could do some crazy shit like this?"

Nico pointedly ignored Abe's question. "So, can you fix it?" he asked anxiously.

"I'm pretty sure that I can," came Abe's quick reply. "But it's going to take some time. That's a custom color ya got there. I can't get this in the human realm. You'll need to go to the Realm of Awe for this."

"Fuck!" Nico let fly the expletive without thinking, and then he caught himself. *No need to take my frustration out on Abe.* He lowered his voice and reigned in his attitude.

"Just do the best you can to replace the window and repair the damage to the body, Abe. I'll take care of procuring the paint later."

Abe was more than happy to oblige.

"You got it, boss. You need a lift somewhere?"

Most Nephilim master the art of "ghosting" (vanishing to travel through space and time to another location) at a very young age. But some things still require a vehicle. Abe was ready to provide the general with a loaner car if needed or have one of his workers drop Nico off anywhere he wanted to go.

"Thanks, Abe, but that won't be necessary. It's been a while since I've been back in the Queen City. I think I will join the Gibborim on patrol tonight."

He looked down at his wristwatch and was just about to send a mental message to Machidiel, his second in command, when Ajuma materialized at the shop.

⚭

Nico forgot what he was about to do or say, so glad was he to see his long-lost friend. Nico loved the members of the Brothers of the

Dark Veil Corps. How could he not? They'd been to The Hells and back together—literally and more than once. But the love he had for Zion Shemyaza and Ajuma Akibeel went deeper than blood. They were closer than most brothers.

Never one to hide his feelings, tears welled in Nico's eyes as he pulled Ajuma in a warm embrace. Ajuma held on tight. Nico could feel the love.

"You are back," Nico said emotionally. "Praise the Ancient of Days, you are back. I cannot tell you how much I have missed you."

Abe made his departure so that the brothers could speak in private.

The last time Nico had seen Ajuma, they had been battling a horde of demons in the Atchafalaya Swamp in 1811. Ajuma had deliberately tried to get himself killed, forcing Zion to banish him. Zion and Nico had to strap him down for transport to Germany and from there to Antarctica, where he remained under tight guard to keep him from offing himself.

Not too many brothers were inclined to freeze their balls off just to pay Ajuma a visit, but Nico and Zion had on several occasions. But Ajuma refused to see them. The rejection stung like crazy. The guards were lifted when Ajuma had finally stopped trying to end his life.

Since there were no Nephilim houses domiciled in the Antarctic, Ajuma had been coming and going as he pleased, carefully avoiding contact with the other Brothers of the Dark Veil and ultimately making a name for himself. Nico had been keeping abreast of Ajuma's exploits for the past hundred years. Ajuma was now known on earth, The Heavens, and The Hells as "The Undertaker," a force to be feared and respected.

It pained Nico to admit that Ajuma hadn't been quite right in the head since the human he fell in love with in the late 1700s died. The Ajuma Nico once knew used to kill only if he had to. But now Ajuma killed because he liked it.

If this is what love does to a male, I don't want any part of it, Nico thought, taking in the emptiness in Ajuma's eyes.

Nico refused to allow a member of the fairer sex to burrow inside the confines of his heart. Love 'em and leave 'em worked just fine for him. He was glad to see Ajuma, but his impromptu appearance could not bode well.

"What brings you to my neck of the woods?"

"I stopped by your house," Ajuma said. "I've been looking for you all night. I tried to mind-meld you as well. One of the Anakins told me you might be here."

Nico didn't want to confess that he'd deliberately sealed his mind off so that no one could disturb him while he was getting his knob waxed.

"Well, now you've found me, brother. What's up?"

"Moultrie has been sighted."

Ajuma's startling green eyes, which had been empty of any emotion, immediately lit up like someone had flipped on a light switch behind them, clearly revealing his bloodthirsty nature.

"Where?" Nico asked, in a deceptively soft voice.

Ajuma's voice was similarly soft. "In Newark."

It was partly because of Moultrie's duplicity that Ajuma was so fucked up. In 1748, Ephraim, the only son of Silas of the House of Armers, went missing. Moultrie, of the Anakin class, once served in the Armers household. It was later discovered that Moultrie was complicit in Ephraim's disappearance. A spy from the third level of The Hells informed a member of the Brothers of the Dark Veil that, for the right price, he would share information relating to the disappearance.

Unfortunately, it had been a set-up. Jihad of the House of Akibeel was one of the Gibborim soldiers serving under Ajuma, was captured while on a fact-finding mission in The Hells. Determined not to leave the soldier's body behind to be raped and desecrated by his demon captors, Ajuma took another trip to The Hells. While he was away, Ajuma lost his pregnant human wife and son.

"Well then," Nico opined, "it looks like I came back east right on time, doesn't it?"

"I have a tape we need to get to Zion. Asap," Ajuma said.

Ajuma had not been given leave by the king to return from Antarctica. Not only had he ended his exile, but he'd left a trail of blood and destruction throughout The Hells and on earth. The king was aware of what he'd been up to.

If Ajuma feels the tape he has is important enough to show himself to Zion, the film must contain some explosive shit, Nico speculated.

The two generals ghosted out of the lot. Ajuma filled Nico in on how he came by the tape on the way.

CHAPTER THIRTY-FIVE

Castle de Haar, The Netherlands

THE ONE THE villagers knew as the Burning One soared through the sky, as naked as the day he was made, his fiery wings blazing as bright as the sun he could no longer see.

Zion Shemyaza, the mighty Nephilim king, felt no shame in his nudity. He knew he was a magnificent, masculine thing of beauty who, though cursed by the artistic hand that created him, was exceedingly fine to look upon.

He'd been awakened by an extremely disturbing dream. As soon as night fell, he instinctively took to the sky, doing that which came naturally to all Seraphim angels.

But instead of flying around the throne of the Ancient of Days, crying "holy, holy, holy," as is a Seraphim's want, Zion found temporary contentment in spreading all six of his glorious wings as he circled the surface of the moon.

And now he sat upon the tip of the brightest star, deep in thought with nothing to keep him company but the sound of meteorites, astcroids, pieces of the moon slicing through the azure blue sky, and his troubled thoughts.

In the dream, Zion had been standing over the casket of someone very dear to him. He didn't know who it was because the casket had been closed. But the pain he felt during the dream lingered well after he woke up, resonating in the center of his chest with a dull, persistent ache.

Something cataclysmic was about to occur. He could feel it. But for the life of him, he could not prepare for it because he didn't know what direction it would come from. Realizing he would not find the answer to any of his questions this night, he vaunted off the star in preparation to fly home.

As Zion descended, he took in the breathtaking view of his estate. The sight of Castle de Haar was one he would never tire of. It was a mini castle, complete with a medieval fortress, towers, ramparts, a moat, and drawbridge. The castle was surrounded by acres of parkland filled with vibrant colors of myriad formal gardens and waterworks. Even to one as ancient as he, the sight was a feast for the eyes and olfactory senses, easily rivaling the French gardens of Versailles in its splendor.

Zion's skin glistened like polished mahogany under the light of the moon when he spread his muscular arms to detract his wings. Minutes later, all three sets of wings were replaced with an ornate group of Enochian symbols that covered his broad back from his shoulders to his muscular buttocks.

His manservant, Jon, dutifully awaited him with a robe fashioned by Anakin artisans from the purest Japanese silk—silk fit for a preternatural king.

Zion recognized the troubled look on Jon's face immediately. *It looks like whatever has been eating at me is about to play itself out, whether I like it or not.* Jon spoke before Zion could ask him what was wrong.

"General Ajuma Akibeel and General Nicodemus Urakabarameel are here to see you on what appears to be pressing business, Sarrum." This was stated in Jon's customary dignified voice.

Zion walked through the door Jon respectfully held open without looking left or right. Although every door on the estate was left unlocked, Zion feared no human intruders. The villagers steered clear of his estate because they thought it was haunted.

Jon could barely keep up with Zion's long-legged strides through the foyer. "Where are they?" Zion asked.

"I placed the generals in your study, Sarrum. I have also offered a libation for their pleasure."

"Very good, Jon," Zion said, turning toward his trusted servant for the first time. "Tell Ajuma and Nico I will be down momentarily." He made his way up the elaborate winding staircase which led to his suite two steps at a time.

Zion quickly changed into a button-down shirt and a comfortable pair of pants before going downstairs to his study to see what Nico and Ajuma wanted to discuss. It had been far too long since he'd seen them.

❧

Five minutes later, the three massive males were standing in the middle of Zion's study. Nico stepped forward to give Zion a manly embrace that required no words. Ajuma followed suit.

This would be the first time Zion had seen Nico since he'd set up headquarters down south, and the first opportunity he had to actually sit down with Ajuma since he'd been forced to banish him to the continent of Antarctica four hundred years ago. It had pained him to do so, but at the time Ajuma had been self-destructive. The banishment had been for his well-being and that of others.

But damn if I don't miss my old friend.

In fact, Zion missed both of them. With a wave of his hand, Zion proffered a seat in a nearby sitting area before he adjusted his pants to sit down.

❧

"How fare you, my brothers?"

Zion and Nico turned their eyes in Ajuma's direction. Ajuma took a moment before answering. These two men were closer to him than blood brothers. They could easily see through any attempt at artifice on his part.

"I no longer want to kill myself if that is what you are asking," came Ajuma's cryptic reply.

It was because of Ajuma's continuous attempts to end his life after losing his human lover and their son that Zion found it necessary to station him in Antarctica.

Ajuma failed to add that he no longer cared whether he lived or died.

"Well, that is a start," Zion said, staring his friend directly in the eye. The last time Zion looked into his old friend's eyes, they had been filled with a painful desperation to end his life. It saddened him to see that instead of healing, there was emptiness.

I shall bring Ajuma back into the fold, but he will require close watching, Zion thought.

In a voice filled with emotion, Zion said, "You know you can come to me any time of the night or day if you ever need anything—even if you just want to talk, Ajuma."

Nico, who had been quiet up to that point, concurred with Zion. "And that goes for me as well, Ajuma. Anytime you need me, I'm here for you, brother."

When Ajuma nodded, Zion asked, "To what do I owe the honor of this surprise visit, gentlemales?"

Ajuma handed Zion the reel of film.

They didn't utter one word while Zion watched it.

"How did you come by this, Ajuma?" Zion asked.

This was the moment Ajuma had been dreading. Not only had

he been hunting demons without prior authorization from his king or the general in whose domain he had been trespassing, but he opened the Nephilim Nation up to potential exposure by leaving behind an eyewitness—not an auspicious return after a four hundred-plus-year banishment.

"I have a confession to make. I have been in the states for the past ten years," he admitted with a guilty look, knowing full well that Zion had not given him leave to return from Antarctica.

"I knew Nico was in Oklahoma. I took advantage of his absence, thinking I could safely hunt on the East Coast without anyone knowing." Ajuma turned first to Zion and then to Nico.

"I apologize for the offense to both of you for returning without your permission, Zion, and for conducting an unauthorized demon hunt in your domicile, Nico."

A solemn nod from Zion and a look of commiseration from Nico was all he received in response to his confession. Zion made a hand gesture which prompted Ajuma to continue.

"Like I said, we were—"

Zion quickly interrupted him. "Wait a minute. You said 'we.' Who was with you?"

"Shit!" Ajuma spat out. He wanted to kick himself for implicating Simeon in this mess.

Who knew that an innocent night out hunting would escalate to an ass-fuck of major proportions? All we wanted to do was slip in and slip out after catching a few fucking demons!

There was nothing for it. Zion's eyes were boring a hole into him. Ajuma knew Zion would not back down until he got some answers.

With a sigh of resignation, Ajuma set out to give Zion the hammer that could very well pound the nail in the coffin of his military career and send him back to Antarctica for the rest of his unnatural life.

"Simeon and I received an anonymous tip about a demon

sighting in the vicinity of the No Name Bar. We came upon four of them while cruising the city. Each was in possession of a human body. It was close to sunrise. We roughed them up, threw them in the back of the van, and split. It was not until we had them back at a safe house I purchased years ago that I realized one of them—the white one—was housing Tyranny. As you know, Tyranny caused grievous injury to Jihad, a Gibborim soldier who once served under me."

Zion and Nico were well aware that Jihad, the Gibborim Ajuma was talking about, was the same soldier Ajuma had risked his life to rescue from Tyranny's clutches in one of The Hells. In doing so, Ajuma lost his wife and child and changed the entire course of his life. There was a bond between Ajuma and that Gibborim that only death could sever.

"When I realized I had Tyranny, I called Jihad. After all he'd been through at that demon's hands, I thought it only fitting he be given the honor of making the kill. It was he who gave me the tape."

Zion found Ajuma's decision to allow the Gibborim the honor of making the kill extremely generous considering all he had lost because of Tyranny.

Ajuma didn't feel it was necessary to tell Zion or Nico that he and Simeon had already tortured and subjected the members of Tyranny's team to the true death before handing Tyranny over. The less Zion knew about that, the better.

CHAPTER THIRTY-SIX

THAT AJUMA RETURNED to North America without prior authorization was not lost on Zion, nor was his convenient omission of the disposition of the remaining members in Tyranny's team. There was a more pressing issue to be addressed. Zion was wise enough to realize that sometimes it is better to praise than to punish.

There was no doubt in either of their minds that most, if not all, of the information tortured out of Tyranny was accurate. Now they had to decide how they intended to use it. Zion was the first to speak.

"First," he said to Nico, "I want the soldier who made the tape promoted to the secret operations division. Give him his own team and free rein to do whatever the fuck he wants to do 'cause I like the way he works."

Nico nodded his head. "Done."

"Next, we need to find that witch," he said with a grimace. Zion made no secret about how he felt about humans, and witches in particular. He abhorred them.

It was written in the Book of Enoch that two-hundred Grigori or Watcher Angels led by Shemyaza, Zion's father, did lust after and lie down with human women, thereby defiling themselves in the eyes of the Ancient of Days.

When the crime against The Heavens became known, in order to save his own skin, Azazel, one of Zion's father's most trusted prefects, told the Archangel Michael that Shemyaza took a human wife and made him and the other prefects swear an oath that they too would take human brides, thus condemning them to a fate similar to his own.

It was a lie. The only crime Zion's father was guilty of was that of loving a faithless human. In fact, he'd been so smitten with Zion's mother, Istahar, that he disclosed to her the explicit name of God. And for that crime, as well as the crime of siring Nephilim abominations, the name Shemyaza would evermore be connected with that of infamous rebellion against the Ancient of Days and the heavenly host.

The prophet Enoch knew Shemyaza's motives were driven by love, not lust, and sought to intercede on his behalf, as well as those prefects who had also taken human wives and sired children out of love. But judgment had been rendered and would be carried out by the Ancient of Days' mighty warrior angels against the condemned angels and their issue.

The seven sons of the precepts, led by Zion and his younger brother, Shiloh, hid the offspring of the condemned angels behind a preternatural dark veil until the sentence was carried out against their fathers. It was Istahar, Zion's own mother and a well-known witch, who had betrayed them to The Satan while they were on the wrong side of the veil.

No matter how Zion felt about human witches, he would have to put his personal feelings aside for the greater good.

"Newark is teeming with witches, Zion. You are asking us to find a veritable needle in a haystack," Nico retorted before raising a glass of whiskey to his lips and drinking deeply.

Zion wasn't the only Nephilim who hated witches. Nephilim tend to keep their distance from humans in general, and especially from those who dabbled in majick. Some witches have the power to invoke demons and angelic beings such as them. It would be foolhardy to trust them. As far as they were concerned, witchcraft and black majick were one and the same.

Jon appeared out of nowhere to top Zion's drink. Zion nodded his thanks, and Jon left the study as quietly as he had entered.

"I am well aware of the difficulty of the task," Zion said to Nico with alacrity. "That is why I want you to put Simeon on it. He has a nose like a bloodhound. If anyone can ferret out any information on the whereabouts of the witch, he can. Once we locate the witch, it will be easy to find the other two thwarts."

"Umm, Zion, there is one more matter we need to discuss," Nico said hesitantly, knowing just how much Zion loathed publicity of any kind. "The body Tyranny appropriated belonged to the son of the mayor of Newark, and someone saw Ajuma and Simeon snatch him. The witness hasn't come forward yet, but it's all over the news. The human feds and state and local police have launched a massive search."

Zion pinched the bridge of his nose, deep in thought. And then he turned toward Ajuma. "It appears this situation is turning into a real shit show, doesn't it, Ajuma?"

"What do you want me to do, Zion?" Ajuma asked hesitantly. He knew he would have to regain Zion's confidence in him. He was anxious to begin immediately.

"I want you to stay in Jersey where Nico can keep an eye on you," Zion said before turning his attention back to Nico.

"Change of plans. Put Simeon on the assignment to locate the eyewitness as well. Tell him to make sure the eyewitness comes up with a case of amnesia," he ordered, holding Ajuma's gaze in a manner that let his old friend know he had not heard the end of this.

Nico nodded his head in assent.

"If any of what Tyranny disclosed is true," Zion said, "we may have to gear up for yet another conflict between the Black and white humans.

I am calling in the Brothers of the Dark Veil. I want all of you here at sundown tomorrow so that we can brainstorm on how best to proceed with this film."

⁘

Twenty-four hours later, seven raucous, muscular, impossibly handsome Nephilim generals were packed inside Zion's office. They had all come at their king's summons: Nico, Boaz, Ajuma, Simeon, Gilead, Rephidim, and Antioch—fearless, dirty-mouthed, irreverent, cold-blooded killers, every one of them.

They drove fast cars, fornicated with loose females, drank hard liquor, and fearlessly lived life in the fast lane. And each one of them would gladly lay down his life for the male standing before them—Zion Shemyaza, the mighty, matchless king of the Nephilim Nation, and the most powerful Nephilim in existence. Zion didn't waste any time getting to the point.

"It has been brought to my attention that Moultrie of the House of Armers is in league with Zuet and is currently in the United States—Newark, New Jersey, to be specific."

Zion nodded his head in Jon's direction, giving the order to play the film. A screen descended from the ceiling. The lights were dimmed, and the film rolled to its bloody conclusion. And now there was nothing left, but a screen covered in snow, static, and jaw-dropping silence. Jon turned the lights on. Rephidim was the first to break the collective silence, issuing a harsh bark of laughter.

"Dayum. Young blood fucked Tyranny's ass up, didn't he?" He stated with his chest rumbling in laughter.

"Damn sure did," Nico agreed with a grin.

"Who the fuck you telling, man?" Gilead concurred, raising his glass for another drink, which Jon hurried to provide.

"Did you see the look on that ass wipe's face when the soldier said, 'I lied,' like he was a fuckin' desperado, or some shit?" Boaz asked.

And then it seemed like everyone was talking at once.

Antioch was bent over in his chair, beset by an uncontrollable bout of laughter. "Muhfuckah was like 'no mas… please don't hurt me no more,' like some kind of fuckin' girl."

Not to be left out, Nico chimed in again. "Somebody needs to give him the dark kiss so that we can kill his ass all over again for being a goddamn pussy. And correct me if I'm wrong, but didn't it look like he shit on himself?"

"Man, why you always got to take it *there*?" Boaz asked, sucking his teeth in disgust. "You'd probably shit on yourself too if that psycho Gibborim had your Black ass strapped to a wall with demon-binding chains."

It got quiet enough to hear a mouse pissing on cotton after Boaz referred to the Gibborim being psycho. Realizing his gaff, Boaz immediately tried to backpedal. But his words had already been released and the damage done. He turned to Simeon, who sat slightly apart from the rest of the brothers, with an apology on his lips. "Listen, Sim, I…"

Simeon cut him off before he could finish. He knew well that his brothers called him Psycho Sim behind his back. Sometimes he questioned his own mental stability. His face was unsmiling when he said, "The demon died without honor."

"He got what he deserved," Ajuma added in a robotic voice.

And just like that, the banter between the brothers resumed, with Ajuma and Simeon remaining quiet, having already said their piece.

The behavior of the Brothers of the Dark Veil would have been considered macabre to an outside observer. But since each of them firmly believed that the only good demon was a dead demon, the methods used to accomplish the end goal were irrelevant. As far as they were concerned, the masked Gibborim deserved the equivalent of a gold star for ridding the universe of one of Zuet's filthy sons.

Boaz raised his glass for a toast. "One down, four more to go."

"I'll drink to that," Zion said. Everyone raised their glass in a silent toast.

Suddenly, Zion was all business. "Simeon, I want you to find that witch and bring her to me, preferably unharmed. I will figure out what should be done with her once I have her." He leaned forward to give Simeon the rest of his instructions.

"Apparently, there was an eyewitness. I need for you to find him or her and erase what they witnessed. Before you go tearing through the city, I recommend you stop in to see the Widow Solonge at The Dark Side Club in Newark. If anyone has information on the witch we seek, it will be her."

Simeon nodded in assent. This was something he excelled at. If the witch was still on this side of creation, he would find her. And thanks to Brother Gilead, who was looking at him with speculation, he already knew the identity of the eyewitness and where she resided.

Zion's eyes landed upon each member of the Brothers of the Dark Veil, one by one. It was time to discuss Moultrie.

"As you know, I am offering a fifty-million-dollar reward to anyone who brings Moultrie in," the king said. "I will double the reward and offer an apprenticeship under the Brothers of the Dark Veil of choice to whomever brings Moultrie in alive."

Antioch let out a long, low whistle. "Damn, Zion. I wouldn't want to be that muthafucka once you get your hands on him!"

Zion's response was deadpan. "No. You wouldn't."

"Hey, Zion," Boaz said, piping in. "What do we get if one of *us* brings Moultrie in?"

"You get to keep your fucking job." Zion's quick response was met with ribald laughter.

"I will put out the word," Gilead said, acting as the Brothers of the Dark Veil scribe.

"You do that, Gil. And while you are at it," replied Zion, handing Gilead the Tyranny torture reel, "make sure this gets sent special delivery to Zuet in Hell."

CHAPTER THIRTY-SEVEN

Shubata, Mississippi.

IT WAS PART of Special Agent Andrew Burkett's daily regimen to run at least fifteen miles. Each new day would find him rising before the sun came up, to run with the moon riding close on his heels, while the rest of the world slumbered.

"Burkett," as he insisted on being called, did his very best thinking when his chest was burning and his legs were cramping from fatigue. During those times, he would test his physical boundaries, stubbornly pushing through the pain. His goal was to experience what he liked to refer to as runner's heaven. That state all real runners strive for, where the spirit takes over the physical body, and you feel like you can fly.

Burkett was on the last leg of his run and sorely in need of a piping hot cup of coffee when he saw one of the agency vehicles parked in front of his temporary digs. He picked up his pace.

⌘

Field Agent, Geneva Garcia, whom all the agents called Gigi, leaned against the agency vehicle, watching her boss's shirtless figure power up the road. From afar, the light sheen of sweat on his torso appeared to glisten as if he had been anointed with precious oil. Gigi's hungry eyes traveled down to his low-riding sweatpants. The sweaty material clung to his flesh, providing a tantalizing glimpse of what lay beneath.

Gigi was the self-appointed coffee gopher. She didn't care if she had to stay up all night with no sleep. It was worth it to get an early morning glimpse of Burkett shirtless with those sweatpants on.

El es magnifico… he is magnificent, she thought, taking a deep inhale to control her runaway emotions.

Truth be told, Gigi could feast her eyes on that man all day and all night and never get tired. But she dared not let him see her doing it. Burkett was all business, all the time.

Pero maldición, ese hombre es una especie de multa, but goddamn that man is some kind of fine, she thought.

Burkett got up every morning at 3:30 A.M., no matter the weather or how late he had been up the night before. You could set your clock by him. Just to prove her point, Gigi glanced at her watch. It was 6:00 A.M. on the dot.

Not only was he fine as hell, but he had a major set of balls to go along with his rugged good looks. They were in rural Mississippi, conducting an investigation in an extremely hostile environment, with hillbilly racists coming out of the woodwork like termites. Her boss, a Negro mind you, goes running in the woods—alone. And from the way those sweatpants were fitting him, he wasn't carrying a weapon—at least not one made of steel. And if he was, she would love to do a body search to find it.

Burkett was either mighty brave or *muy loco.* Gigi had yet to decide which.

Gigi camped out beside the agency car, daydreaming about running her tongue along the flat planes of Burkett's ripped belly. By the time Burkett made his way to where she was standing, she was lost in a particularly pleasant daydream, with a coffee in each hand: a sweet and light for herself and a black with no sugar for her boss.

"Is one of those for me, Gigi?" Burkett asked, snapping the agent out of her erotic reverie.

"Oh, I am so sorry, sir. Yes, this one is for you," she responded, looking flustered. He always made her feel this way. She handed him the coffee.

Coffee seemed to be Burkett's only vice. He didn't drink. He didn't smoke. As far as Gigi knew, he didn't have a woman in his life. Other than drinking a ton of bitter black coffee all day long and being one of the most intense men she'd ever met, the brother lived the life of a monk.

Burkett nodded his thanks for the coffee, choosing to ignore how Gigi automatically tensed up around him. He took a long, satisfying swallow from the cup.

"Any word on those prints yet?"

"Yes, sir," Gigi said, glad to focus on something other than the uncomfortable sensation generated by the close proximity to her attractive boss. She issued her report while following Burkett up the steps. She was having a hard time maintaining her focus with his tight, sweaty glutes in front of her.

"Word came in this morning. The prints lifted in the Stretch shed and the DeLonge barn are an exact match. We don't, however, have a match in the database."

"I suspected as much," Burkett replied, digging his keys from the mailbox.

Four whites were murdered in Meridian. They were Sheriff Edgar DeLonge, Deputy Lester Stretch, Louise Sadie Krutchner, and her father, Neusome Krutchner.

They lifted fingerprints in the shed where Stretch was murdered that did not belong to any of the occupants of the Strretch residence. Gigi confirmed that the same set of fingerprints were found in the stable where Sheriff DeLonge was murdered and in the Krutchner trailer. Burkett was disappointed they didn't get a hit in the FBI database, but not surprised. That would make things too easy. He had learned long ago that nothing for him was ever going to be easy.

He was up for the challenge, even though all they had to go on were some photos someone leaked to the press and three sets of unidentifiable fingerprints on the property of two of the victims. *We have our work cut out for us*, Burkett thought.

"I think it's time we shake up the natives. Give me twenty minutes to shower and shave, Gigi. We are going to have a one-on-one with Stretch's grieving widow." With that, he downed the rest of the coffee and headed for the shower.

From what Burkett's field agents could garner over the last few days, Lester Stretch was a real piece of work. He was a good ole Mississippi boy with a decidedly racist bent who didn't mind beating on the Negroes in Meridian just for kicks. Burkett's staff had done a cursory investigation of Stretch's wife, but he was curious to see what kind of woman would marry a man like him. It was with those salient facts in mind that Burkett approached the Stretch residence with Gigi by his side.

Burkett rang the doorbell four times. After the fourth ring, he raised his hand to knock. That was when a woman who bore an uncanny resemblance to Bette Davis in *Whatever Happened to Baby Jane* answered the door in one of those cotton floral duster things no woman should allow herself to be seen in. The garish combination of purple, orange, and pink flowers on the cotton duster was almost more than Burkett could take.

"What do you want?" the woman demanded, with narrowed eyes and a scowl on a face that had seen far too much sun exposure and far too many early morning cocktails. It was only 10:00 A.M., and Burkett could smell the liquor seeping through her pores.

But who am I to judge? Burkett thought. *It has to be happy hour somewhere on the planet.* It was obvious they had come at an inconvenient time. Too bad Burkett didn't give a damn.

"Good morning, ma'am," he said in his best Sidney Poitier, *Guess Who's Coming to Dinner* voice. "I am Special Agent Andrew Burkett with the Federal Bureau of Investigation, and this is my partner, Field Agent Geneva Garcia." Burkett and Gigi flipped their badges open for her inspection.

"What? You got wax in your ears? I didn't ask you to introduce yourselves. What do you want?" she repeated none too kindly.

Susan Stretch could tell by their demeanor and by the way they were dressed that they were law enforcement officers of some kind. The police and the FBI had been swarming over her property like cockroaches ever since she went into the shed to feed their dog and found the dog and her husband, Lester, dead. She'd been drunk ever since and intended to stay that way. Maybe if she drank enough, she would stop seeing the grisly sight of her decapitated dog and her dead husband or, at the very least, pass out. She'd do just about anything to give her mind a rest from the rage that was boiling inside her like a kettle left too long on the stove.

CHAPTER THIRTY-EIGHT

S USAN STRETCH DIDN'T know what pissed her off more, the fact that she was the overweight fifty-seven-year-old widow of a renowned womanizer or that the FBI sent a nigger and a spick to find out who killed him.

"Are you Susan Stretch?" Burkett asked politely.

Burkett considered himself an expert on the human psyche. He sized Susan Stretch up the minute she opened the door. Lester Stretch had been a philanderer who spent more time laying-up with whores and drinking with his friends, than he spent with his fat, frumpy wife.

Stretch wasn't anybody's prize, but his widow is probably thinking a rotten husband is better than none at all. She is clearly hurting. As the saying goes, hurt people hurt others. His Black face would serve as a target for her pain. Burkett was more than ready for her.

"Yeah, I'm Susan Stretch. What of it?"

"I would like to extend my condolences in the loss of your husband, Mrs. Stretch," Burkett said in a voice that was clearly rehearsed. Now that the formalities were out of the way, Burkett wasted no time cutting straight to the chase.

"I know that you have been questioned extensively by the local police and my agents, and I apologize for any inconvenience. We have a few additional questions we need to ask regarding your late husband, if you don't mind. May we come in?"

"Yes, I do mind. And, no, you cannot come in! I don't allow nig—"

She stopped short of releasing the racial epithet that was begging to force its way out of the back of her throat. Something in Burkett's eyes warned her. She caught herself when she saw the bulge of a pistol in Burkett's jacket pocket, a pistol he purposely revealed as a not-too-subtle warning.

You can't be too careful when you are around them, she thought, looking between Burkett and Garcia. *I don't want to join my husband on a slab in the morgue—or worse. Maybe he and the spick will rape me.*

Andrew knew what time it was. He represented everything the Susan Stretches of the world were afraid of, but too ashamed to admit. He was clean-cut, intelligent, well-educated, and held a position of authority over her. This type of fear always manifested into hatred.

Burkett watched her intently as she pushed an errant strand of bleached blonde hair behind her ear. After a generous heave of her chest, she started anew.

"I don't allow nigras in my house without my husband being present and never through the front door," she said, trying to dig the knife of the insult in deeper.

Susan Stretch need not have wasted her time. As a part of his great society initiative to eliminate poverty and racial injustice, President Lyndon B. Johnson formed the Special Task Force for Race-Related Crimes.

Burkett was the first Black to head the task force and, as such, was under the intense scrutiny of the president and FBI Director J. Edgar Hoover. He had dealt with far harsher verbal treatment from the FBI director than Susan Stretch could ever dish out. She didn't own the vocabulary or the intelligence to penetrate Burkett's steely armor. He learned to take it on the cuff by living thirty-three years in black skin and being in the military.

Gigi blended into the background, allowing Burkett to take the lead. She was quiet but ever observant. Burkett was a consummate professional at all times, a disciplined control freak who liked to line things up before he knocked them down.

Not for one second did Burkett betray his true feelings for the ill-kept woman standing before him, even though Gigi knew for a fact that he hated the sight of her and wanted nothing more than to feed her the tail end of his pistol. Through the entire exchange, Burkett maintained the same professional demeanor he had when Susan Stretch first opened her front door.

Instead of verbally lighting into Susan Stretch, he reached into his pocket and whipped out his trump card, one of the four gruesome black-and-white photos of the lynching someone leaked to the press.

The photo he was holding clearly showed the grinning faces of Lester Stretch, Sheriff Edgar DeLonge, Louise Sadie Krutchner, and about thirty others standing around three bodies hanging from the Shubata Bridge.

Yeah, bitch. You can act like you didn't know your husband was a murdering, racist, sonofabitch if you want to, but I know better, he thought, chuckling to himself.

Burkett didn't believe in coincidence. It was not lost on him that Stretch, DeLonge, Louise Sadie Krutchner, and her father Neusome Krutchner, who was not in any of the photos, were victims of vicious murders on the same night the lynchings took place. There had to be a connection, and he was determined to find it.

Despite the orders from his commander-in-chief, Burkett's sole purpose for visiting this pissant town in this backwoods state of home-grown racists was to find out who those Black victims were and prosecute their killers.

If the person or persons responsible for murdering Stretch and his cronies get caught up in my net at the same time, then so be it; otherwise, fuck 'em. I stopped taking orders from white men a long time ago. They just don't know it.

"What do you know about this?" Burkett asked, placing the photo directly in Susan Stretch's line of vision. His lips turned up in a wolfish smile. Her face went ghost white. She held on to the door sill to keep from falling.

Burkett and his agents questioned the individuals identified in the photos more than once, only to be given a Mississippi stonewall at every turn. He knew he would get little or no cooperation at the onset, but he had to go through the motions. When offered his current position, Burkett's only proviso had been to have total autonomy in choosing the agents on his team. All members of Burkett's team were minorities, which made it especially difficult to get information from whites, who would just as soon spit on them than answer any of their questions.

Three cold-blooded murders were committed on the Shubata Bridge. The photos that were burning a hole in Burkett's pocket were the proof of it. Yet no one would admit to seeing or hearing anything or knowing where the bodies are. In fact, most of the people questioned had been downright surly, especially the ones identified in the leaked photos.

His interviews with the resident Negroes didn't yield much information either. They were acting as if the Grand Wizard of the Klan was holding a knife to their necks. They were afraid, and Burkett couldn't blame them. They had to live here after the FBI was gone. No one wanted to end up swinging from the Shubata Bridge.

It didn't help that the media had arrived in Meridian *en masse*, right along with representatives of the NAACP, CORE, and every other Black organization he could think of. During a live interview, the governor of Mississippi threatened to lynch some more niggers if they didn't clear out of his state.

This was not Burkett's first rodeo. He joined the ROTC program while at Morehouse College. He did a five-year stint in the military, where he served on the military police, all in preparation for joining the FBI. He applied a dogged and determined methodology to all his investigations.

I will learn the identity of the Negro victims and find their bodies, even if I have to slice open the bellies of every gator in Mississippi to do it, he vowed.

❧

Two days later, Burkett got an unexpected break. It came in the form of James "Jimmy Lee" Lawson, who parked outside the temporary FBI offices in downtown Meridian in broad daylight. His truck was loaded with all of his belongings.

Lawson strode up to the front desk to offer Burkett an anchor to hold on to during a time when he was feeling uncharacteristically disheartened by his progress in the investigation, or more particularly, the lack thereof. Holding a tattered straw hat in his hands, Jimmy Lee asked the receptionist if he could speak with the man in charge about the François' murders. She quickly ushered him into Special Agent Burkett's office.

Burkett stood to shake Lawson's hand, sizing him up in less than ten seconds. He was your typical Mississippi farmer, wearing a pair of Gomer Pyle overalls and a somber expression.

"Why did you decide to come forward when no one else in town was inclined to do so?" Burkett asked, after offering Lawson a seat.

"I'm leaving Mississippi for good," Lawson replied. "I want to do the right thing before I go." The pronouncement was made in a firm tone with a heavy southern accent.

"Do you mind if we take notes?" Burkett asked.

"Take all the notes you want."

Burkett picked up the phone and issued instructions to his secretary. "Send in Agent Garcia, and hold all of my calls."

Gigi entered moments later, dressed in a black suit and white blouse, pen and pad in hand. She nodded in Lawson's direction and took the vacant seat next to him.

"I knew the victims well," Lawson said without being prompted. "In fact, I worked on their farm part-time."

Burkett issued a series of questions. Lawson's responses to each were straight-forward and candid.

Of course, Jimmy Lee made no mention of Elizabeth or the bodies he helped bury. Burkett wished him well when he was done with his questions.

To avert any untoward reprisals, Burkett ordered two of his field agents to personally escort Lawson out of town. Should he need to question him further, Burkett knew how to find him.

❧

"We now know the names of the victims and the circumstances of their death," he said as soon as Lawson departed. "Lawrence Alexander 'Fruit' François, twenty-eight; his brother Johnny Heathcliff 'Junior' François, twenty-seven and their nephew Calvin Lionel François, fourteen."

Investigative work entails patiently connecting the dots, something Burkett was exceedingly good at. They now had something tangible to work with. Burkett and Gigi checked the tax records to see the status of the François farm. Not only did they own the farmland free and clear, but the land had apparently been in their family for five generations.

Next, they scoured the Census Bureau records. According to the 1960 census, the occupants of the farm were Lawrence and Johnny François, their widowed sister, Elizabeth Anne François, and their nephew Calvin. This revelation raised a new question.

"Where is Elizabeth? If she is a widow, why is she using her maiden name, and why is there no legal record of her husband's death?"

Did the racist mob wipe out the entire François family? Burkett wondered. *And if so, why didn't Lawson mention Elizabeth François when they spoke?*

Burkett was prepared to round up his team and head out to the François farm, where he hoped to get some answers. But then his phone rang.

The strident voice of his secretary sounded over the speaker. "I know you requested I hold all of your calls, sir, but I think you will want to take this."

Burkett was on the line for less than a minute before he hung up and turned to Gigi.

"My brother is dead," he said in disbelief.

Gigi wanted nothing more than to wrap her arms around him to console him, but was fearful anything she said or did would be unwelcomed. Instead, she said, "I am so sorry for your loss, Burkett. Who will take over this case while you are away at the funeral?"

"I'm not going anywhere," he said, all business. "Let's go."

⚜

The François Farm

Evidence of a scuffle and a shootout was immediately apparent as soon as the agents exited their cars. Bullets were embedded in the wood surrounding the front porch, and spent rifle shells littered the front yard. Burkett ordered most of the team to search the grounds, while the remaining agents searched the interior of the house and the area surrounding it.

Burkett had his agents search every inch of the François farm, including ancillary structures, without coming up with much, other than that there had been a violent altercation in front of the farmhouse. Burkett was about to call it a day and reconvene the following morning when one of his field agents shouted, "Sir! I think you might want to take a look at this!"

The shit had hit the fan. They found a human skull and a femur. Burkett called in the FBI forensic team. By the time they were done, the François land looked like someone had set off land mines everywhere. They retrieved the skeletal remains of fifteen bodies and three fresh kills that Burkett would bet a year's pay belonged to Lawrence, Johnny, and Calvin François.

"Tag 'em and bag 'em," Burkett ordered. He couldn't trust the local authorities as far as he could throw them. The bodies would be shipped to the FBI forensic lab in Jackson for identification.

Gigi silently watched the forensic team load the bodies into the transport wagon.

"Sir, it looks like we got ourselves a serial killer."

CHAPTER THIRTY-NINE

1294 Arlington Avenue, Plainfield, New Jersey 07060

"YOU OKAY, GOOD friend?"

Since early evening, there'd been a steady stream of people in and out of the Burkett residence for the post-funeral repast. Althea joined Loretta in her bedroom, where she'd closeted herself to escape the uncomfortable crush.

"It depends," Loretta replied softly.

"On what?" Althea asked, taking her hand.

"On whether all of those hypocrites have left my house," Loretta riposted.

While some came with good intentions, Loretta was keenly aware that others harbored personal agendas because of who they thought she was, a question she was hard-pressed to answer herself. All of them were friends or associates of her late husband and barely tolerated her.

"I swear, Althea," she said, looking her best friend in the eyes for the first time that day. "If one more person comes up to me and says, 'I'm so sorry for your loss,' I'm going to lay them out and bury them right next to Albert."

Her off-color comment generated a brief laugh between them at

Trudy Scott's expense. The old harridan, who'd boldly asked Loretta how many life insurance policies she had on Albert, was probably downstairs nursing a bottle of gin and disparaging the widow's name. Everyone thought she'd married Albert to get her hands on his money. Now that he was dead, they assumed she would be cashing in big time.

If only they knew, Loretta thought bitterly.

⋙

Earlier that week, Loretta showed up at the funeral home to make Albert's final arrangements, with all three life insurance policies she'd found in Albert's office in hand. It took a little over an hour to make the arrangements and less than a minute to tear down what little hope she had left.

She replayed the events of that day in her mind, beginning at the point where the funeral director said, "I'm sorry, Mrs. Burkett. All three policies have been cashed in."

Her first reaction had been to assure the funeral director that someone at the insurance companies must have made a mistake. She'd even insisted he check again because Albert was a good businessman and couldn't possibly have cashed in all three of the policies. But there was no mistake. The policies were no longer viable.

Loretta had yet to locate Albert's Last Will and Testament. Luckily, she'd taken Sister Jenkins's advice and held off reporting Albert's death to get the money out of the bank before the accounts were frozen and the probate process triggered. She learned the full extent of her financial situation when she went to the bank to withdraw enough cash to cover ancillary funeral expenses.

Every one of the bank accounts was overdrawn. That was also when she received the devastating news that the Arlington Avenue residence and the building housing the restaurant were in foreclosure, and a long line of creditors were waiting like bloodthirsty vultures for Albert to make good on his debts. Dead men can't pay bills.

Under the law, the loved ones of the dearly departed are left to bear the burden. Albert's creditors wasted no time informing Loretta that she was now responsible for Albert's debts.

Loretta had to sell her furs and several pieces of jewelry to scrape up the money to bury Albert. She was destitute. Each time Loretta thought things couldn't possibly get any worse, they did.

She returned home after settling the funeral home account to find a beat-up brown Pontiac parked in front of her house. An unsavory-looking character was sitting behind the wheel. He got out of the car to meet Loretta at the door and introduced himself as Frankie Palermo, a self-proclaimed New York money broker whom Albert had borrowed money from at an exorbitant interest rate. The loan was in default. He said he wanted his money in a week's time, or else.

Loretta got sick to her stomach every time she thought of the way his evil eyes had raked her body. Loretta was no dummy. She recognized a threat when she saw one.

If Albert wasn't dead already, she probably would have killed him herself. Then, as now, she wrapped her arms around her waist and cried.

"Please, don't cry, Loretta. God has a plan for you. Everything is going to be alright," Althea assured her.

If only that was true, she thought.

⁓

When Pastor Nelson announced the call to the altar for those in need of prayer during Albert's funeral service, Loretta was the first one up front and on her knees, praying for direction and forgiveness.

She looked over at the pew that was customarily occupied by Leila and Leroy Fuller and their daughter Renee, and began to weep.

It was empty, and everyone in the church knew why. But few of them knew what she knew. She had been there.

Renee Fuller didn't make it out of the No Name Bar as Loretta had hoped. She'd been brutally beaten and raped and was in University Hospital fighting for her life. The news of her attack was traveling through the church grapevine before sunrise the next morning.

Try as she might, Loretta couldn't erase from her memory what she'd seen on that dark street in Newark during the wee hours of the morning, any more than she could shake the sense of guilt that was eating away at her like the worst kind of cancer for not getting Renee to safety.

The mayor's son and the horrible men with him—men who weren't really men—had been in the bar earlier that night. She had seen them.

Just as sure as I know there is a God, I know things will never be right in my life unless I do the right thing.

First, I need to get these people out of this house. And then she paused, looking at Althea, whose earnest gaze was focused on her, clear-eyed and true. *I must confess and apologize for bringing Althea into this mess I helped to create.*

Lastly, I need to go to the police, and let them know I saw the mayor's son and the men with him. And most importantly, I can identify the men—or whatever they were—who most likely had taken him.

Of course, she would omit the fact that one of them had a lethal set of fangs and the ability to turn into ten exact replicas of himself, or how another spat fire while single-handedly pummeling the mayor's son and the men with him to a bloody pulp.

No one will believe me anyhow. Shit, I can barely believe what I saw, she thought.

She would never forget the look in the eyes of the man who sat behind the wheel of the van. They were haunting, frightening, and eerily beautiful, invading her dreams and disrupting her thoughts since she'd seen him.

Once I go to the police, everyone will know my shame. They will know that on the night my husband died I was in a seedy bar with another man, that I'm a liar and a cheat and would have played the whore if things had gone according to plan. But I can't put it off any longer.

Maybe the mayor's son knows something about Renee's attacker. If I have information to assist the police in finding him, they can question him. Loretta knew that if she was going to do this, it had to be now, while she still had the courage.

"I wasn't with Albert on the night he died," she began, diving right in.

"I know," Althea replied, interrupting her confession. "I called that night to speak with you. Albert assumed you were spending the night with me."

"I'm so sorry," Loretta said in a voice barely above a whisper. Althea was quick to assure her.

"There is nothing for you to be sorry about, dear friend. Nor do we have to speak about why you led Albert to believe you were with me, at least not tonight. I love you like a sister. Nothing you can do will change that. How about we get these folks out of your house so that you can get some rest?"

⋙

Almost everyone had come bearing containers, beverages, pots and pans of food, and well-rehearsed, disingenuous expressions of condolence. Loretta had no idea where she would put all that food until Althea and Sister Jenkins rolled up their sleeves and offered to stay behind to put away what they could, pack the rest for the needy, and tidy up.

Albert would have loved all this food, Loretta thought,

subconsciously rubbing the area above her heart to ease the ache that refused to leave.

"Thank you so much, Althea, for everything. The past few days have been pure hell. I couldn't have made it without you."

Loretta's voice trembled with emotion when her best friend finally took off her apron and prepared to leave. Althea had been by Loretta's side through it all.

"You're welcome, dear friend. If you need anything, anything at all, sweetheart, I am just a phone call away."

"Please feel free to call on me as well," Sister Jenkins chimed in. She'd stayed behind to lend a helping hand.

The heavyset woman who sang in the gospel choir had a heart as pure as gold. Loretta knew she meant every single word when she said she could call on her, as sure as she knew she wouldn't take her up on the offer. Sister Jenkins, a widow herself, had already shared a great deal of information with her. Loretta dared not impose.

Loretta stood on her front porch, staring at the stars, long after Althea and Sister Jenkins drove away. The delicious smell of sweet juniper and almond drifted onto the porch, wrapping its arms around her. She recognized the first fragrance, but had no idea what the source of the second was. All she knew was that she liked it and found it oddly comforting considering, well, everything.

CHAPTER FORTY

THE AROMA OF Simeon's Amsterdam Shag hand-rolled cigarette formed a cloud around his head, drifting on the wind, as he stood across the street from the home of the human whose name he now knew was Loretta Burkett. The mighty Nephilim general had been observing the comings and goings through the fragrant mist since mid-evening. And now there was a growing stack of discarded cigarettes at his feet.

Simeon tried to convince himself that his reason for being there was to track the woman down to ensure she didn't repeat what she'd seen in Newark to the human authorities. And yet here he was, standing in the park across from her home, borderline stalking her, chain-smoking, and wishing he could talk to her or maybe even touch her.

She'd been easy to find. Simeon gave Gilead her license plate number. Gilead accessed the human DMV database and ran her plates for her name, address, and phone number. He also informed Simeon of her husband's recent death.

And now she is a woman all alone, with no man to protect and care for her, Simeon thought, marshaling every ounce of power he had to keep from springing to her aid when she began to cry. He stamped the hand-rolled beneath his feet as she stood to go back inside.

"Fuck it," he muttered, throwing caution to the wind. Taking a deep breath, he ghosted into her house just before she locked the door behind her.

⮜

Something about the tight configuration of the plastic-covered furniture inside the cramped confines of the Burkett house triggered the pulsing sound of living, breathing walls pressing against Simeon's body, threatening to crush him in increments. Simeon didn't do well in close spaces.

I can't breathe, he thought, his anxiety mounting.

The cold-blooded Nephilim general, whose depraved exploits had earned him the moniker Psycho Sim throughout The Hells and beyond, would have panicked and torn the Burkett house to pieces to get out of there had it not been for his sudden desire to ease the woman, who was equally distressed.

⮜

This was the moment Loretta dreaded—being left alone in this hideous house of hatred and despair. She couldn't even bathe in peace without the memory of her perverted father-in-law pressing his rheumy eye to cracks in the wall to spy on her whenever she was unclothed. Not only did her mother-in-law know what her husband was doing, she hated Loretta for it. Loretta never told Albert about his father or how glad she'd been when the bastard finally died.

The house turned on Loretta the day after her mother-in-law died. Since then, other than a few minutes here and there, Loretta tried not to spend any significant time alone in what she referred to as the house of heartaches, and never at night.

How can I explain the feeling I get when I know something hateful is hiding behind every closed door? Thanks to Albert, I don't even have enough money to stay at a hotel. She staggered up the stairs with the sweet fragrance of almond trailing her steps.

Loretta felt him before she saw him. She was halfway up the stairs when she turned to find the man she'd seen in the van. He was in her house, gazing up at her from the bottom of the stairs with a frightening intensity, his heat scorching her flesh. Somehow she had known she would see him again.

She couldn't move. She couldn't speak. She could barely think.

It took but a moment for Loretta to come to her senses, and when she did, her first instinct was to make a run for it. She sprinted up the stairs, tripping once and banging her knees before she gained the top step. She made for her bedroom.

Once inside, she slammed the door shut, threw the lock, and pressed her back against the door, her heart drumming to an unnatural cadence that screamed of death. As she glanced up, she saw him inside her bedroom, and her knees nearly buckled.

⨎

Simeon moved at a superhuman rate of speed to block Loretta at the door, covering her mouth to cut off what he suspected would have been an epic scream.

Loretta stood stock still, afraid to breathe as he drew closer, leveling his body against hers to sniff her like a wild animal courting its mate.

From up close, Simeon found the human to be even more striking than he'd previously thought. Even with her face frozen with fear, he found her indescribably beautiful.

The last thing I want from this woman is fear.

Simeon caged her in, forcing her to feel his heat. He pressed one hand against the door above her head. The other hand remained against her lips.

"Look at me," he commanded, desperate to look into the eyes that had haunted him since he'd last seen her.

Simeon's dominant nature craved the essence of a submissive female. Having no will to do anything but obey, Loretta complied without hesitation. He growled at her responsiveness as the rock-hard evidence of his desire strained beneath the fine-hewn material of his custom-made trousers.

Her skin was as smooth and clear as a calm river at midnight, without a pore or blemish, and her lips so soft and full he ached to taste them. But it was her eyes that captivated him. They were the color of warm cognac and filled with a sadness that mirrored his own. He couldn't help but wonder why she had been out so late and why she had been alone.

She is far too lovely to be walking in one of the most dangerous areas of Newark late at night. No male worth his salt would allow his woman to go out unprotected against the evils of the night, he thought, drawing even closer to inhale the fresh, sweet smell of her.

Loretta issued a sweet moan of surrender and no protest when Simeon placed his hands on both sides of her head, sinking his long, powerful fingers in the mass of soft, thick natural coils framing her heart-shaped face. He kissed her, forcing her lips apart to invade her sweet, hungry mouth with his talented tongue. An electric current traveled from Simeon's lips to the base of his dick, metaphorically jerking him off to the rhythm of her pounding heartbeat.

Loretta felt something routing around inside her mind, but his masterful kiss and the proximity of his warm body robbed her of both good sense and free will. She could not have fought him if she wanted to.

At that moment, Loretta would have willingly given him any-thing he wanted, anywhere he wanted it—on the ground in front of her house, on the roof of the car—hell, he could have taken her on top of her husband's freshly dug grave for all she cared.

Loretta moaned in his mouth, offering him her breath and more. She pressed her hands inside his shirt to score the surface of his hot flesh with the tips of her sharp nails. Simeon growled at her responsiveness, grinding her into the door as he blazed a trail of passionate kisses from her lips to her throat. Loretta gasped at the mixture of pleasure and pain, wantonly raising her leg to meet his need, as he sank his fangs in.

Just as quickly as the soul-stripping majick began, it stopped, and he was no longer there, leaving Loretta leaning against the bedroom door with her hand against her heart, gasping for air, and wondering what the hell had just happened.

Having done the unforgivable, Simeon ghosted across the street, waiting for his fangs to retract and his lust to subside. He'd tasted the sweetness of her blood and her kisses. He knew he couldn't stay away from her, any more than he could stay away from the private sex dungeon in the basement of Solonge Shemyaza's nightclub.

Even if she were not a human, I will never be good enough for her. I am darkness, and she is light.

CHAPTER FORTY-ONE

ELIZABETH ARRIVED IN Plainfield, New Jersey, just past sunset on a humid Thursday evening. She drove the old farm truck twenty miles per hour to better take in the tree-lined streets and well-tended homes, pegging the place referred to as the Queen City as more town than city.

A friendly tap on the horn from the driver behind her reminded her where she was and why she was there. She immediately picked up speed. Within minutes, she arrived in the bustling downtown area.

Elizabeth viewed her surroundings with the sense of wonder one would expect from a small-town farm girl who finds herself smack-dab in the middle of an unknown city. She slowed down yet again, this time keeping pace with the traffic, to take in a multitude of businesses far exceeding anything she'd seen in Meridian.

Colored folks were driving shiny Chevy Impalas and Cadillacs, making her beat-up old pickup truck stand out like a horse and buggy in Beverly Hills. Despite the oppressive humidity, clean-cut Colored men in well-fitted suits and bow ties stood on the corner hawking bean pies, fish sandwiches, and *The Final Call* Newspaper while Colored families brandished copies of *The Watchtower* less than a block away.

Heavyset evangelists, dressed in all white, handed out religious tracts and quoted scripture. Background music coming out of an establishment with Brooks Record Shop emblazoned in the front window competed to drown out the voices of the holy rollers.

Brown-skinned girls and boys walked the streets with stylishly cut afros and bell bottom pants, their heads held high. Loretta remained skeptical, even though she saw nobody remotely resembling a Sheriff DeLonge to steal the joy in their eyes or the youthful pride in their stride.

I know those pale-faced devils are here, lurking in the shadows, ready to pounce, she thought. *Because isn't that always the case?*

Front Street and the areas surrounding it were literally bursting at the seams with pedestrian commerce. Elizabeth found it difficult to secure a parking spot, as the stores remained open until nine on Thursday nights. It appeared many of the residents were taking advantage of the late shopping hours. She finally spied a spot on Somerset Street in front of Robert Hall and Harry's Township Clothiers and sped up to take it.

"We have to find somewhere safe to lay our heads," she said, talking to Àse like she was human. "But first we have to find ourselves a job."

If Elizabeth knew one thing for sure and two things for certain, it was that white folks don't truck with strangers, especially Colored ones. Down south, Colored folks are liable to be victims of harassment by the local police the minute they set foot in town.

Until now, Elizabeth had never stepped foot outside of Mississippi and didn't know what to expect in New Jersey. For that reason alone, she slipped Lucille Ball inside her satchel for protection, just in case something jumped off. She grabbed Àse's carrier and got out of the truck.

"Damn if it don't feel good to stretch these legs," she said aloud, closing and locking the truck behind her.

᪥

Elizabeth was oblivious to the attention she generated in her brother Junior's dungarees. More than a few male eyes were on the sway of her hips as she walked the downtown area, hoping to see a Help Wanted sign in one of the windows.

Coming from Meridian, where Phil's Local Tack and Feed was the anchor establishment, she was overwhelmed by the number and variety of stores she saw. There was Bamberger's, Woolworth, and McCrory's on one end and Teppers, Rosenbaum's, Sears, and Montgomery Ward on the other with countless retail and eating establishments in between, all frequented by Colored people.

She would not learn until much later that none of the establishments she marveled over were owned or managed by Colored people, and that things were not much different in Plainfield than they were back in Mississippi.

Elizabeth stopped at a convenience store on her way back to the truck. She purchased a newspaper, a bottle of pop, and a bag of chips, more determined than ever to get a job and find somewhere to live in this unique city where the ancestors saw fit to place her.

That night, Elizabeth and Àse slept inside the truck beneath a blanket of stars.

᪥

Loretta opened her eyes the next morning with a pounding headache and her skin feverish to the touch. Confused to find she was still wearing yesterday's clothing down to her high heels, she assumed she'd crawled in bed suffering a wicked hangover, even though she couldn't recall imbibing any alcohol. The pain in her head intensified when she tried to remember anything past Althea and Sister Jenkin's departure the night before.

Groaning, she struggled to sit up in bed, only to lie back down to escape the blinding illumination from the bedside reading lamp and the bright sunlight streaming through the open bedroom window, both of which were vying for the privilege to make her throw up.

What time is it? She raised her arm to cover her sensitive eyes from the blaring light, waiting for the world to stop spinning.

Loretta remained in a prone position for another minute, her stomach roiling and her pulse pounding like a bass drum inside her head.

While going through Albert's office, she found a certified letter from the bank's attorney informing Albert of the foreclosure on The Melting Pot building and the pending auction of the restaurant contents to the highest bidder. She had no choice. She had an appointment with Albert's attorney at one o'clock to see what she could do, if anything, to stave off the sale. She attempted to sit up again, this time succeeding.

The upcoming appointment and the fact that in four days Palermo would come for his money weighed heavily on her spirit. The thought that she'd have to do everything alone was devastating.

Albert is dead, she reminded herself on a whimper.

Loretta sent up a silent prayer that the attorney could arrange for an extended grace period to give her time to figure things out and got out of bed.

❧

Loretta walked to the bathroom in her robe and slippers, wondering how long it would be before Public Service turned the lights off or the city cut off the water.

It has been less than twenty-four hours since I put my husband in the ground, she thought, stirring up an already boiling pot of anxiety. *I have no idea what to do.*

For as long as Loretta could remember, there'd always been a man to take care of her needs. Having to rely upon herself was a task she deemed herself woefully inadequate to accomplish.

Here I am, she thought, *a twenty-nine-year-old widow with no job—my fault—and no skills to get a job, also my fault. But the monstrous pile of debt I'll never be able to pay off if I live to see a hundred and the slimy loan shark my late husband owes money to, is one hundred percent Albert's fault,* she thought bitterly.

I've come full-circle—haunted, desperate, and hunted.

She closed and locked the bathroom door behind her, a habit she adopted when she was seven years old. That was when her cousin, who was fifteen years her senior, started coming into the bathroom while she was bathing to rape her.

Loretta knew better than most that a locked door was merely a coping mechanism, and that it represented little to no protection against someone hell-bent on doing harm. For Loretta, it was more so a mental security blanket which afforded her a modicum of comfort.

She stood before the vanity, taking in her appearance with a critical eye, frowning at her reflection. The unforgiving morning light revealed a wan complexion, dark circles beneath her eyes, and a bright red hickey with two inflamed puncture marks on the left side of her neck, which she assumed was the result of a spider bite while she slept.

She washed and dried her face and brushed her teeth, then turned on the shower. The ancient pipes clanked and banged in protest as she adjusted the temperature, filling the tight space with steam.

"Instead of the security Albert promised me on the day we exchanged our wedding vows, all he's left me is a boatload of debt and fucking problems." She shook her head and hung her robe on the back of the bathroom door.

Loretta snatched the shower curtain back to step beneath the stream of steaming hot water, growing angrier by the moment—not at her late husband, but at herself for perpetuating the same behavior again and again and foolishly expecting a different result.

She took her frustration out on the expensive bar of French mill soap Albert purchased for her, vigorously lathering her washcloth and then her body. Her mind immediately returned to Chet, Renee, and what happened at the No Name Bar.

Why can't I remember driving home? Loretta wondered. The mere thought of that fateful night elicited a sharp, stabbing pain in the center of her brain.

She thought she heard the familiar squeal of the front door opening and closing and froze.

Someone is in the house, she mouthed, suddenly terrified.

She turned off the shower water to listen. A steady drip, drip, drip of the shower faucet kept pace with her pounding heart as the heavy tread of her late mother-in-law's distinctive, uneven footfall advanced up the stairs.

She slapped her hand over her mouth to keep from screaming the house down when the intruder paused after stepping on the third step from the bottom that always screamed when stepped on.

Frantic with fear, Loretta's eyes combed the bathroom searching for something—anything she could use to defend herself—finally landing on the plunger. Soapy water dripped off her body and pooled on the tile floor as she stepped out of the tub to scramble into her robe.

Shaking all over, she grabbed her makeshift weapon and, afraid to take a breath, waited as whoever was on the other side of the door turned the knob.

The shrill ring of the phone sliced through the silence, followed by the sound of the uneven tread descending the stairs and the front door opening. Loretta had no idea how long she sat on the bathroom floor sobbing. When she finally mustered the courage to open the bathroom door and venture out, the housed reeked of her late mother-in-law's signature fragrance, *Le Air du temp*. The front door lay wide open, and it was dark out.

Loretta got dressed, hurriedly threw some clothes in a satchel, and got the hell out of there.

CHAPTER FORTY-TWO

A S LUCK WOULD have it, Elizabeth secured an interview for a position in the housekeeping department at Green Brook Manor Nursing Home on her second day in Plainfield. There was an opening for the 3–11 P.M. shift. She took it.

Through conversations with her new coworkers, she learned the landscape of what was frequently known as The Plainfields was much more complex than she initially thought.

The Township of South Plainfield is in Middlesex County. The Township of North Plainfield is located in Somerset County. Both North and South Plainfield abut opposite ends of the Queen City, known as simply Plainfield, which boasts both east and west ends, in Union County. Green Brook Manor Nursing Home is located in the Township of North Plainfield.

Elizabeth and Àse camped out in the farm truck every night for nearly two weeks. She would let Àse out to run wild and arrive at work early enough to wash up before she started her shift. Like clockwork, her beloved companion would be waiting to greet her at the end of her shift with bloody paws and the gift of a dead bird or mouse locked between her teeth.

The routine Elizabeth established was finally paying off. The following morning, she circled two rentals of interest, one on Arlington

Avenue and the other on Berkeley Terrace, both in Plainfield. Armed with a job, a week's pay, and the local newspaper, Elizabeth set out to find a place to live.

❧

"Let's gas the truck up and find us someplace to live," she said to Àse, who let out a loud meow in agreement. She pulled into a gas station on Somerset Street for a fill-up and directions.

"I know that motherfucker sees me waiting here," she said, frowning after the white gas attendant bypassed her to wait on the car behind her for the second time. Instead of causing a scene, she rolled her eyes and sucked her teeth.

Focusing her attention elsewhere, she caught the tail end of an exchange between a slender, Colored man with a mountain of hair stuffed beneath a red, black and green wool cap and a scholarly looking Colored man. They were discussing the merits, or lack thereof, in following the teachings of the Honorable Elijah Muhammad over Haile Selassie.

Everywhere Elizabeth turned, she saw Colored people trying to convince somebody to follow whatever it was they believed in. It seemed every one of them was searching for what Elizabeth already had: the knowledge of who she was, where she came from, and an awareness of the spirit flowing through her; for all the good the knowing had done her and her family.

"It wouldn't make a damn bit of difference if Colored folks know every secret under the sun as long as white folks are in charge," she mumbled after the white gas attendant ignored her to tend to yet another white customer. Praying she'd have enough gas to get her where she needed to go, she pulled out of the gas station, itching to give the attendant the finger.

❧

The landscape changed significantly once Elizabeth left the down-town area of Plainfield for the residential one. It soon became evident that the west end of the city was where most of the Colored people lived, with Park Avenue being the great divide between the haves and the have-nots.

On the Colored side of town, little girls with nappy pigtails counted off a youthful cadence of "ten, twenty, thirty, forty," as they jumped double Dutch on the uneven sidewalk pavements while little boys played touch football in the middle of the street. She suspected they were totally oblivious to the turmoil roiling around them and the opportunities they were destined to forfeit merely because of the color of their skin.

The ancestors must have been all tapped out from the long ride between Mississippi and Jersey because not only did the sun go into hiding in the middle of the afternoon, but it began to rain so hard Elizabeth could barely see a foot in front of her.

She never possessed a good sense of direction. It was only through the grace of the Creator and her beloved elevated ancestors whose shoulders she stands upon that she got from Mississippi to Jersey without any serious mishaps.

Once the rain began to fall, Elizabeth got all turned around. She didn't know where the hell she was. She pulled over to get her bearings and wait out the flash storm.

Elizabeth just about jumped out of her skin when a nice-looking muscular youth with an infectious smile yanked the passenger-side door of her truck open, jumped in, and shut the door behind him.

What kind of place is this where folks jump in your car without so much as a by your leave? Elizabeth thought, pinch-lipped.

Elizabeth was of half a mind to reach under her car seat for her sawed-off shotgun and bust a Mississippi bullet in his young ass, but something stopped her.

"Before you get upset, ma'am," he said, making a calming gesture with his hands, "I need a really big favor. Please hear me out. If I don't get home within the next fifteen minutes," he continued, glancing at his watch, "my granny is gonna have my hide for dinner. Please, lady. Could you please give me a ride home right now so I can beat my granny home before she gets out of choir rehearsal?" he pleaded, as rainwater streamed down his face.

The truth of the matter was that he'd slipped out of the house to spend some quality time with his girlfriend, and now he had to haul ass before his granny returned home and found him gone. Colored kids were coming up missing in Jersey, his cousin Daniel among them. His grandmother issued explicit instructions for him not to leave the house.

Elizabeth glanced down at the gas gauge. Thanks to that nasty-ass gas attendant, she was getting perilously close to "E."

"I promise it's not far," he assured her.

Something in the kid's manner reminded Elizabeth of her son Calvin, causing her to immediately soften her expression.

"What's your name, Sugah?"

"My name is Henry Smith. But you can call me Muscles," he replied proudly, extending his wet hand for a shake.

Elizabeth wasn't too keen on physical contact under the best of circumstances, especially with strangers. You never know what demons are attached to their spirits. But she shook the young man's hand all the same, thinking he must have been raised right. At least he had good manners.

"My name is Betty Johnson," she said, trying her alias on for size. "You can call me Miss Betty. You know you like tah scared the living daylights out of me."

Muscles said he was sorry, and Betty believed him.

She scrutinized Henry "Muscles" Smith. She could smell mannish all over him. He was in that delicate stage between boy and manhood, where dreams are as big as the sky and the possibilities are endless—that is, until somebody makes him feel like he's less than a pile of hot horse shit, or he gets himself lynched.

The boy in him had to report back to his grandma's house before dark, while the man in him sported a big old hickey on the side of his neck, which told Betty he'd been messing around with somebody's daughter. Young Henry was still wet behind the ears and smellin' himself, alright.

Betty couldn't help but think about Calvin and what kind of man he would have grown up to be, had he been given half a chance. Thankfully, the rain stopped as quickly as it started.

"Okay, I'll give you a ride under one condition." Betty didn't miss Henry's immediate sigh of relief. "Do you know how to get to 1294 Arlington Avenue?"

The smile that came over that kid's face was bright enough to make the sun come out of hiding.

"Yes! I know exactly how to get there," he said excitedly. "My granny lives on the same street!"

"Well then, I think you got yourself a ride," Betty said, smiling back.

The rest of the time was spent with Muscles telling Betty which streets to turn on. A few minutes later, Betty was pulling in front of 1294 Arlington Avenue. Muscles' destination was two houses down.

"Thanks, Miss Betty. I really appreciate this ride," he said, opening the door to the truck.

"You're welcome, Sugah. And Muscles," she said, making him pause in his departure.

"Yes, ma'am, I mean, Miss Betty?" he added, staring at her nervously.

Muscles had been so intent upon getting to his grandma's house before she returned home that he hadn't noticed just how pretty Miss Betty was.

"I don't want to hear about you jumping in anybody else's car, ya hear? It's dangerous. Something bad coulda happened to you."

"I won't, Miss Betty. I promise."

"Alrighty then, wish me luck."

"Good luck, Miss Betty. And thanks again for the ride!" He jumped out of the car and sprinted to his grandmother's house.

CHAPTER FORTY-THREE

PALERMO HAD TAKEN to showing up at random times of the day and night to season his previous threat. After Loretta's last encounter with the frightening loan shark, she made a point to pay close attention to her surroundings so that he wouldn't catch her off guard ever again. She believed she was doing a stellar job of giving Palermo the slip.

Afraid to have a repeat performance of the bathroom debacle, Loretta hightailed it to Newark to stay at Althea's house, where she remained for nearly a week. Althea didn't ask her why she didn't want to stay in her own house, and Loretta didn't volunteer the information.

How in the world could she explain her belief that the spirit of her mother-in-law was haunting her?

Loretta would never forget what Althea told her after Albert's funeral. Her exact words had been, "God got you."

Those three words made Loretta realize she couldn't hide out in Newark forever. Determined to no longer live in fear, Loretta went home and trusted that the lord would work things out.

She placed an ad in the *Courier* for a boarder and hoped having someone else in the house would both discourage any future visitations and ease her financial burden.

Last night was the first time she'd slept in her own bed all week. Admittedly, she slept with her bedroom door locked, the lights on, and a bible at the head and foot of her bed, but at least she'd done it.

Loretta had even ventured out for groceries. She circled the block three times to make sure she wasn't being followed, parked around the corner from where she lived, and entered her house through the back door. She couldn't get her key in the lock quick enough.

Once she made it inside, Loretta pulled back the curtain in the living room just enough to peer out, sighing in relief when she didn't see the infamous brown Pontiac parked out front. All she could do was drop to her knees and praise the lord. God must have heard her prayers because a few hours later, a woman named Betty Johnson showed up.

⚬

"It's not much, but it's clean and comfortable," Loretta said while leading Betty up the stairs to the third-floor attic bedroom.

"I lost my husband a while back. This used to be his and his younger brother's childhood bedroom. I never have any guests, so I thought I would rent it out, you know, to help with the expenses." She opened the bedroom door.

"There is attic space and a crawl space annexed to the bedroom if you need to store anything. You can gain access to the attic down the hall, right next to the bathroom."

"I have a cat," Betty said hesitantly. Àse chose that moment to let out a loud "meow" in the pet carrier. "Her name is Àse."

"Well now, that's an odd but pretty name," Loretta replied.

"It means power."

Loretta peeped inside to get a look at the feline in question. "Oh my!" she exclaimed. "What happened to her eye?"

"She lost it in a fight with a bobcat," Betty responded. "She survived. The bobcat did not."

"Well, I see no reason your pet cannot stay just as long as you clean up behind her," Loretta said.

"Thank you." Betty let out a noticeable sigh of relief. She and Àse were a package deal. If Àse could not stay, neither could she.

Now that the issue of her beloved pet was off the table, Betty was becoming optimistic.

She liked Loretta Burkett immediately. There was something sad and extremely vulnerable about her. Betty wondered if the spirit of the big fat man that followed them upstairs was draining her joy. She could see the spirit just as clearly as she could see Loretta. She wondered who he was and why he had not gone into the divine light.

She put her bag and the pet carrier down and walked into the comfortably appointed, airy room. It was perfect. The walls were painted a soft shade of peach. There was a queen-sized bed with crisp white sheets and a gingham print bedspread. A hot summer breeze lifted the matching white curtains dressing the windows. The room smelled of fresh lemon, and the dark hardwood floor had a sheen that comes from Murphy's Oil and elbow grease.

"I'll take it!" Betty said, turning to her new landlady with a tremulous smile. The smile diminished in increments after her hasty outburst, finally disappearing altogether. She cleared her throat.

"I mean, I would love to take it. How much is the rent?" she asked anxiously.

Loretta noted Betty's anxiety. She could tell from Betty's clothes that she had fallen on hard times. She could also sense something inherently decent about her. Bottom line, Loretta was sick and tired of going to sleep with the lights on. She was tired of being afraid in her own house. It sure would be nice to have someone else in the house with her. She decided right then and there to rent the room to Betty.

"Well, since you have come all the way from Mississippi and will need time to get on your feet—and believe me, I know how that is—how 'bout you pay me fifty dollars a week? You are more than welcome to use the washer and dryer in the basement and the kitchen, but if you want a phone in your room, you will have to set up your own line. Does that sound reasonable to you?"

Betty was so happy, she wanted to kiss Loretta. Instead, she nodded with a tentative smile on her face. She had enough for two weeks' rent. She was determined to take up residence in this lovely house, fat spirit and all.

"Yes! That sounds absolutely perfect!" She blurted out.

❧

Betty was settling into her new life in Plainfield as well as could be expected—that is, if you don't take into account that she had yet to shed a single tear over the loss of her family. Whenever someone asked Betty about her family, she told them she had no one.

She hadn't been in Loretta Burkett's house a full week before she went to work on DeLonge's severed head. She'd kept it on dry ice all the way from Mississippi. Her first night on Arlington Avenue, she waited until Loretta went to sleep, wrapped it in plastic and buried it in the backyard.

Ten days later, she waited for Loretta to leave for choir rehearsal to dig the head up. The easiest way to clean a skull is by the maceration method. The head was already in an advanced stage of decay. Nature and excessive heat did most of the work. Betty took the stinking skull down to the basement to remove as much of the flesh and brain matter as she could. Then she placed the bloody skull inside a container and covered it with tap water. When Loretta mentioned the foul smell coming from the basement a few days later, Betty told her a rodent probably crawled inside a wall and died.

Every few days, Betty would water the rose bushes with the smelly water and put fresh water in the bucket holding the head. She laughed to herself when Loretta remarked on how nicely the roses were blooming. Once the water stopped stinking, Betty went about the thankless task of rinsing the skull and manually scrubbing off any remaining tissue. She did this in the washbasin next to the washing machine in Loretta's basement.

Once the skull was clean, she submerged it in a tub of hydrogen peroxide to whiten and sterilize it. A few days later, Betty removed the skull from the peroxide, rinsed it, and allowed it to dry on the altar she'd set up in the storage area annexed to her bedroom.

⁓

Betty secured the rental in Loretta Burkett's home on a Friday, and not a minute too soon. The Monday after she moved in, the old faithful farm truck that carried her from Mississippi to Jersey decided it had enough. The engine stubbornly refused to turn over when she put the key in the ignition. Until she could fix or replace the truck, Betty had no choice but to hoof it home each weeknight.

It was hot as hell on that first day Betty laced up her sturdy shoes, walked to Park Avenue, and caught the number eighteen bus to North Plainfield. She got off the bus at Green Brook Road and made the short walk to Rock Avenue to the nursing home with relative ease.

Getting home from work proved to be a bit more challenging. Betty worked the 3–11 P.M. shift. The bus from North Plainfield stopped running before she got off work. She could not spare the money for cab fare. Betty walked for the better part of a month before she and a coworker named Thomas started messing around, after which he started giving her a lift to and from work.

Betty and Thomas came together for the first time in one of the nursing home supply closets. Betty was looking for some Drano to clear out a clogged sink in one of the patient's bathrooms, and Thomas was looking to get the pipe in his pants unclogged. Without a word, he locked the door behind him and pulled the pants to

Betty's uniform down just far enough to slide inside her warm place nice and easy. Ten minutes later, Betty was exiting the supply closet with something closely resembling a serene expression and a pleasant soreness in her insides.

They soon established a routine, whereby Betty would sneak Thomas up to her room at least once a week and on Saturday evenings. It was comfortable and fun between her and Thomas, with no strings attached, just the way Betty liked it. Betty didn't know how Loretta would feel about her entertaining a man in her house, and she didn't intend to find out.

She intended to keep on sneaking Thomas upstairs until an opportune time arose to delicately broach the subject with her nice landlady.

CHAPTER FORTY-FOUR

"ARE YOU SURE you don't want to join me for church this morning?" Loretta asked with an anxious smile. She'd asked Betty the same question last Sunday and the Sunday before. Both times she had received a resounding, albeit polite, "No, thank you."

Betty's room was on the third floor of the house. It was difficult to tell if she was home. Loretta placed her ear to the bedroom door, waiting for a response from within.

She heard a rustling sound on the other side of the door and said, "I know you will enjoy the service. We have a dynamic pastor."

Loretta had become extremely fond of Betty in the short period she had been renting from her. It was nice to have someone else in the house, especially at night. Prior to Betty's arrival, Loretta had been a nervous wreck, imagining spooks behind every shadow and monsters lurking behind every door. There was a quiet strength about Betty. Her presence calmed Loretta's spirit and made her forget her troubles, at least for a little while.

"Thank you, but no, thank you," Betty said through the closed bedroom door. "I had a really hectic week at work. I think I will sleep in. Maybe next time," she added politely, knowing full well that the words "next time" actually translated to "nevah gonna happen."

Loretta was nothing if not persistent. She was determined to harvest a new servant for the lord. She made a mental note to ask Betty again next Sunday before making her way back downstairs and out the door.

If Loretta had known Betty's history, she could have saved herself a lot of time and trouble. The last time Betty set foot in a church was after that bastard of a husband of hers beat her second baby out of her. She remembered dropping to her knees at the altar, begging God to stop the agonizing cramps in her belly and save her unborn child. When her prayers went unanswered, she swore she would never step foot in a church again.

Nah, as much as I like my new landlady, I am going to have to pass on the church invite and the white Jesus that goes along with it, she thought humorlessly.

Betty didn't need a church. Her body was her temple. She would rely on *Damballah Weddo*, her spirit guides, and the elevated ancestors if she needed help.

Besides, Betty was not alone. She had a big, brawny man lying in her bed with an impressive hard-on that needed tending. They'd been drinking and fucking all night long. She planned to ride him one more time before she sent him home.

Loretta can do all the praying she wants, Betty thought. *I would much rather spend this lazy Sunday morning on all fours with some hard meat inside of me.*

Betty had been living in Jersey for a little over three weeks before she got lucky. Three weeks is a long time for a passionate woman to go without a man.

Before she met Thomas, she used to wake up each morning feeling like she was standing at the edge of a cliff, hardly able to breathe. Over time, a hunger built up inside of her, making her toss and turn in her sleep. The sultry nights only added to her frustration. Betty never did cotton to sticking her fingers inside her aching place. She craved the delicious weight of a man on top of her.

She raised her finger to her lips, signaling Thomas to remain silent. She waited until Loretta backed the car out of the driveway before taking his nice hard morning boner inside her mouth. She closed her eyes, delighting in the sweet, sticky taste of herself on him. Betty didn't need to go to church. The way Thomas was chanting "oh lawd" over and over again, as her head bobbed up and down on him, she knew it would not be long before he would be worshipping at the altar between her thighs. She didn't stop sucking on him until she polished every trace of herself off him.

A gust of hot wind rode through the open bedroom window to lift the edges of the white gingham curtains. The breeze danced on the surface of their sweaty skin for a moment before going still. Although the bedroom was hot as an oven, the heat didn't stop Betty from straddling Thomas, nor did it stop her from sinking her slick body down on his hardness until the sweaty, curly hairs between their respective thighs met. Thomas wasn't holding like the feds, but he had enough to please. She could feel him real good.

Betty started doing spiritual readings and skull work on the side to earn some extra money to repair the truck. It worked out well, since Loretta spent nearly all day in church on Sundays, leaving Betty free run of the house to do whatever she wanted. She had a reading scheduled in three hours. She wanted Thomas gone way before then.

With the specific goal of getting Thomas out of the house in mind, Betty grabbed hold of his shoulders at the same time that he grabbed hold of her fat ass, and she rode that man as if her life depended on it. She rode Thomas as if the house was on fire, and the burning ceiling was about to cave in. She rode him like she had to get the last nut of her entire life before the house burned to the ground. She rode him like he was the dream man she could never have.

"Damn, Betty, you got some goddamn good pussy," Thomas exclaimed, slapping her ass cheeks until they jiggled. Thomas was a big, Black, South Carolina, *Geechee* man, with a pretty white smile and a fine set of bowlegs. He wasn't a fancy lover with grand gestures and flowery words, but he got the job done.

Betty let go of his shoulders to hold on to the headboard, allowing her heavy breasts to swing in his face. Thomas looked like he had died and gone to heaven. He did a slow pump and grind against her sweat-slick body, bobbing his head to latch onto Betty's pebble-hard nipples with his hungry lips. He'd been dreaming about those titties and the secrets she was hiding under her unflattering uniform since the first day she walked past him at work, with her tall, fine, chocolate self.

Betty wasn't shy. She pounded her sweet nether lips against Thomas so hard, his ashy toes were curling into the sheet.

Slinging a heavy mop all day and walking home every night for nearly a month had slimmed Betty's buxom farm-fed size-sixteen frame down to a nice tight size twelve real quick. Despite the rapid weight loss, Betty still had curves in all the right places. Thomas couldn't get enough of her.

There is majick in sexual energy—sweet majick. Their bodies propelled the headboard into the wall, creating a staccato rhythm loud enough for that sweet sex energy to travel through the open bedroom window to kiss the ivy clinging to the side of the house.

Thomas was gibbering pure Gullah nastiness when Betty spread her thick thighs so that he could get a good look at what he was moving around in. She slid one hand between her legs to rub herself in a circular motion, building up the friction she needed to gain her release. She was a lusty lover. Her sexual essence was strong. All she had to do was close her eyes and imagine the lips suckling at her breasts and the hardness stirring the pot of juice inside her willing body belonged to her dream lover, and her female essence came down like Niagara Falls.

"Dis some good, ole, country, snappin' pussy!" Thomas shouted, before sucking in a breath to shoot his wad. Betty threw her head back to ride the wave of her orgasm.

There is something a little obscene about pleasuring yourself on a Sunday morning, especially if you are under the microscope of broad daylight, with Àse relaxing on the sill of the open window and the sound of your neighbor's gospel music filtering in.

Betty slumped against Thomas, totally spent. Now that the urgency of her need had been assuaged, she wanted Thomas gone— not now, but *right* now. She could no longer stand the sight of him. She made her desires evident when he tried to kiss her and even more so when he asked if he could take a shower with her before his departure. Betty didn't do kissing, and she damned sure didn't want to shower with anyone.

Those acts required a level of intimacy Betty was ill-equipped to provide, ranking on a par with going to church with a man or meeting his entire family for Sunday dinner. Betty could tell Thomas's feelings were hurt. She couldn't bring herself to care.

He needs to take his funky ass home and shower there.

No sooner did the door close behind Thomas before Betty was up and out of the bed. She changed the stained bedding, after which she took a quick shower. She crawled between a set of crisp, clean sheets that didn't hold a single trace of Thomas, as happy as a fat cat in a cool bowl of cream.

The sound of the next-door neighbor's Sunday morning gospel music drifted into her bedroom window. The words "Blessed assurance, Jesus is mine; Oh what a foretaste of glory divine," were the last words Betty heard before she drifted off to sleep and into a vivid dream in which she saw two women from the Motherland.

They were naked from the waist up, with heavy tribal scarification covering their faces and torsos. One had a hatchet for lips, and the other's lips were oversized razor blades. Both were bending forward to give Betty the kiss of spiritual and physical death.

CHAPTER FORTY-FIVE

BETTY ROSE FOR work the next day weighed down in spirit. She easily interpreted the troubling dream.

Somebody is talkin' shit behind my back, she surmised. *Beloved Elevated Ancestors and Spirit Guide Egun, please reveal the guilty party to me so that I can deal with them accordingly.*

Betty knew something was off when Thomas didn't pick her up for work on Monday afternoon. She doubted the rides would continue now that he had seen her true colors.

So be it. That's okay. I was walking before I met him, and I can keep on walking, she thought, stepping off the porch to make the short hot walk to the bus stop.

That's when she saw them: two fat black crows with cold human eyes, sitting on the telephone line in front of the house. She would have paid them no mind had it not been for their eyes following her every move and her recent dream. Something bad was gonna happen. She just knew it.

⌘

"Betty, you need to take care of room 215 right now."

The young nurse issued the order and kept walking past Betty, automatically assuming her order would be carried out. Betty wasn't

295

accustomed to taking orders from anyone. She was about two seconds from sticking her foot up that nurse's skinny ass. Instead, she slipped inside the break room and put a little sumthin' sumthin' inside that low-fat shit she eats for lunch.

If you don't know who ya messin' with, you need to ask somebody, bitch, she thought, making her way to her cart.

She walked into the supply room to find Thomas replenishing his supplies. They exchanged a brief look but did not speak to each other. She could see by the look in his eyes and his overall demeanor that he still wanted her. He soon proved her right by brushing up against her when she bent over to pick up a bottle of the industrial cleaner they used to mop the floors.

His sex was hard as new math. The brief contact caused a temporary stirring in Betty's loins. She intentionally ignored it. It was Thomas who had been spreading rumors about her with the nursing home staff.

I can't stand a man who gossips and whines like a baby. You can rub against me all you want, Thomas. Trust and believe, that ship has sailed. She gathered everything she needed and left without a backward glance.

⤌

Betty entered room 215 to find soiled bed linen and vomit splatter on the floor. The sour stench of vomit, piss, and shit was coming from a wizened gray-haired harridan who had called Betty a nigger the Friday before.

I hope that bitch chokes the next time she throws up, Betty thought vindictively. Emitting a sigh of resignation, she got to work cleaning up the nasty mess.

The day sped by quickly. Betty looked at the clock behind the second-floor nurse's station on her way to the next room. It was

9:00 P.M. She had two more hours to go before quitting time and six rooms left to clean. She was right on schedule.

Betty worked methodically, moving from room to room, emptying the wastepaper baskets, cleaning the bathrooms, and mopping the floors like a robot. She accomplished her duties, no matter how distasteful, without feeling or thought, stubbornly refusing to think about anything other than putting one foot in front of the other to perform the tasks she was being paid for.

She never called a patient by their given name, preferring instead to identify them by their sickness or their room number. For example, she referred to the patient in room 219 as "heart attack" and the patient in the bed next to 221 as "pain-in-the-ass stroke."

Betty always saved room 279 for last. The patient in 279 was a convicted serial killer and a member of an organization called NAMBLA, The North America Man/Boy Love Association, where grown men get their rocks off by molesting little boys.

Huh, leave it to white folks to start a club doing some scary shit like that, Betty thought.

Room 279 went rogue and started snatching kids off the street. Betty did not know exactly what 279 did to his victims, but she clearly overheard an aide say he ate choice parts of them and hid what was left of their bodies when he was done.

That ain't nuthin' but some sick white people shit, she thought, nodding in disgust. *You won't catch no Colored folk killin' a bunch of kids and eatin' 'em. That's for damn sure. And now I gotta clean his damn room!*

The medics were wheeling that smart-mouthed nurse out on a stretcher as Betty pushed her cleaning cart down the hall.

৶

With aching arms and a sense of fatigue that went past anything physical, Betty dragged the heavy bucket and mop to the end of the hallway. She took a deep calming breath before she opened the door.

The patient whose room she was about to enter was under twenty-four-hour police guard. Three cops from the Union County Sheriff's Department rotated on guard duty. Betty was fearful one of them would make a connection between her and the woman who had gone missing in Mississippi and try to haul her Black ass downtown for questioning. She knew to keep her head down and her mouth shut while in their presence. For once she was grateful most white folks think all Coloreds look alike.

Considering the string of dead bodies she left in Mississippi, Betty did not feel comfortable while in the presence of white people in general and white police in particular. She doubted she ever would. She was relieved when she entered the room to find the pudgy cop on duty sprawled in the seat, slack-jawed, and fast asleep with a newspaper spread open on his lap. A soft snore slipped past his thin lips. He was out cold.

Two seventy-nine's dark brown, pain-filled eyes followed Betty's every move as she silently went about setting the room to rights. As a precaution, and to ensure the safety of the nursing home staff, the police required that he be shackled to the hospital bed at all times.

After mopping the floor, Betty leaned against the mop handle to get a real good look at him. Two seventy-nine was a godawful mess. While he was awaiting trial in the Union County Jail, several inmates attacked him in the communal shower. Apparently, even the most hardened criminals take exception to heinous crimes committed against innocent children.

Black and blue marks covered his arms. Deep purple bruises covered his face and throat, and his lips were splattered with cuts.

He was deathly pale, with limp strands of wispy brown hair plastered to his forehead. Betty imagined his skin would be clammy to the touch. He'd suffered extensive damage to his internal organs, particularly his heart, lungs, and kidneys, which explained the respirator, heart monitor, and kidney dialysis machine.

Betty could tell by the cast of his swollen lips that he wanted to say something, but the trach tube in his throat prohibited him from speaking. For the first time since the death of her son and brothers, the corners of Betty's lips turned up in a genuine smile.

I'm glad they fucked him up. I wished they had killed him.

Betty was amused by the shackles because 279 wasn't in any condition to do shit to anybody. The shiny silver shackles around his wrists matched the railings on both sides of the hospital bed. The prison jewelry was in direct contrast to the wires connecting him to the life-sustaining machinery which was taking up most of the space in the room. If it were up to Betty, she would smother that piece of shit in his hospital bed. Better yet, she would do to him exactly what he'd done to his innocent victims, except for the fucking and cannibalism part.

And to think the local police were kicking in doors and dragging Colored men out of their homes in the middle of the night to stand in line-ups. All the while, this sick piece of shit was right next door in Westfield, snatching and killing innocent little kids and eating 'em, she thought bitterly. *Not only does he live to stand trial, but they make sure he gets the best medical care available. If he was Colored and living in Mississippi, he'd be skinned alive and hanging from a poplar tree for killing all of those little white boys. Hell, a couple of Colored kids been missing in Plainfield for weeks, and ain't nobody getting upset about that.* Betty had to force herself to calm down because of the sheer injustice of it.

Rumor had it the authorities hoped to keep him alive long enough for him to disclose the location of the bodies of nine of his victims, so that the families could have closure.

Betty stood at patient 279's bedside, literally willing him to die. Suddenly, whether by providence or happenstance, he stopped breathing. A series of alarms sounded, jerking the derelict cop awake.

Before Betty knew it, the room was flooded with medical personnel feverishly working to keep the patient alive. Betty knew it was too late. She felt the ice-cold touch of his spirit rubbing against her as it departed the room, leaving the smell of a thousand rotten eggs behind. She mumbled, "See you in hell, bastard," and silently slipped out of the room.

CHAPTER FORTY-SIX

PLACING THE EVENTS of the day behind her, Betty punched out in preparation for the long, hot walk home. Since she and Thomas were no longer speaking, she could forget about a lift. It was nearly October, close to midnight, and an unprecedented ninety-eight degrees out.

I'm not looking forward to the walk home, but I'll be double damned if I ask that pathetic Geechee for a ride. She grabbed her stuff out of her locker and headed for the exit. The humidity smacked her in the face as soon as she stepped outside.

As Betty walked, she noticed that every tree had fliers with pictures of two kids on them. Daniel Calhoun and Ernie Wilson were the last of a string of Colored youths who had gone missing in the area. The cops couldn't blame this one on 279, whose given name was Morris Fischer. All his victims were white, and he was already in custody when the last two kids went missing.

Betty was about a block away from the nursing home when a police cruiser pulled up alongside her with the passenger window rolled down. Its occupant was a member of Plainfield PD. The fact that the cop was cruising out of his jurisdiction immediately raised Betty's hackles.

The cream cheese bagel she had eaten earlier that day was

curdling in her belly, making her feel as if she needed a bowel move-ment. Betty knew what she was feeling was nothing but a good old-fashioned dose of self-righteous anger, the kind of impotent anger that makes you sick to your stomach and gets you in a heap of trouble if you don't keep your shit in check.

The cops in Plainfield had a reputation, and it was not a good one. There were only five Colored cops on the force and, according to Loretta, they were treated worse than Mississippi slaves. The last thing Betty needed tonight was a confrontation with one of those white devils in blue. The cop slowed the car to a near-stop and motioned Betty over.

He may think I look dumb 'cause I'm Colored, but I damn sure ain't stupid. He's out of his effin' mind if he thinks I'm getting in that squad car, Betty thought.

She kept walking, keenly aware of his malicious gaze on her. The cop did not say a word. But then again, he didn't have to. His intent to intimidate was patently clear. Too bad his tactic didn't work on Betty. She'd already been through the worst thing that could possi-bly happen to her.

I guess that peckerwood's wolf mama and jackal pappy forgot to tell him that you ain't supposed to fuck with folks who ain't afraid to die, Betty thought bitterly, as she ate up the distance between Green Brook Manor and 1294 Arlington Avenue with long measured strides. Betty knew the cop was shadowing her to start some trouble.

He's lucky I don't have "Lucy," "Ricky," "Fred," or "Ethel" with me, she thought, *because if I did, I would show him the true definition of trouble.* "Punk ass motherfucker!" she mumbled under her breath.

"Ain't it funny?" she said to the universe. "I ain't done a god-damn thing to this asshole. He hates me just because I'm Colored. Well guess what, motherfucker? I hate you too! Shit! Things ain't no better here in the north than they are in Mississippi." She sneered. "You can run all you want, but you can't outrun ya skin.

I'll tell you one thing," she said, continuing to talk to herself as she walked and getting madder by the minute. "You let him get his ghost-faced ass out of that cop car and fuck with me tonight. I got something for him." She fisted her set of house keys, prepared to aim for his eyes and then go for the throat the minute he got close enough.

The thought of fighting the cop off with a set of house keys somehow struck Betty as funny. She laughed like a patient in the psych ward at Green Brook Manor. She stopped laughing the minute the cop drove off, thinking the only reason the bastard moved on was because he probably found himself a better target. By the time Betty made it to the intersection of Somerset and Front, she understood who the cop's next target was, and got sick to her stomach.

Three Colored youths, all male, were walking down Somerset Street toward Front Street when the cop demanded they come to the squad car for questioning. Betty's breath hitched in her chest when she recognized one of the kids was her young neighbor Muscles, whom she'd grown very fond of.

It was about 11:30 P.M. The downtown area was lit up like Times Square but empty as a schoolyard at midnight. Three Colored kids and a racist cop is a guaranteed prescription for trouble. This was the something bad she feared would happen.

One of the more vocal youths replied to the cop's baseless command. "For what? We ain't do nothing."

That was all the excuse the bastard in blue needed. He jumped out of the car with his gun drawn. The kids broke camp, all three of them running in separate directions.

Betty picked up her pace.

The cop caught one of the kids on Park Avenue and dragged him into the United National Bank parking lot. Betty said a silent prayer of thanks that it was not Muscles. She ducked behind a parked car across the street to conceal herself. She was in no position to get in

Plainfield PD's crosshairs. If they were to get wind of the carnage she left back in Mississippi, they would throw her Black ass *under* the jail, or worse.

Betty's mind may not care whether she lived or died, but apparently her body gave a damn about what happened to it. She was forced to hide and watch the sordid scene unfold right before her eyes.

⁂

What Betty witnessed that night blasted through the brick wall of numbness encasing her heart. It forced her to feel everything she'd kept banked inside since Fruit, Junior, and her son were murdered.

The sounds that kid made while the cop repeatedly struck him with the butt of his pistol reminded Betty of the brutal blows Calvin must have endured at the hand of DeLonge and his vigilantes. The boy's ragged screams ripped away the tenuous scab that was holding Betty's sanity together, allowing the darkness to rise to the surface and bubble over.

There was no more sass, no bravado, just a scared, young Colored boy begging the cop not to kill him. The kid was screaming for his mother, his father, for *somebody* to help him. And all he had was broken Betty, kneeling behind a car across the street, as an impotent witness. This was somebody's child being beaten worse than a dog. Like it or not, Betty's hands were metaphorically tied.

The cop was merciless. He beat the kid until his chest started heaving and sweat dripped off his face. He beat him until his arm got tired and his hat fell off his head. The sonofabitch beat on that kid long after he stopped moving. And Betty witnessed it all.

Betty couldn't help but wonder. *Did my baby scream like that? Did he call my name? Did he beg his murderers for mercy?*

The thought was too much for her to bear. She clapped both hands over her mouth to keep from screaming as scalding hot tears burned the flesh on her cheeks. She knew there was nothing she could do. She could not protect this kid any more than she had protected her son. The reality nearly broke her.

Finally exhausted, the cop lowered his weapon. He dug deep inside his pocket and planted a small plastic bag containing white powder in the kid's pocket. And then the bastard had the gall to read the unconscious kid his rights.

"You are under arrest for possession of a controlled substance with intent to distribute within a thousand feet of a school." He then dragged the unconscious youth to the nearby squad car and threw him in the back.

Betty waited until the taillights on the cop car diminished and disappeared before hurrying across the street to retrieve the forgotten hat. It had his name inside the sweaty rim: "Paul R. Pressley."

She hurried home, glancing over her shoulder every few seconds. The streets were dark and deserted. She could see no one, yet she sensed she was being followed.

Betty's instincts were dead on. Hindrance assigned the demon, Agares, the task of locating the human named Elizabeth François, and so he had. Agares, who had shapeshifted into the form of a crow, was shadowing her every step, taking great pains not to be seen.

Not only had his master commanded Agares to determine her location, but he threatened him with a thousand tortures if he so much as touched a hair on the human's head. Curious to see first-hand what it was about this particular human that held his master so enthralled, the demon drew closer. From what Agares could see, the human had very little hair to speak off. In fact, her hair was less than three inches long all over. Agares, who preferred the long, thick bushy locks of ancient African queens, could not see her appeal. In his excitement at having run his prey to ground, Agares brushed against a dead tree limb, causing it to crack.

Betty stopped in her tracks and turned toward the noise. Her narrow-eyed gaze appeared to cut through the bushes concealing the demon. Even though Agares knew she could not see him, he knew she sensed his presence. He looked into her dark luminous eyes, and he knew why Hindrance wanted her so badly. The human's eyes were lit with a fire that could only have originated in The Hells.

She is a daughter of darkness.

CHAPTER FORTY-SEVEN

Blood Falls Mansion, coordinates 162°16288'E77°43.329'S,

Southern Victoria Land, McMurdo Dry Valley, Antarctica.

AFTER TIRELESSLY SCOURING the east coast in search of the human thwart his king charged him to locate, and coming away empty-handed, General Simeon Ramuel opted to shapeshift into the form of a Wandering Albatross for his return trip home.

He had hoped the long arduous flight from the US to the frigid climes of the Antarctic would take him back to his former implacable lack of emotion, so that he could clear his mind of Loretta Burkett's sweet surrender, and do his job.

Despite Simeon's best efforts, when he touched down in his front yard shortly before daybreak, unbidden memories of Loretta's lush body, coupled with the exquisite taste of her rich human blood, threatened to be his undoing.

The unfamiliar emotions superseded Simeon's awareness of an elderly Caucasian human whose inquisitive milky-blue eyes were even now tracking his every move. He assumed the man was a member of the nearby US Army research facility, but was too weary in mind, body and spirit to do anything about it. He willed his body to convert to its comely male form, and thought no further on the matter as he strode up the walkway to enter his house.

Upon entering, Simeon found General Ajuma Akibeel, who'd already made himself at home, sitting in his great room with a stiff drink in hand. Simeon was a loner. However, this time, the General who prized solitude above all things, welcomed the company. There was much on his mind that he wished to unload.

❧

Simeon walked past Ajuma naked as the day he was born, and without a word, made his way upstairs, taking two steps at a time. He returned moments later, tying the sash of a black silk robe around his waist.

"How fare thee?" he asked by way of greeting.

"I am well," Ajuma replied, extending a battle-hardened hand in brotherhood, which Simeon readily accepted.

"Were you able to garner anything of value from Solonge?" Ajuma asked, referring to the infamous Nephilim soothsayer, who resides among humans on the wrong side of the Dark Veil.

"No. I have not seen Solonge," Simeon replied cryptically, evading eye contact as he made his way to the well-stocked bar to pour himself a drink.

How do I explain my hesitance to address Solonge without explaining the longstanding acrimony she has for me? Simeon wondered. *Solonge would sooner give information to a demon than aid me in my quest.*

Ajuma raised a glass of absinthe to his lips before speaking. "Care to elaborate?" He patiently awaited Simeon's response as the strong spirit burned a fiery trail from his throat to his belly.

"I have searched everywhere but New Jersey. There is no way that I can go anywhere in that State, and not see her, if only from a distance," Simeon confessed, bowing his head in shame.

Ajuma didn't need to ask who Simeon was referring to. He

suspected Simeon's unusual attraction to the human named Loretta Burkett. Simeon's next words proved his suspicion correct.

"I purchased the deeds to the human's house and business," Simeon blurted out.

"What do you intend to do with the properties, brother?"

"Nothing at all," Simeon replied.

"Both properties were up for sheriff's sale. I intend to ensure she has a roof over her head for as long as she wants or needs it."

Simeon didn't add that he would protect her with his life or that he'd placed a spiritual shield of protection around her residence to ensure her safety. But he didn't have to, because Ajuma saw what was in Simeon's heart, even if he could not.

Simeon has strong feelings for this human, Ajuma thought, heaving a sigh of commiseration. He knew better than most that relationships between humans and Nephilim never end well, and that Simeon was in for a world of pain.

May the Ancient of Days have mercy on him.

McMurdo Research Station, the Southern Tip of Ross Island, approximately 850 miles north of the South Pole

"I tell you, Josh, I know what I saw!"

World-renowned geologist Admiral Craig C. Goodie rose from his chair to lock eyes with his first and second in command, Lieutenant Commanders, (LCDR) Joshua Shinn, and Scott Ferrara, with a mutinous expression.

Shinn and Ferrara are part of a task force headed by Admiral Goodie, funded by the National Science Foundation, and coined Operation Deep Freeze V. The study involves the United States Air Force, Navy, Army, and Coast Guard, and provides operational and logistical support for scientific research activities in Antarctica.

Although significantly younger than Goodie, who was knocking on the door to his nineties, Shinn, a botanist and Ferrara, a biologist, were well-known, respected scientists in their own right. Both could attest that, despite his advanced age, Craig Goodie's tall, stoop-shouldered frame housed a surprisingly fit body and an exceptionally brilliant intellect.

"I was out before dawn, collecting microbe specimens about a mile away from McMurdo Dry Valley, when I observed the largest Wandering Albatross I'd ever seen. Its sharp talons and hooked beak could easily capture and tear a man apart," he repeated for what seemed like the hundredth time.

"It was flying due northeast towards Blood Falls with a wingspan of at least 10.4 meters. I hopped on the skidoos (snowmobile), and tracked it to the mansion on Blood River, where the predatory avian landed in the front yard. Moments later, it turned into a muscular, naked black man.

It was minus thirty degrees out with blustery winds, and yet, "the thing," because I dare not characterize what I saw as a man, strolled up the walkway to the porch just as nice as you please. Taking his time as if the sub-zero temperature and gale force winds had absolutely no physical effect on him at all, he walked inside and closed the door behind him. It was then that I noticed a replica of the Wandering Albatross carved into the surface of the front door and tattooed on his back," he concluded.

Shinn exchanged a look of disbelief with Ferrara, thinking their esteemed leader had finally lost all of his marbles. Shinn was the first to respond.

"Craig, that can't be possible. No way can a human withstand those temperatures unclothed, even for a minute, without going into shock. And I don't even want to address the improbability of a predatory avian transporting into a man, or vice versa," he replied respectfully.

"I am not accustomed to being made out a liar," Craig reposted, before adding in a softer, but decidedly more conciliatory tone, "Of course, I know what I saw was impossible, Josh."

"I believe you, Craig," Scott interjected softly. "I say we pay the owner of the mansion a surprise visit."

∽

A dense blanket of fog rolled in, shrouding the vast icy landscape in a caliginous mist, as the three scientists sliced through the snow, dressed like Inuks in their Army-issued skidoos. The sudden advent of fog made it difficult to see more than a foot ahead.

In seemingly no time at all, Blood Falls, the five-story tall waterfall that flows red, briny water onto Lake Bonney, appeared out of nowhere, leaving them spellbound.

They shut off their transport to take in the edifice constructed of ice, steel, and glass that sat on the edge of the falls like a picture in a frame. Its stark, haunting beauty stained the backdrop of fresh-fallen snow like a blood-red ruby on a canvas of pristine white.

Admiral Goodie shouted over the harsh winds to be heard.

"Blood Falls flows from Taylor Glacier into West Lake Bonney. The microbe-rich waters of the falls is derived from iron salts in the ice that oxidize when exposed to oxygen," he explained, pointing at the blood-red portion of the waterfalls that was frozen in place.

"So. Do we walk up to the door and ring the bell?" Scott asked.

"You say the bird turned into a black man?" Josh asked.

"Yes," Craig replied over the angry sound of the wind.

"Well, then, I say we force our way in," Josh stated, pulling a gun from his pocket.

∽

Simeon and Ajuma smelled the humans from a mile away.

"It appears the Caucasian who witnessed me flying home this

morning has returned with reinforcements," Simeon said, stating the obvious.

Their superior sense of hearing picked up the cadence of three distinctive sets of heartbeats sounding as loud as a symphony of base drums.

"Isn't that what Caucasoid humans always do, stick their long pointy noses where they don't belong? Why not make it easy for them?" Ajuma suggested, unlocking a side door with his mind.

"Yes. Why not, brother," Simeon responded, dropping fang and bulking up for battle as two of the three men breached his place of peace. One of them walked to the front door to allow the third break-in artist entry.

"The Whites are far too curious for their own good," Ajuma opined, watching the men on one of five security screens.

"Too bad, curiosity killed the cat," Simeon added, placing his drink on a coaster.

"I hear there is no police force, judiciary, or prisons on Antarctica. Anyone suspected of a crime is subject to the laws of their country of origin," Ajuma stated, his breath hitching in excitement.

"You are correct, brother. That being said, I say we give the Caucasoid home-invaders a warm welcome," Simeon stated, locking the doors with his mind and trapping the scientists inside for all time.

CHAPTER FORTY-EIGHT

601 High Street, Newark, NJ 07102

SOLONGE OF THE House of Shemyaza tore her gaze away from her crystal ball with an inscrutable expression.

I have witnessed the beginning of the end, she thought, grimacing from the wicked pulsing pain that was her constant companion. *The human witches will cast their spell and unleash an unspeakable evil upon humanity and the Ancient of Day's holy angels. The skies will rain blood.*

With shaking hands, she covered her ruined face to prepare for her uninvited guest. *The die has been cast. And there is nothing anyone could do to stop it. There will be dark days ahead.*

After centuries of isolation behind the Dark Veil, Solonge chose to take her chances among low vibrational humans than continue to live among members of the Nephilim Nation who despise or fear her.

It is far better to sit high and look low in a city filled with weak, unsuspecting humans than to abide in splendor among my own.

Few know Solonge is the anonymous owner of "The Dark Side",

an underground nightclub that caters to fallen angels, Nephilim, devils, demons, imps, witches, warlocks, mages; and other things "that go bump in the night." She'd opened the well-known preternatural meeting place as a designated no kill zone for one purpose.

One day, Zuet's son Hindrance and the other demons responsible for killing my children and destroying my life will walk through the door of this club. And when they do, I fully intend to make them pay for their crimes.

On the rare occasions when Solonge consents to a private audience, she is garbed in a black-on-black shador, identical to those worn by Sunni and Shiite Muslim women. Tonight was no different. Everything was covered but one eye. She wore a black patch over the other one.

Solonge was seated behind a desk that dwarfed her wizened figure when Simeon arrived on the date and time she'd expected him. Solonge knew things, often before they occurred.

"Well, to what do I owe this unexpected visit, General Ramuel?" she asked, knowing full well the only reason this ruthless Brother of the Dark Veil would deign to grace her establishment with his murderous presence would be for information, to satisfy his dark desires, or a little of both.

Maybe I will hand my enemies over to the psycho Nephilim who is standing in front of me right now, she thought, looking at Simeon with a speculative expression.

Or better yet, how about I leave my enemies to the none-too-tender mercy of the sadistic Gibborim soldier who filmed the torture session King Zion thinks no one knows about, she added, with her face twisted beneath her nijab in something resembling a grin.

Until the day I have Hindrance in my sights, I intend to keep the doors to The Dark Side open to one and all, she vowed, holding on to the decision that frequently placed her in a perfect position to see and hear things she would not ordinarily be privy to.

❧

"I seek information about a witch the Ancient of Days has designated as a thwart against Zuet. Have you knowledge of the one I seek?" Simeon asked, getting right to the point.

"Of course I do," she said while lifting an ornate teapot to pour some tea into a delicate matching cup. Simeon waited patiently while she struggled with the heavy teapot, shaking his head to indicate he did not desire a cup when she offered to pour a second cup for him. Solonge did not return her attention to Simeon until after she poured a healthy dollop of whiskey from a bottle she pulled out of her desk drawer.

Well-aware of the horror that lay hidden beneath Solonge's layers of dark clothing, Simeon turned away as she raised her nijab to take a sip. He swallowed to keep his gorge from rising.

He can't stand to look at my ugly face, Solonge thought, laughing to herself. *Fucking hypocrite! I know what you and that monster Ajuma Akibeel did to those white scientists.*

❧

Just about every Nephilim youth learned the sad story of Solonge and her husband Tremaine on their parent's knee. Simeon had been the one to track her down, but it was Generals Ajuma Akibeel, Nicodemus Urakabarameel and their King, who rescued Solonge from the 5th level of the hells after Hindrance and his vicious imps had at her and her two children. They'd been too late to save her children, but were able to get Solonge out.

Simeon shook his head to remove the stain on his memory of the damage the demons had wrought on the once beautiful female;

wondering if the Generals and their king had done her a favor by saving her life.

It may have been kinder to let her die, he surmised. *But I didn't come here to speculate on the mercy of euthanasia. I came here to get information about a witch.*

§

"The one you seek is lying in a hospital, riddled with cancer and close to death. Her name is Sharon Samuels. You are already too late to save her, or this city, Simeon," she warned. "Both she and the city will be reborn, and many of you along with it. There is nothing you can do for the Samuels human; but there is hope you might reach the other one in time."

Simeon said: "Wait a minute," with a frown. "I was told there were three."

"There were. But one of the human thwarts, a preacher of a church not twenty-five miles from here, is as good as dead already. There is nothing you can do to save him. I saw his death in my crystal ball. If you don't move quickly, the last of the human thwarts will die as well."

Solonge took another sip of the heavily laced tea, allowing Simeon time to mull over her cryptic words about the ultimate demise of two of the three thwarts, the destruction and rebirth of the city, and the potential effect the foregoing occurrences would have on the members of the Nephilim Nation.

No matter how much she was pressed, Solonge never gave a straight answer to a question; always preferring to change the subject or respond in parables. Tonight was no different.

"General Ramuel, will you be returning this evening to satisfy your unique needs?" She asked as Simeon made to take his leave. "I can have a room and a succubus ready for you.

Not in the mood?" she taunted when he ignored her barbs.

"Perhaps you can invite the human female whose home and business you recently paid off? I'm sure she will be more than happy to reward you for your generosity." Simeon's sharp intake of breath was all the reward Solonge needed.

Simeon temporarily froze with his hand on the door. Time stood still as the sadistic, Nephilim warrior turned to level Solonge with a narrow-eyed, chilling stare. Solonge met his gaze boldly.

Simeon squelched his desire to rip Solonge's hideous head from her shoulders and slam her frail body against the wall until she was a pile of bloody pulp.

I don't know where to start my search for the other thwart, so you get to live another day, bitch, he thought, ghosting away from the object of his cold, calculated rage.

He had a very long night ahead of him.

CHAPTER FORTY-NINE

1294 Arlington Avenue, Plainfield, NJ 07060

WHAT WAS THAT?

Loretta sat up in bed like a ball fired from a smoking cannon. She'd been nursing an overall sense of disquiet for the past week and hadn't had a good night's sleep since. The feeling intensified when she returned home from bible study to find a letter from the bank informing her that the house and the Melting Pot building were sold at sheriff's sale to S. Ramuel & Company.

The only information the bank would give Loretta when she called was that the principal shareholder of the company was an out-of-state developer. The letter stated the contents of the Melting Pot were to be sold at auction on a date to be advised.

As troubling as the news was, Loretta couldn't concern herself with the ramifications of the recent sale.

Someone is in my house.

She remained as still as a post, straining to hear the house speak over the soft drone of voices on the TV.

I could've sworn I heard someone walking around in the kitchen, she thought, frowning.

Chalking it up to an overactive imagination, she expelled an exaggerated sigh of relief when her irrational fear was met with a poignant, mocking silence.

"This must be what hell feels like," Loretta said to no one in particular.

She wiped the avalanche of sweat pouring from her brow and slid closer to the side of the bed nearest to the door, leaving the real estate to the right empty in remembrance of the flawed, insecure man who'd once slept there.

Yes. I miss Albert. Especially on nights like this, she silently confessed, acknowledging that the TV served as a woefully inadequate substitute for her husband's slightly annoying and sorely missed masculine snores.

Her eyes scanned the environs of the bedroom, taking in the prison of her own making. Before retiring for the night, Loretta had closed and locked the bedroom door, and wedged a chair beneath the doorknob, barricading herself inside the stifling hot bedroom as securely as a death row inmate's prison cell.

The night before, she'd done everything short of nailing the windows shut, to protect herself from a ghostly incursion, effectively trapping herself inside what amounted to a roiling five-hundred-degree oven of fear.

The sealed window, barricaded door, and the fact that every light in the room was on was, in Loretta's mind, proof-positive that she was no longer operating with a full deck. That she was seeing and hearing stuff that wasn't there escalated her self-diagnosis to a level of bat shit, certified, crazy, and she knew it.

Loretta lowered her head to the pillow, lying directly in the path of hot air flowing from the ineffective box fan sitting on a folding chair at the foot of her bed.

She laid there, counting the highway of prominent cracks in the ceiling, afraid of what might come next.

❧

Shouldn't Betty be home by now? Loretta wondered, trying to shake off the debilitating fatigue and the uncomfortable feeling of someone or something watching her.

She glanced at the clock on her nightstand, rubbing her eyes against the harsh glare of the brightly lit room. The green numerals on the clock's face read 11:49 P.M.

A few minutes later, the dreaded sign-off video appeared on the TV. A decidedly white male voice alerted the viewing public of the end of broadcasting for the night, followed by the playing of the Star-Spangled Banner. The screen then filled with snow, and the unpleasant sound of static eclipsed the contents of her mind. Loretta wanted to turn the lights and the TV off, but she was as afraid to leave the psychological security of her bed, as she was to see what lay behind the curtain of darkness.

It was now 12:01 A.M.

Awful things happen after midnight, she thought, gnawing at the flesh on her bottom lip, a nervous habit she'd adopted as a young child. *At least they do for me.*

Loretta offered to pick Betty up from work. And as desperately as she needed the money, had even informed Betty of her intention to waive her rent until she could get that beat-up old truck of hers up and running. She'd been willing to do just about anything to have another living, breathing, human being in the house to mitigate her fear. She'd been dumbfounded when Betty declined her offer.

Why in the world would she turn down a free ride? It's hot as hell out there. Shit. I'd have jumped at the offer, she thought, melting under the heat of the brightly lit room, and conceding that Betty Johnson remained an enigma, albeit a welcomed one.

There'd been a string of missing people in Newark, Irvington,

Camden, and East Orange, all of them Colored. And now the evil specter of vulnerability had attached itself like a poisonous clinging vine to the City of Plainfield, threatening to choke the inhabitants of the predominantly Negro city with its patent evil, uncertainty, and parlous-driven terror.

She squeezed her eyes shut against the horrific mental image of Daniel Calhoun and Ernie Wilson rotting in shallow graves with maggots crawling out of their eyes, ears, noses, and mouths. They'd been among the most recent residents to disappear.

Loretta liked to think she stayed awake long after her bedtime, solely out of concern for Betty. She was far too ashamed to admit that she did so out of raw visceral fear—a fear that proved to be justified when she heard a stealthy footfall on the cracked step leading upstairs, the one with a loose floorboard that always squeaked.

Someone is definitely my house.

❧

"Please be Betty," Loretta prayed as rivulets of sweat flowed from her temple to mingle with the salty tears burning her eyes.

The hum of the box fan did little to ameliorate the thick heat in the room or block out the heavy tread of footsteps ascending the stairs. Loretta held her breath, afraid to so much as breathe. This time she knew she wasn't imagining things.

She sat up in the bed as someone or something made its way down the hallway. The dreaded footfalls she'd previously discounted as a figment of her imagination resumed, stopping outside her bedroom door.

Loretta quaked as three evenly paced knocks shook the aged, wooden door, each pound demanding entry.

"Betty? Is that you?" she whispered in a weak, shaking voice she no longer recognized as her own.

Betty gets off work at 11:00 P.M. It will take her at least thirty minutes to walk from North Plainfield to Plainfield in all this heat, she thought, mentally calculating her tenant's every step. *It's almost midnight. She should be home by now.*

A trail of fire and ice galloped down her spine when her inquiry was met with heavy breathing.

"Oh, God," she whispered, scouring the room in search of a means of escape, and finding none. Loretta didn't know who or what was on the other side of that door. But it damn sure wasn't Betty.

She reached for the only weapon she had, a dog-eared copy of the King James Bible, and began to pray.

"You are my refuge and my fortress, my God, in whom I trust," she chanted over and over until her lids grew heavy and the familiar words of the 91st psalm became a drunken slur on her lips.

In seemingly no time at all, her mouth dropped open and the muscles in her beautiful face went slack as she slipped into the REM state of slumber, where dreams and reality become one.

⁊

Loretta's mind traveled on the wings of Morpheus to the rocky mountain of Prenter, West Virginia, and more specifically to a one-bedroom shotgun shack issued to the employees of The Red Parrot Coal Mining Camp.

It was the dead of winter and cruelly cold out. Loretta stood outside the structure barefoot, and clad in nothing but her night clothes. She shivered, with her arms wrapped around her waist, as a fierce wind and snow drifts swirled around her bare feet. Desperately cold, she made her way on painfully stiff feet to the front door, and raised her hand to knock.

When her knock went unanswered, Loretta took a deep breath, and with stiff, frozen fingers, turned the icy doorknob. She entered the residence with trepidation, praying she would not be mistaken for a burglar and gunned down on sight.

Loretta forced the door shut and pressed her back against the smooth surface of the worn wood, but not before an unwelcomed gust of wind crept in behind her to advance its cruel agenda.

The blood supply previously held in abeyance as nature's protection against frostbite chose that moment to expand and flood her extremities. She grimaced at the painful pulse, throb, and tingle of her fingers and toes.

Loretta struggled to adjust her vision to the dim interior lighting, the source of which was a sole candle sitting atop the mantle of a wood-burning fireplace. She held her breath to listen, as the errant wind whistled through the thin walls. She prayed that the wind wouldn't extinguish the piteous flames offered by the candle, or the waning embers of the fireplace, and plunge her into total darkness.

The combined flames of the candle and the fireplace held steady, and Loretta's presence went unchallenged, eliciting a heartfelt sigh of relief.

CHAPTER FIFTY

"HELLO. IS ANYONE home?" Loretta asked, in a voice drowned out by the angry cry of the wind, her teeth chattering out of control.

The floor plan of the structure was simple and oddly familiar. From what Loretta could see, the rooms were lined up one after the other, with the living room first, then a bedroom, and the kitchen bringing up the rear. Although the house was clean and tidy, Loretta saw no evidence of electricity or indoor plumbing.

Reminding herself that this was naught but a dream, she doused her fear and pushed away from the door to follow a muffled sound coming from the next room. She made her way from the living room to the soul of the house, where a pleasant mixture of cinnamon, cloves, and white sage greeted her.

There was no time for speculation as the curtain to the dreamscape opened, drawing Loretta's attention to the largest piece of furniture in the sparsely decorated room, a king-sized brass bed.

A white man was sitting with his back against the cheap brass headboard like a Nordic king, his pale eyes locked on Loretta with a lascivious expression.

He chose that moment to allow the covers to fall away,

deliberately revealing his meaty fist pressing the bright red curls of a woman's skull against his groin.

"I don't want to see this," Loretta whispered, as if she was viewing the opening credits to a horror movie she'd seen many times before.

"Loretta," came a soft whisper from somewhere behind her.

Loretta turned from the lascivious sight at the sound of her name.

There stood her late husband, Albert, looking as dapper as ever in the navy-blue two-piece suit, white shirt, and navy, sky-blue, and crème silk tie she'd buried him in.

"This is just a dream," Loretta told herself, closing her eyes to keep from toppling over the cliff of irreversible insanity.

She fought to convince herself that she was not going stark-raving mad. Failing abysmally, her brain shut down, and she slumped to the floor, fainting dead away.

❦

Arlington Avenue

By the time Betty made it to Arlington Avenue, her clothing was drenched in sweat and her hands were shaking uncontrollably—not from anger, but from something far more sinister.

She was consumed with a hatred and rage similar to that which had driven her to embark upon the murderous rampage in Mississippi, only this time it was exponentially stronger because she now had a new victim to expend her bottomless pit of pain on. Betty was hell-bent on making Officer Paul Pressley suffer for every slight and injustice against humanity from the beginning of time.

"There was nothing I could do to help that kid without bringing attention to myself. But I swear before the Divine Creator and every single one of my Ancestors and Spirit Guides who walk in the fucking dark, that cop's days are numbered!" Betty said aloud.

So consumed was she with rage that she failed to hear her

ancestors' screaming out a warning for her to beware the demon who was keeping pace with her movements across the street like a destructive storm cloud.

Determined not to lose sight of his quarry, Agares chose that moment to shoot across the street to follow Betty up the walkway.

The demon was hovering above her, waiting for her to open the door and enter the house, when he slammed into an invisible force field so solid, he literally saw stars. For now, his intent to defy his master's orders and slip inside the house on the human's coattails was effectively thwarted. He was still trying to recover when Betty slipped inside the house, and locked the door behind her.

There was nothing for it. Agares was forced to wait outside the house to see which lights the human turned on and off before sending a telepathic message to his master.

Loretta woke up on a piss-soaked mattress. The back of her upper thigh burned like she'd been branded with a hot poker, and the inside of her head pounded like someone was beating the errant poker upside her head like a bass drum.

The only thing that kept Loretta from bashing her head against the wall and tumbling into fear-induced madness was the welcomed sight of Betty standing inside her open doorway.

CHAPTER FIFTY-ONE

"WHERE IS SHE?" Hindrance growled as every flying creature within a two-mile radius took to the sky, vacating the scene.

Agares side-eyed Hindrance's gargantuan set of scaly demon horns and the long, slimy, reptilian, tail writhing behind him with envy.

Hindrance seeks to frighten the human to death before he snatches her out of her home. What could be more frightening to a human than to find a seven-foot horned demon at the foot of their bed? Well played, Hindrance. Very well played, though I doubt the human in question has any concept of what fear is.

Keeping his opinion to himself, Agares pointed his beak toward the brightly lit attic room in the house the human had entered. Anxious to see the demon at a disadvantage, the demonic lackey failed to warn Hindrance of the demon-repelling force field that felled him earlier, a force field Agares suspected had been put in place by something other than a human.

Hindrance strode across the street and up the narrow human walkway with single-minded intent—that being to enter the human residence and drag her down to The Hells with him. He was fully prepared to rip anyone and anything to shreds who dared get in his way.

Hindrance stood before the weathered red door, poised to enter, when he felt a tentative tug on the base of his ultra-sensitive horns.

Before he could determine what was happening or do anything to circumvent it, an invisible hand of fire snatched him by his horns, causing him to soar through time and space to points unknown.

❧

324 Prescott Place, Plainfield, New Jersey 07063

Even the most seasoned alchemist would be hesitant to invoke one such as Hindrance with naught but the protection of a pentagram between them. However, the one known on the urban streets of New York, New Jersey, and Maryland as The Wizard was not your average run-of-the-mill alchemist. Nor was he altogether human.

Holding the original sigil King Solomon used to bind demons in the year 930 BCE, The Wizard uttered the name of the demon he sought for the third and final time.

The walls of the thirty-some-odd-year-old structure trembled, and a cloud of throat-clogging, black sulfurous soot filled every inch of the filthy basement wherein he stood. Rats, roaches, mice, and myriad winged vermin scurried for cover, as a tsunami of dust escaped the damp, dank ceiling and mold-mottled walls. The Wizard hastily cloaked himself in invisibility and floated to the eves of the spider-webbed ceiling to await the arrival of his reluctant guest.

Moments later, Hindrance landed on his scaly knees with a loud boom. He was smack-dab in the center of a demon-binding pentagram and looking none too pleased about it.

"Who dared invoke me!" he shouted, spewing acid spittle while spinning around in search of the human culprit he intended to kill. "For surely this is an invocation orchestrated by a human."

One of the many reasons demons despise humans is because of the ability some possess to invoke angelic and demonic beings in ritual and bend them to their will.

The thought of a human's role in his invocation fermented into a violent outburst of anger, strong enough to cause a row of filthy glass apothecary jars containing indiscriminate substances to crash to the floor. The demon howled as a ricochet of breath-snatching rage surged through his body.

As quickly as it was ignited, the demon's fiery rage was extinguished as if doused with a bucket of sanctified holy water prayed over by the pope. The uncontrollable rage was replaced by a cunning inherent in all things demonic. The demon rose on his haunches to better get the feel of his surroundings.

There was but one small basement window, and it was blacked out, allowing no light to filter in. Hindrance released a low rumbling growl, his porcine snout twitching speculatively at the distinctive smell of more than one human. He grew still, allowing his preternatural vision to slice through the inky darkness, revealing animal cages hanging from thick chains bolted into the beams of the ceiling. There were four of them, all occupied by humans, three of whom bore deep puncture wounds near their carotid arteries. The occupant of the fourth cage, a female whose throat had been ripped open, was dead.

Blood-red demon eyes rose to meet the terrified gazes of three sniveling, whimpering humans with rags stuffed in their mouths. Two melanated and one white, all were frightened beyond measure as they awaited their fate.

"Ah, I see that you've met my other guests," came a disembodied voice from points unknown inside the basement. "Allow me to make the introductions," The Wizard said affably as he floated from his ceiling perch on a slide made of thin air.

"The young man on the left is Daniel Calhoun, and the one next to him is his good friend, Ernest Wilson. The pale-faced gentleman to the far right is Martin Lewis, a long-distance truck driver who happened to be in the right place at the wrong time. As to the lone female, well, let's just say her time on earth is up."

When Hindrance realized what and who had the temerity to invoke him, he went ballistic.

"You lowlife, stinking, accursed Nephilim!" Hindrance bellowed, followed by a blistering string of filthy epithets in *Dimoori Sheol*, the universal tongue spoken in The Hells.

Hindrance allowed his evil reptilian eyes to roam the length of the Nephilim with repugnance, nearly going off the deep end when his discomfiture was met with a low, taunting rumble of disrespectful laughter. Unable to restrain himself, Hindrance leapt into the air, snarling like a rabid beast with acid slobber dripping from his snout.

As if he had a front-row seat inside the demon's mind and the ability to divine his intentions, the Nephilim swept one side of his long velvet cloak aside to reveal the sigil of King Solomon.

Hindrance slammed into the invisible wall separating him from his intended prey, reeling from the impact. He raised his arm to cover his face like Count Dracula faced with a crucifix, a necklace made out of garlic, and a lethal blast of the noon-day sun, yelping like a whipped cur to the mocking music of The Wizard's sinister laugh.

The black bristling hairs that landscaped the demon's massive heaving chest rose and fell like lethal spikes as he sat on his hind haunches, trying to pull himself together as he formulated his next move.

Blood-red demon eyes locked with the bright-yellow orbs of the Nephilim in a metaphoric preternatural standoff. Hindrance was the first to turn away, deciding it best to play along until he could determine the true purpose of the invocation.

To think that I'd been within seconds of taking Elizabeth François before this half-breed mongrel invoked me, he thought, as the unforgettably sweet scent of the human's dark soul lingered in the doorway of his swine-shaped snout. *That alone shall serve as grounds for me to present this piece of shit with the true death*, he thought.

Like it or not, at least for now, he was inexplicably bound by the pentagram and the sigil. Enraged, he stood to pace the confines of the circle, awaiting The Wizard's next move.

CHAPTER FIFTY-TWO

"**A**LLOW ME TO introduce myself," Hindrance's captor said, bowing with an exaggerated flourish. "My name is Moultrie, formerly of the House of Armers. But you, my new demon friend, may call me The Wizard."

"Spare me your posturing. I know who the fuck you are," Hindrance spat with narrow-eyed speculation. "You are known throughout The Heavens, The Hells, and the caves inhabited by those of your kind as the lowest kind of bottom-feeder. You are a traitorous half-breed angel, diviner, necromancer, and a practitioner of the black arts, whom it appears the demons in The Hells would do well to keep their eyes on," he concluded.

"High flattery coming from a demon, I think," The Wizard responded, nonplussed.

"Despite your unwarranted condemnation, I recall that it was me who delivered the son of a high-ranking member of the Nephilim Nation to your father in the 1700s, and at great peril to myself, I might add. I am now an enemy of the Nephilim Nation, on the Preternatural Most Wanted List, and have an obscene bounty on my head. And wasn't it you who brokered the deal?"

Choosing to ignore the Nephilim's reminder of the infamous

deal he'd cut in the 1700s on behalf of The Satan, the demon retorted, "And you were paid handsomely for your services.

For what purpose was I invoked, Nephilim?" Hindrance demanded in a gravelly voice that sounded like that of a beast with a mouth full of jagged rocks.

"I desire to enter into a pact with you," The Wizard replied, just as bold as you please.

Moultrie would not be the first wizard to sell his soul to a demon to gain wealth and power. But he would have the dual distinction of being the first Nephilim and the only alchemist holding the lauded rank of Arch mage Wizardry to do so.

Arch mage wizards are far too powerful and intelligent to engage in a dance with the devil, and Nephilim generally steer clear of demons unless they are trying to kill them. That has always been the way of things.

"You know the drill, half-breed," the demon sneered. "If you want to make a pact with me, you must first pledge to give your soul over to me fifty years from now. I will also demand a solid gold coin from you on the first Monday of each month. Then, and only then, will I entertain your request, Nephilim."

The demon said the word "Nephilim" as if someone had taken a dump in his mouth. Fifty years was but a blink in the eye of time for a demon, especially one as ancient as he. Hindrance rubbed his greedy hands together in anticipation of the gold that would grease his leathery palms. He couldn't wait to get his hands on the Nephilim and the brand-new soul he would control.

And when I do…

A predatory growl completed the thought for him.

The Nephilim's face was lost in the shadows of his velvet hood, making it virtually impossible for the demon to read his expression or divine his thoughts. The part of The Wizard's head that was visible beneath the hood bore tattoos of runic symbols and mystic lettering Hindrance could not decipher.

This one who calls himself a wizard must be very powerful, Hindrance thought. *It will be good to have one such as him under my influence.*

Hindrance held his breath, hoping the hated Nephilim would consent to his terms.

❧

The Wizard's red-rimmed yellow eyes glowed like bright lanterns behind the folds of his hood. He knew exactly what Hindrance was thinking. Instead of agreeing to his terms to enter into a pact, the cagey Nephilim came back with a counteroffer.

"I will not give up what is left of my soul, demon. Nor will I pay a monthly tribute to you of any kind. However," he said, raising a long clawed finger to punctuate a point, then added in a blasé tone, "I *can* give you the means by which to take down one of your father's most hated enemies—that is, if you are interested." The Wizard toyed with the bloodstone in his pocket. He awaited the demon's response, his expression inscrutable. Hindrance's response was immediate.

"And why in The Hells would I put my trust in the likes of you?"

Hindrance had to give the cocky motherfucker credit. The half-breed son of a cur had a big set of brass balls on him.

How 'bout I rip off those brass balls with my bare claws and shove them down your treacherous throat for pulling me away from my future bride before I was done with her, he thought, as an unaccustomed bout of worry set in.

Elizabeth Anne François is intuitive, resourceful, and bound to make a run for it should she sense anything untoward. That could prove problematic in light of the plans I have for her. I must be about my business. What could this talking pile of dung possibly want from me that any one of my brothers can't provide?

The Wizard could see the wheels in Hindrance's wicked brain turning. *Hindrance is probably wondering why I came to him with my request and not his brothers Travail, Salacious, or the wicked Incarnadine, all of whom are in better standing with their sire. The answer is simple.*

"Why would you enter into a pact with me?" The Wizard replied with a question of his own, in preparation for the "I gotcha" moment he had up his sleeves.

"Because if you don't agree to my terms, I will be obliged to tell your daddy what became of your brother, Tyranny," he said with an evil grin.

The demon's sharp intake of breath was all the evidence he needed to confirm his barb had struck home.

Hindrance judiciously chose to ignore the comment about his brother, Tyranny, until his adversary revealed what he knew, if anything.

You don't fool me, demon, The Wizard thought. *He's trying to figure out whether I am bluffing, and if not, how much I actually know.*

The Wizard deduced all this as the three horns protruding from Hindrance's forehead twitched out of control and his black leathery wings flapped in aggression.

Test me if you dare, The Wizard crowed, watching Hindrance nervously pace back and forth inside the periphery of the summoning circle, obviously deep in thought.

I know EVERYTHING. The Wizard chortled to himself with malicious glee, barely able to control himself.

Hindrance inhaled the familiar stench of death that hung in the air like yesterday's raw sewage before speaking. The jackal-faced demon leveled his dead reptilian eyes on The Wizard.

"Does the information you have and your silence come with a price?" he asked, knowing the answer before the words were uttered.

"Why, of course," said The Wizard calmly. "Doesn't everything?"

"Tell me what you know. I will let you know if it is worth my time and consideration," Hindrance said cagily.

"Very well," The Wizard responded, pausing a moment for dramatic effect.

"I know that it was you who, as the human thugs say, dropped a dime on your brother, Tyranny. You knew he and his team were on assignment at the No Name Bar. You gave the intel to a known Nephilim sympathizer who, in turn, shared the information with two rogue Brothers of the Dark Veil. The rest, as they say, is history. And, Hindrance, I recommend you not try to lie your way out of this because the Nephilim sympathizer is in my employ."

⸏

"Tell me what you want in return for this information and your continued silence, half-breed," Hindrance said, deciding not to waste time in useless denials. He'd been set up, stuffed, and trussed as effectively as a Thanksgiving turkey. "I will give you whatever you ask within reason," he hastily added.

"I want the immediate release of a prisoner you are holding on Sha'are Zalmuwet (*The Hell of Seven Hells*)." The Wizard made the demands as if he owned all seven levels of The Hells and everything in it.

"Who is this prisoner whose freedom you seek?" Hindrance demanded.

When The Wizard uttered the name of the prisoner he wanted released, Hindrance took a step back, stunned by the unmitigated gall of him.

"What you ask is impossible, half-breed. I know for a fact the prisoner you seek is long dead. My father is powerful, but even he cannot raise the dead. You ask too much, half-breed," Hindrance spat.

The Wizard uttered the word "Liar," in response to Hindrance's impassioned speech. He had spies on all seven levels of The Hells. He knew for a fact that not only was the prisoner he asked for still very much alive but that Hindrance's brother, Incarnadine, was holding him in *Castellum Regnum Mortuorum*, a maximum-security prison located on Sha'are Zalmuwet.

"What is your second request?" Hindrance asked, deciding to ignore the blatant insult for now.

"I demand Daywalker status."

"You are a lowly Anakin," Hindrance said with a sneer. "No Anakin in the history of creation has ever enjoyed Daywalker status."

Nephilim society is based upon angelic hierarchy, with those descended from Seraphim, Cherubim, and Throne angels making up the nobility. Nephilim descended from Dominions, Virtues, and Powers make up the Gibborim or military/middle class. Those with third-sphere angelic blood, namely the Principalities, Archangels and Angels, such as The Wizard, make up the lower or working class.

Hindrance, on the other hand, was a full-blooded angel, albeit a fallen one, with not one drop of accursed human blood flowing through his angelic veins. The demon belonged to the angelic order of the Powers or Potentates before the Ancient of Days expelled him from The Heavens.

The demon's words rattled The Wizard more than he cared to admit. He didn't need anyone to remind him of his low birth, least of all, a demon.

The Wizard shook off his anger at the demon's caustic words and returned to the business at hand. He had risen too high to allow the vicious words of a demon to lay him low.

If Hindrance doesn't want the information I'm offering, someone else will. The male I intend to betray has many enemies, all of whom are literally standing in line to give him the true death. I shall sell the information to the highest bidder.

"Very well then," The Wizard said.

His body became transparent as he prepared to ghost away.

Hindrance shouted, "Wait!" to stay him.

"Perhaps I was a bit hasty," he said in an attempt to halt The Wizard's departure. "I did not say I wouldn't grant your requests." He reluctantly humbled himself in the face of his enemy.

"I will have to consult with my father before granting your wishes. One of my emissaries will seek you out in the human realm once my father has made his decision."

"Excellent!" came The Wizard's eager response.

"Very well then," Hindrance said, albeit grudgingly. "Now tell me what you know."

He bit his tongue in an effort to restrain himself from adding the disrespectful "half-breed" he always tacked at the end of every sentence when addressing a Nephilim.

The Wizard wasn't fooled by Hindrance's sudden capitulation. One snake always recognizes another.

The demon thinks to trick me, The Wizard thought, clearing his throat.

"I know where one of the Brothers of the Dark Veil lays his head," he confessed.

Hindrance hissed with excitement. *This was even better than I anticipated.*

The Brothers of the Dark Veil are Nephilim demon hunters who are personally responsible for diminishing the population in The Hells by the trillions. Hindrance had proof that it was one of the Nephilim behind Tyranny's recent disappearance.

Surely, he must be dead, right? My father must never learn that it was me who dropped the anonymous tip that facilitated the ambush of my brother and his posse of low-level demons.

The half-breed angels maintain primary residences behind the Dark Veil, an impenetrable mystical wall erected by their collective power. However, they frequently keep residences among humans in the cities where they hunt and kill demons. No demon has ever been able to ascertain the location of one of these houses… that is, until now.

Hindrance got all warm and mushy inside at the prospect of killing one of his most hated enemies. *The reward I will receive from my father will be magnificent… and the power.* Suffice it to say, his demon dick got hard just thinking about it.

Hindrance's wicked brain was working overtime. He wouldn't delude himself into thinking the self-proclaimed wizard could be trusted. After all, he was a traitor to his own people.

In this instance, I shall have to take a chance. The stakes are too high and the potential rewards too great not to. If I play my cards right, I may well come out of this with everything I desire.

The Nephilim's hated voice sliced through the demon's ruminations.

"I will gladly share my information with you," The Wizard said as if they were friends and not possessed of the most vile souls in existence. "That is, after I receive both Daywalker status and the prisoner I requested."

"You see, I know where the Nephilim 'Money Man' lays his head. Give me what I ask, within a fortnight, and I will lead you to General Rephidim Turel's doorstep."

GLOSSARY

Anakin	Working class Nephilim.
Ancient of Days and Attiq Yomin	Nephilim names for God.
àṣẹ	Divine Power.
BODV	Acronym for "Brothers of the Dark Veil".
Brothers of the Dark Veil	Nephilim King's personal honor guard. First Generation descendants of the officers who served under the Watcher Angel Shemyaza. Generals of the Gibborim armies. Nephilim royalty.
Conjure Woman	A female who is feared and admired, with the power to heal or harm.
Damballah Weddo Vévé	A serpent deity; one of the oldest and wisest of the Voodoo Loa.
Dark Kiss	A ritual where a Nephilim can bring a human from the brink of death by the exchange of blood.
Daywalker	All Nephilim are cursed with advanced xeroderma pigmentosum, a disease which causes their skin to burn in sunlight. Given the right circumstances, The Brothers of the Dark Veil can sometimes walk in the sun; thus they are called "Daywalkers" among the Nephilim people.
Demon	Fallen angels and the imps, gnomes, monsters, and little beasties that serve under them.
Doula or Baby Catcher	One who provides emotional and physical support during the delivery of a baby.
Elevated Ancestors	A deceased ancestor that has taken an active role in the lives of living family members.

The Fall	Period of time when wicked/rebellious angels were cast out of the Heavens.
The Fallen	Members of the celestial choir that were cast down from the heavens by the Ancient of Days to rule over the Seven Hells.
Feeding	Drinking blood.
Gateway	A portal from earth to the heavens and the hells.
Ghosting	A means of Nephilim travel.
Gibborim	Members of the Nephilim military.
He Whose Name I Dare Not Speak	Phrase residents of the Hells use when referring to God.
Heredity Hedge Witch	These are witches who are born into a witch family and brought up learning about the shamanic aspect of witchcraft with a strong earth-based spiritualty.
Hoodoo Nation Sack	The "nation sack" is a form of mojo or "root bag" women use to keep a man faithful.
Houses of the Nephilim	Nephilim royalty consist of 12 major Houses (Anane, Arazyal, Armers, Asael, Batraal, Ertael, Samsaveel, Saraknyl, Shemyaza, Turel, Yomyael and Zavabe). The highest is that of the King, "Shemyaza."
King Solomon's Grimoire	A mystically inspired textbook of magic with instructions on how to cast spells, create magical objects and evoke and invoke angels, spirits and demons.
Lao	The Loa or Lwa are Voodoo spirits and Orisha gods, respectively.
Lay down tricks	Hoodoo ritual where an item is laid down, buried, hidden, or thrown where the target can walk over it unawares, to achieve a specific result.
Maroon	Community of escaped slaves in the Atchafalaya Swamp.

Mind Meld	Nephilim telepathic means of communication.
Mind Swipe	A forceful mental invasion to erase human memories.
Mojuba	Loosely translated to mean, "I salute or pay homage" to the Ancestors.
Nephilim	Half angel/half human preternatural beings descended from the Watcher Angels that landed upon Mt. Heron during the time when the Prophet Enoch walked among men.
Nyny (pronounced, "nee nee")	Ancient Kemetic greeting, meaning "hello".
Oogun Ika or Oogun Burburu	Practitioners of sorcery or black majick seeking to harm, kill or destroy the property of someone through the use of negative rituals.
Orisha	African Pantheon of gods and goddesses.
Realm of Awe	The gateway to paradise; a place where angelic beings who walk in darkness transition after the "true death."
Rephaim	Members of the Nephilim aristocracy.
Root work	A practice that originated in the antebellum south, supporting the belief that illnesses can be caused and cured by herbs, medicine, and majick.
Sarrum	A title of honor accorded the Nephilim King.
The Satan	A title of honor accorded Zuet, the King of Darkness.
The True Death	A death which even immortals cannot return from.
Sons of Zuet	Tyranny, Hindrance, Salacious, Travail and the youngest; Incarnadine a/k/a Lucifer.
Vessel	A human who gives birth to a child fathered by one of the Fallen.

Vilokan	A City beneath the sea where the Voodoo Iwa are said to reside, heaven.
Voodoo Priestess	A sacred female practitioner of the Voodoo tradition (also known as a Mambo or Manbo) with religious and spiritual authority to perform rituals.
Watcher Angels	Elite corps of angels sent from heaven to earth to watch over man. "The sons of God saw the daughters of man and found them to be fine."
Zion Shemyaza	King of the Nephilim; the oldest and most powerful Nephilim in existence.
Zuet	The Satan, ruler of all seven levels of the Hells.

ABOUT THE AUTHOR

Carolyn is a bibliophile. She purchased Rosemary Roger's *Sweet Savage Love* in 1974 and fell in love with the main characters. The storyline was raw, violent, and sensual while maintaining historical integrity. From that day forward, she was hooked on historical romance. She is a hopeless romantic. Please don't judge her!

The historical romance genre took off like a rocket, giving female writers the autonomy to write true-to-life erotica with a backdrop of historical fact. To date, the genre has minimal representation from people of color. Carolyn was determined to change that by writing books for and about people of color which appeal to male and female readers. She was not ready to act upon it until she came across *The Book of Enoch* and the Watcher Angels, who were beguiled by the loveliness of earthly women and begat children with them - Nephilim. The rest, as they say, is history.

Carolyn has a weakness for wide-brimmed hats, stilettos, hard to find books, music, and a good bottle of cabernet. She loves to travel, cook, and spend time with family and friends. She resides on the U.S. East Coast with her spirit guides and her cast of otherworldly fictional characters.

Are you interested in connecting with Carolyn?
Here's how you can do it.

Website: https://www.carolynhollandwrites.com

E-Mail: Carolynhollandbooks@gmail.com